When the Tides Hold Us

THE TIDES BETWEEN US, BOOK 3

Written by Diane Kann

Brought to you by Volans Galaxy Press

Published by Kannceptual Creations LLC

An imprint of Volans Galaxy Press

ISBN: 978-1-971356-32-7

Printed in the United States of America

First Edition, January 2026

Contents

Dedication

To all the dreamers who found their anchor,

To the hearts that learned to embrace permanence,

And to the quiet courage it takes to choose love,

Again and again, in the face of every storm.

May you find your own Port Blossom,

A place where your deepest aspirations can take root,

Where the scent of salt and possibility mingles,

And where the rhythm of the waves whispers promises of forever.

This story is for you, for the journey of self-discovery,

For the bravery to build a life that feels like coming home,

And for the profound truth that sometimes,

The greatest adventures are found in settling down,

In weaving your life with another,

And in creating a sanctuary of love,

Against the backdrop of a world that so often rushes past.

May you always find strength in shared purpose,

And solace in the unwavering embrace of a love that endures.

For the quiet strength found in commitment,

And the beautiful, unfolding story of two souls

Finding their forever, together.

CHAPTER ONE

The Calm Before the Storm

Sunlight, a warm, buttery wash, spilled through the tall windows of the Port Blossom Animal Rescue's main office, chasing away the last lingering shadows of dawn. Dust motes, tiny dancers in the ethereal light, pirouetted in the golden beams that slanted across the worn wooden floor. The air, still cool from the night, was a comforting blend of freshly brewed coffee, the faint, earthy scent of hay from the nearby stables, and the distant, rhythmic sigh of the ocean. Outside, the mournful cries of gulls punctuated the gentle roar of the waves, a soundtrack Mara had come to associate with peace, with home.

Mara knelt on the floor, her fingers laced through the soft fur of a wriggling litter of puppies. They were barely a few weeks old, their eyes still adjusting to the world, their tiny bodies a tumble of clumsy paws and eager yips. Each one was a testament to resilience, a small miracle nursed back to health under her care. A wave of pure contentment washed over her, so potent it felt almost tangible. This was it. This was the heart of it all – these vulnerable lives entrusted to her, the quiet satisfaction of nurturing them, of knowing she was making a tangible difference. The frantic energy of the puppies was infectious, and a genuine, unrestrained smile bloomed on her face as she gently stroked a particularly boisterous sable-colored pup. Its tiny tail thumped against her hand like a miniature drumbeat.

A few feet away, Eli sat at his desk, the worn leather of his chair creaking softly as he shifted. The morning sun caught the silver threads woven through his dark hair, and his brow was furrowed in concentration, not from stress, but from engagement. He was poring over a stack of adoption applications, his gaze thoughtful as he scanned the hopeful faces and heartfelt pleas for forever homes. His movements were economical, his presence a steady, grounding force in the lively chaos of the rescue. Yet, his eyes, more than once, drifted from the papers to Mara, a quiet affection softening his features. He watched the way her brow furrowed slightly in concentration as she examined a tiny mewling creature, the way her shoulders relaxed when a puppy settled contentedly in her lap. It was these small, intimate moments, woven into the fabric of their everyday lives, that Eli cherished. They were the quiet anchors in the often-turbulent sea of running a rescue, the silent affirmations of the deep, abiding love that had bloomed between them in this little corner of the world.

The main office, usually a hive of activity, was in a rare state of quiet repose. This morning, it was just them, the animals, and the gentle rhythm of their shared life. The adoption applications laid out before Eli were more than just forms; they represented futures, second chances, the culmination of countless hours of hard work and dedication. He carefully considered each one, picturing the animals finding loving homes, imagining the joy they would bring to their new families. He remembered the day he first walked onto the Port Blossom Animal Rescue grounds, a whirlwind of organized chaos and earnest passion, and Mara, then the fiercely independent operations manager, had begrudgingly but efficiently shown him the ropes. He'd been drawn to her spirit, her unwavering commitment to the animals, even as she projected an air of untouchable self-sufficiency. Now, months later, that self-sufficiency had softened, giving way to a shared vulnerability and a deep, comfortable intimacy that felt as natural as the ebb and flow of the tides.

Mara shifted, her movements fluid and unhurried as she gathered the puppies into a soft blanket. She hummed a low, tuneless melody, the sound a gentle counterpoint to the puppies' soft whimpers. She felt a profound sense of gratitude for this moment, for this life. Port Blossom, with its salty air and weathered charm, had become more than just a place; it was the beating heart of their shared world. The rescue, a beacon of hope for countless animals, was their sanctuary, their shared purpose. And Eli... Eli was the steady, unwavering lighthouse in her often-stormy sea. His quiet strength, his gentle humor, his unwavering belief in her, had a way of grounding her, of reminding her of the beauty and resilience of love.

Eli let out a soft sigh, a sound of pure contentment, as he placed a particularly promising application into a 'pending' pile. He glanced at Mara again, the sunlight catching the stray strands of hair that had escaped her ponytail, framing her face with a soft halo. He loved the way she was so completely absorbed in the task at hand, her entire being focused on these small, helpless creatures. It was a reflection of her heart, a heart so large it seemed capable of holding all the broken and forgotten souls of the world. He had often wondered, in the early days, if her passion for the rescue was a way to keep people at a distance, a shield against the perceived vulnerability of deeper connection. But as he had come to know her, to truly see her, he understood that it wasn't a shield, but an extension of her being. Her love for these animals was a pure, unadulterated expression of the love she was capable of giving, a love he was now the fortunate recipient of.

He remembered a conversation they'd had just weeks ago, over a shared mug of tea after a particularly demanding day. Mara had confessed, her voice quiet and laced with a vulnerability he rarely saw, that she'd always assumed she was destined for a solitary life, a life of perpetual motion, always moving on before roots could truly take hold. "I was afraid," she'd admitted, her gaze fixed on the flickering flame of a candle, "that if I stayed too long, if I let myself be truly seen, I'd inevitably disappoint. Or worse, I'd be left behind." Eli had reached for her hand then, his thumb stroking the back of hers, his voice steady and reassuring. "You'll never disappoint me, Mara," he'd said, his eyes holding hers. "And you'll never be left behind. We're building this, together.

We're each other's home now." The memory brought a warmth to his chest, a quiet affirmation of the journey they were on.

The gentle nuzzle of a puppy against her cheek brought Mara back to the present. She scooped up the tiny creature, its warmth seeping into her hands. She looked over at Eli, who was now carefully organizing the adoption files, his movements precise and efficient. He was so different from the restless wanderer she had once imagined herself to be. He was solid, dependable, a man who had found his place and was determined to build upon it. He spoke of the rescue not just as a job, but as a legacy, a responsibility he embraced with every fiber of his being. And he spoke of their future, their life together in Port Blossom, with a quiet certainty that had, at first, unsettled her, but now, soothed her to her very core.

He caught her looking and offered a soft, knowing smile. It was a smile that conveyed a thousand unspoken words – of shared understanding, of deep affection, of the quiet joy of simply being in each other's presence. Mara returned the smile, a sense of profound peace settling over her. The distant cries of the gulls, the gentle lapping of waves against the shore, the happy snuffles of the puppies in her lap – it was all a symphony of contentment. This was the calm. The beautiful, precious, fragile calm before the storm. She didn't know what lay ahead, what challenges the day, or the future, might bring. But in this moment, bathed in the golden light of a Port Blossom morning, with Eli by her side and a litter of puppies demanding her attention, she felt utterly, completely at peace. The world outside the office walls, with its unpredictable currents and hidden dangers, felt a million miles away. Here, in the heart of the rescue, their shared life unfolded in a tapestry of quiet devotion, punctuated by the joyous yips of new beginnings. It was a scene of perfect domesticity, a tableau of two souls who had found their anchor in each other and in the shared purpose that bound them together. The air was thick with unspoken promises, with the quiet hum of a life built on love, compassion, and the unwavering hope for a brighter future for all creatures, great and small. And for Mara, at least, this was everything.

The tranquil morning at Port Blossom Animal Rescue, a sanctuary carved from salty air and shared purpose, was about to be subtly disrupted. Eli, lost in the quiet rhythm of reviewing adoption applications, found his focus gently nudged by the soft ping of an incoming email. The sound, usually just another digital whisper in the background of their busy lives, seemed to carry a different weight today. He glanced at his screen, his brow lifting in mild surprise. It was from the prestigious Oceanic Research Institute – the very institution he'd sent a speculative application to months ago, a hopeful shot into the vast blue of possibility with little expectation of a return call. Now, a missive from them sat in his inbox, a stark contrast to the comforting familiarity of the puppy-littered floor and Mara's quiet humming.

He opened the email, his fingers moving with a practiced efficiency that belied the subtle shift in his demeanor. The screen glowed with crisp, official text, detailing an offer that was both breathtaking and daunting. It spoke of cutting-edge research, of marine conservation initiatives that could genuinely alter the trajectory of endangered species, and of a leadership role that carried the weight of significant responsibility. This wasn't just another job prospect; it was a potential nexus point, a confluence of his deepest passions and aspirations, a life-altering prospect that had materialized from the ether of his professional dreams. He read through the proposal, his gaze scanning the ambitious research projects and the scope of the conservation efforts. The words painted a vivid picture of a life dedicated to the ocean's most pressing issues, a life far removed from the shores of Port Blossom, yet intimately connected to the very essence of the marine world he so adored.

Mara, her attention momentarily diverted from a particularly fluffy terrier mix currently attempting to scale her knee, noticed the subtle change in Eli. His usual relaxed posture had tightened, a almost imperceptible tension creeping into the set of his shoulders. The thoughtful contemplation that usually graced his features when reviewing applications had deepened into something more profound, a quiet introspection that suggested a world unfolding behind his eyes, a world separate from the immediate comfort of their shared space. He didn't speak, didn't sigh, didn't offer any outward indication of the email's contents, but Mara, attuned to the nuances of his presence, felt the shift. It was like a change in the atmospheric pressure before a storm, a subtle tremor beneath the surface of their serene morning.

Eli continued to read, absorbing the details of the offer. The institute was renowned, a global leader in marine biology and conservation. The research projects described were exactly the kind that had fueled his academic pursuits, the kind that demanded innovation and a deep understanding of the ocean's intricate ecosystems. Leading a significant conservation initiative was more than just a career advancement; it was an opportunity to make a tangible, lasting impact on the very environments he felt most compelled to protect. He imagined himself in a laboratory, surrounded by state-of-the-art equipment, collaborating with leading scientists, and venturing out on expeditions to study whales, to protect coral reefs, to understand the delicate balance of marine life. It was a powerful allure, a siren song that resonated with the core of his ambitions.

He reached the section detailing the proposed compensation and benefits, then the timeline for a potential decision. The offer was generous, reflecting the prestige of the role and the institute. It also implied a swift transition, a demand for a decision that would necessitate a significant upheaval. He scrolled to the bottom, his finger hovering over the "reply" button. The vastness of the opportunity was undeniable, a testament to years of hard work, dedication, and a quiet persistence in pursuing his academic and professional goals. Yet, as his gaze drifted from the screen to the sun-drenched office, to Mara's easy smile as she coaxed a hesitant puppy into a warm embrace, a different kind of weight settled upon him. It was the weight of implication, of choices that would ripple far beyond his own life.

He closed the email, not deleting it, but minimizing the window, tucking the digital artifact away as if it were a delicate, fragile specimen. The information, however, wouldn't be so easily contained. It had already begun to permeate his thoughts, weaving itself into the fabric of his morning. The dream of impacting marine conservation on a grander scale, a dream he'd almost allowed himself to forget, had suddenly become a tangible possibility, a starkly illuminated path diverging from the one he was currently walking. He looked at Mara again, her face alight with the simple joy of her work, and a quiet contemplation settled over him. The peaceful rhythm of their lives, the comfortable intimacy they had cultivated, suddenly felt like a precious, delicate thing, something that would be tested by the winds of ambition and opportunity. He knew, with a certainty that settled deep in his gut, that this email was more than just a job offer; it was a crossroads, and the journey ahead, whatever he chose, would be profoundly different. The weight of it, he realized, was already settling upon him, a quiet but insistent pressure that promised to reshape the landscape of their shared future. He pushed the laptop slightly away, the smooth, cool surface suddenly feeling foreign under his fingertips, a stark reminder of the world that existed beyond the comforting confines of the rescue, a world that was now, undeniably, knocking at his door.

The afternoon sun, which had earlier bathed Port Blossom Animal Rescue in a warm, benevolent glow, now cast long, slanted shadows across the kennels. Eli had managed to tuck the Oceanic Research Institute's offer into a mental sidebar, a monumental decision pressing in on him, but one he'd relegated to the back burner for the moment. The immediate, tangible needs of the rescue had a way of demanding their due, of anchoring him firmly in the present, however turbulent it might be. He was in the small office, ostensibly reviewing the meager remaining supplies of dog food, when Mara burst through the door, her usual cheerful demeanor replaced by a stark, almost frantic urgency.

"Eli," she began, her voice tight, breath coming in shallow gasps. "You need to see this. Now." Her eyes, usually so bright with a blend of compassion and resilience, were wide with a fear that sent a chill down Eli's spine, a fear that had nothing to do with his own internal deliberations. He pushed aside the half-empty bag of kibble, his attention snapping to her. Mara held her phone aloft, her fingers trembling slightly as she scrolled through an email.

"What is it?" he asked, his voice a low rumble, his gaze fixed on the distress etched onto her face. The air in the small office, usually filled with the comforting scent of disinfectant and faint doggy musk, suddenly felt charged with an electric tension, a prelude to a storm far more immediate and devastating than any Eli had been contemplating.

"The Harrison Foundation grant," Mara whispered, her voice barely audible above the distant barks and whimpers from the kennels. "It's... it's frozen. All of it." She turned the phone towards him, the screen illuminating her pale face. The email, stark and impersonal, laid out a bureaucratic nightmare. A critical administrative error, a misplaced comma in a funding request that had been overlooked for months, had triggered an immediate freeze on all disbursements. The foundation, known for its steadfast support of animal welfare organizations, had placed Port Blossom on a probationary status, demanding a full audit before any funds would be released. And the audit, according to the email, could take weeks, if not months.

Eli read the words, his mind struggling to grasp the enormity of the situation. The Harrison Foundation grant wasn't just a piece of their funding; it was the lifeblood of Port Blossom. It covered the bulk of their operating costs – the food, the medical supplies, the salaries, the essential veterinary care that kept their rescued animals healthy and adoptable. Without it, the sanctuary was, quite literally, facing imminent collapse. The comfortable, if modest, stability they had painstakingly built was now teetering on the brink of oblivion.

"Frozen?" Eli repeated, the word feeling foreign and absurd on his tongue. "What do you mean, frozen? It's just an administrative error, isn't it? They'll fix it, won't they?" His voice held a note of disbelief, a desperate attempt to cling to a semblance of normalcy.

Mara shook her head, her eyes glistening. "They said it's standard procedure. Until the audit is complete, no funds can be released. And that could be... weeks, Eli. We have enough food for maybe ten days, if we stretch it. The vaccinations for the new litter of puppies are due next week. Dr. Albright's bill from last month for the stray cat with the broken leg... we haven't even paid that yet. This isn't just a setback, Eli. This is... this is catastrophic."

The knot of dread that had been subtly tightening in Mara's stomach since she'd read the email now felt like a vise, crushing the air from her lungs. She sank onto the worn office chair, her gaze unfocused, seeing not the familiar posters of happy adopted animals on the wall, but the looming specter of closure. She pictured the faces of the animals they cared for, the hopeful eyes of the dogs and cats who had found refuge within these walls, and the sheer terror of what would happen to them if Port Blossom was forced to shut its doors. These were not just animals; they were individuals with personalities, with stories, with a desperate need for a second chance. She had poured her heart and soul into this place, sacrificing personal time, sleep, and even her own savings at times to ensure its survival. To see it all threatened by a single, careless mistake... it was almost unbearable.

Eli walked over to her, placing a hand gently on her shoulder. He could feel the tremors running through her. "We'll figure something out, Mara," he said, his voice steady, a practiced calm he didn't entirely feel. He was already mentally calculating their emergency fund – a woefully inadequate buffer for a crisis of this magnitude. He knew the grant's specifics, the lifeline it provided, the critical services it enabled. He thought of the recent influx of strays after the storm that had hit the coast last month, the increased demand for their services, the constant need for more resources. And now, this.

"Figure something out?" Mara echoed, her voice cracking. "Eli, 'figuring something out' usually involves more than a few weeks. We're talking about hundreds of animals. Food, medicine, vet bills that are already piling up. We can't just magic more money out of thin air. The adoption fees barely cover our daily expenses as it is. This grant... it's everything." She buried her face in her hands, her shoulders shaking. The image of the sleek, official letter from the Oceanic Research Institute, a beacon of a different kind of future, felt a million miles away, an almost cruel irony in the face of this immediate, devastating reality. His own professional aspirations, which had seemed so weighty just hours ago, now felt trivial, a distant dream overshadowed by the very real crisis unfolding at their doorstep.

Eli knelt beside her, his gaze sweeping across the cramped office, taking in the stacks of paperwork, the overflowing inboxes, the worn but functional equipment. This was their sanctuary, a haven built on dedication and an unwavering love for animals. He remembered the early days, the sheer grit it had taken to get Port Blossom off the ground, the countless hours spent fundraising, cleaning, and advocating. He understood, perhaps better than anyone, the immense effort that had gone into securing that grant, the meticulous planning and compelling proposals that had convinced the Harrison Foundation to invest in their mission. And now, a bureaucratic snafu threatened to unravel it all.

He knew Mara wasn't prone to hysterics. When she said this was catastrophic, she meant it. He reached for the phone, his fingers hovering over the keypad. There were other foundations, smaller grants, local businesses they could appeal to. But the scale of the need was immense. The Harrison grant was designed to cover their operating expenses for the entire year. Replacing that income, even partially, would require an unprecedented fundraising effort, one that would demand every ounce of their energy and ingenuity.

"Okay," Eli said, his voice firm, cutting through Mara's despair. He took a deep breath, pushing down the rising tide of his own anxieties. "Okay. Let's not panic. We have ten days of food, you said? That's a start. We need to inventory everything. Every bag of kibble, every bag of litter, every medication. We need to know exactly where we stand. Then, we need to call Dr. Albright and explain the situation, see if we can work out a payment plan. I'll call the Harrison Foundation myself. I need to speak to someone directly, understand the exact timeline and what we can do to expedite this audit."

Mara looked up, her eyes red-rimmed but a flicker of resolve returning to them. "I already called them. They said it's a standard procedure. They can't expedite it. The auditors are booked solid for months." Her voice was heavy with the weight of that news.

Eli's jaw tightened. Months. The word hung in the air, a death knell. He stood up, pacing the small confines of the office. The idyllic calm of the morning felt like a distant memory, replaced by a chilling premonition of the storm that had truly broken. This was more than just a financial crisis; it was an existential threat. The sanctuary, a place of hope and healing, was now a beacon of vulnerability. He felt a surge of protectiveness, a fierce determination to shield this place, and the animals within it, from the harsh realities of the world. He looked at Mara, her face a picture of weary determination, and he knew they were in this together, facing a challenge that would test them in ways they had never imagined. The future of Port Blossom, once so bright with the promise of continued work and growth, was now shrouded in a chilling shadow of uncertainty.

He picked up his laptop, the weight of it feeling heavier than usual. He needed to see the grant documentation, to understand the exact nature of the administrative error. Information was power, and right now, they needed every shred of it they could get. "Show me the email again, Mara," he said, his voice regaining some of its earlier steadiness, a nascent plan beginning to form in the chaos. "Every detail. We'll go through it line by line. We have to. Because if this grant is truly frozen for months, then we have to be resourceful. We have to be creative. We have to fight for this place." He met her gaze, his own eyes reflecting a newfound intensity, a quiet resolve that, despite the dire circumstances, offered a sliver of hope. This wasn't just about saving a facility; it was about saving lives, about preserving the sanctuary they had built with their own hands and hearts. The shadow at Port Blossom was deep and unsettling, but perhaps, just perhaps, they could find a way to outrun it, or at least, to navigate through it.

The stark reality of the Harrison Foundation's frozen grant settled over Mara like a shroud, each tick of the office clock amplifying the dread. Eli's words, meant to be reassuring, echoed in the small space, but they couldn't quite fill the void left by the email's chilling pronouncement. *We'll figure something out.* She wanted to believe him, to cling to that promise like a life raft in a rising tide. But even as she turned her mind to the immediate, desperate logistics of the next few days – inventorying supplies, stretching meals, concocting a plan for emergency fundraising – a quiet, persistent worry began to unfurl in the back of her mind, a worry that had little to do with kibble shortages and everything to do with the man standing beside her.

Eli's usual focused intensity, the way his brow would furrow when he was deep in thought, seemed different now. It wasn't just the weight of the rescue's imminent collapse that etched itself onto his face. There was a subtle distance in his eyes, a contemplative gaze that seemed to look past her, past the overflowing kennels, and into some uncharted territory within himself. He moved with a practiced efficiency, his hands sorting through invoices and supply lists with a familiar dexterity, but his movements lacked their usual fluidity. He was present, undeniably, his actions geared towards addressing the crisis, yet he also felt… elsewhere.

She caught him staring out the window more than once, his gaze fixed on the distant, shimmering expanse of the ocean that Port Blossom overlooked. The vast, indifferent blue seemed to mirror a certain stillness in him, a quiet resignation that both unnerved and intrigued her. It was a look she'd seen before, fleetingly, in moments of profound decision-making, but now it seemed to linger, a permanent fixture. He'd mentioned the Oceanic Research Institute's offer, a seemingly life-altering opportunity, and while the immediate crisis had forced it to the back of his mind, Mara wondered if it hadn't burrowed deeper, a seed of potential change taking root even as the ground beneath their current reality began to crumble.

Their shared dream, the very foundation of Port Blossom Animal Rescue, had always felt solid, an unshakeable edifice built on mutual passion and countless hours of shared labor. They had poured their hearts into this place, their lives intertwined with the needs of the animals they rescued. She trusted Eli implicitly, had always seen them as an indivisible unit, facing every challenge head-on, together. But lately, she sensed a subtle shift, a widening aperture between his outward focus on the rescue and some inner, private world. Was this pre-occupation solely a product of the Harrison Foundation's sudden withdrawal of support, or was it something more personal, a yearning for a path untaken, a different kind of future that suddenly felt within reach, even amidst the chaos?

She tried to dismiss the thought, pushing it away as the desperate machinations of a mind under immense pressure. This was no time for introspection about their individual aspirations; this was about survival. They had hundreds of mouths to feed, lives dependent on their immediate action. Eli was a problem-solver, a doer. He would rally, he would find a way. That was who he was. He wouldn't let this place, their shared legacy, fall apart without a fight.

Yet, the quiet hum of his unspoken thoughts was a new, unsettling melody in the familiar soundtrack of the rescue. He was a man of deep conviction, but also of quiet contemplation. His silences, usually filled with a comforting presence, now felt weighted with unspoken questions. Had the offer from the Oceanic Research Institute, with its promise of groundbreaking scientific discovery and a world beyond the daily grind of animal welfare, stirred a deeper ambition in him? An ambition that, perhaps, Port Blossom, in its current state of precariousness, could no longer fulfill?

Mara watched him as he spoke on the phone, his voice low and measured, a stark contrast to the tremor she'd felt in his hand earlier. He was coordinating with Dr. Albright, attempting to negotiate an extension on the outstanding bill for the injured stray cat. Even in this moment of intense pragmatism, his concern for the cat's well-being was palpable, a testament to the core of his being. But there was an underlying weariness, a subtle slump of his shoulders that spoke of more than just the immediate financial strain. It was the weight of leadership, yes, but perhaps also the weight of diverging paths.

She knew he needed space to process, to strategize, to simply breathe amidst the whirlwind. She wouldn't pry, wouldn't add to his burden by voicing her own nascent anxieties about his internal landscape. Her role, for now, was to be the anchor, to tackle the immediate, tangible tasks that would keep the rescue afloat for the next few days. She would rally the volunteers, organize the donation drive, write the desperate appeals to their supporters. She would be the outward-facing force, the one who projected an unshakeable resolve, even if her own heart was aflutter with unease.

But as she turned back to the stacks of paperwork, her mind still whirring with contingency plans, a small part of her couldn't help but observe the subtle shifts in Eli's demeanor. The way his gaze would drift towards the horizon, as if searching for a different shore. The almost imperceptible sigh that would escape him when he thought no one was listening. She understood the pressure, the immense responsibility he carried. She shared it. But she also knew Eli, knew the quiet currents that ran beneath his steady surface. And in the face of this storm, she worried about the silent choices he might be making, the internal compass that might be subtly recalibrating, guided by a different star. The dream they'd built together was strong, resilient, but dreams, she was learning, were vulnerable things, susceptible to the winds of circumstance and the quiet whispers of individual longing. She could only hope that their shared vision was strong enough to weather this unexpected gale, and the unspoken winds that seemed to be blowing through Eli's own heart. She took a deep breath, her own resolve hardening, and turned back to the immediate task at hand, a silent prayer on her lips for their shared future, and for the man who was both its architect and, she feared, its potential wanderer. The calm before this particular storm had been a deceptive, fragile thing, and the true tempest, she suspected, was only just beginning to gather its strength.

The salt-laced air kissed Mara's cheeks as she walked beside Eli along the familiar stretch of Port Blossom beach. The tide was going out, leaving behind a slick, glistening canvas of sand that mirrored the vast, star-dusted canvas of the night sky above. The rhythmic symphony of waves crashing against the shore was a sound deeply woven into the fabric of her life, a constant, comforting bassline against the sometimes-cacophonous melody of running Port Blossom Animal Rescue. Tonight, however, that familiar rhythm felt tinged with a new, subtle dissonance, a counterpoint born of unspoken anxieties and the chilling reality of their current predicament.

Eli walked with his usual long, unhurried stride, his silhouette a familiar, grounding presence against the deepening twilight. His hand, rough and strong from countless hours of work, brushed against hers, a fleeting contact that sent a familiar warmth through her. She leaned into it slightly, a silent acknowledgment of their shared journey, their shared burden.

The conversation had been light, a gentle ebb and flow of mundane observations about the day, the sea birds calling their final farewells to the receding light, the faint glow of distant fishing boats bobbing on the inky water. Yet, beneath the surface of their words, a more profound dialogue was unfolding, a silent conversation that Mara desperately wanted to bring into the open.

"I was thinking," Mara began, her voice soft, almost swallowed by the murmur of the ocean, "we could try a small community bake sale next weekend. Maybe set up a few tables outside the rescue. You know, keep it low-key, but let people know we're still here, still fighting." She laced her fingers with his, her thumb tracing the calluses on his palm. "We could get the kids from the art class to make some signs, maybe even have a few of the adoptable dogs come out for a bit. It might... lift spirits, you know? Ours and theirs."

Eli's grip tightened almost imperceptibly. "That's a good idea, Mara," he said, his voice even, yet something in its measured tone made her heart hitch. It was the kind of response that was kind, that was supportive, but it lacked the usual spark of collaborative enthusiasm, the quick ignition of shared purpose that had always characterized their brainstorming sessions. It felt like a concession, rather than a contribution.

She watched his profile, the sharp line of his jaw softened by the moonlight. His gaze was fixed on the horizon, a place where the ocean met the stars in an ethereal blur. It was the same gaze she had seen earlier, the one that seemed to look beyond the immediate crisis, beyond their shared world. "We'll need to order more flyers too," she continued, pushing gently, trying to steer the conversation back to the tangible, the actionable, the present. "And I was thinking about reaching out to the local newspaper again. A human interest piece, perhaps? Focus on a specific animal, tug at some heartstrings."

He nodded slowly, his eyes still distant. "Yes, that sounds sensible."

Sensible. The word hung in the air, a dry leaf in the salty breeze. Sensible was what you did when you were managing a crisis. But it wasn't the word she craved. She craved passion, she craved the fierce, unwavering determination that usually burned so brightly in him. Where had it gone? Had it been extinguished by the Harrison Foundation's abrupt withdrawal, or was it being siphoned away by a different current altogether?

They walked in silence for a while, the only sound the persistent whisper of the waves. Mara's mind churned, a frantic attempt to decipher the quiet eddy in Eli's demeanor. He had mentioned the Oceanic Research Institute's offer in passing, a distant, almost theoretical possibility that had been immediately overshadowed by the rescue's very real, very immediate financial crisis. But the way he had spoken of it then, with a flicker of something akin to awe, a subdued excitement that had been quickly masked, had lodged itself in Mara's memory. It was a world away from the constant, often heartbreaking, demands of Port Blossom. A world of scientific discovery, of vast, unexplored frontiers, of a different kind of impact.

Was that the source of the distance? Was he mentally packing his bags, already mentally charting a course for that distant, starlit horizon? The thought was a cold, sharp pebble in her shoe, a constant, nagging discomfort. She knew, with a certainty that settled deep in her bones, that he had to tell her. The offer, the potential change, was a significant part of his life, a potential fork in their shared road. And the fact that he hadn't, that he was still holding it back, felt like a betrayal, not of intent, but of an essential, unspoken contract between them.

"It's just... it's been a tough few days," Mara said, her voice deliberately casual, an attempt to create an opening without forcing it. "With everything. The grant, the bills... it makes you re-evaluate things, doesn't it?" She risked a glance at him, her heart thrumming a nervous rhythm against her ribs. "What we're doing here. If it's enough. If it's what we want, long-term."

Eli finally turned to her, his eyes, usually so clear and direct, now held a shadowed depth. He met her gaze, and for a fleeting moment, she saw a flash of the internal struggle, the conflict that had been simmering beneath his calm exterior. He opened his mouth as if to speak, a faint furrow appearing between his brows, the familiar sign of intense thought. Then, he closed it again, a subtle shake of his head.

"We'll get through this, Mara," he said, his voice low and steady, a familiar anchor in the swirling uncertainty. "We always do."

But the assurance felt like a well-worn cloak, draped over a more complex reality. It was a comforting sentiment, but it didn't address the question she had implicitly asked – not about their ability to survive, but about their shared future, about the paths they were truly walking.

He squeezed her hand again, a more deliberate gesture this time, as if trying to convey reassurance through physical contact. "Port Blossom is our life. Yours and mine. We built it together."

And yet, the unspoken question hung between them, as vast and as silent as the ocean itself. Was it still *their* life? Was he still as committed to building it, brick by painstaking brick, as she was? Or had the allure of a different kind of building, a different kind of construction, begun to captivate his gaze? The Oceanic Research Institute. The words themselves conjured images of laboratories, of groundbreaking discoveries, of a world that felt infinitely more abstract and perhaps, to Eli, more profoundly fulfilling than the daily, often messy, reality of rescued animals.

She understood his silence, on one level. This was not the time for difficult conversations about personal ambitions and potential career shifts. The rescue was teetering on the brink. The immediate need was for unity, for unwavering focus on survival. Voicing her anxieties, forcing him to confront his own internal divisions, would only add to the immense pressure he was already under. He needed her support, her steadfastness, her outward projection of confidence, even if her inner world was a landscape of burgeoning doubts.

But the silence was a heavy thing, a physical presence between them. It amplified every doubt, every fleeting thought. It created space where there had always been connection. It was the quiet intruder, the phantom guest at their intimate dinner, the subtle chill that permeated their shared space.

"I know," she murmured, her voice a little tighter than she intended. "And we will. We have to." She forced a smile, trying to imbue it with the conviction she didn't fully feel. "Maybe we should focus on the bake sale logistics tomorrow. I can start a signup sheet for volunteers."

Eli's gaze softened slightly as he looked at her, a hint of apology in his eyes. "Yes. Volunteers. That's a good start." He paused, then added, almost as an afterthought, "And maybe... maybe we can talk later. Properly. About... everything."

The promise, however tentative, was a lifeline. "I'd like that," she said, a genuine warmth finally surfacing in her voice. "Very much."

They continued their walk, the familiar comfort of the beach slowly reasserting itself, the rhythm of the waves a balm to her unsettled spirit. But the unspoken question, the one that hummed beneath the surface of their words, remained. It was a question of loyalty, of ambition, of the very definition of their shared dream. And as they walked, side by side, under the indifferent gaze of a million stars, Mara knew that the calm before this particular storm had been a fragile, deceptive thing. The real tempest, she feared, was not the one brewing over Port

Blossom's finances, but the one gathering strength in the quiet, uncharted territory of Eli's heart. He needed to tell her. She needed him to tell her. But for now, the ocean kept its secrets, and so, it seemed, did he. The stars offered no answers, only a vast, silent expanse that mirrored the growing distance she felt between them, a distance measured not in miles, but in the unarticulated hopes and fears that now lay between the crashing waves and the starlit sky.

Chapter Two

Cracks in the Foundation

Eli found himself drawn to the quiet sanctuary of Dr. Ramirez's study, a room that always seemed to hum with the accumulated wisdom of decades dedicated to the ocean's mysteries. Books, their spines bearing the weight of scientific inquiry and conservation efforts, lined the walls from floor to ceiling, creating an atmosphere of profound respect for the natural world. The scent of aged paper and faint traces of pipe tobacco, Dr. Ramirez's occasional indulgence, hung in the air, a comforting aroma that always settled Eli's nerves. He'd driven over directly after his tense walk with Mara on the beach, the unresolved weight of his unspoken thoughts pressing down on him with an almost physical force. He needed to talk, to unpack the bewildering tangle of his emotions with someone who understood the currents that pulled at him, both professionally and personally.

Dr. Ramirez, a man whose silver hair and gentle smile belied a sharp intellect and a formidable career in marine biology, gestured towards a worn leather armchair positioned by a large window overlooking a meticulously kept garden. "Eli, my boy," he said, his voice a low rumble, like the distant swell of a calm sea. "Come in, sit down. You look like you've wrestled a kraken and lost."

Eli managed a weak smile as he sank into the chair, the leather creaking softly in protest. He ran a hand over the smooth, cool surface, his gaze drifting to the framed photographs on the desk: Dr. Ramirez in his younger days, standing beside a research vessel; a close-up of a vibrant coral reef; a majestic whale breaching the surface. These images represented a lifetime of dedication, a path Eli felt increasingly torn between. "Something like that, Dr. Ramirez," he admitted, his voice betraying the weariness he felt. "Just... a lot on my mind."

Dr. Ramirez poured two glasses of water from a crystal carafe, handing one to Eli. "The Institute," he stated, his tone knowing. It wasn't a question. Eli had shared his initial excitement about the Oceanic Research Institute's offer weeks ago, a professional coup that had momentarily eclipsed the looming crisis at Port Blossom. But then the Harrison Foundation's funding had been abruptly cut, and the conversation had shifted to survival, to bake sales and flyers, to the immediate, desperate need to keep the rescue afloat. Eli had, in his attempt to shield Mara and the rescue from further worry, deliberately downplayed the significance of the Institute's offer, letting it recede into the background as a distant, improbable dream. But the offer had not gone away. It had solidified, the details becoming concrete, the timeline pressing closer, and with it, Eli's own internal conflict had intensified.

"Yes," Eli confirmed, taking a slow sip of water. The cool liquid did little to quench the dryness in his throat. "The Institute. They've formally offered me the lead research position. The one we discussed." He paused, gathering his thoughts, the words feeling heavy and cumbersome as they formed in his mind. "It's... it's everything I've worked for. The chance to lead a project on deep-sea hydrothermal vents. The technology they have, the access to unexplored regions... it's incredible, Dr. Ramirez. Truly groundbreaking." He looked around the study, at the testament to a life lived in pursuit of scientific discovery. "It's the kind of work that could make a real difference, a tangible impact on our understanding of ocean ecosystems."

Dr. Ramirez nodded, his expression thoughtful. He leaned back in his own chair, his hands clasped loosely over his stomach. "I'm not surprised, Eli. Your proposal was exceptional, and your passion for that particular field is undeniable. You have a rare gift for seeing the patterns, for connecting the dots where others see only chaos. That's precisely what the Institute is looking for." He met Eli's gaze, his eyes kind but direct. "It's a remarkable opportunity. A career-defining one."

And therein lay the crux of Eli's torment. The opportunity was immense, a dazzling professional peak that beckoned with the promise of fulfillment and recognition. But standing at the base of that peak was Port Blossom, and more specifically,

Mara. The thought of leaving her, of leaving the life they had so painstakingly built together, felt like a physical wrench. "I know," Eli said, his voice quieter now, the initial excitement dulled by a profound sense of conflict. "And that's... that's the problem. I'm so excited about the prospect, the research... but I can't shake this feeling, this crushing guilt, about leaving everything behind. Leaving *her* behind."

He gestured vaguely, as if to encompass the entire scope of his dilemma. "Mara. Port Blossom. They're my life, Dr. Ramirez. We built the rescue from nothing. Every late night, every stressful fundraising event, every moment of doubt we've overcome together... it's all intertwined. And now, to walk away from it... it feels like a betrayal." He ran his hand through his hair, a gesture of frustration. "Especially now, when they need us most. The Harrison Foundation pulling out... it's a disaster. And I'm standing here, contemplating a dream job on the other side of the country, while Mara is here, fighting tooth and nail to keep the doors open."

Dr. Ramirez listened patiently, his gaze never wavering, allowing Eli the space to articulate his deepest fears and reservations. He understood the inherent conflict of ambition versus loyalty, the agonizing calculus of personal dreams colliding with shared commitments. He had faced similar crossroads himself, albeit decades ago, when the lure of a prestigious international fellowship had clashed with his burgeoning relationship with his late wife.

"Eli," Dr. Ramirez began, his voice gentle but firm, "ambition and love are not mutually exclusive. They are often, in fact, the two most powerful forces in a person's life, and navigating their currents can be the most challenging voyage of all." He leaned forward, his tone becoming more earnest. "You have dedicated years to Port Blossom, to nurturing that rescue, to saving lives. That commitment is undeniable, and Mara knows it, just as she knows your drive for scientific exploration. This offer doesn't negate your past contributions; it speaks to your future potential."

"But the timing," Eli interjected, the word tasting like ash in his mouth. "It's just... the worst possible timing. How can I even consider it when Mara is so stressed, so overwhelmed? How can I have this conversation with her, knowing it might break her heart, or worse, make her feel like I'm abandoning her when she needs me most?"

"Ah, the conversation," Dr. Ramirez said, a knowing smile playing on his lips. "That's the knot you're trying to untie, isn't it? The fear of the conversation itself." He paused, letting the truth of his observation settle. "Eli, honesty is the bedrock of any strong relationship. And while this conversation will undoubtedly be difficult, it's far more damaging to let it fester, to let the unspoken create a chasm between you. Mara is strong, Eli. She's a fighter, as you well know. She deserves the truth, the whole truth, about your aspirations, just as you deserve her understanding and support. She might be hurt, she might be worried, but she will also, I believe, respect your candor."

He picked up a small, smooth stone from his desk, turning it over in his fingers. "Think of it this way. Your skills, your knowledge, your vision – these are unique. The work you propose at the Institute is vital. It's not just about your personal advancement; it's about contributing to a broader understanding that could, in the long run, benefit countless marine ecosystems, perhaps even those that Port Blossom strives to protect indirectly. You have a responsibility, not just to yourself and Mara, but to the knowledge you can unlock."

Eli leaned his head back against the chair, the soft leather a welcome contrast to the tension in his shoulders. He knew Dr. Ramirez was right, of course. He always was. But knowing what to do and being able to do it were two entirely different oceans. He pictured Mara's face, the worry lines etched around her eyes, the fierce determination that fueled her every action. How could he add to her burden, even with the best intentions?

"I just don't know how to start," Eli confessed, his voice barely above a whisper. "It feels... selfish. All this talk of groundbreaking research, when she's worried about paying for food for the animals. It feels like I'm living in a different world."

"You are living in two worlds, Eli," Dr. Ramirez corrected gently. "And that's the challenge of a full life. You are deeply rooted in the immediate, tangible work of Port Blossom, and you also have the capacity and the ambition to explore the vast, abstract frontiers of scientific discovery. These are not contradictory; they are complementary aspects of who you are."

He placed the stone back on his desk. "The key is to find a way to communicate this complexity. Acknowledge the difficulties at Port Blossom. Express your unwavering commitment to supporting Mara through this crisis. And then, and only then, share your excitement and your dilemma regarding the Institute's offer. Frame it not as a choice between two things, but as a decision that requires careful consideration of all the interwoven threads of your life. And importantly, Eli, make it clear that your decision will be made in partnership with her, not in spite of her."

He paused, his gaze fixed on Eli. "Don't let the fear of the unknown, the fear of her reaction, paralyze you. The greatest disservice you could do to your relationship with Mara would be to deny her the opportunity to be your partner in this, to let her wonder, to let doubt fester. You built Port Blossom together. Let her be a part of building your future, whatever shape that may take."

Eli felt a sliver of the tension begin to dissipate, replaced by a fragile sense of clarity. The path forward was still daunting, shrouded in the fog of uncertainty, but Dr. Ramirez had provided a compass, a guiding star. He needed to be honest. He needed to be brave. He needed to trust Mara, and he needed to trust their shared foundation.

"You're right," Eli said, his voice stronger now, more resolute. "I have to tell her. I can't keep this hidden. It's not fair to either of us." He looked at Dr. Ramirez, a newfound sense of purpose in his eyes. "Thank you, Dr. Ramirez. I... I needed this. More than you know."

Dr. Ramirez offered a warm smile. "That's what mentors are for, Eli. To help navigate the storms, to remind you of the strength of your anchor, and to encourage you to hoist the sails when the winds are right. Now, go. Have that conversation. And when you've figured out the next steps, whatever they may be, know that you have my full support."

As Eli rose from the armchair, he felt a subtle shift within him. The weight hadn't entirely disappeared, but it had transformed. It was no longer a crushing burden of secrecy, but the bracing challenge of an impending, necessary confrontation. He would face it, for Mara, for Port Blossom, and for the truth that would ultimately strengthen their bond, no matter how turbulent the waters ahead. The research might be on the other side of the country, but his heart, he knew, was right here, tangled inextricably with Mara's, and that was a truth he finally felt ready to confront.

The fluorescent lights of the Port Blossom office hummed with a relentless, almost accusatory buzz, a stark contrast to the usual comforting murmur of the sea that Mara associated with her sanctuary. But sanctuary felt a million miles away tonight. The door to Dr. Ramirez's study, a room steeped in the quiet wisdom of marine biology and the comforting scent of aged paper and pipe tobacco, was firmly closed behind Eli as he'd left, leaving Mara alone with a gnawing unease and a mountain of urgent, pressing problems. The conversation had been… difficult. Eli's unspoken anxieties, now laid bare, had settled over her like a thick, unfamiliar fog. His ambition, his dream job that would take him across the country, felt like a shadow cast over the fragile life they had so painstakingly built together. But dwelling on that, on the potential fissures in their shared future, would do neither of them any good. Not now. Not when the immediate threat to Port Blossom loomed so large.

She turned her attention back to the overflowing inbox on her laptop, the cursor blinking impatiently, a silent demand for action. The rescue's financial situation was dire, a fact that had been a low thrum of anxiety for months, but since the Harrison Foundation's abrupt withdrawal of funding, it had escalated into a deafening roar. The emergency fund was depleted, operating costs were spiraling, and the looming payroll was a specter that haunted her waking hours and infiltrated her dreams. She knew, with a certainty that settled deep in her bones, that she couldn't afford to be overwhelmed. She had to be pragmatic. She had to be surgical.

Mara pulled a fresh notebook from the drawer, its pages crisp and unblemished, a blank canvas for the chaos she was about to impose upon it. She flipped to the first page, her handwriting bold and decisive as she penned "Port Blossom Financial Deep Dive – October." Below it, she added a sub-heading: "Immediate Actions & Long-Term Viability." She wasn't just looking for quick fixes; she needed to understand the systemic issues, the cracks in the foundation that had allowed them to reach this precipice.

Her fingers flew across the keyboard, opening spreadsheets that felt more like intricate puzzles than simple financial reports. She started with the most recent quarter, meticulously cross-referencing invoices, receipts, and bank statements. The hours blurred into a single, unbroken stretch of intense focus. The world outside the office – the distant sound of gulls, the gentle lapping of waves against the docks, even the occasional siren wail from the town – faded into insignificance. Her universe had contracted to the glowing screen and the columns of numbers that danced before her eyes.

She remembered Eli's frustration during the last board meeting, his exasperation with what he'd termed "unaccountable expenditures." At the time, she'd been too preoccupied with securing a grant for new diving equipment to delve too deeply into his concerns. Now, those words echoed in her mind, a prescient warning she had, perhaps, dismissed too easily. Eli, for all his occasional idealism, had an uncanny knack for spotting imbalances, for seeing the subtle discord in complex systems. And his current emotional turmoil, while concerning, didn't negate his professional insight.

Mara sipped her lukewarm coffee, the bitter taste a familiar companion to late nights. She traced the lines of a budget allocation for animal care. The figures seemed... high. Higher than she would have expected, even with the rising cost of specialized diets and veterinary care. She pulled up the corresponding invoices from the past six months, her brow furrowed. There were multiple entries for a particular brand of premium fish food, a brand that, she distinctly recalled, had been flagged as prohibitively expensive during an earlier budget review. Had they switched suppliers without a formal board decision? Or was this simply a case of miscategorization?

She moved on to the veterinary expenses. The numbers were even more perplexing. Several large, recurring payments were listed under "specialized consultations," but the corresponding documentation was vague, lacking the detailed reports she'd expect for complex treatments. One entry, a significant sum for a single procedure, was attributed to an external clinic she didn't immediately recognize. A quick search revealed it was a highly specialized facility, known for treating exotic marine life, located nearly three hours away. Why would Port Blossom be utilizing such a resource without her direct knowledge or approval, especially when their local veterinarian, Dr. Davies, was both competent and considerably more affordable?

A knot of unease tightened in Mara's stomach. This wasn't just about the Harrison Foundation's withdrawal. This was about internal inconsistencies, about financial decisions that seemed to have been made in a vacuum. She felt a prickle of anger, a sense of betrayal not just by the circumstances, but by a potential lack of transparency within the very organization she poured her heart and soul into.

She decided to tackle the donor outreach next. The grant applications were her forte, a meticulous process of research, writing, and persuasive argumentation. But individual donor relations were a more delicate dance, requiring a personal touch, a genuine connection. She pulled up the database of past supporters, their names a familiar roll call of individuals and businesses who had, at one time or another, believed in their mission. She started with the most recent major donors, the ones who had contributed during the last successful fundraising drive.

She crafted an email, her fingers hovering over the send button. She needed to be direct but not desperate. She needed to convey the urgency of their situation without sounding like a charity case. She emphasized the critical work they were doing, the success stories that had resulted from their efforts, and the immediate need for their continued support to keep those operations running. She attached a concise, updated financial summary, highlighting the impact of the Harrison Foundation's funding cut.

As she sent the email, a notification pinged on her screen. A reply. Her heart leaped with a flicker of hope. It was from Mr. Henderson, a local businessman who had been a consistent, albeit modest, contributor for years. His response was brief and to the point: "Mara, deeply concerned to hear of your funding difficulties. I've always admired the work you do. I'm not in a position to make a substantial pledge right now, but I'd be happy to host a small, informal gathering at my home next month. We could invite a few like-minded friends, perhaps make a small, collective donation to help tide you over. Let me know if this is of interest."

A small spark of warmth ignited in Mara's chest. It wasn't a lifeline, but it was a lifeline nonetheless. A chance to connect with potential supporters, to share the Port Blossom story in a more intimate setting. She immediately replied, her words filled with genuine gratitude, confirming her interest and offering to discuss details.

She then moved on to the smaller, recurring donors, the ones who contributed monthly, who formed the bedrock of their operational stability. She drafted a slightly different message, one that acknowledged their consistent support and reassured them that their contributions were still making a significant impact, even in these challenging times. She felt a pang of guilt, knowing that she couldn't guarantee the continuity of every program, the certainty of every rescue.

Hours later, the office was silent save for the rhythmic clicking of her keyboard and the distant sigh of the ocean. Mara stretched her stiff neck, her eyes gritty from staring at the screen. The spreadsheets were filled with her annotations, circled figures, question marks, and hastily scribbled notes. She had identified several areas of concern: the unusually high spending on premium animal feed, the unexplained external veterinary bills, and a discrepancy in the accounting for equipment maintenance.

She decided to pick up the phone and call Dr. Davies, their regular veterinarian. She explained her inquiry in general terms, framing it as a review of past expenditures to ensure optimal resource allocation. Dr. Davies was polite but direct. He confirmed that Port Blossom's account with him had been inactive for the past three months. When Mara pressed further, asking about any referrals to specialized clinics, he seemed surprised. "Mara, I haven't referred anyone to an external specialist in quite some time," he stated. "If there were complex cases requiring advanced care, I would have handled them myself, or at the very least, discussed the necessity of outsourcing with you or Eli."

A chill snaked down Mara's spine. Dr. Davies was a man of integrity, meticulous in his record-keeping and always transparent in his dealings. His words confirmed her deepest fears. The external veterinary bills were not only unexplained, they were potentially fabricated, or at the very least, grossly misrepresented. The implications were staggering. This wasn't just poor financial management; this was something far more serious.

She hung up the phone, her hand trembling slightly. She looked at the spreadsheet again, at the column of figures representing "specialized consultations." These were thousands of dollars, diverted from the rescue's core mission, from the animals in their care, from the very purpose for which donors entrusted them with their hard-earned money.

She knew she couldn't confront Eli with this information just yet. He was already wrestling with his own monumental decision, and layering this new crisis on top of his personal turmoil would be unfair, overwhelming. But she also knew she couldn't let it fester. The integrity of Port Blossom, the trust of their supporters, and the well-being of the animals were paramount.

Mara opened a new document, her fingers finding the familiar rhythm of typing. She began to meticulously document her findings, cross-referencing dates, invoice numbers, and amounts. She attached copies of the relevant documents, creating a clear, irrefutable trail of the financial discrepancies. She didn't know who was responsible, or why this had happened, but she was determined to uncover the truth.

Her mind raced, piecing together fragments of information. The premium fish food. The specialized veterinary care. The lack of documentation. It all pointed towards a deliberate misdirection of funds. But who would do such a thing, and to what end? Was it a desperate attempt to cover up a personal debt? Or something more sinister?

She pulled up the records for equipment maintenance. Again, the figures seemed inflated. There were several large payments for "engine overhaul" and "hull repair" for boats that, to her knowledge, hadn't undergone significant maintenance in over a year. She recalled a conversation with Leo, their head mechanic, a few weeks prior. He'd mentioned that the rescue boats were in surprisingly good condition, considering their age, and that most of their maintenance needs were routine. He'd even commented on how fortunate they were to have avoided any major, costly repairs.

The pieces were beginning to form a disturbing picture. A pattern of inflated invoices, questionable expenditures, and a general lack of transparency that seemed to permeate the financial operations of Port Blossom. She felt a surge of protectiveness, a fierce resolve to safeguard the rescue, not just from external threats, but from internal rot.

Mara decided to reach out to Sarah, a former volunteer who had a background in accounting. Sarah had always been incredibly organized and had a sharp eye for detail. Perhaps she could offer a fresh perspective, an objective analysis of the numbers. Mara drafted a brief, carefully worded message, explaining that she was conducting a thorough review of Port Blossom's financial records and had encountered some anomalies she needed help understanding. She didn't want to alarm Sarah unnecessarily, but she desperately needed a second opinion.

As she waited for Sarah's reply, Mara pulled out her phone and scrolled through her contacts. She hesitated for a moment, then dialed Eli's number. He'd said he'd be at Dr. Ramirez's for a while, and she knew he was wrestling with his own difficult decisions. But she couldn't keep this to herself any longer. She needed to share the burden, to have a sounding board, even if he was grappling with his own storm.

"Hey," she said softly, her voice a little hoarse. "Just checking in. How are you doing?"

A pause, then Eli's voice, laced with weariness, came through the line. "Hey, Mara. I'm... okay. Just talking things through. How about you? Still buried in numbers?"

"You have no idea," she replied, a humorless chuckle escaping her lips. "Eli, I found something... something concerning. In the financial records. About the veterinary expenses and boat maintenance." She paused, choosing her words carefully. "It looks like there might have been some significant overspending, maybe even some... discrepancies. I'm trying to get to the bottom of it, but it's complex."

Another pause, this one longer, heavier. Eli sighed. "Discrepancies? What kind of discrepancies?"

Mara explained, her voice steady, detailing the unusual veterinary bills, the lack of documentation, and the inflated maintenance costs. She mentioned Dr. Davies' confirmation of no recent external referrals. Eli listened intently, his silence punctuated by the occasional sharp intake of breath.

"That doesn't make any sense," Eli finally said, his voice taut with concern. "Leo said the boats were fine. And Dr. Davies is one of the most honest people I know. If he's saying that, then..."

"Then the invoices don't add up," Mara finished for him. "I'm going to be digging deeper tomorrow. I've asked Sarah, from accounting, to take a look too. I just... I wanted you to know. Before things potentially get messy."

"Messy is an understatement, Mara," Eli said, his voice grim. "This is... this is bad. If someone has been deliberately... misusing funds..." He trailed off, the unspoken accusation hanging heavy in the air.

Mara felt a wave of exhaustion wash over her, but also a renewed sense of determination. "I know," she said. "But we'll figure it out, Eli. We always do. Right now, I need to focus on understanding the extent of it. And then we'll deal with it. Together."

"Together," Eli echoed, the word a quiet promise. "Always together. Mara, I... I'm so sorry I didn't pay closer attention to this. I've been so caught up in the Institute offer, in all of this... I let it slide. I should have been more vigilant."

"Don't do that, Eli," Mara said, her voice firm. "We're a team. And right now, I need you to focus on what you need to focus on. I'll handle this. I'll get to the bottom of it." She didn't say "I'll handle it alone," but the implication was there, a silent acknowledgment of the different battles they were currently fighting.

"No," Eli said, his voice suddenly resolute. "We'll handle it together. This is Port Blossom, Mara. It's our rescue. Our responsibility. I'll be back as soon as I can. We'll go through this together, line by line."

Mara felt a small, fragile sense of relief bloom in her chest. The financial storm was raging, the cracks in the foundation were becoming alarmingly clear, but she wasn't facing it entirely alone. And as she looked at the glowing screen, at the complex web of numbers that represented both a crisis and a challenge, she knew one thing with absolute certainty: she would not let Port Blossom crumble. She would fight for it, meticulously and relentlessly, until every last anomaly was exposed, every misplaced dollar accounted for, and the foundation of their rescue was once again solid and secure. The path ahead was daunting, but for the first time that evening, Mara felt a flicker of hope, a quiet strength that came from facing the truth, however uncomfortable it might be.

Eli found himself adrift in a sea of research, the glow of his laptop screen a surrogate sun in the quiet study at Dr. Ramirez's. The offer from the prestigious Oceanic Dynamics Institute was a siren song, its melody promising intellectual stimulation, cutting-edge research, and a trajectory that could redefine his career. He'd spent hours poring over the institute's website, delving into the biographies of its lead scientists, each one a titan in their respective fields, their names synonymous with groundbreaking discoveries. He read about projects that aimed to unlock the secrets of deep-sea ecosystems, to develop sustainable aquaculture practices that could feed a growing world, and to create predictive models for marine climate change – initiatives that resonated deeply with his scientific soul.

He scrolled through project proposals, his fingers tracing the complex diagrams and dense scientific jargon. One project, in particular, caught his eye: the development of advanced bio-luminescent sensors for tracking plankton migration patterns. It was the kind of intricate, multi-faceted problem that made his scientific mind sing. The institute had the resources, the talent, the sheer intellectual horsepower to tackle such ambitious endeavors. He could see himself there, collaborating with leading minds, pushing the boundaries of marine biology, making a tangible impact on a global scale. The thought sent a jolt of exhilaration through him, a feeling he hadn't experienced in years, a sensation of being on the cusp of something truly significant.

He read about the institute's state-of-the-art facilities – electron microscopes that could see the building blocks of life, high-pressure chambers that mimicked the crushing depths of the ocean floor, and vast computational clusters that could process unimaginable amounts of data. It was a playground for a scientist, a place where curiosity was not just encouraged but actively cultivated and rewarded. He imagined the discussions in the lab, the late-night debates fueled by coffee and shared passion, the thrill of discovery.

Yet, with each glowing review, each testament to the institute's unparalleled contributions to science, a counter-narrative began to weave itself into the fabric of his thoughts. It was a narrative that began with a simple image: Mara's hands, calloused and stained with salt and sea, gently tending to a rescued seal pup. It was the sound of the Port Blossom bell, signaling a successful rescue, the triumphant cry of gulls overhead, the comforting rhythm of the waves against the docks. It was the quiet satisfaction of seeing a rehabilitated dolphin released back into the vast expanse of the ocean, a tangible testament to their shared purpose.

He found himself comparing the glossy brochures of the institute with the worn, dog-eared pages of his own research notes, meticulously filled with observations of local marine life, the precise measurements of water salinity, and the careful documentation of rescue efforts. The institute offered a life of grand, sweeping gestures, of global impact. Port Blossom offered something quieter, something more intimate, something deeply rooted in the immediate, the tangible, the community they served.

He read an article about the institute's relocation program for its researchers, a perk that boasted the opportunity to experience diverse marine environments across the globe. A wave of unease washed over him. It was an exciting prospect, a chance to explore the world's oceans, but it also meant prolonged absences, a constant state of flux. It meant leaving Mara behind, not for a few weeks or months, but potentially for years at a time, if he were to truly immerse himself in the institute's long-term projects.

He pictured Mara, her brow furrowed in concentration as she navigated a complex financial report, her unwavering dedication to Port Blossom evident in every line she wrote. He remembered the late nights they'd spent together, side-by-side in the dimly lit office, the shared fatigue, the quiet companionship that had become the bedrock of their relationship. The institute's offer, while intellectually dazzling, seemed to cast a shadow over that shared space, that shared life. It was a life built on the quiet hum of purpose, on the shared understanding of their work's immediate impact, on the deep, abiding love that had grown between them amidst the salty air and the calls of the sea.

He imagined the conversations they'd have, or rather, the conversations he would be having with himself, trying to explain the allure of distant oceans and abstract scientific pursuits to the woman who found her fulfillment in the tangible reality of their coastal haven. How could he convey the thrill of a theoretical breakthrough when she was holding a cold, injured seabird in her hands, her sole focus on its immediate recovery? The institute's world was one of grand hypotheses and global solutions, while his life with Mara was grounded in the everyday miracles of their rescue, in the quiet dedication to the creatures who needed them most, right here, right now.

He looked at a photograph on the institute's homepage – a sleek, modern laboratory with scientists in pristine white coats working with gleaming equipment. It was a world away from the organized chaos of the Port Blossom rescue center, with its scent of disinfectant, fish food, and the faint, salty tang of the ocean, a world that, for all its imperfections, felt undeniably like home. He remembered the day they'd found the injured harbor seal pup, tangled in discarded fishing gear, its eyes wide with fear. Mara, her movements gentle and reassuring, had soothed the distressed animal while he'd meticulously worked to free it. That shared moment, that raw, unfiltered act of compassion, held a weight that no groundbreaking scientific discovery could ever truly replicate.

He found himself scrolling back through his emails, re-reading Mara's messages. Her calm, rational tone as she outlined the rescue's financial woes, her unwavering focus on finding solutions, her quiet strength in the face of overwhelming adversity. He knew she was currently embroiled in a deep dive into their finances, wrestling with the fallout from the Harrison Foundation's withdrawal. He'd left her to it, wanting to give her space to handle the immediate crisis, while he grappled with his own internal turmoil. But now, the weight of his own decision felt heavier, burdened by the knowledge of the battles she was fighting on his behalf, on behalf of Port Blossom.

The institute offered him a chance to explore the unknown, to delve into the mysteries of the deep. But the life he had built with Mara was its own kind of exploration, a journey into the depths of shared commitment, of unwavering support, of a love that had weathered its own storms and emerged stronger. He saw a photo of a researcher on an expedition, bundled in cold-weather gear, standing on a remote, icy coastline. It was a stark contrast to the image of Mara, her face flushed with exertion as she heaved a net full of kelp onto the dock, her smile radiant despite the sweat beading on her forehead.

He began to see the offer not just as a career opportunity, but as a fundamental choice about the very essence of his life. Did he crave the intellectual prestige of a world-renowned institute, or did he cherish the quiet, profound satisfaction of making a difference in his own backyard, with the woman he loved? The institute promised a life of grand narratives, of global recognition. Port Blossom offered a life of quiet purpose, of deep connection, of a love story woven into the very fabric of their community and the lives of the creatures they saved.

He closed his laptop, the room plunging into a softer, more familiar twilight. The silence was no longer filled with the hum of digital ambition, but with the gentle murmur of the sea, a sound that had always been the soundtrack to his life with Mara. He thought of her, alone in the office, poring over spreadsheets, her strength and resilience a constant source of inspiration. He knew, with a clarity that had been eluding him for days, that the most groundbreaking research he could ever undertake was right here, in the quiet, shared life he had built with her. The offer from the institute was a powerful lure, a testament to his achievements, but it was a path that diverged sharply from the one they had chosen together, a path that led away from the warmth of their shared home and the quiet, unwavering purpose that bound them. He had to decide not just what kind of scientist he wanted to be, but what kind of man, what kind of partner, he wanted to be. And as the waves whispered against the shore, the answer began to crystallize, not in the dazzling allure of distant horizons, but in the steadfast glow of a love that had become his truest north.

The scent of salt and fried calamari, usually a comforting balm, did little to soothe Mara's frayed nerves. She watched Eli across the small, scarred table at 'The Salty Siren,' their usual haven for post-work decompression. The flickering candlelight cast dancing shadows on his face, highlighting the worry lines etched around his eyes, lines that seemed deeper tonight than usual. He'd always been so open, his thoughts and feelings as clear as the tide pools at low ebb. But lately, a fog had settled between them, a subtle but persistent barrier that made her heart ache.

"The sea bass was particularly good tonight," Mara offered, forcing a smile. She gestured with her fork towards the remnants on his plate, a desperate attempt to inject some normalcy into the heavy silence that had descended almost as soon as their food had arrived. "Almost as good as Mrs. Henderson's, and you know how I feel about that." She waited for his usual playful retort, his easy chuckle. Instead, he just nodded, his gaze distant, fixed on something beyond the condensation-streaked window.

"Hmm. Yeah, it was," he murmured, his voice flat, lacking its usual warmth. He picked up his water glass, swirling the ice cubes as if contemplating a complex scientific equation. Mara's stomach tightened. This wasn't just stress about the rescue's finances, though that was certainly a dark cloud hanging over them. This was something else, something more personal, and it was keeping him from her.

"Eli," she began, her voice softer now, laced with a concern she couldn't quite disguise. "Are you alright? You've been so... quiet. For days, now." She reached across the table, her fingers brushing against his, a silent plea for connection. He didn't pull away, but he didn't quite meet her touch either, his hand remaining stubbornly still beneath hers.

He finally looked at her, his eyes troubled. "It's just... a lot, Mara. The Harrison Foundation pulling out, the upcoming bills... it's all weighing on me." He pulled his hand away gently, toying with the edge of his napkin. "We're going to have to make some tough decisions. About the new equipment, maybe even some of the outreach programs."

Mara's heart sank further. She knew all of this. She was living it, breathing it, dissecting every ledger and grant proposal with a fierce determination. But Eli's reticence was a different kind of burden. He was usually her anchor, the steady presence who could dissect a problem with logic and find a solution. Now, he seemed lost at sea himself. "We'll figure it out, Eli," she said, her voice firm, trying to project a confidence she didn't entirely feel. "We always do. That's what we do. We face it together."

He gave her a weak smile, a fleeting ghost of his usual warmth. "I know. You're amazing, Mara. Truly." His gaze, however, still held that faraway look, that hint of something unsaid, something he was wrestling with alone. He wanted to tell her about the Oceanic Dynamics Institute, about the offer that had landed in his inbox like a meteor, burning bright with promise and peril. The words were lodged in his throat, a knot of ambition and fear. How could he even begin to explain it? How could he articulate the intoxicating allure of cutting-edge research, of global impact, when their immediate reality was a desperate struggle to keep their beloved rescue center afloat?

"There's something else, isn't there?" Mara pressed, her intuition screaming at her. She could feel the invisible wall between them growing higher, thicker. "It's not just the rescue, is it?" She watched his reaction closely. He shifted in his seat, his gaze dropping back to his water glass.

"What makes you say that?" he asked, his tone carefully neutral, but she heard the slight tremor in his voice. It was the sound of someone trying to build a dam against a rising tide.

"Because you're not here, Eli," she said, her voice barely a whisper. "You're physically here, at dinner with me, but your mind is miles away. And it has been for weeks." She felt a pang of guilt for pushing, but the silence was becoming unbearable, a chasm widening with every unanswered question. "You've been so distracted, so... distant. Did something happen at Dr. Ramirez's? Did you hear something about the grant proposals?"

He shook his head, a little too quickly. "No, no. Nothing like that." He took a large gulp of water, as if to wash away the truth. He wanted to tell her about the institute, about the incredible projects, the chance to work with brilliant minds, the opportunity to push the boundaries of marine science on a scale he had only ever dreamed of. But the thought of her face, the potential disappointment, the fear of disrupting their shared life, kept him silent. He saw her image, her unwavering dedication to Port Blossom, her fierce protectiveness of their small community, and the words caught in his throat like a snagged fishing line.

"Then what is it?" Mara's voice was laced with a quiet desperation. "Please, Eli. Talk to me. Whatever it is, we can face it. But you have to let me in. This... this distance... it's starting to feel like a crack in the foundation." She looked at him, her heart aching with the unspoken gulf that had opened between them. She saw the conflict warring within him, the scientific ambition battling with his love for her, for their life here. And the silence, the terrible, suffocating silence, was the loudest confession of all. He was wrestling with something enormous, something that was changing him, and it terrified her. She could sense the potential for a seismic shift, a tremor that could shake the very ground they stood on.

Eli felt the weight of her gaze, the unspoken question hanging heavy in the air. He wanted to explain, to pour out the conflicting emotions churning within him. The Oceanic Dynamics Institute. The offer. The potential to reshape his entire career, to contribute to global scientific endeavors on an unprecedented scale. It was everything he had ever worked for, a dazzling pinnacle of achievement. But the thought of the words leaving his mouth, of seeing the implications dawn in Mara's eyes, was paralyzing. He pictured her hands, stained with salt and fish scales, mending a torn net, her brow furrowed in concentration. He saw her face, alight with joy as a rescued otter was released back into the wild. That was his world, their world, built on tangible acts of compassion, on the immediate needs of their coastal haven. The institute offered a different kind of world, one of abstract theories and far-reaching discoveries, a world that felt a million miles away from the comforting rhythm of their shared life.

He cleared his throat, the sound rough. "It's just... the pressures, Mara. The financial strain is immense. I've been doing a lot of thinking about... the future. About what we can realistically achieve here, given the constant struggle." He chose his words carefully, skirting the truth like a ship navigating treacherous shoals. He couldn't bring himself to mention the institute directly, not yet. The guilt was a physical ache in his chest. He saw how much she poured into Port Blossom, how much of herself she gave, and the thought of introducing a destabilizing element, a choice that could pull him away from her, felt like a betrayal.

Mara's brow furrowed. "What do you mean, 'realistically achieve'?" she asked, her voice tight with a sudden, sharp anxiety. "Are you saying you want to give up? After everything we've done?" The accusation hung in the air, unintentional but potent. She watched him, searching his face for a flicker of his usual resolve, but found only a troubled uncertainty.

He flinched at her words, at the implication. "No! Of course not," he said, his voice rising slightly. "That's not what I meant at all. I'm just... I'm worried, Mara. Worried about us. About the stress this is putting on you, on us." He reached for her hand again, this time his grip firmer, more desperate. "You're working yourself to the bone. And I... I feel like I'm not doing enough. Like I'm not... providing enough security."

His words, meant to reassure, only amplified Mara's unease. 'Providing enough security.' It sounded so unlike him, so... practical, almost detached. He was a scientist, a man driven by a passion for discovery, for understanding the intricate workings of the natural world. This sudden focus on financial security, on 'providing,' felt out of character, like a poorly rehearsed line. She remembered the fierce pride in his eyes when he'd secured the grant for the new marine rehabilitation unit, the sheer joy he'd derived from the scientific challenge, not the funding.

"Eli," she began again, her voice a low murmur, laced with an unspoken question. "There's something more. I can feel it. You're holding something back. Is it... is it something someone said? Or something you read?" She remembered his hours spent on his laptop, his usual research dives into plankton migration or ocean currents replaced by something more intense, more introspective. He had been lost in his own world, and she had given him space, respecting his need for quiet contemplation. But now, that quiet felt like a deliberate wall.

He finally met her gaze, and for a fleeting moment, she saw a flicker of the truth in his eyes, a desperate yearning to confess, to share the burden. But it was quickly masked, replaced by that familiar, troubled expression. He wanted to tell her about the job offer, about the prestigious Oceanic Dynamics Institute, about the chance to lead groundbreaking research that could impact the world. He knew he should. It was the right thing to do, the honest thing. But the words refused to form, a tangled mess of ambition, guilt, and fear. He saw the image of her, her fierce dedication to Port Blossom, her quiet strength, and he couldn't bear to dim that light, to introduce doubt or fear into the sanctuary they had built together.

"It's just... the weight of it all, Mara," he said, his voice strained. "The responsibility. Sometimes I wonder if we're cut out for this. If I am." He looked down at his hands, those hands that had so expertly manipulated delicate scientific equipment, that had so gently nursed injured sea creatures. Now, they felt heavy, inadequate. The offer from the institute, a beacon of opportunity, felt like a betrayal of the life they had meticulously crafted, a life built on the salty air and the unwavering pulse of their shared purpose. He could see the allure of the institute, the promise of intellectual fulfillment, but it felt like a path that would lead him away from her, away from the quiet, profound intimacy they shared.

Mara reached for his hand, her touch gentle but firm. "We are cut out for this, Eli," she said, her voice unwavering. "We're a team. And you are brilliant. Don't ever doubt that." She squeezed his hand, trying to impart some of her own resilience. But she could feel the tremor of his unspoken turmoil, a disquiet that went beyond the immediate financial crisis. It was a personal storm brewing, and she was on the outside, looking in, the wind and rain whipping around her, the distance between them a vast, unsettling ocean. She knew, with a certainty that chilled her to the bone, that he was wrestling with a decision that would change their lives, and the silence was the most terrifying part of all. It was a silence pregnant with possibility, with uncertainty, with a future she couldn't yet see, but could already feel shifting beneath her feet.

The salt-laced air, usually a comfort, now felt heavy, charged with unspoken anxieties. Mara found herself adrift in a sea of introspection, the flickering lamplight of The Salty Siren casting long, dancing shadows that mirrored the disquiet swirling within her. Eli's silence, a more profound rift than any financial worry, had forced her inward, and what she found there was a familiar, unwelcome companion: the ghost of her own hesitations. She traced the rim of her wine glass, the cool condensation a stark contrast to the heat of her burgeoning realization.

Her past relationships. The thought sent a shiver down her spine. They were a tapestry woven with threads of passion, yes, but also with the persistent, undeniable pattern of her own avoidance. She had always been the one to pull away, the first to seek the solace of her own space, the one who equated deep commitment with a cage. Independence had been her mantra, her shield, her meticulously crafted escape route. She remembered the whirlwind romance with Liam, the artist whose vibrant spirit had once seemed to promise a world of color, only for her to retreat when his talk turned to shared apartments and a future painted in permanent hues. Then there was David, the steady, reliable lawyer, whose quiet proposal had sent her fleeing into the anonymity of a solo backpacking trip across Europe, her heart a drumbeat of panicked freedom.

She had always justified it, of course. It was about preserving herself, about not losing her identity in the embrace of another. It was about the thrill of the unknown, the boundless possibilities that stretched out before an unattached soul. She had cultivated an image of the free spirit, the woman who answered to no one, who charted her own course. And for a long time, that had felt liberating, empowering. But now, sitting across from Eli, watching the troubled lines deepen around his eyes, she understood that her fiercely guarded independence had also been a form of fear. It was a fear of permanence, a fear of the irrevocable choice, a fear of what might be lost when the boundaries blurred and two lives became inextricably intertwined.

And Eli. Her Eli. The thought of him, his quiet strength, his unwavering belief in her, the way he saw the best in her even when she couldn't, it made her chest ache with a love so profound it was almost terrifying. They had built something beautiful here, something real, in Port Blossom. The rescue center, their shared dream, was a testament to their collaboration, their resilience, their deep, abiding connection. She loved the scent of the sea, the cry of the gulls, the comforting rhythm of their days. She loved the way Eli's hand fit into hers, the quiet understanding that passed between them with a single glance. She loved the life they had forged, brick by salty brick.

But the idea of *settling*. The word itself felt heavy, loaded. Settling down, truly settling down, meant more than just sharing a life; it meant an absolute, unwavering commitment, a declaration that this was it, this was forever. It meant closing the door on other possibilities, on the vast, open horizon she had so long cherished. And the familiar anxiety, that prickle of unease, began to surface, insidious and unwelcome. It whispered doubts in her ear, conjuring images of a future where her own ambitions might be stifled, where the exhilarating freedom she had always craved might be traded for the comforting, yet confining, predictability of domesticity.

She looked at Eli again, his gaze fixed on the distant, star-dusted ocean. He was wrestling with something, she knew it. And in his struggle, she was forced to confront her own. Was his silence born of external pressures, or was it a reflection of the internal battles she herself had been waging, albeit unconsciously? She had always admired his decisiveness, his ability to face challenges head-on. Now, she saw a flicker of something she recognized in him – a deep-seated apprehension, perhaps, about the very permanence she was only now beginning to acknowledge within herself.

This wasn't just about the rescue center's precarious finances, though that was a tangible weight. This was about the unspoken future, the potential for their lives to diverge, for a choice to be made that would irrevocably alter their shared trajectory. And her instinct, the old, ingrained instinct, was to brace herself, to prepare for the possibility of retreat. But with Eli, it was different. Retreating from him felt like tearing away a piece of her own soul.

The realization washed over her, both sobering and strangely liberating. She had to acknowledge this pattern, this ingrained fear of permanence, if she ever wanted to build something truly lasting with Eli. It wasn't enough to love him, to cherish their life together. She had to actively choose it, not out of obligation or inertia, but out of a conscious, willing embrace of forever. That meant confronting the voice that told her independence was paramount, that commitment was a trap. It meant understanding that true freedom wasn't the absence of ties, but the ability to choose those ties willingly, to bind herself to someone with open eyes and a courageous heart.

She took a deep breath, the salty air filling her lungs, a cleansing ritual. She looked at Eli, her gaze steady, no longer seeking answers in the darkness, but finding them within herself. She loved him. She loved their life. And she was ready, finally, to acknowledge that the most profound adventure wasn't always about forging new paths, but about deepening the one already walked, about laying down roots, about choosing to build a future, not just a present. The fear of permanence was still there, a faint echo in the chambers of her heart, but for the first time, it was being drowned out by the growing certainty of her love, and the quiet, determined resolve to face whatever came next, together. It was a choice, a conscious decision to step away from the allure of perpetual possibility and to embrace the rich, enduring beauty of a life chosen, a life shared, a life made permanent by love. This introspection wasn't an endpoint; it was the beginning of a new phase, a crucial step in her own growth, a testament to the profound impact Eli and their shared world had on her willingness to finally, truly, belong.

CHAPTER THREE

Confronting the Unspoken

The night had settled over Port Blossom with a velvet hush, the kind that usually promised peace. But tonight, for Mara, it was a fragile calm, a thin veneer over the churning waters of her own introspection. She sat on the porch swing, the rhythmic creak a counterpoint to the frantic beat of her heart, her gaze fixed on the sliver of moon painting a shimmering path across the inky ocean. Eli's silence had been a tangible thing for weeks, a heavy shroud that had settled between them, muffling their usual easy banter, their shared laughter. It had forced her to excavate her own buried fears, to confront the ingrained patterns of her past, the ones that whispered of independence as a shield and commitment as a cage. She had come to a fragile understanding, a dawning acceptance that her fiercely guarded autonomy had also been a form of fear, a fear of the irrevocable, of the beautiful, terrifying prospect of forever. She loved Eli. She loved their life, the rescue center, the scent of salt and sea, the quiet strength he exuded. And she was, she had realized, ready to choose it, to choose *him*, with all the courage she could muster.

Then, he was there. He sat beside her on the swing, his presence a familiar warmth that nonetheless sent a fresh tremor through her. He didn't speak immediately, and the silence stretched, thick with the unspoken words that had been accumulating between them. She could feel the tension radiating from him, a coiled spring of something she couldn't quite decipher. His hand, calloused and strong, reached out, his fingers brushing hers. It was a simple gesture, yet it held a universe of unarticulated emotion. Mara turned her head, her eyes meeting his in the dim moonlight. The usual playful spark in his gaze was replaced by a profound weariness, a shadow she hadn't seen before.

"Mara," he began, his voice a low rumble, laced with an emotion that tightened her chest. "There's something I need to tell you. Something I should have told you a long time ago." He paused, his thumb tracing small, absent circles on the back of her hand. "It's... it's not easy."

She nodded, her throat suddenly dry. "I know, Eli." She squeezed his hand, a silent invitation for him to continue, to unravel the mystery that had been tightening its grip around them.

He took a deep, shaky breath, his gaze drifting out to the restless sea. "You know how I've been doing a lot of... thinking lately? About the rescue center, about our future?" Mara's heart gave a lurch. This was it. The conversation she had been both dreading and, in a strange way, anticipating.

"Yes," she managed, her voice barely a whisper.

"Well, it's more than just thinking," he confessed, his gaze finally returning to her, pleading and raw. "I've been... I've been offered something. A job." He winced, as if the words themselves pained him. "A really significant opportunity. Back in the city. It's... it's a dream job, Mara. The kind I used to fantasize about when I was just starting out."

Mara's breath hitched. The city. The word hung in the air, alien and sharp. She had always known his roots were there, his past. But this... this felt like a direct challenge to the life they had built, to the very foundation of their shared dreams in Port Blossom. A prestigious offer. His dream job. The implications cascaded through her mind, a torrent of shock and disbelief.

"What... what kind of job?" she asked, her voice trembling slightly.

Eli's jaw tightened. "It's with that architectural firm I interned with years ago. The one that does all the high-profile, sustainable urban development projects. They want me to lead a new division. It's a huge step up, Mara. The kind of work that could really make a difference on a larger scale. More resources, more impact." He was speaking quickly now, a torrent of words that seemed to spill out of him, desperate to be free.

Mara listened, her mind reeling. She pictured him, brilliant and driven, excelling in that world. It was so undeniably *him*. And yet, the thought of him there, away from the salty air, away from their quiet life, away from her... it was like a physical blow. "But... you've always loved it here," she stammered, her voice thick with unshed tears. "The rescue center, Port Blossom. You built this life with me."

"I know," he said, his voice cracking. "And that's what's killing me, Mara. That's why I haven't said anything. Because every time I think about it, about leaving this... about leaving *you*... it feels like I'm tearing myself in half." He finally turned to face her fully, his eyes dark with a pain that mirrored her own burgeoning fear. "This is the hardest thing I've ever had to do. Because I love you, Mara. More than anything. And the thought of walking away from you, from what we have, from this life... it's unbearable."

His confession hung in the air between them, heavy and suffocating. Mara felt a complex swirl of emotions rise within her. There was the sting of betrayal, the hurt that he had kept this from her for so long, that he had wrestled with such a monumental decision in silence. But beneath that, a fragile tendril of understanding began to unfurl. She saw the genuine anguish in his eyes, the conflict that had clearly been tearing him apart. He wasn't a villain; he was a man caught between two powerful desires, two competing futures.

"You... you were offered this a while ago?" she asked, her voice barely audible.

He nodded, his gaze never leaving hers. "A few weeks ago. I've been going back and forth, trying to reconcile it all. Trying to find a way it could work. But there's no easy answer, Mara. It's a complete relocation. A complete shift."

Mara's mind raced. A few weeks. While she had been grappling with her own anxieties about permanence, about commitment, he had been faced with a choice that threatened to shatter their shared reality. The irony was almost unbearable. She had been fearing the slow creep of domesticity, the potential loss of her independence, and he was being offered an escape route, a grand adventure that would take him far from her.

"So, what are you saying, Eli?" she asked, the words laced with a desperate plea for clarity. "Are you saying you're going to take it?"

He ran a hand through his hair, his frustration palpable. "I don't know, Mara. That's the brutal truth. Part of me... the part that's always been ambitious, that's always strived for more, that's always wanted to leave a mark on the world... that part of me sees this as an incredible opportunity. A chance to do work that matters, to build something significant." He turned back to the ocean, his shoulders slumping. "But then I think about this. About you. About the rescue center. About the life we've built here. And it feels like... like everything I've ever wanted."

He fell silent again, and Mara felt the weight of his indecision pressing down on her. Her initial shock was beginning to recede, replaced by a gnawing fear. The fear that her own hesitations about commitment had, in a twisted way, pushed him towards a different kind of future. The fear that his dreams, so different from her own quiet aspirations, would ultimately pull him away.

"It's not just about the job, is it?" she said, her voice softer now, a dawning realization settling in. "It's about... what you want from life. What you're looking for."

Eli nodded slowly. "It is. And I'm so torn, Mara. I love this place. I love the quiet, the connection to the sea, the work we do. But I also... I have this drive. This need to achieve, to build on a larger scale. And when this offer came... it felt like a validation of that part of me that I've been trying to suppress, because I thought it wasn't compatible with what I have with you."

He turned back to her, his eyes pleading for her to understand. "I was so afraid of losing you if I even considered it. And I was so afraid of resenting you, of resenting this life, if I turned it down without truly exploring it. So I just... I held it all in. I tried to find a way to make it all fit, and I couldn't. And the longer I kept it from you, the more it ate away at me."

Mara's own fears, the ones she had so recently begun to confront, resurfaced with a vengeance. Her ingrained tendency to retreat, to protect herself from the potential pain of loss, warred with the deep, abiding love she felt for Eli. She saw the struggle in him, a mirror of her own internal battle. His ambition, his drive for something more, was a part of him she had always admired, and now, it was the very thing that threatened to pull them apart.

"So, what do we do?" she asked, the question laced with a vulnerability she rarely allowed herself. She was no longer bracing for retreat; she was standing firm, ready to face the storm with him.

Eli reached out, his fingers gently cupping her cheek. His touch was electric, a silent apology and a desperate plea all at once. "That's what I don't know," he whispered, his thumb stroking her skin. "I don't know how to reconcile these two worlds. My love for you, for our life here, and this... this pull towards something else. It's like I have to choose between my heart and my ambition. And the thought of losing either... it's devastating."

He pulled her closer, his forehead resting against hers. "I'm so sorry, Mara. I never wanted to hurt you. I just... I got lost in it. In the possibilities, in the conflict. And I let the fear paralyze me, just like you said I do sometimes." He paused, a faint, self-deprecating smile touching his lips. "Maybe we're more alike than I realized."

Mara leaned into his embrace, the familiar scent of him, of sea salt and honest work, a comforting anchor in the turbulent sea of their emotions. His confession, raw and unvarnished, had ripped open the carefully constructed façade of their quiet life. The unspoken had finally been spoken, and the air between them crackled with the aftermath, with the weight of his revelation and the dawning realization of its profound implications. Hurt, confusion, and a deep-seated fear for their future warred within her, but beneath it all, a flicker of resolve ignited. She had finally acknowledged her own fear of permanence, and now, Eli was facing a similar crossroads. Their shared vulnerability, their mutual struggle, was a painful, yet perhaps essential, step in the evolution of their love. The moon continued its silent journey across the sky, casting its ethereal glow on the fragile, yet enduring, bond between them. The path ahead was uncertain, shrouded in a mist of difficult choices, but for the first time, they were facing it together, with the truth laid bare between them. The confession, though devastating, was also a form of honesty, a necessary excavation that might, paradoxically, lead to a stronger, more resilient foundation for whatever came next. The silence that followed was no longer heavy with secrecy, but with the profound weight of shared truth, a testament to a love that was willing, finally, to confront the unspoken.

Mara's breath hitched, a tiny, almost inaudible sound lost in the vastness of the night. Panic, cold and sharp, pierced through the fog of shock. Eli, her Eli, the steady anchor of her world, was contemplating a life that didn't include Port Blossom, didn't include *her*. The image of him, brilliant and ambitious, leading a prestigious firm in the city, flickered behind her eyes, a stark and unwelcome contrast to the salt-laced air and the familiar scent of drying nets that defined their present. A tremor ran through her, a visceral fear of loss that threatened to unravel the fragile peace she had only recently found within herself. The fear wasn't just of losing him, but of losing the quiet, deeply satisfying life they had meticulously woven together, a tapestry of shared dreams and everyday moments.

Her initial instinct, the one honed by years of self-reliance, was to retreat, to build walls around her reeling heart. But the warmth of his hand, still resting on her cheek, the raw vulnerability in his eyes, held her tethered. She didn't lash out, didn't accuse. Instead, a profound weariness settled over her, a different kind of exhaustion than the one she'd seen in Eli. It was the exhaustion of grappling with her own deeply ingrained patterns of fear, the ones that whispered that happiness was always conditional, always fleeting. And now, confronted with his potential departure, those whispers amplified into a deafening roar. She felt a desperate need to understand, not just the offer itself, but the man who had held it so close, so secret, for weeks.

"Weeks?" Mara's voice was barely a whisper, each syllable heavy with the weight of his confession. The word hung between them, a stark reminder of the time he had spent wrestling with this decision in solitude, while she had been navigating her own internal landscape, believing their future was a shared, solid ground. "You've... you've known about this for weeks, Eli?" The hurt, sharp and unexpected, lanced through her. It wasn't just the news of the job; it was the silence, the exclusion, that stung the deepest. She had been opening herself up, daring to believe in forever, and he had been harboring a secret that threatened to blow it all apart.

He nodded, his gaze dropping to her lips, a silent apology. "I... I've been trying to figure it out, Mara. Trying to find a way that it could work without... without hurting you. Without losing you." His voice was rough, thick with an emotion that mirrored the turmoil raging within her.

Mara pulled back slightly, just enough to see his face clearly in the moonlight. Her independent spirit, the very core of who she was, flared, a protective instinct rising to meet the threat. Yet, beneath it, a deep, unwavering love for him thrummed, a counterpoint to the rising tide of fear. "But... why wouldn't you tell me, Eli?" she asked, her voice trembling, the vulnerability she so rarely showed now laid bare. "We're a team, aren't we? We talk about things. Especially things this big. This... this feels like a betrayal, not just of our relationship, but of... of trust." The words tumbled out, a desperate plea for an explanation, for a way to bridge the chasm that had suddenly opened between them. She needed to understand his perspective, to see the world through his eyes, even if it meant facing a future she hadn't dared to imagine.

He flinched, as if struck. "I know. And I'm so, so sorry, Mara. That's... that's the part that's been tearing me up. The fact that I kept it from you. But I was so afraid, Mara. So incredibly afraid of your reaction. Of what it would mean if you thought I was unhappy here, or that I was looking for an escape." He ran a hand through his hair, his movements agitated. "I've seen what happens when people get too comfortable, when they stop striving. And this offer... it felt like a lifeline, in a way. A chance to prove something to myself, something I thought I'd lost."

Mara swallowed, the knot in her throat tightening. She understood striving. She understood the drive to prove oneself. It was part of what had drawn her to Eli in the first place – his quiet determination, his inherent goodness, his passion for building something meaningful. But this... this was different. This was a choice that could redefine their entire existence. "So, you felt like you had to hide this part of yourself from me?" she pressed, her voice regaining a measure of steadiness, though the tremor remained. "This ambition? This need to... to do something bigger?" The question was loaded, a gentle probe into the depths of his unspoken desires, and her own insecurities that had perhaps contributed to his silence.

Eli's gaze met hers, raw and honest. "Yes," he admitted, his voice low. "Partly. Because I love what we have here. I love the rescue center, the community, and I love *you*, Mara. More than anything. And I didn't want anything to jeopardize that. I thought if I didn't even consider it, if I just focused on what we have, that would be enough. That *you* would be enough." He paused, a flicker of self-reproach crossing his features. "But that's not fair, is it? To you, or to me. To pretend that part of me doesn't exist, that it doesn't yearn for... for different challenges."

His admission hung in the salty air, a testament to his internal conflict. Mara felt a surge of empathy, a recognition of the fear that had paralyzed them both, albeit in different ways. Her own journey to embracing commitment had been a slow, arduous climb, fraught with the ghosts of past hurts. She had grappled with her fear of losing herself, her independence, in the embrace of a shared life. Eli, it seemed, was now facing a similar dilemma, but from the opposite direction – the fear of losing his identity, his ambition, in the quiet comfort of their love.

"It's not about not being enough, Eli," she said, her voice softer now, imbued with a newfound understanding. "It's about... acknowledging all the parts of ourselves. The parts that are strong, the parts that are scared, the parts that dream of different horizons." She took a deep breath, the scent of the ocean filling her lungs, a grounding sensation. "I've been doing a lot of thinking too, you know. About my own fears. About the idea of permanence, of settling down. And I've realized that my independence, as much as I cherish it, can also be a shield. A way to keep myself safe from getting hurt."

She met his gaze, her own eyes reflecting the moonlight. "And I've realized that I *want* this, Eli. I want our life here. I want *you*. And I'm ready to choose that, fully, without reservation. But that doesn't mean I don't understand the pull of something else. The allure of a different path." She reached out, her fingers brushing his, a silent offering of understanding and support. "What I need, more than anything, is to know that we can face this together. That whatever you decide, whatever we decide, it's a decision we make as a team."

Eli's hand tightened around hers, a silent affirmation. "I don't want to leave you, Mara," he murmured, his voice thick with emotion. "The thought of coming back to an empty house, of not having you here to share my day, to hear about your rescues... it's unbearable. This place, this life... it's everything I thought I wanted. It's *you* that I want." He paused, his thumb stroking the back of her hand. "But this opportunity... it's a chance to build something on a scale I've only dreamed of. To leave a mark. And I've always been driven by that, by that desire to create, to achieve."

A fresh wave of unease washed over Mara. The words "leave a mark" echoed in her mind, a stark contrast to the quiet, profound work they did at the rescue center, work that touched individual lives, that mended broken wings and hearts. Her own mark had always been made in the subtle shifts, the quiet victories, the gradual healing. His ambition seemed to demand a grander stage, a louder applause. "And you think you can't do that here?" she asked, her voice laced with a hint of defensiveness. "You think that Port Blossom, and the rescue center, and our life together... that it's not enough to satisfy that part of you?"

Eli sighed, a heavy sound that seemed to carry the weight of his indecision. "I don't know, Mara. That's the honest truth. I've tried to make it fit, to convince myself that this is enough. But when this offer came... it felt like a confirmation of that other ambition, that drive I've always had. And the thought of turning it down, of letting that dream slip away... it's hard. It's like I'd be burying a part of myself." He turned to face her fully, his eyes dark and searching. "And the thought of taking it, of leaving you... that's even harder."

He drew her closer, his arm wrapping around her waist, pulling her against him. Mara leaned into his embrace, seeking solace in the familiar warmth of his body, the steady beat of his heart against hers. The scent of him, a comforting blend of sea salt and honest work, was a potent reminder of their shared life, of the home they had built together. "It's like I have to choose between my heart and my ambition," he whispered against her hair, his voice laced with despair. "And the thought of losing either... it's devastating."

Mara's own heart ached for him, for the impossible choice he was being forced to make. She understood the yearning for purpose, for impact. She felt it every day at the rescue center, the quiet satisfaction of making a difference, of easing suffering. But Eli's ambition seemed to crave a different kind of recognition, a different scale of achievement. "I don't want you to have to choose, Eli," she said softly, her hand resting on his chest, feeling the powerful rhythm of his heartbeat. "But I also don't want you to resent me, or our life here, because you feel like you sacrificed something so important."

She pulled away slightly, just enough to look him in the eye again. The fear was still there, a cold knot in her stomach, but it was tempered by a newfound resolve. She had spent so much of her life guarding her heart, fearing the vulnerability that came with deep connection. But in facing this with Eli, she was discovering a strength she hadn't known she possessed. "I love you, Eli," she said, her voice clear and steady, devoid of the tremor that had underscored her earlier words. "I love our life. I love the rescue center. And I'm ready to commit to this, to *us*, with everything I have. But that doesn't mean we can't acknowledge your dreams, your ambitions. We just have to figure out how they fit. Or if they can fit."

He cupped her face, his thumbs tracing the curve of her cheekbones. His eyes, so full of turmoil moments before, now held a flicker of hope, a dawning understanding. "You're not angry?" he asked, his voice a hushed question.

Mara offered a small, sad smile. "Angry? I'm hurt, Eli. I'm scared. And I'm confused. But I'm not angry. Because I see you. I see your struggle. And I know that you're not trying to hurt me. You're just trying to figure out who you are and what you want, just like I have been." She leaned into his touch, her gaze holding his. "And I think... I think we need to figure it out together."

He pulled her close again, burying his face in her hair. "You're incredible, Mara," he murmured, his voice muffled. "You always have been. I'm so lucky to have you."

She clung to him, the steady rhythm of his breathing a soothing balm to her frayed nerves. The confession, so devastating in its implications, had also been a catalyst, a force that had stripped away the pretense and laid bare their deepest fears and desires. The unspoken had been spoken, and the air between them, though heavy with uncertainty, was no longer choked with secrets. A fragile hope began to bloom within Mara, a belief that perhaps, just perhaps, their love was strong enough to navigate this uncharted territory. The path ahead was shrouded in mist, the decisions they faced monumental, but for the first time, they were facing it together, not as two individuals harboring separate dreams, but as a united front, ready to confront the unspoken truth that had threatened to divide them. The moonlight continued to cast its gentle glow, illuminating not just the fear, but the enduring strength of their shared bond, a testament to a love that was willing, finally, to confront the most difficult truths, together.

The scent of disinfectant and the faint, metallic tang of desperation clung to the air in the veterinary clinic. Mara traced the condensation ring left by her untouched coffee cup on the sterile counter, her gaze fixed on the incubator where a fragile cluster of kittens lay, their tiny chests heaving with labored breaths. Each wheeze was a stab to her heart, a stark reminder of the impossible arithmetic they were facing at the rescue. The grant, their lifeline for the past year, had vanished like mist at dawn, leaving them exposed and vulnerable. And now, this.

Dr. Evans, his face etched with concern, emerged from the examination room, pulling off his gloves with a sigh. "Mara, they're weak. Very weak. This strain of panleukopenia is aggressive. They need constant IV fluids, broad-spectrum antibiotics, and around-the-clock monitoring. It's going to be... expensive."

The word hung in the air, heavy and suffocating. Expensive. It was a word Mara had become intimately familiar with in the weeks since the grant's denial. It had started with the gradual depletion of their emergency fund, then the painful decisions about cutting back on non-essential supplies. Now, it was about life and death, about the agonizing calculus of a budget against the desperate plea in the eyes of a tiny, suffering creature.

"How expensive, Doctor?" Mara asked, her voice tight, betraying the tremor she fought to control. She had always prided herself on her resilience, her ability to find solutions, to stretch every dollar until it screamed. But this felt different, like standing at the edge of an abyss with no safety net.

Dr. Evans consulted his notes. "For this level of intensive care, for all five of them, we're looking at conservatively... upwards of three thousand dollars. And that's if there are no complications. Honestly, Mara, even with the best care, the prognosis is guarded. But they're fighters, and they deserve every chance."

Three thousand dollars. Mara's mind raced, a frantic hamster on a wheel. Three thousand dollars that they simply didn't have. The rescue's coffers were scraped bare. The regular donations, while loyal, were barely enough to cover the day-to-day costs of food, bedding, and basic vaccinations for the dozens of animals already under their care. The sudden influx of these five critically ill kittens had been a cruel twist of fate, a devastating blow right when they were already reeling.

"I understand," Mara said, forcing a calm she didn't feel. "Thank you, Doctor. I'll... I'll figure it out." She met his gaze, her own filled with a fierce determination that masked the gnawing fear. She wouldn't let these kittens die because of a funding shortfall. Not on her watch.

Back at the rescue center, the atmosphere was a palpable mix of bustling activity and hushed anxiety. The news of the kittens' critical condition had spread like wildfire, casting a pall over the usually cheerful sanctuary. Sarah, her most dedicated volunteer, approached Mara with a worried frown.

"Mara, have you heard about the kittens? Dr. Evans just called me. Are we... are we going to be able to afford it?" Her voice was laced with apprehension. Sarah had a particular soft spot for the kittens, often spending her own free time bottle-feeding the most vulnerable.

Mara leaned against the doorframe of the main kennel, the familiar scent of dog fur and hay doing little to soothe her frayed nerves. "It's going to be tough, Sarah. Really tough. We're looking at close to three thousand dollars for their intensive care."

Sarah's eyes widened. "Three thousand? Oh, Mara... Where are we going to get that kind of money? We've barely managed to keep our heads above water this month. The bulk food order is due next week, and I'm not sure we have enough even for that without cutting back on the more nutritious brands."

The reality of their precarious financial situation hit Mara with renewed force. It wasn't just about the kittens; it was about the entire rescue. The grant had been a significant portion of their operational budget, and its absence had created a gaping hole that felt impossible to fill. Every single animal that came through their doors relied on their ability to provide adequate food, shelter, and medical care. Now, that ability was in serious jeopardy.

"I know," Mara said, her voice low. "I've been racking my brain. We need to do something, and we need to do it now. I'm going to start by calling some of the local businesses. See if anyone can help. And we'll launch an emergency online appeal. Every little bit will count."

Over the next few days, Mara and her small team threw themselves into a whirlwind of fundraising efforts. They organized an impromptu "Kitten Shower" at the local community center, transforming it into a festive, yet urgent, plea for donations. Flyers plastered the town, detailing the plight of the orphaned kittens and the rescue's ongoing struggle. Mara spent hours on the phone, her voice growing hoarse, explaining their mission to skeptical business owners and hopeful donors alike. Some offered generous contributions, a welcome balm to their financial woes. The local bakery donated all proceeds from their weekend bake sale, and the pet supply store offered a substantial discount on food and medical supplies. But it wasn't enough. Not nearly enough.

The online appeal, though shared widely on social media, yielded a trickle rather than a flood of donations. The outpouring of sympathy was heartening, but sympathy didn't pay veterinary bills. Mara found herself caught in a constant cycle of anxiety, the weight of responsibility pressing down on her with an almost physical force. Sleep became a luxury, snatched in short, restless bursts between frantic calls and sleepless nights spent worrying about the fragile lives depending on her.

One evening, as she sat alone in her small office, surrounded by stacks of invoices and donation receipts, Mara found herself staring at a photograph of the five kittens. They were impossibly tiny, their eyes still closed, nestled together in a soft blanket. A wave of despair washed over her, so profound that it threatened to buckle her knees. She had always been the one to find a way, to pull a rabbit out of a hat. But this time, it felt like the hat was empty, and the rabbit had already vanished.

She thought of Eli, of his quiet strength, his unwavering support. But the conflict that had been simmering between them, the unspoken tension surrounding his potential city job, made her hesitate to burden him further. He had his own dreams, his own ambitions, and she didn't want to add her own anxieties to his already heavy load. She had to be strong, for them, for the rescue.

The relentless pressure of running a non-profit, of being constantly on the brink, was taking its toll. Mara felt a weariness seep into her bones, a fatigue that went deeper than just physical exhaustion. It was the emotional toll of bearing witness to so much suffering, of constantly fighting for resources, of knowing that so many desperate pleas for help went unanswered because they simply lacked the capacity. She had poured her heart and soul into the rescue, believing in its mission with every fiber of her being. But there were days, like today, when the sheer immensity of the task felt overwhelming, when the constant struggle threatened to erode her optimism, her very belief in their ability to make a difference.

The kittens' plight was a stark, poignant symbol of their ongoing crisis. It was a microcosm of the larger battle they were fighting, a battle for survival against the ever-present specter of financial ruin. Mara closed her eyes, taking a deep, shaky breath. She couldn't afford to break down. Not now. Not when those tiny lives depended on her. She had to find a way. She *had* to. The unspoken fear of failure, of letting down the animals and the people who depended on them, was a constant, gnawing ache. But beneath that fear, a flicker of defiance ignited. She wouldn't give up. Not on the kittens, not on the rescue, and not on the hope that they could, somehow, find a way through this overwhelming crisis. The fight for their survival had just begun.

The news, like a rogue wave, breached the quiet shores of Port Blossom and spread with an astonishing speed. Whispers of the rescue's dire financial straits, of the five fragile lives hanging precariously in the balance at the veterinary clinic, and of Mara's desperate scramble for funds, rippled through the quaint coastal town. It wasn't just a few concerned souls who heard; it was as if the very heart of Port Blossom began to beat in unison with the rescue's struggling rhythm.

Mara, buried beneath a mountain of invoices and the gnawing anxiety of dwindling resources, was almost unprepared for the tidal wave of support that began to crest. It started subtly. Mrs. Gable, the owner of the charming little yarn shop on Main Street, a woman known more for her prickly demeanor than her generosity, called Mara personally. "Heard about your predicament, dear," she'd rasped into the phone, her voice surprisingly gentle. "I've set aside a box of my finest wool. Could be useful for keeping those little ones warm, or perhaps for some craft sales if you decide to go that route. And I've put a donation jar on my counter. Every little bit helps, they say." Mara, touched by this unexpected kindness from a woman she'd always perceived as distant, felt a flicker of hope ignite within her.

Then came the call from Tom, the burly, jovial owner of "The Salty Dog," Port Blossom's most popular pub. "Mara, my girl! Heard you're in a bit of a pickle. The lads and I were thinking. How about we host a 'Paws for a Cause' night next Saturday? We'll do a special menu, a portion of the proceeds go to the rescue. And I'll get a band to play, no charge. We'll make it a real shindig!" His enthusiasm was infectious, a much-needed balm to Mara's weary spirit. A pub night. It was audacious, unplanned, and exactly the kind of bold stroke they needed.

The volunteer response was equally overwhelming. Sarah, her most devoted helper, seemed to multiply her efforts. She coordinated a rota for extra cleaning shifts at the rescue, ensuring that the existing residents received the extra attention they deserved while Mara's focus was necessarily divided. Young Liam, who usually spent his Saturdays kicking a football in the park, arrived at the rescue with a stack of flyers he'd designed himself, eager to help distribute them around town. Even Mr. Henderson, the reclusive retired librarian who rarely ventured out, surprised Mara by showing up with a box of gently used blankets and a quiet offer to help organize donated items. The rescue, once a haven for the abandoned, was now becoming a beacon for the community's compassion.

Eli, observing this groundswell of support, found his own anxieties easing, replaced by a deep sense of pride and gratitude. He'd always known Port Blossom was a special place, a town where neighbors looked out for each other, but this went beyond mere neighborliness. This was a town rallying around a cause it believed in, a collective outpouring of heart that resonated deeply with him. He saw the way Mara's shoulders, perpetually hunched with the weight of responsibility, began to relax. He saw the flicker of genuine joy in her eyes when a significant donation arrived, or when a new volunteer offered their time. This community, he realized, was not just a place to live; it was a living, breathing entity, a testament to the kind of life he and Mara were building.

The "Paws for a Cause" night at The Salty Dog was a spectacular success. The pub was packed to the rafters. Locals, from the youngest teenagers to the oldest mariners, turned out in force. The air buzzed with laughter and the lively strumming of a local folk band. A silent auction, hastily assembled with donations from local artisans and businesses – hand-painted pottery, artisanal jams, vouchers for local services – saw bidding wars erupt with good-natured ferocity. Mara, overwhelmed, circulated through the crowd, accepting donations, thanking people, her heart swelling with each passing hour. Eli stayed close, his hand occasionally finding hers, a silent anchor in the delightful chaos. He watched her, seeing not just the dedicated rescuer, but the woman he loved, radiating a warmth and gratitude that was palpable.

By the end of the night, the donation buckets were overflowing, and the tally from the silent auction was staggering. It wasn't the full three thousand dollars they desperately needed for the kittens, but it was a monumental leap forward, a substantial injection of hope into their depleted coffers. The generosity of Port Blossom had exceeded their wildest expectations. Local businesses, inspired by The Salty Dog's initiative, continued to offer their support. The town's only florist organized a special "Petal for Paws" promotion, donating a percentage of their sales. The little independent bookstore offered a discount to anyone who donated to the rescue. It felt as though the entire town had adopted the rescue, and by extension, its vulnerable charges.

This outpouring wasn't just about the money, though that was undeniably crucial. For Mara, it was a profound validation. It was an affirmation that her tireless efforts, her sacrifices, her unwavering dedication to these animals, were seen and valued by the community she served. It chipped away at the isolating burden of responsibility she had been carrying. She wasn't alone in this fight. The rescue wasn't just her dream; it was a shared endeavor, a collective commitment. This was the tangible impact of the life they had chosen to build together in Port Blossom, a life woven into the fabric of this close-knit community.

Eli felt it too, a deep satisfaction that transcended the financial relief. He'd always been drawn to the idea of community, of belonging. He'd seen enough of the world to know that such genuine connections were rare. Port Blossom offered that in spades, and the rescue was its vibrant, beating heart. Witnessing the town rally around Mara and her mission solidified his belief that they had made the right choice, that this coastal haven was precisely where they were meant to be. He saw the rescue not just as a sanctuary for animals, but as a catalyst for human connection, a place that brought out the best in people. This shared purpose, this communal spirit, was a powerful force, a testament to the enduring strength of human kindness and the profound impact of a life dedicated to compassion. The unspoken anxieties that had sometimes shadowed their future in Port Blossom began to recede, replaced by a quiet confidence and a profound sense of belonging. They were not just residents;

they were part of the heart of Port Blossom, and Port Blossom, in turn, was undeniably part of theirs.

The hum of the refrigerator was the loudest sound in the small kitchen, a counterpoint to the quiet intensity that had settled between Mara and Eli. The remnants of a hastily prepared dinner – pasta salad, half-eaten bread – sat on the counter, forgotten. Outside, the familiar chorus of crickets had begun their nightly serenade, a stark contrast to the unspoken melody of apprehension that filled the space between them. The overwhelming success of "Paws for a Cause" had left Mara buoyant, a feeling that was now being gently deflated by the looming shadow of the decision that lay before them.

"I'm so grateful," Mara began, her voice barely a whisper, tracing the rim of her untouched water glass. "Truly, Eli. The town... it was incredible. I don't know how I would have managed without everyone's support. Without *your* support." She looked up, meeting his gaze, and saw the familiar warmth there, a warmth that always had the power to soothe her, but tonight, it also highlighted the complexity of their situation.

Eli reached across the table, his hand covering hers. His touch was grounding, a familiar anchor. "You don't need to thank me, Mara," he said, his voice low and steady. "This is your passion. Your life. I'm just here to help you navigate it." He paused, his thumb gently stroking the back of her hand. "And that offer... it's not something I want, Mara. It's just... an opportunity. A way to provide a certain kind of security, a path I thought we both might want."

Mara's chest tightened. She knew he was trying to reassure her, to let her know that his heart was firmly planted in Port Blossom, with her. But the words, however well-intentioned, also underscored the stark reality of what he was being asked to sacrifice, or at least, what he was *perceiving* as a sacrifice. "I know," she managed, her voice thick with emotion. "I know you're not trying to leave. It's just... when you talk about it, it sounds like a fallback plan, Eli. And you deserve more than a fallback plan. You deserve... a first choice. A life that excites you, that you're passionate about, not just something you're settling for because it's convenient or because I'm here."

He squeezed her hand, a silent plea for her to understand. "Mara, Port Blossom *is* what excites me. You are what excites me. The offer... it's a complication, yes, but it's not a desire. My desire is to build a life here, with you. To see this rescue thrive, to see you happy and fulfilled. That's my first choice. This other thing... it's just a piece of paper, a potential future that was presented to me, and I have to consider it, as any responsible person would, especially when it involves our shared future. But it doesn't hold a candle to what I have here with you."

The honesty in his eyes was disarming, and for a moment, Mara felt a wave of relief wash over her. He wasn't secretly yearning for a different life, for a city skyline or a bustling corporate world. He was here, with her, in this small, sometimes chaotic, but undeniably loving life they were building. Yet, the weight of the decision remained. The financial stability the offer represented was a siren song, a promise of relief from the constant tightrope walk of keeping the rescue afloat. It was a tangible solution to a problem that gnawed at her every waking moment.

"But what if it's not enough?" she whispered, the fear a cold knot in her stomach. "What if the rescue... what if it never becomes financially sustainable? What if I can't ever pull myself out of this constant scramble for funds? Then what, Eli? You'll have put your dreams on hold for a sinking ship. And I can't bear the thought of being the reason you resent me, or resent this life." Her gaze dropped to their intertwined hands, her knuckles white. "I need to know, deep down, that we're building something solid. Not just for the animals, but for us. For our future. And right now, that future feels so... precarious."

Eli gently tilted her chin up, his gaze unwavering. "Mara," he said, his voice firm yet tender. "I know you're afraid. I see it, and I understand it. Your fear comes from a place of immense love and dedication to this rescue, and to me. But you have to trust me when I say that my commitment to you, to us, is unwavering. That offer... it represents a certain kind of security, yes. But the security I feel with you, in this life we are building, is far more profound. It's the security of knowing I'm with the person I love, doing something meaningful, even when it's difficult."

He leaned in, his forehead resting against hers. "We knew this wouldn't be easy. Building a rescue from the ground up, in a town that, while supportive, isn't exactly overflowing with wealthy patrons, is a monumental task. There will be challenges. There will be moments of doubt. But we face them together. That's what we promised each other, isn't it? Not just the good times, but the hard ones too."

Mara closed her eyes, breathing in the scent of him, a comforting blend of sea salt and something uniquely Eli. He was right. They had spoken about the difficulties, about the sacrifices. She had envisioned financial strain, long hours, the emotional toll. But she hadn't fully anticipated the profound personal pressure, the weight of feeling responsible for another person's potential happiness, for their future.

"It's just... I've always dreamed of a life where I didn't have to worry about the money," she confessed, the words tumbling out in a rush. "Where I could focus solely on the animals, on providing them with the absolute best care, without the constant threat of closure looming over my head. I've dreamed of a stable home, of maybe even starting a family someday. And while I love this rescue with all my heart, I worry that it's consuming that dream. That it's asking for too much, not just from me, but from you."

Eli pulled back slightly, his eyes searching hers. "And you think I don't have dreams, Mara? You think I'm just content to drift along? I have dreams too. Dreams of seeing you thrive, of building a family with you, of having a home filled with laughter and love. And yes, I dream of financial security too. But those dreams don't exist in a vacuum. They are intertwined with you, with us. If this rescue is what makes you happy, if it's where your heart truly is, then my dreams must also find a way to encompass it. That offer... it's a potential shortcut to some of that security. But it's not the only way. And it's certainly not the way I'd choose if it meant sacrificing what we have here."

He let go of her hand and stood, walking over to the window, his back to her. He stared out into the darkness, a silhouette against the faint glow of the porch light. "The truth is, Mara," he said, his voice softer now, more introspective. "When I first came to Port Blossom, I was adrift. I was looking for something. A purpose. A place to belong. I found that here, with you, and with this rescue. It's given me a sense of community, a sense of contribution that I'd been missing. The thought of walking away from that... it's not easy. It's not something I do lightly."

He turned back, his expression earnest. "But then this offer came. And it forced me to really examine what I want. And what I want is *you*. It's this life. The challenges and all. I've learned that true security isn't just about a steady paycheck or a big house. It's about having a partner you can rely on, a shared vision, and the courage to face whatever comes your way, together." He walked back to the table, sitting down again, his gaze locking with hers. "So, yes, the offer is a difficult thing to navigate. It's a tempting glimpse of a different kind of future, one that might offer a certain kind of ease. But it's not the future I *want*. Not when the alternative is building something real, something meaningful, with you, right here."

Mara felt a prickle of tears in her eyes, but they were tears of a different kind now – tears of relief, of gratitude, and of a deep, abiding love. His words were a balm to her anxious soul, a reassurance that her fears, while valid, were not the only truth. He saw her struggles, he understood her anxieties, and he was choosing her, choosing their shared life, even with its inherent uncertainties.

"I'm scared, Eli," she admitted, her voice trembling. "I'm so scared of failing. Of letting everyone down. Of letting *you* down."

"You won't," he said, his voice unwavering. "We won't. We'll figure it out, Mara. Together. This rescue is a part of you, and now, it's a part of us. And we're not going to let it go. We'll find a way. We always do." He reached for her hand again, interlacing their fingers. "The conversations are difficult, I know. But they're necessary. And the fact that we can have them, that we can be this honest with each other, that's the foundation we need. That's what makes this strong. That's what makes us strong."

He squeezed her hand again, a gentle affirmation. "So, let's not pretend this isn't hard. Let's acknowledge the weight of it, the potential sacrifices. But let's also remember why we're doing this. Because we believe in this. We believe in each other. And we believe in the future we're building, right here, in Port Blossom."

Mara leaned her head against his shoulder, the tension in her body slowly beginning to ease. The honesty, though raw and painful at times, had indeed begun to rebuild the bridge between them, not by erasing the difficulties, but by acknowledging them and choosing to walk across them together. The offer was still there, a complication they would have to address. But it no longer felt like a looming threat to their relationship, but rather, a challenge they would face as a united front. The difficult conversations, she realized, were not the end of their dreams, but the necessary building blocks for them. They were the conversations that solidified their commitment, strengthened their resolve, and reminded them that even in the face of uncertainty, they had each other. And in Port Blossom, that felt like the greatest security of all. The crickets chirped outside, their melody now a soothing lullaby, a gentle reminder of the life they were choosing, the life they were fighting for, together. The path ahead was still uncertain, still fraught with the potential for bumps and detours, but for the first time in a long time, Mara felt a quiet confidence settle within her. They would face it all, hand in hand, in the heart of this town that had, against all odds, become their home.

CHAPTER FOUR

Weighing the Options

The silence that followed Eli's departure was a different kind of quiet than the one that had held them captive earlier. It wasn't heavy with unspoken fears or the metallic tang of apprehension. Instead, it felt expansive, a vast canvas upon which Mara could begin to sketch her own truths. She watched him walk away, the porch light casting long shadows that seemed to stretch and bend with his retreating form, and a profound sense of calm settled over her. He had laid bare his heart, his desires, his unwavering commitment, and in doing so, had gifted her the space to examine her own.

She stayed at the kitchen table long after the hum of the refrigerator had become a monotonous drone, the half-eaten pasta salad a testament to a meal interrupted by life's complexities. Her gaze drifted to the framed photograph on the wall – a candid shot of her and Eli laughing at the summer fair, his arm slung comfortably around her shoulders, her head tilted back in mirth. It was a snapshot of a moment, yes, but it also held the promise of countless more. The worry about financial security, about the precariousness of the rescue's future, still lingered at the edges of her mind, a persistent hum like the refrigerator. But it no longer felt like an insurmountable wall. Eli's unwavering belief in them, in their ability to weather any storm together, had chipped away at that wall, revealing a sturdy foundation beneath.

But the conversation had unearthed something else within her, a quieter, more insidious fear that had shadowed her for years. It was the fear of being truly rooted, of permanent belonging. She had always been a wanderer, a seeker, her life punctuated by moves, by the careful construction and subsequent deconstruction of temporary shelters. Even Port Blossom, with its growing embrace, its welcoming faces, had felt, in some unspoken way, like another chapter in a book of transient stories. Her dreams had always been just out of reach, shimmering on the horizon, always a little further down the road, a little more polished, a little more *permanent*. And she had been so afraid that *this*, this life with Eli and the rescue, this messy, beautiful, uncertain existence, wasn't it. That it was too small, too imperfect to hold the weight of her deepest desires.

She needed air. She needed space. She needed to walk, to let the rhythm of her own footsteps echo the shifting landscape of her heart. Slipping on a light jacket, Mara stepped out into the cool night, the salty air a familiar balm against her skin. She didn't head for the rescue, nor for the quiet streets of the town. Instead, her feet carried her instinctively towards the winding path that led to the cove.

The cove was their sanctuary, the place where their tentative connection had deepened into something undeniable. It was where they had shared stolen moments under the vast expanse of the night sky, where he had first confessed his feelings, and where she had begun to see beyond the immediate challenges of her life to the possibility of a shared future. The moonlight painted a shimmering silver path across the water, transforming the familiar scene into something ethereal. The gentle lapping of the waves against the shore was a soothing, rhythmic mantra, each ebb and flow a reminder of the constant, yet ever-changing nature of life.

She found her usual spot, a smooth, sun-warmed boulder nestled amongst the dune grass. Sitting down, she pulled her knees to her chest, her gaze fixed on the horizon. The vastness of the ocean always had a way of putting things into perspective. The anxieties that had felt so suffocating just hours before now seemed to shrink, becoming mere specks against the immensity of the sea and sky.

Eli's words echoed in her mind.

"My desire is to build a life here, with you." And then her own confession, raw and vulnerable: *"I've always dreamed of a life where I didn't have to worry about the money... Where I could focus solely on the animals... I've dreamed of a stable home, of maybe even starting a family someday. And while I love this rescue with all my heart, I worry that it's consuming that dream."*

She had been so focused on the *lack* – the lack of funds, the lack of security, the lack of a perfectly polished future – that she had failed to see the *abundance* that was already present. Eli. His love. His unwavering support. The growing sense of community in Port Blossom. The very animals she poured her heart and soul into, each one a testament to her dedication and their collective efforts.

Her fear of permanence, she realized, was a well-worn cloak she had draped around herself for protection. It was easier to keep moving, to keep searching, than to truly settle, to truly invest in something that might, one day, break her heart. But Eli wasn't a temporary stop. He was a destination. And the rescue, the place that had once felt like a constant struggle, was slowly transforming into a shared dream, a tangible manifestation of their combined hopes and efforts.

She had always equated 'home' with a physical structure, a place with solid walls and a locked door. But sitting there, with the cool night air on her skin and the sound of the ocean in her ears, she understood that home was more than just bricks and mortar. It was a feeling. A sense of belonging. A place where your heart felt safe, where you were loved and accepted, flaws and all. And that place, she now understood with startling clarity, was not a geographical location, but a person. It was wherever Eli was.

The offer of a different future, a future of financial ease and perceived stability, still lingered, but its allure had faded. It represented a path of least resistance, a shortcut that bypassed the very things that made life, and their love, meaningful. True security, she echoed Eli's sentiment, wasn't found in a bank account or a prestigious job title. It was found in shared commitment, in mutual trust, in the quiet understanding that you had someone to face the world with, no matter what storms raged.

She thought back to their early days in Port Blossom, to the hesitant smiles, the tentative conversations. She had been so guarded, so wary of opening herself up, of allowing herself to be truly seen. She had kept a part of herself locked away, a secret reserve that she could fall back on if things went south, if the rescue failed, if... if Eli left. But he hadn't left. He had stayed. He had invested. He had shown her what it meant to be truly present, to be fully committed. And in doing so, he had earned the right to her own vulnerability, her own full investment.

The waves continued their timeless rhythm, a gentle reminder that change was not something to be feared, but an inherent part of existence. Her dream of a stable home, of starting a family – those dreams hadn't been consumed by the rescue. They had simply evolved. They now included the rescue, woven into the fabric of their shared aspirations. The rescue wasn't an obstacle to her dreams; it was a part of them. It was a testament to her passion, and a place where Eli had found his own sense of purpose.

She closed her eyes, picturing their lives in the years to come. Not a grand, perfectly curated existence, but a life filled with the laughter of children, the happy barks of adopted dogs, the quiet companionship of shared meals, and the ongoing fulfillment of their mission. A life that was built, not on the shaky foundation of fear, but on the bedrock of love and shared purpose. It wouldn't be easy. There would still be challenging days, moments of doubt, financial anxieties. But they would face them together. That was the commitment. That was the promise.

A single tear traced a path down her cheek, not of sadness, but of release. The heavy cloak of fear, of past hurts and ingrained patterns, was finally beginning to slip from her shoulders. She wasn't a wanderer anymore, not in the way she used to be. Her heart had found its anchor, its true north, in Port Blossom, in the rescue, and most importantly, in Eli.

The word "home" no longer felt like a foreign concept. It was the warmth of Eli's hand in hers, the scent of dog biscuits and sea salt that permeated their small house, the shared smiles over a late-night cup of tea. It was the understanding that even when the path ahead was unclear, they had each other, and that was more than enough. It was everything.

She stood up, brushing the sand from her jeans. The moonlight still illuminated the cove, but now, it didn't just highlight the beauty of the place; it illuminated the beauty of her own evolving heart. She had spent so long looking for a perfect, permanent future, only to realize that the most profound sense of belonging, the truest definition of home, was already here, in the messy, imperfect, and utterly perfect life she was building with Eli. The decision wasn't about choosing between an offer and the rescue. It was about choosing to fully embrace the life they were creating, together. And in that realization, Mara felt a profound sense of peace, a quiet strength that had been simmering beneath the surface, finally ready to bloom. She turned and began the walk back, her steps lighter, her gaze no longer fixed on the distant horizon, but on the path immediately before her, a path illuminated by the steady glow of her own rediscovered sense of belonging.

Eli found himself back in his study, the sleek brochure for the Seattle institute resting on his desk. The crisp, glossy paper now felt less like a beacon of opportunity and more like a weighty reminder of a path not taken, or perhaps, a path he was now actively choosing to avoid. He'd reviewed the offer a dozen times since Mara's quiet departure into the night. Each perusal had been a whirlwind of professional ambition, a frantic scramble to quantify the intangible benefits of prestige, resources, and groundbreaking research. But tonight, with the echo of Mara's newfound clarity in his mind, his approach had shifted. The lens through which he viewed the offer was no longer solely his own; it was filtered through the shared reality they were building.

He picked up a pen, not to sign, but to meticulously dissect. The salary figures, once so dazzling, now seemed like a mere footnote. He scribbled them down, then circled them with a resigned sigh. Yes, it represented financial security, a level of comfort that would undeniably ease some of the burdens Mara had spoken of with such quiet resignation. It was the kind of security he'd always assumed was the ultimate prize, the bedrock upon which a stable future was built. But then he paused, the pen hovering over the paper. What was the *true* cost of that security? He'd seen the spark in Mara's eyes when she spoke about the rescue, about the resilience of the animals, about the community they were fostering. That spark, that fierce, unwavering passion, was a currency far more valuable than any monetary figure.

He turned his attention to the research opportunities. Advanced labs, cutting-edge technology, the chance to collaborate with leading minds in his field. These were the things that had initially drawn him to the offer, the siren song of scientific advancement. He could almost feel the intellectual stimulation, the thrill of discovery. He imagined the accolades, the publications, the tangible markers of success that his younger self would have chased with reckless abandon. But a deeper, more resonant ambition had begun to take root in Port Blossom. It wasn't the ambition for personal glory, but for shared impact. The rescue, in its own way, was a laboratory of sorts – a place where compassion met practicality, where science was applied not for abstract acclaim, but for tangible good. He was learning, growing, and contributing in ways he hadn't anticipated, and more importantly, he was doing it alongside Mara.

The thought of leaving Port Blossom, of uprooting their carefully constructed lives, sent a familiar pang of unease through him. He pictured the quiet rhythm of their days: the early morning mist rolling in off the bay, the cheerful chaos of the rescue's morning rounds, the shared silence over dinner, the comfortable weight of Mara beside him as they watched the stars. These weren't grand, dramatic moments, but they were the substance of his contentment. He traced the outline of the rescue's logo on a discarded flyer. It was more than just a building; it was their shared sanctuary, a testament to their resilience and their commitment. It was a place where their individual strengths converged, creating something greater than the sum of their parts.

He considered Mara's well-being. Her journey had been one of cautious healing, of tentatively opening her heart to the possibility of love and belonging. Port Blossom had become her haven, the rescue her purpose. The thought of extracting her from that environment, of forcing her to navigate a new city, a new professional landscape, a new set of social circles, felt like a betrayal of the trust she had placed in him. He remembered the vulnerability in her eyes when she'd spoken about her past, the fear of being uprooted, of losing what little stability she had found. His own professional ambitions, however compelling, could not justify inflicting that kind of uncertainty upon her. Her peace, her happiness, had become inextricably linked with his own.

He imagined the city of Seattle. Bustling, vibrant, a hub of innovation. It held a certain allure, a promise of a different kind of life. But as he pictured it, it felt sterile, impersonal. He saw himself lost in the anonymity of a large metropolis, his contributions, however significant, likely to be swallowed by the sheer scale of it all. Here, in Port Blossom, his impact was undeniable. He saw it in the wagging tails, the contented purrs, the relieved sighs of adopters. He saw it in Mara's smile, in the way she leaned into him, her fear visibly receding with each passing day.

The financial aspect resurfaced, a persistent whisper of practicality. He acknowledged the appeal of not having to worry about every invoice, every unexpected vet bill. He understood Mara's anxieties, her deep-seated need for a safety net. But he also recognized that he had inadvertently become a part of that safety net. His presence, his willingness to share the burden, had already begun to alleviate some of her concerns. And his skills, honed through years of dedicated practice, could undoubtedly be leveraged to improve the rescue's financial standing. It wasn't about a quick fix, but about building sustainable solutions, together.

He picked up a photograph from his desk – a candid shot of him and Mara, taken during one of the rescue's adoption events. They were both beaming, surrounded by a flurry of happy dogs and even happier families. In that moment, there was no thought of profit margins or grant applications, just pure, unadulterated joy. It was a snapshot of a life lived with purpose, a life rich with meaning. That was the kind of life he wanted to continue building, not just for himself, but with Mara. The Seattle offer, in comparison, felt like a solitary pursuit, a glittering prize that would ultimately leave him feeling empty.

He closed his eyes, picturing their future. Not a future defined by professional accolades or financial windfalls, but a future woven from shared experiences, quiet moments of connection, and the unwavering commitment to a cause they both believed in. He saw himself by Mara's side, not as a visitor or a temporary partner, but as an integral part of the Port Blossom community, of the rescue's story. He saw them weathering the inevitable storms, not with fear, but with the quiet confidence that comes from knowing you have a steadfast partner by your side.

The allure of the Seattle institute began to dissipate, like mist burning off in the morning sun. It was a tempting offer, a validation of his skills and his potential. But it was also a distraction, a detour from the profound sense of fulfillment he had discovered right here, in Port Blossom. He realized that true success wasn't measured by external validation or material wealth, but by the depth of connection, the richness of purpose, and the enduring strength of love.

He picked up the brochure again, his gaze lingering on the institute's imposing skyline logo. It represented a world of possibilities, a world he had once aspired to conquer. But now, he saw it for what it truly was: a different path, one that would lead him away from the life that had unexpectedly captured his heart. He laid the brochure down, a sense of quiet certainty settling over him. His deliberation was over. The answer was clear. His future, the one that truly mattered, was not in Seattle. It was here, in Port Blossom, with Mara. He reached for his laptop, not to draft a reply to the institute, but to begin mapping out strategies for the rescue's long-term sustainability. The real work, the fulfilling work, had just begun.

The glossy brochure for the Future Institute lay open on Eli's desk, its crisp edges a stark contrast to the worn, familiar pages of the rescue's latest veterinary journal. He'd spent the morning rereading the email confirming his visit, a knot of anticipation and trepidation tightening in his stomach. Seattle. The word itself conjured images of towering glass buildings, a relentless urban hum, and a scientific landscape that promised to be at the forefront of his field. He'd agreed to the visit not out of a burning desire to accept, but out of a need to silence the nagging voice of 'what if.' He had to see it, touch it, breathe its air, to truly understand if the glittering offer held the substance he craved, or if it was merely a mirage.

The flight itself was a blur of recycled air and a quiet hum of engines, a stark departure from the salty breeze and the gentle lapping of waves he'd grown accustomed to in Port Blossom. As the plane descended, the sprawling urban canvas of Seattle unfolded beneath him, a mosaic of concrete and steel stretching to the horizon. It was undeniably impressive, a testament to human ambition and innovation. Yet, as he navigated the bustling airport and hailed a cab, a subtle unease began to creep in. The sheer scale of it all, the anonymity of the crowds, felt overwhelming.

The Future Institute was an imposing structure, a monument to modern architecture. Gleaming metal and expansive glass panels reflected the perpetually overcast sky, giving the building an almost ethereal, detached quality. Eli stepped out of the cab, the cool, damp air a stark contrast to the relative warmth of Port Blossom. He was greeted by a receptionist with a perfectly coiffed bob and an unnervingly placid smile. Her efficiency was undeniable, her words clipped and precise as she directed him to the designated meeting room.

Inside, the atmosphere was a symphony of hushed efficiency. The air was cool and sterile, scented faintly with something vaguely antiseptic. The meeting room itself was sleek and minimalist, all polished chrome and muted tones. He was introduced to Dr. Aris Thorne, the lead researcher, a man whose sharp features and intense gaze suggested a mind perpetually at work. Thorne's handshake was firm, his smile tight, more a professional courtesy than a genuine warmth. He spoke of cutting-edge equipment, of breakthroughs in genetic sequencing, of the institute's unparalleled success rates.

"We believe in pushing the boundaries, Dr. Hayes," Thorne stated, gesturing towards a large screen that displayed complex molecular structures. "Our research here isn't just about incremental progress; it's about revolutionizing the field. We attract the brightest minds, individuals driven by a singular focus on scientific advancement."

Eli listened intently, his professional curiosity piqued. The technology on display was indeed state-of-the-art, far beyond anything he'd encountered. He imagined the hours spent in these advanced labs, the thrill of discovery, the potential for groundbreaking publications. Thorne outlined several ongoing projects, each more ambitious than the last. There was the gene-editing initiative for rare autoimmune diseases, the development of novel diagnostic tools for early cancer detection, and a long-term project exploring the neurological underpinnings of advanced cognitive function.

"Our resources are virtually limitless," Thorne continued, his voice gaining a slight inflection of pride. "We provide our researchers with everything they need to succeed. Think of the potential, Dr. Hayes. The impact you could have."

As Thorne spoke, Eli found himself observing the subtle dynamics of the room. The other team members who joined the discussion were equally focused, their conversations revolving almost exclusively around data, hypotheses, and experimental outcomes. There was an undeniable intellectual energy, a shared dedication to their work. Yet, it felt... contained. Isolated. He saw no casual camaraderie, no shared jokes, no easy laughter. When a minor technical issue arose with the projector, the problem was solved with swift, unemotional precision. There was no shared sigh of exasperation, no eye-rolling good-naturedness that often punctuated the occasional mishap at the rescue.

Thorne then offered him a tour of the facilities. They walked through immaculately clean laboratories, each equipped with the latest machinery. Eli saw automated centrifuges, high-resolution microscopes, and an array of specialized equipment he could only dream of. He saw sterile workspaces, meticulously organized, where every pipette and petri dish had its designated place. The sheer sophistication was breathtaking.

"We maintain a rigorous protocol for everything," Thorne explained as they passed a team of researchers in sterile suits working within a sealed environment. "Minimizing contamination, maximizing accuracy. It's essential for the integrity of our work."

Eli nodded, appreciating the scientific discipline. But as he observed, a stark contrast began to form in his mind. He remembered the controlled chaos of the rescue's veterinary clinic, the joyous barks and purrs that filled the air, the shared sense of purpose that animated every interaction. He recalled the way Sarah, the dedicated vet tech, would hum off-key while meticulously cleaning surgical instruments, or how young Liam, the intern, would bound in each morning, his enthusiasm infectious even on the most exhausting days. He thought of Mara, her quiet competence as she tended to a frightened animal, her gentle reassurance to a worried adopter. These weren't sterile, isolated moments; they were infused with a warmth, a human connection, that was entirely absent here.

"And what about the community aspect?" Eli found himself asking, the question escaping before he could fully formulate it. "The integration of findings, the collaboration beyond immediate project teams?"

Thorne blinked, as if the question were an unexpected anomaly. "We have regular departmental meetings, of course. And interdisciplinary symposia are held quarterly. Our researchers are encouraged to publish and present their work extensively. That's how findings are disseminated."

Eli pressed on, sensing a gap he couldn't quite articulate. "I mean, more informally. The kind of synergy that arises from shared experiences, from building something together outside of the strict confines of research. Like, do you have…?" He trailed off, unsure how to phrase it without sounding naive. He thought of the rescue's weekly potluck dinners, the impromptu brainstorming sessions fueled by coffee and a shared passion for their mission, the way everyone pitched in, regardless of their role, when a crisis arose.

Thorne's expression remained neutral, though a flicker of something akin to confusion crossed his eyes. "We foster a highly collaborative environment within research groups. Individual researchers are recognized for their contributions. Our focus is on individual scientific excellence and its collective contribution to the institute's overall objectives."

Eli realized then that the very foundation of the Future Institute's success – its rigorous, specialized, and highly individualized approach – was also its greatest limitation, at least for him. It was a place designed for singular brilliance, for minds dedicated solely to the pursuit of knowledge in a vacuum. There was no room for the messy, unpredictable, yet profoundly rewarding entanglement of human lives that had become the fabric of his existence in Port Blossom.

He pictured Mara's face, the way her eyes crinkled when she laughed, the quiet strength that radiated from her. He thought of the shared burdens and triumphs at the rescue, the collective sigh of relief when a difficult surgery was successful, the shared joy in finding a forever home for a long-term resident. That was the environment that had nurtured him, that had helped him heal, that had made him feel truly alive. This, in contrast, felt like a beautifully constructed, highly efficient machine, devoid of a soul.

Later, as he sat in a sterile cafe within the institute's complex, sipping an impeccably brewed, yet uninspired, latte, Eli watched the institute's employees go about their day. They moved with purpose, their faces often set in masks of concentration. Conversations were brief, functional. There was a distinct lack of spontaneous interaction, of the easy camaraderie that characterized his colleagues at the rescue. Even the support staff, from the security guards to the administrative assistants, seemed to exist in their own professional orbits, rarely crossing paths in a way that suggested genuine connection.

He pulled out his phone and scrolled through photos of Port Blossom. A picture of a boisterous group of volunteers after a successful fundraising event, their faces flushed with exertion and shared accomplishment. Another of him and Mara, silhouetted against a sunset over the bay, their arms around each other. He felt a pang of longing so intense it was almost physical. The contrast was stark, almost jarring. The Future Institute offered him the pinnacle of scientific prestige, unparalleled resources, and the chance to contribute to groundbreaking research. But it couldn't offer him what Port Blossom had so unexpectedly, and so profoundly, given him: a sense of belonging, a shared purpose, and a love that was deeply rooted in the everyday realities of their lives.

The sterile environment, the clinical efficiency, the singular focus on individual achievement – it all served to highlight what was truly important to him. It wasn't just about the science; it was about the people with whom he practiced it, the community he served, and the life he was building, piece by precious piece, with Mara. The allure of Seattle, once so potent, now felt diminished, overshadowed by the vibrant, messy, and deeply fulfilling reality he had found. He realized, with a clarity that settled deep within his bones, that his future, the one that held true happiness and purpose, lay not in the sterile brilliance of this institute, but in the warm, beating heart of Port Blossom.

The drive back from Seattle felt longer, each mile that separated him from the gleaming, sterile towers of the Future Institute a measure of the growing certainty in Eli's heart. He'd left the city with a clear head but a heavy heart, the weight of decision pressing down on him. The glittering offer, which had once represented the zenith of his professional aspirations, now felt like a gilded cage. He'd seen the future of veterinary science, and while it was undeniably brilliant, it was also undeniably cold. He found himself craving the familiar scent of salt and sea, the cacophony of barking dogs and concerned meows, the warmth of human connection that permeated every corner of the Port Blossom Animal Rescue.

He'd booked a call with Ben for that evening, a ritual they'd fallen into whenever one of them faced a significant crossroads. Ben, with his pragmatic outlook and unwavering loyalty, was the anchor Eli often needed to steady his often-turbulent thoughts. As the familiar blue dot of Port Blossom appeared on the GPS, Eli felt a surge of relief. He was almost home, and soon, he'd be able to articulate the complex emotions that had been swirling within him.

The video call connected, and Ben's cheerful, slightly rumpled face filled the screen. "Eli! How was the great Seattle adventure? Did they offer you the keys to the kingdom of cutting-edge veterinary medicine?" Ben's grin was wide, and Eli could see the stacks of paperwork behind him, a familiar sight in Ben's home office, which doubled as his unofficial rescue command center.

Eli managed a weak smile. "It was... an experience, Ben. Very impressive. State-of-the-art facilities, brilliant minds, endless resources. Everything you'd expect." He paused, choosing his words carefully. "But it also felt... sterile. Like a beautifully engineered machine, operating in a vacuum. There was no warmth, no real sense of community beyond the immediate research teams. It was all about individual achievement, about pushing boundaries in isolation."

He went on to describe the institute, the hushed corridors, the focused intensity of the researchers, the almost clinical detachment that permeated the atmosphere. He recounted his conversation with Dr. Thorne, the emphasis on individual contributions and the disconnect he felt when he inquired about a more organic, community-driven aspect to their work. "They talked about dissemination of findings, about interdisciplinary symposia," Eli explained, his voice tinged with a newfound frustration. "But it wasn't the same as... you know. Us. The potlucks, the spontaneous brainstorming sessions, the way everyone pitches in when things get tough, regardless of their official title. That's where the real magic happens, Ben. That's where the innovation and the soul of our work comes from."

Ben listened intently, his usual jovial expression softening into one of thoughtful consideration. He leaned forward, his elbows resting on his desk. "I hear you, Eli. It sounds like they're offering you a chance to be a brilliant cog in a very large, very efficient machine. But you're not just a cog, are you? You're the heart and soul of a lot of what we do here. And frankly, Port Blossom wouldn't be the same without your... messy, unpredictable, brilliant self."

Eli felt a flush of warmth spread through him. Ben always knew how to cut through the noise. "That's exactly it," Eli agreed. "I realized that in Seattle, I'd be sacrificing a huge part of myself. The part that thrives on connection, on shared purpose, on the sheer joy of building something meaningful with people you care about." He thought of Mara, her quiet strength and unwavering support, the way their lives had become so beautifully intertwined in the fabric of Port Blossom. "And Mara," he added, his voice softening. "I don't think I could build a life with her in a place where work is that... all-consuming and isolating. Our life here, it's not just about the rescue. It's about the walks on the beach, the impromptu dinners, the late-night talks. It's about the community we've built together."

Ben nodded slowly. "And that's a powerful thing, Eli. Don't ever underestimate that. I see the way you and Mara look at each other, the way you support each other's passions. That's not something you can just pack up and move to a sterile lab. That's a foundation. That's home." He gestured around his cluttered office. "Look at this. It's a mess, right? Paperwork everywhere, half-eaten sandwich on the side. But it's *my* mess. It's the chaos of a life lived with purpose, with people I care about. I wouldn't trade it for all the polished chrome in Seattle."

Eli smiled, a genuine, unforced smile. "That's what I needed to hear, Ben. I kept thinking I *should* want the prestige, the resources, the chance to be at the absolute cutting edge. But when I was there, all I could think about was what I'd be leaving behind. The tangible, everyday reality of what makes me happy."

"The shiny new toy versus the comfortable, beloved blanket," Ben quipped. "You're choosing the blanket, Eli, and that's a sign of wisdom, not weakness. Besides," he leaned closer to the camera, a mischievous glint in his eyes, "think of the stories you'd miss out on! The rescued kitten who decided the best place to sleep was inside a freshly laundered pair of scrubs. The dog who figured out how to open the treat cupboard. Seattle might have groundbreaking research, but Port Blossom has Barnaby trying to herd the entire volunteer staff every Saturday morning. Which one sounds like more fun to you?"

Eli chuckled, the sound coming easily and freely. "Barnaby, definitely. No contest."

"Exactly," Ben said, his voice firm. "You've got something special here, Eli. Mara, the rescue, this quirky little town. Don't let the allure of a bigger, shinier version of success make you forget that. You're already successful, my friend. You're living a life that's rich in meaning and love. That's the real prize."

They talked for a while longer, dissecting the nuances of Eli's experience, Ben offering practical advice on how to professionally decline the offer from the Future Institute while maintaining a good relationship. Eli felt lighter than he had in weeks. The knot of anxiety in his stomach had loosened, replaced by a quiet sense of resolve. He knew, with absolute certainty, that his path lay here, in Port Blossom, with Mara, and with the animal rescue.

The following day, Eli found himself seeking out Sarah, another long-time fixture at the rescue, known for her uncanny ability to balance fierce pragmatism with a deep well of empathy. He found her meticulously cleaning out the kennels, her movements efficient and purposeful. "Sarah," he began, "do you have a minute? I wanted to pick your brain about something."

Sarah wiped her hands on her apron and turned, her brow furrowing slightly in concern. "Eli, you look like you've seen a ghost. What's going on?"

Eli explained his visit to Seattle, the offer he'd received, and the internal turmoil it had caused. He spoke of the impressive facilities and the groundbreaking work, but also of the overwhelming sense of disconnect he'd experienced. "It felt like a place where I could advance my career exponentially," he confessed, "but at the cost of... everything else. My connection to the community, the collaborative spirit, the sheer joy of working alongside people I genuinely like and respect."

Sarah leaned against the kennel door, her expression thoughtful. "Seattle," she mused. "Impressive. But... is it *you*, Eli? Is it what you actually want, or what you think you *should* want?" She gestured around the bustling rescue. "Look at this place. It's chaotic, it's messy, and half the time we're running on fumes and sheer willpower. But it's *ours*. We built it. We pour our hearts into it. And we do it together. Remember when Buster came in, that terrified German Shepherd mix who wouldn't let anyone near him? Thorne's institute would probably have a team of behaviorists and cutting-edge tranquilizers. We sat with him for hours, day after day, just being present. And you, Eli, you were the one who finally got him to take a treat from your hand. That wasn't about resources; it was about patience, compassion, and connection. That's the kind of work that matters, isn't it?"

Eli felt a surge of emotion. Sarah, with her no-nonsense approach, had a way of cutting straight to the heart of things. "That's it exactly," he said, his voice thick. "I saw the potential for immense scientific achievement in Seattle, but I also saw the potential for immense personal loss. I'd be trading the depth of our relationships here for the breadth of their research. And honestly, Sarah, I don't think I can make that trade."

"And Mara?" Sarah asked gently, her eyes holding his. "What about her? You two have built something beautiful here. Is a life in Seattle compatible with that?"

Eli pictured Mara's radiant smile, the way she'd supported him through his own personal struggles, the quiet strength she brought to their shared life. "That's the hardest part," he admitted. "I can't imagine pulling her away from everything she loves here. And even if we did, I don't know if I could be the partner she deserves in that kind of environment. I need this connection, this sense of belonging, to be my best self. And she deserves that best self."

Sarah reached out and squeezed his arm. "You're a good man, Eli. A good vet, and a better friend. It takes courage to walk away from something that promises so much, especially when it's something you've worked so hard for. But it takes even more courage to choose happiness, to choose what truly nourishes your soul, even when it's the harder path." She smiled, a warm, genuine smile that crinkled the corners of her eyes. "You have a good foundation here, Eli. A strong one. Don't let anyone tell you that means you're not ambitious enough. It means you're wise enough to know what truly matters."

Her words resonated deeply. The external validation of a prestigious position in Seattle felt hollow compared to the internal validation of knowing he was choosing a life aligned with his deepest values. He was choosing connection over isolation, community over individual achievement, and, most importantly, he was choosing a future with Mara, a future built on shared love and purpose. The decision, once a daunting mountain to climb, now felt like a clear, sunlit path. He wasn't just weighing options; he was weighing his own heart, and his heart was firmly rooted in Port Blossom.

The hum of the fluorescent lights in the Port Blossom Animal Rescue's small office always seemed to amplify Mara's thoughts, turning them into a low thrumming that vibrated just beneath her skin. Today, however, the hum felt less like an annoyance and more like a steady, insistent beat, mirroring the newfound rhythm of her own heart. The conversation with Eli the previous evening, his quiet revelation about the sterile allure of the Seattle offer and his deep-seated need for connection, had been a catalyst. It had cleared away the lingering fog of uncertainty, leaving her with a sharp, crystalline clarity about her own desires and, more importantly, her own agency. She had been waiting, passively, for *their* future to unfold, a future she envisioned with Eli, rooted firmly in Port Blossom. But now, she understood. The future wasn't something that simply happened; it was something you built, brick by painstaking brick, with intention and unwavering effort. And she was ready to start laying the foundation.

Her gaze swept across the worn oak desk, a familiar landscape of overflowing inboxes, adoption papers waiting for signatures, and a scattering of well-loved animal care manuals. Tucked amongst them was a thick binder, its pages dog-eared and heavily annotated, a testament to weeks of research and nascent planning. This was her "Port Blossom Rescue – Future Forward" initiative, a project she'd initially approached with a hesitant optimism, a quiet hope that it might resonate with the board. Now, it felt like an urgent mission. She wasn't just hoping anymore; she was *doing*. She smoothed a hand over the cover, a determined smile playing on her lips. Eli had chosen Port Blossom, had chosen *them*, because of the soul of this place, the tangible warmth of its community, the interwoven lives they were building. It was her responsibility, and her privilege, to ensure that the sanctuary that housed so much of that heart had a future as vibrant and enduring as their own burgeoning love.

The first hurdle, as always, was the board. A well-meaning, if sometimes overly cautious, group of individuals whose dedication to the rescue was unquestionable, but whose financial foresight could, at times, feel like a relic of a bygone era. Mara admired their commitment, their years of service, but she also knew that enthusiasm alone wouldn't keep the lights on, wouldn't cover the ever-increasing veterinary bills, or fund the much-needed expansion of their quarantine facilities. She'd spent the past week poring over the rescue's financial reports, a task that had initially felt daunting, but had soon become a puzzle she was determined to solve. She'd identified areas where expenses could be trimmed without compromising care, but more importantly, she'd pinpointed opportunities for growth, for diversified income streams that went beyond the traditional bake sales and donation jars.

She opened the binder, her fingers tracing the headings of the proposal she'd meticulously drafted. "Project Pawsitive Impact: Innovative Fundraising Strategies for Port Blossom Animal Rescue." It was a bold title, she knew, but it reflected the ambition she now felt coursing through her. She'd broken it down into actionable steps, each one designed to engage the community in new and exciting ways. There was the "Sponsor a Shelter Star" program, a tiered sponsorship system where individuals could symbolically adopt one of the long-term residents, receiving regular updates, photos, and even a personalized "thank you" note from their chosen animal. This wasn't just about the money; it was about fostering a deeper emotional connection, turning passive donors into active advocates.

Then there was the "Rescue Rendezvous" event series. She envisioned a monthly gathering, each with a unique theme. A "Yappy Hour" at a local dog-friendly brewery, a portion of the proceeds going to the rescue. A "Kitten Cuddle Cafe" in collaboration with the town's beloved coffee shop, offering a serene space for people to de-stress and interact with adoptable kittens. A "Pet Portrait Paw-ty" with local artists offering quick, affordable sketches of beloved pets, with a commission going to the rescue. These events weren't just fundraisers; they were community builders, opportunities to weave the rescue even more tightly into the fabric of Port Blossom life, creating a network of support that was as strong as it was widespread.

She'd even proposed a "Rescue Runway" fashion show, featuring adoptable animals walking (or being carried) alongside local celebrities and community leaders, showcasing the charm and unique personalities of the animals available for adoption. It sounded a little whimsical, perhaps even a touch audacious, but Mara believed in the power of joy, of creating positive, memorable experiences that would leave people with a lasting impression of the rescue and its incredible residents. She knew she had to present these ideas not just as hopeful suggestions, but as well-researched, financially viable plans. She'd spent hours calculating potential revenue streams, estimating costs, and outlining marketing strategies, all with the goal of demonstrating her thoroughness and her unwavering commitment.

Beyond the immediate fundraising initiatives, Mara had also dedicated a significant portion of her energy to exploring grant opportunities. This was a more complex undertaking, involving meticulous research into eligibility criteria, understanding the specific focus areas of various foundations, and crafting compelling narratives that highlighted the rescue's impact and its vital need for support. She'd discovered several local and regional foundations that aligned with animal welfare, conservation, and community development, and she was meticulously working on tailoring applications to each one.

She picked up a thick stack of printed grant guidelines, her brow furrowed in concentration. One, from the "Coastal Community Foundation," specifically supported initiatives that strengthened local non-profits and enhanced community well-being. Another, the "Green Paw Foundation," focused on organizations that promoted sustainable animal care and provided rehabilitation services. These weren't just abstract funding sources; they represented tangible opportunities to secure resources for critical upgrades. She envisioned using grant money to finally replace the aging, inefficient heating system in the main kennel building, a project that had been on the back burner for years due to its prohibitive cost. She also dreamed of expanding the veterinary clinic's diagnostic capabilities, perhaps investing in a digital X-ray machine, which would significantly improve diagnostic accuracy and speed up treatment for critically ill animals.

She flipped through a draft of a grant proposal, her pen hovering over a section describing their community outreach programs. She wrote about the mobile adoption unit that visited underserved areas, bringing the joy of animal companionship to those who might not otherwise have access. She detailed their junior volunteer program, which instilled a sense of responsibility and compassion in young people. She spoke of their partnerships with local schools, offering educational talks on responsible pet ownership. These were the stories that resonated, the evidence of the rescue's deep and meaningful impact on the Port Blossom community, the very essence of what made this place special, and what she and Eli were fighting to preserve.

She paused, a wave of emotion washing over her. It wasn't just about securing the rescue's future; it was about solidifying *their* future. Every grant she applied for, every fundraising event she planned, was a declaration to Eli, and more importantly, to herself, that she was all-in. She wasn't just passively accepting his decision to stay; she was actively demonstrating that their shared life here was a worthwhile investment, a future brimming with potential and purpose. She wanted him to see her not just as a supportive partner, but as a proactive force, someone who was willing to roll up her sleeves and fight for the life they envisioned together.

The phone on her desk buzzed, startling her. It was Sarah, calling to confirm the volunteer schedule for the upcoming weekend. "Hey Mara," Sarah's voice was warm and familiar. "Just wanted to touch base about Saturday. We've got a lot of intakes coming in, and Barnaby's already started trying to organize the entire volunteer crew into a parade."

Mara laughed, picturing the energetic Border Collie already trying to herd the early arrivals. "Sounds about right," she replied, her voice filled with a newfound lightness. "I'll be there early. Actually, Sarah, I was hoping we could chat for a few minutes before things get too hectic. I've been working on some ideas for the rescue, some new fundraising initiatives, and I wanted to run them by you."

There was a brief pause on the other end. "New fundraising? That's fantastic, Mara! You know you've got my full support. What have you been cooking up?"

Mara explained her "Project Pawsitive Impact," outlining the Sponsor a Shelter Star program and the Rescue Rendezvous events. As she spoke, she felt a growing confidence, a sense of empowerment that bloomed with each word. Sarah listened intently, interjecting with enthusiastic questions and practical suggestions. "A Yappy Hour? Mara, that's brilliant! The Salty Dog Pub would be perfect for that. And the Kitten Cuddle Cafe? People are going to go crazy for that!"

By the time they ended the call, Mara felt a renewed sense of purpose. Sarah had offered invaluable insights, her practical experience a perfect complement to Mara's ambitious vision. She'd also agreed to help Mara flesh out the details for the "Rescue Runway" event, her own knack for organization proving invaluable. This wasn't a solo endeavor; it was a collaborative effort, a testament to the strength of the community they were a part of.

Later that afternoon, Mara found herself at the town hall, meeting with Mayor Thompson. She'd requested the meeting to discuss the possibility of securing a small, long-term lease on a neglected plot of land behind the existing rescue building. Her vision was ambitious: a dedicated outdoor agility course for dogs, a secure space for larger dog playgroups, and perhaps even a small, enclosed garden area where cats could safely experience the outdoors. It was a long shot, she knew, but she felt a compelling urge to think big, to envision a future for the rescue that was not only sustainable but also enriched the lives of the animals in their care.

Mayor Thompson, a man whose pragmatic approach was softened by a genuine fondness for the town's animal inhabitants, listened patiently as Mara laid out her proposal. He knew Mara, knew her dedication, and he'd witnessed firsthand the positive impact the rescue had on Port Blossom. He'd also seen the wear and tear on the current facilities, the constant need for repairs and upgrades.

"An outdoor agility course, you say?" Mayor Thompson mused, tapping his pen against his chin. "And expanding the play space. That's a considerable undertaking, Mara. We'd need to see a solid financial plan, of course. Grants, community fundraising... you understand."

"Absolutely, Mayor," Mara replied, her voice steady and assured. "I've been developing a comprehensive fundraising strategy, and I'm also actively pursuing grant opportunities. This isn't just a wish list; it's a carefully considered plan for enhancing our facilities and expanding our services, all aimed at better serving the animals and the community." She then elaborated on her "Project Pawsitive Impact," explaining the innovative fundraising events and the grant applications she was preparing. She spoke with a passion and conviction that was palpable, her belief in the rescue's potential shining through.

Mayor Thompson nodded slowly, a flicker of genuine interest in his eyes. He appreciated her proactive approach, her willingness to go beyond the expected. "You've certainly done your homework, Mara," he admitted. "And I see the dedication you have for this rescue. It's something special for Port Blossom. Let's see what we can do. I'll have my assistant look into the specifics of that land parcel. In the meantime, keep developing those plans. Show me you can make it happen, and I'll do my best to help you make it a reality."

As Mara walked out of the town hall, a sense of exhilaration washed over her. It was a small victory, a single step in a long journey, but it was a step taken with purpose, with a clear vision of the future. She pulled out her phone, her fingers flying across the screen as she typed a message to Eli: "Just had a meeting with Mayor Thompson about expanding the outdoor space. He's open to it! Feeling so energized right now. This place is worth fighting for. "

She imagined Eli's smile, the warmth that would spread through him at the news. This was more than just building a better rescue; it was building a future for them, a life that was rich with shared purpose and unwavering commitment. She was no longer waiting for life to happen; she was actively shaping it, brick by brick, dream by dream, right here in the heart of Port Blossom. And in that act of creation, she found a profound sense of peace and a burgeoning resolve that felt as solid and enduring as the very ground beneath her feet.

Chapter Five

The Turning Tide

Eli's phone buzzed on the worn surface of his nightstand, the vibration a low thrum against the quiet of his apartment. The caller ID, a familiar string of numbers, brought a familiar flutter of apprehension to his chest. He'd been expecting this call for days, ever since he'd returned from his initial visit to the institute in Seattle, the sterile air of the lab still clinging to his clothes like a phantom scent. He knew what they were going to say, what they were offering. And he knew, with a certainty that had been slowly solidifying over the past week, what his answer had to be.

He took a deep breath, the cool morning air doing little to quell the turmoil within him. Mara was still asleep in the guest room, her presence a comforting weight in the house that he was slowly beginning to call his own. He'd spent the night replaying their conversation, the quiet intensity of her gaze as she'd spoken about her vision for the rescue, the way her eyes had lit up when she'd described her ambitious plans for community engagement. He'd seen a reflection of his own deepest desires in her passion – the yearning for connection, for a life built not just on individual achievement, but on shared purpose and the quiet, profound beauty of belonging.

He finally answered the call, his voice a little rougher than usual. "Dr. Thorne," he began, the formal address feeling both foreign and strangely fitting. "To what do I owe the pleasure?"

The voice on the other end, smooth and professional, spoke of research grants, state-of-the-art equipment, and the kind of groundbreaking discoveries that had once been the sole focus of his ambition. He listened, his mind calmly absorbing the details, the offer laid out with all the allure and prestige he had once craved. They painted a vivid picture of a life dedicated to pure science, a life unburdened by the practicalities of running a non-profit, a life that promised accolades and recognition within the scientific community. It was, in many ways, everything he had worked towards for years, the culmination of countless late nights and relentless dedication.

But as the institute representative continued, Eli found himself increasingly drawn to the subtle undertones of his own life, the quiet hum of contentment he'd discovered in Port Blossom. He thought of the eager faces of the volunteers at the rescue, the hopeful eyes of the animals awaiting adoption, the steady, grounding presence of Mara. He remembered the feeling of accomplishment he'd experienced when helping a shy dog finally trust a new handler, the quiet joy of seeing a litter of kittens find their forever homes. These were not the achievements that would be published in prestigious journals, but they were achievements nonetheless, deeply felt and intrinsically rewarding.

"I appreciate the offer, Dr. Sterling," Eli said, his voice now firm and steady. "You've presented a compelling case, and the research opportunities you've outlined are undeniably exciting. However, I must respectfully decline."

There was a brief, surprised silence on the line. "Decline? Dr. Thorne, are you certain? This is a unique opportunity, one that could redefine your career trajectory."

Eli smiled faintly, a genuine, unforced smile that reached his eyes. "I am certain. My career trajectory, as you call it, has taken a rather unexpected but profoundly fulfilling turn. I've realized that my true calling lies not solely in the pursuit of scientific discovery in isolation, but in building something tangible, something that enriches the lives of others, both human and animal. And I've found that in Port Blossom."

He went on to explain, not with regret, but with a quiet certainty, about the life he was choosing. He spoke of Mara, not just as a romantic partner, but as a kindred spirit, a force of nature whose passion for the rescue ignited a similar fire within him. He described the community, the inherent value he found in contributing to its well-being, in being a part of something larger than himself. He acknowledged the allure of Seattle, of the advanced facilities and the cutting-edge research, but he couldn't shake the feeling that it was a path that would ultimately lead him away from the very things that had come to mean the most to him.

"I understand that this might seem like a step backward to some," Eli continued, choosing his words carefully. "But for me, it's a step forward. A step towards a life grounded in purpose, in connection, and in love. I've been searching for a sense of belonging, Dr. Sterling, a place where I can contribute meaningfully, and I've found it here. The work Mara is doing at the rescue, the potential for growth and impact... it resonates with me on a level that scientific advancement alone, as groundbreaking as it may be, cannot quite touch."

He listened as Dr. Sterling offered further inducements, a more flexible research schedule, additional funding for his personal projects, but Eli's decision was made. He thanked him again for the offer, reiterating his gratitude for their interest, but his resolve was unwavering. He knew that this was not a decision born of impulse, but of deep introspection. He had wrestled with the possibilities, with the ghosts of his former ambitions, but in the end, the quiet pull of a life shared, a life built with Mara in this charming, imperfect town, had won.

As he ended the call, a profound sense of peace settled over him. The weight he hadn't fully realized he'd been carrying for the past week lifted, leaving him feeling lighter, more centered. He walked out of his bedroom, the morning sun streaming through the living room window, casting long shadows across the familiar space. He found Mara in the kitchen, already brewing coffee, her back to him as she hummed a soft tune.

He walked up behind her, wrapping his arms around her waist and resting his chin on her shoulder. She started slightly, then leaned back into his embrace, a contented sigh escaping her. "Morning," she murmured, her voice still thick with sleep.

"Morning," Eli replied, his voice warm and filled with a newfound sense of purpose. He held her for a moment longer, soaking in the simple intimacy of the gesture. He knew that this was just the beginning, the start of building the life they'd both envisioned, a life woven together with shared dreams and unwavering support.

"I took a call this morning," he said, his voice soft against her hair.

Mara turned in his arms, her eyes questioning. "From Seattle?"

Eli nodded, his gaze meeting hers. He saw the flicker of worry in her expression, the unspoken question hanging in the air. He squeezed her hands gently. "Yes. From Seattle. And I told them... I told them I'm staying."

A slow smile spread across Mara's face, widening until it reached her eyes, filling them with a radiant joy that mirrored the sunbeams dancing around them. She didn't need to ask for details, didn't need a grand pronouncement. She understood. She saw the quiet triumph in his eyes, the deep satisfaction that radiated from him. She reached up, her fingers tracing the line of his jaw, her touch a silent confirmation of everything they had found in each other.

"Oh, Eli," she whispered, her voice thick with emotion. "That's... that's wonderful."

He lowered his head, his forehead resting against hers. "It is. It really is. I realized... I realized that the research I want to do, the impact I want to make, it's here. With you. In this community." He pulled back slightly, his eyes searching hers. "I want to build this life with you, Mara. This Port Blossom life."

Mara's breath hitched, a tear escaping and tracing a path down her cheek. She didn't bother to wipe it away. "And I want to build it with you," she replied, her voice a steady promise. "Every single brick."

The coffee machine hissed, signaling the end of its brewing cycle, but neither of them moved. They stood there, holding each other, the quiet certainty of their shared future settling around them like a warm embrace. The decision, once a source of agonizing deliberation, now felt like the most natural, the most right, thing in the world. Eli had made his choice, not out of obligation or compromise, but out of a deep, resonant understanding of where his heart truly belonged. He had chosen connection over isolation, a shared life over solitary ambition, and in that choice, he had found a happiness more profound than any he had ever imagined. The tide had truly turned, and it was carrying them, together, towards a future brimming with promise.

The familiar scent of disinfectant, animal feed, and something vaguely floral, undoubtedly Mara's chosen brand of hand soap, greeted Eli as he stepped through the back entrance of the Port Blossom Animal Rescue. The late morning sun, a cheerful presence that had finally broken through the persistent coastal mist, illuminated dust motes dancing in the air. He found Mara not in her usual office, where paperwork usually threatened to spill onto the floor, but out in the main kennel area. She was kneeling, a gentle smile gracing her lips as she spoke in hushed, soothing tones to a boisterous terrier mix, its tail a blur of ecstatic motion. A half-emptied bag of kibble lay beside her, and she'd clearly been interrupted mid-task. The scene was one of controlled, heartwarming chaos, the kind that had so quickly come to feel like home to him.

He paused for a moment, simply watching her. There was a grace in her movements, an innate understanding of the animals that transcended mere expertise. She radiated a quiet confidence, a groundedness that he'd come to rely on. He felt a profound sense of peace settle over him, the echoes of his decision resonating within him like a perfectly struck chord. The sterile laboratories of Seattle, the ambitious research proposals, the accolades he'd once chased with single-minded intensity – they all seemed a distant, almost irrelevant dream now. His reality, his ambition, his *life*, was here, in this place, with this woman.

Taking a steadying breath, Eli walked towards her. The clatter of kennels, the occasional bark, the soft murmur of Mara's voice

– it all blended into a symphony of purposeful activity. As he drew closer, the terrier, sensing his approach, momentarily shifted its attention, its perky ears swiveling in his direction. Mara followed its gaze, her smile widening as she saw him. She rose to her feet, brushing stray strands of hair from her forehead with the back of her hand.

"Hey," she said, her voice warm and welcoming, though a hint of curiosity flickered in her eyes. He looked different today, she thought. There was a lightness about him, a serenity that hadn't been there before, even in their happiest moments. It was as if a great weight had been lifted, and she sensed, with a flutter of her heart, that whatever had been pressing on him had finally resolved itself.

He didn't immediately launch into an explanation. Instead, he walked the few remaining steps until he was directly in front of her, his gaze locking with hers. The noise of the rescue seemed to fade, the world narrowing to just the two of them. He reached out, his hands gently closing around hers. Her skin was warm, slightly roughened from her work, and he held them firmly, anchoring himself.

"I got the call this morning," he began, his voice low and steady, devoid of any of the apprehension that had marked his previous conversations about the Seattle offer. "From the institute."

Mara's breath hitched slightly, her eyes searching his. She'd known this day was coming, had braced herself for whatever his decision might be. A small knot of anxiety tightened in her chest, a familiar companion whenever the future felt uncertain. She offered a small, encouraging smile, a silent plea for him to share whatever was on his mind.

Eli squeezed her hands, a gesture of reassurance. "They made a very... compelling offer, Mara. State-of-the-art facilities, unlimited research funding, the chance to work on projects that could genuinely change the world. It was, in many ways, everything I'd worked towards for years." He paused, a faint smile touching his lips as he saw the tension in her shoulders ease ever so slightly. "It was the kind of offer that, a few months ago, I would have jumped at without a second thought. It represented a culmination of all my past ambitions."

He continued, his voice deepening with emotion, "But as they were talking, laying out all the prestige and the potential for scientific acclaim, all I could picture was this. You. This place. The work we're doing here." He gestured vaguely around them, taking in the bustling kennels, the determined glint in Mara's eyes, the undeniable vibrancy of the rescue. "I realized that the life they were offering, the life of pure, solitary scientific pursuit, wasn't the life I wanted anymore. It wasn't the life that made me feel... whole."

He looked directly into her eyes, his own reflecting a profound sincerity. "My heart isn't in Seattle, Mara. It's here. With you. And with this community." The words, spoken with such conviction, hung in the air between them, potent and clear. "I told them no. I respectfully declined the offer."

A gasp escaped Mara's lips, soft and involuntary. Relief, so potent it felt like a physical wave, washed over her, loosening the tight knot in her chest and making her knees feel weak. She hadn't realized how tightly she'd been holding her breath, how much she'd been dreading the possibility of him choosing a path that would take him away from her, away from Port Blossom. Her eyes, already glistening with unshed tears, now overflowed, hot drops tracing paths down her cheeks. She made no move to wipe them away, letting the pure joy of the moment wash over her.

"Oh, Eli," she whispered, her voice thick with emotion, barely audible above the happy barks of the dogs. "Are you... are you sure?"

He smiled, a genuine, radiant smile that crinkled the corners of his eyes. "More sure than I've ever been about anything in my life." He lifted one of her hands, bringing it to his lips and pressing a gentle kiss to her knuckles. "The work you're doing here, Mara, the impact you're making on these animals, on this town... it's extraordinary. And I want to be a part of it. Not just as a supporter, or a partner, but as someone who's fully invested, side-by-side with you."

He laced his fingers through hers again, his grip firm and reassuring. "I want to help build this rescue into everything you envision. I want to be here to face the challenges with you, to celebrate the triumphs with you. I want to make our life here permanent, Mara. This is where I belong."

Mara's heart swelled with a gratitude so immense it was almost overwhelming. She'd loved Eli from the moment she'd realized the depth of his kindness, the quiet strength beneath his reserved exterior. But in that moment, seeing the unwavering certainty in his eyes, the profound commitment in his voice, her love for him deepened, solidifying into something even more profound. The possibility of him leaving had been a dark cloud hanging over her, a constant undercurrent of fear that had threatened to overshadow the joy she found in her work and in their burgeoning relationship. Now, that cloud had dissipated, replaced by a brilliant, golden sunshine.

"And I want to build it with you, Eli," she vowed, her voice ringing with a newfound strength and joy. "Every single brick. I love that you're choosing this, choosing *us*. It means more than you can possibly imagine." She leaned forward, her forehead resting against his, her eyes closed as she savored the feeling of his presence, the warmth radiating from him. The tension that had subtly underscored their interactions for weeks, a quiet hum of unspoken anxieties about his future, had completely evaporated. In its place was a profound sense of ease, a shared understanding that felt as solid and comforting as the ground beneath their feet.

He pulled back slightly, his thumbs gently stroking the back of her hands. "I know we'll have our challenges," he admitted, his gaze steady. "This isn't an easy path. Running a rescue is demanding, and there will be days when it feels overwhelming. But I want to face them with you. I want to be your partner in this, in every sense of the word." He looked around the kennel, then back at her, his expression radiating a quiet determination. "I've spent so long chasing my own ambitions, Mara. But I've realized that the greatest ambition, the most fulfilling pursuit, is building a life of purpose with someone you love."

Mara's smile widened, a tear finally escaping and tracing a glistening path down her cheek. She didn't try to stop it. It was a tear of pure, unadulterated happiness. "And I love you, Eli," she whispered, the words a simple, powerful declaration. "More than I ever thought possible."

He brought her hands up to his chest, pressing them against his heart. She could feel the strong, steady beat beneath her palms, a rhythm that now seemed perfectly in sync with her own. "And I love you, Mara," he replied, his voice filled with a quiet certainty. "This is my home now. You are my home."

The boisterous terrier, sensing the shift in energy, let out a happy bark, nudging Mara's hand with its wet nose. She laughed, a bright, clear sound that echoed through the kennels. "Looks like we have some adopters to introduce," she said, her eyes still shining with joy as she looked at Eli. "But first..."

Before he could even react, she reached up, cupped his face in her hands, and pulled him down for a kiss. It wasn't a rushed or tentative kiss, but one filled with a deep, abiding love and a profound sense of relief. It was a kiss that sealed their commitment, a silent promise of a shared future built on love, purpose, and the unwavering belief in the extraordinary life they were creating together, right here, in the heart of Port Blossom. The turning tide had indeed brought them to a shore where they could finally anchor themselves, together.

The air in Mara's small office, usually a vibrant hub of activity, now hummed with a different kind of energy. It was a focused, determined quiet, punctuated by the soft scratch of pens on paper and the gentle click of keyboard keys. The earlier chaos of the kennels, filled with the joyous barks of newly adopted pets and the quiet reassurance of Mara's voice, had receded, replaced by the intricate work of securing the Port Blossom Animal Rescue's future. Eli, his lab coat replaced by a practical, comfortable sweater, sat beside Mara at her desk, the shared space suddenly feeling much larger, imbued with the weight of their joint commitment. The Seattle offer, once a looming shadow, had receded into irrelevance, its brilliance dimmed by the radiant glow of a shared purpose.

Mara, her brow furrowed in concentration, was meticulously outlining her fundraising strategies, her natural optimism now tempered with a strategic pragmatism. "Okay, so the 'Paws for a Cause' bake sale brought in more than we anticipated," she murmured, ticking off an item on a long list. "And Mrs. Henderson's 'Adopt-a-Kennel' initiative is already exceeding its target for the month. The community's response has been... overwhelming, in the best possible way." She looked up at Eli, her eyes shining with a gratitude that mirrored his own. "It's like they've been waiting for us to signal that we're here to stay, that we're fighting for this place. Their support is a lifeline, Eli. A genuine lifeline."

Eli nodded, his gaze fixed on a complex spreadsheet detailing projected expenses and potential income streams. He'd spent the morning immersed in the data, his analytical mind, once focused on molecular structures, now dissecting the financial health of the rescue. "It is," he agreed, his voice carrying a new kind of authority, one born not of academic prestige but of genuine investment. "And we need to build on that momentum. The immediate influx of donations is crucial, but we can't rely solely on spontaneous generosity. We need a robust, diversified plan for long-term sustainability."

He tapped a section of the spreadsheet. "Your initial strategies are brilliant, Mara, hitting the emotional core of the community while also offering tangible ways for people to contribute. But we need to layer in more structured approaches. I've been researching grant opportunities – national foundations that focus on animal welfare, local government grants for community betterment projects. There are avenues we haven't even begun to explore." He met her gaze, a spark of excitement igniting in his eyes. "Imagine what we could do with a consistent grant stream. Upgrading the veterinary facilities, expanding our outreach programs, perhaps even investing in a dedicated transport vehicle for animal rescues further afield."

Mara's breath hitched. These were dreams she'd long harbored, ideas that had often felt impossibly distant, weighed down by the constant struggle for basic funding. "A transport vehicle?" she breathed, her voice filled with wonder. "We could reach so many more animals. We could pull from shelters that are already at capacity, bring them here where they have a better chance."

"Exactly," Eli confirmed, his enthusiasm infectious. "And it's not just about the money itself. It's about building a reputation, establishing ourselves as a professional, reliable organization. Grants require detailed proposals, clear objectives, and demonstrable impact. That means robust record-keeping, rigorous evaluation of our success rates, and a clear vision for the future. All things," he added with a gentle smile, "that my scientific background has prepared me for."

He pushed a stack of papers towards her. "I've started drafting a proposal for the 'Coastal Communities for Animal Well-being' grant. It's a local initiative, but the funding is substantial. I've focused on our role in addressing pet overpopulation, our educational programs for responsible pet ownership, and our success in finding permanent homes for even the most challenging cases. I've also included a section on our plans for expansion and how we intend to become a model for other smaller rescues."

Mara picked up the documents, her fingers tracing the crisp edges. The proposal was thorough, meticulously researched, and written with a clarity that spoke volumes about Eli's dedication. It wasn't just an application; it was a testament to his belief in their mission. "Eli, this is... incredible," she whispered, a lump forming in her throat. "You've done so much already. I was so focused on the immediate crisis, on keeping the lights on and the kennels full, that I almost forgot about the bigger picture."

"We'll do it together," he said, his voice firm. "Your understanding of the rescue's operational needs, your connection with the animals and the community, and my ability to navigate the bureaucratic and financial landscapes – it's a potent combination, Mara. We're not just partners in this personal journey anymore; we're partners in building something lasting." He reached across the desk, his hand covering hers. His touch was warm, grounding, a silent affirmation of their shared future. "Think about partnerships, too. Beyond grants. Are there local businesses that might be willing to sponsor a kennel, a specific program? Vets who might offer pro bono services for complex cases in exchange for recognition? We need to weave ourselves into the fabric of this town, Eli. Become indispensable."

Mara's mind, now cleared of immediate anxieties, began to whir with possibilities. "Dr. Ramirez at the Port Blossom Veterinary Clinic... she's always been supportive, though her own practice is demanding. Perhaps we could offer her a dedicated space for emergency consultations, or a plaque on the clinic wall acknowledging her contribution. And 'The Salty Dog' pet supply store downtown – they already do a small donation box, but a more formal partnership, maybe featuring our adoptable animals in their window display, could be huge." She paused, a thoughtful expression on her face. "And what about collaborations with other non-profits? The local historical society, for instance. We could host joint events, cross-promote our causes. It's about building a network of support, isn't it? A whole ecosystem of care."

"Precisely," Eli agreed, a smile playing on his lips. He loved seeing her mind work, the way her passion translated into actionable ideas. "It's about demonstrating our value, not just to the animals, but to the entire community. We're not just a place where lost pets go; we're a resource, an educator, a symbol of compassion. When people see us thriving, it reflects well on Port Blossom as a whole." He leaned back, a sense of contentment washing over him. The spreadsheets, the grant proposals, the strategic planning – it was all so different from his previous work, yet it felt infinitely more rewarding. This was tangible. This was real. This was building a life, brick by brick, with the woman he loved.

"I've also been thinking about volunteer recruitment and training," he continued, drawing her attention back to the task at hand. "A strong, dedicated volunteer base is essential for operational efficiency. We need to formalize our training protocols, offer ongoing support, and create a sense of community amongst the volunteers themselves. A happy, well-trained volunteer is a loyal volunteer."

Mara nodded enthusiastically. "Yes! And we need to make sure our volunteers feel appreciated. Little things, like a monthly

'Volunteer Spotlight' in our newsletter, or a small appreciation event at the end of each quarter. It's about creating a culture of gratitude, mirroring the one we want to foster for our donors and partners." She picked up a pen and began sketching out a new section in her notebook. "And perhaps a tiered volunteer program? Offering more specialized training for those who want to take on leadership roles, or focus on specific areas like behavioral training or event planning."

The conversation flowed seamlessly, a collaborative dance of ideas and aspirations. Hours passed, marked not by the ticking of a clock but by the growing pile of meticulously organized documents and the increasing sense of purpose that filled the small office. The late afternoon sun cast long shadows across the room, painting a warm, golden hue that mirrored the optimism blooming within them. The immediate crisis had been averted, the immediate financial strain eased by the outpouring of community support. Now, they were laying the foundation for something far more enduring.

"We need to think about branding too," Eli mused, tapping his chin. "Our logo is functional, but does it truly capture the spirit of the Port Blossom Animal Rescue? Does it convey the warmth, the hope, and the professionalism we're striving for?"

Mara considered this, her gaze drifting to the framed photographs of happy adopted animals adorning the walls. "I've always loved the idea of a logo that incorporates the lighthouse symbol of Port Blossom," she offered. "It represents guidance, safety, a beacon of hope for those lost at sea, much like we are for animals in need. Perhaps a stylized lighthouse with a paw print integrated into it?"

Eli's eyes lit up. "That's brilliant, Mara! It's instantly recognizable, deeply tied to our location, and subtly communicates our mission. We can use that across all our communications – our website, our social media, our merchandise. It creates a unified identity, a recognizable symbol of our commitment." He made a note on his notepad. "I can research graphic designers who specialize in non-profit branding. We want something impactful, memorable, and representative of the incredible work you do here."

As the conversation continued, weaving through fundraising strategies, grant applications, partnership ideas, volunteer management, and branding initiatives, a profound sense of partnership solidified between them. It wasn't just about saving animals anymore; it was about building a sustainable, thriving organization that would serve the Port Blossom community for years to come. Eli, who had once seen his future in the sterile confines of a research lab, now saw it here, amidst the organized chaos of rescue operations, side-by-side with Mara, their shared vision a powerful force driving them forward.

The scent of disinfectant and animal feed, once just background noise, now felt like the perfume of a shared purpose. The gentle barks and meows from the kennels were no longer just the sounds of animals needing care; they were the affirmations of a mission worth fighting for. They were the soundtrack to a future they were actively, deliberately, and lovingly building together. The turning tide had indeed brought them to a shore where they could not only anchor themselves but also construct a sanctuary, a testament to their love, their commitment, and their unwavering belief in the transformative power of compassion. Securing the rescue's future was no longer just a task; it was a promise, whispered in every grant proposal drafted, every partnership explored, and every loving glance exchanged between them. It was a promise etched in the very foundations of the Port Blossom Animal Rescue, a promise of hope, resilience, and a brighter tomorrow for every creature that crossed their threshold. The work ahead was immense, the challenges undeniable, but with their combined strengths and their shared love, they were ready to face it all.

The storm had passed, leaving behind a landscape scrubbed clean, vibrant under a sky that promised an endless stretch of blue. For Mara and Eli, it felt as though a personal tempest had also subsided, revealing a clarity and a strength they hadn't fully appreciated before. The frantic energy of the preceding days, the gnawing anxiety that had threatened to capsize their hopes, had receded, leaving in its wake a profound sense of calm and a renewed appreciation for the quiet solidity of their shared life. Eli's decision to remain in Port Blossom, to dedicate his considerable intellect and growing passion to the rescue, was no longer a tentative step but a firm, decisive stride. It was a commitment that resonated in the way he looked at Mara, in the way he spoke about their future, a future now inextricably linked with the weathered charm of their coastal town.

Mara felt it too, a settling in her soul that was deeper and more genuine than any she had experienced before. The transient nature of her past, the constant ebb and flow of uncertainty, had been replaced by a steadfast anchor. Port Blossom, once a temporary refuge, now felt like home in the truest sense of the word. This wasn't just about owning a building or running a business; it was about planting roots, about becoming an integral part of the community's tapestry. The near-disaster had served as a stark reminder of what truly mattered, not just to her, but to the people who had rallied around them, who had shown such unwavering support. Their collective response had been a testament to the power of shared values, a palpable demonstration of a community's heart.

"I keep replaying that night," Mara confessed, her voice soft as she traced the rim of her coffee mug, the morning sun warming her face through the kitchen window. "The fear that we might lose everything. And then, seeing everyone show up... Mrs. Henderson with her casseroles, the teenagers from the high school offering to help clean, even old Mr. Fitzwilliam, who usually grumbles about everything, was out there with a shovel." A small smile touched her lips. "It was humbling, Eli. Truly humbling."

Eli, who was meticulously sorting through a stack of thank-you cards, paused and met her gaze. His eyes, usually filled with a quiet intensity, held a depth of emotion that spoke volumes. "It was more than humbling, Mara. It was… inspiring. It showed us what this place, this community, is capable of. It showed us that we're not alone in this." He set down the cards, his attention fully on her. "And it solidified my decision, more than any grand pronouncement ever could. I want to be part of that, Mara. I want to contribute to that spirit, to that resilience. I want to build something here, with you."

The sincerity in his voice, the quiet conviction that underpinned his words, sent a tremor of joy through her. It was the assurance she had craved, the tangible proof that their shared journey was not just a fleeting detour but a deliberate, cherished destination. "And I want that too," she replied, her own voice thick with emotion. "I want us to be part of this town, to contribute in ways that matter. Not just to the animals, but to the people too. We've seen firsthand how much good can come from people connecting, from people caring."

The work ahead, though still daunting, no longer felt like a burden. Instead, it was infused with a fresh sense of purpose, a shared mission that fueled their days. They had weathered the storm, and now, in its aftermath, they were emerging stronger, their bond forged in the crucible of adversity. The near-loss had sharpened their focus, clarifying their priorities and reinforcing their commitment to each other and to the rescue. They understood, with a profound clarity, that their partnership extended beyond their personal relationship; it was a professional alliance built on mutual respect, complementary skills, and a shared vision for a more compassionate future.

"I've been thinking about the grant applications," Eli continued, his mind already shifting to the practicalities. "With this renewed community backing, we have a much stronger narrative. We can highlight the immediate outpouring of support as proof of our vital role in Port Blossom. It's not just about asking for funds; it's about demonstrating impact and community investment." He picked up a notebook, his fingers already sketching out ideas. "We can tailor proposals to specifically address needs that were made apparent during the crisis – perhaps emergency preparedness funds, or a program focused on supporting vulnerable pet owners during difficult times."

Mara nodded, her own thoughts coalescing into a similar stream. "And we can leverage the volunteer energy too. We need to formalize that enthusiasm, give people clear roles and responsibilities, and create a sustainable volunteer program. That's a resource that can significantly reduce our operational costs and expand our reach. Imagine expanding our foster network, or having dedicated teams for community outreach and education." She paused, a thoughtful expression settling on her face. "We've always been a small, scrappy rescue, Eli, but now... now we have the opportunity to become something more. Something bigger."

"Exactly," Eli agreed, his voice laced with a quiet excitement. "We have the foundation, the community support, and now, a clearer vision. This isn't just about keeping the doors open anymore; it's about growth. It's about becoming a hub for animal welfare in this region. That means investing in our infrastructure, expanding our veterinary services, and developing more robust adoption and rehabilitation programs." He looked at her, a gentle smile softening his features. "And it means building a life here, together. A life that's grounded in purpose and sustained by love."

The feeling of permanence, of a future unfolding with a sense of deliberate intention, was a revelation for Mara. She had spent so long reacting to crises, putting out fires, that the idea of proactively building something solid, something lasting, felt both exhilarating and a little surreal. "I used to think that 'settling down' meant giving up on dreams," she admitted, her gaze drifting towards the bustling kennels, where a new litter of kittens was being carefully introduced to a shy, older cat. "But I see now that it's the opposite. It's about finding the place and the people where your dreams can truly take root and flourish."

Eli reached across the small desk, his hand covering hers. His touch was warm, reassuring, a silent promise of unwavering support. "And we've found that place, Mara. Together. This rescue, this town... it's where we belong." He squeezed her hand gently. "The Seattle offer... it feels like a lifetime ago, doesn't it? A distraction from what was always meant to be."

"It does," she whispered, her heart swelling with gratitude. "It was a wake-up call. A reminder that sometimes, the greatest opportunities aren't found in grand horizons, but right here, in the life we're already building." She leaned into his touch, a sense of deep contentment washing over her. The anxieties of the past had receded, replaced by a quiet confidence in their shared future. They had faced a challenge, a true test of their resilience and their bond, and they had emerged not only intact but stronger, more determined, and more deeply in love than ever before. The turning tide had brought them to a new shore, one where they could finally build their sanctuary, brick by brick, paw print by paw print, together. The path ahead was clear, illuminated by the steady glow of their renewed purpose and the unwavering warmth of their shared commitment. They were ready to embrace whatever came next, knowing they would face it as a united front, their hearts full of hope and their hands ready to build.

The soft glow of string lights draped across the rescue's outdoor patio cast a warm, inviting ambiance. Laughter, like the gentle lapping of waves against the shore, mingled with the contented chirps and contented purrs of the animals in their respective quiet zones. It was an evening painted in hues of gratitude and nascent joy, a deliberate pause to savor the stillness after the storm, both literal and figurative. Mara, her eyes sparkling with a happiness that had long been dormant, leaned against Eli, her hand resting lightly on his arm. The air thrummed with a quiet magic, a testament to the resilience of their spirits and the unwavering support of their community.

"Can you believe it?" Mara murmured, her gaze sweeping over the gathering. "Just a few weeks ago, we were staring at the possibility of losing everything. And now... look at this." She gestured to the scene around them – familiar faces animated with conversation, plates laden with delicious food prepared by local vendors they had supported, and the undeniable sense of shared victory that permeated the very atmosphere. The rescue, battered but unbowed, was on a path to recovery, and their relationship, tested by fire, had emerged not just intact, but profoundly strengthened. This gathering wasn't just a celebration of survival; it was a vibrant affirmation of their future, a future inextricably woven into the fabric of Port Blossom.

Eli's arm tightened around her, his own contentment a palpable presence. "I can believe it, Mara," he replied, his voice a low rumble of pleasure. "Because I've seen what we're capable of. What *we* are capable of, together. And I've seen what this community is capable of. It's... humbling, in the best possible way." He turned his head, his lips brushing her temple. "It's exactly what I envisioned when I decided to stay. A place where we build, we grow, and we're supported by people who believe in what we're doing."

Their small gathering was a carefully curated blend of those who had been instrumental in their recent trials and those who had always been pillars of their Port Blossom existence. Mrs. Henderson, her usual apron replaced by a crisp, elegant dress, was regaling a small group with an animated anecdote about a particularly stubborn goat she'd once owned, her laughter ringing with genuine mirth. Across the patio, young Liam, one of the high school volunteers whose tireless efforts during the cleanup had been invaluable, was earnestly explaining the intricacies of cat behavior to a captivated Mr. Fitzwilliam, the town's resident curmudgeon, who surprisingly, was nodding along with an almost-smile on his face. The transformation in him, as in so many others, was a quiet miracle in itself.

Maya, the owner of the bustling bakery that had provided much of the evening's delectable spread, clinked her glass against Mara's. "To new beginnings, and to the best darn animal rescue this side of the coast!" she declared, her eyes twinkling. "Seriously, Mara, Eli, you two are an inspiration. The way you handled everything... and the way the town pulled together... it's just incredible."

Mara felt a warmth spread through her chest, more potent than the crisp rosé she was sipping. "We couldn't have done it without you, Maya. Or any of you," she said, her voice catching slightly as she looked around at the faces beaming back at her. "This isn't just our victory; it's Port Blossom's. It's proof of what we can achieve when we come together."

Eli chimed in, his gaze meeting Mara's with a depth of shared understanding. "And it's proof of what can happen when you have the right people by your side. Mara, you've poured your heart and soul into this place, and seeing it thrive, seeing this community embrace it... it's everything." He raised his own glass. "To Mara, for her unwavering dedication, her incredible compassion, and for being my partner in every sense of the word."

The toast was met with a chorus of "Hear, hear!" and clinking glasses. Mara's cheeks flushed, a private smile shared between her and Eli that spoke volumes of their journey. The tentative steps they had taken together, the doubts and anxieties that had once clouded their horizon, now seemed like distant echoes, fading into the comforting hum of their shared present.

Among the guests were also the representatives from the local veterinary clinic, Dr. Ramirez and her team, whose swift and expert care had been critical in saving many of the animals, particularly during the immediate aftermath of the crisis. They were discussing future collaborative efforts with Eli, their conversation a testament to the strengthened partnerships forged through shared adversity. The rescue's financial stability, while not yet fully restored, was on an upward trajectory, thanks to a combination of renewed community trust, the promise of grants Eli was diligently working on, and the overwhelming generosity of local businesses and individuals.

"The grant applications are looking promising, Mara," Eli had confided earlier in the week, a rare lightness in his voice. "With the documented outpouring of community support, we have a compelling narrative. It's not just about our need; it's about our integral role in this town. They see that now. They understand what this rescue means to Port Blossom."

Mara had nodded, a sense of relief washing over her. "And the volunteer program is already taking shape. We had an unprecedented number of sign-ups after the cleanup. People want to help, Eli. They want to be involved. We just need to channel that energy effectively." She had spent hours that week designing training materials and outlining new roles, envisioning a robust system that would empower volunteers and expand the rescue's reach.

Now, watching her volunteers laugh and connect, she saw the fruits of that potential. The evening was a living embodiment of their shared vision. It was more than just providing shelter and medical care for animals; it was about fostering a compassionate ecosystem, a place where kindness flowed in multiple directions, from humans to animals, and from one human to another.

A gentle nudge from Eli brought Mara back to the present. "Thinking about the future again?" he asked, his eyes warm.

"Always," she admitted with a smile. "But now... it feels less like a daunting mountain and more like a beautiful landscape we're exploring together." She sighed contentedly. "I used to think that building a life meant sacrificing dreams. But this... this is a dream realized. It's a life filled with purpose, with love, and with the constant, reassuring presence of every wagging tail and grateful purr."

The scent of salt air, mingled with the aroma of Maya's signature lemon bars, was a comforting perfume. The clatter of dishes from the makeshift buffet, the murmur of conversations, the occasional happy bark – it all wove together into a symphony of domestic bliss, a scene Mara had once only dared to imagine. The rescue grounds, once a place of frantic activity and the ever-present hum of worry, now felt like a sanctuary.

"Remember that evening, not too long ago, when you were wrestling with the decision to stay?" Eli asked, his voice soft. "You were so torn, thinking about what you were leaving behind, what you were giving up."

Mara leaned her head on his shoulder. "I remember. And I remember how scared I was that I'd made the wrong choice. But looking at all of this, at us... I know I didn't." She looked up at him, her eyes shining. "This is where I'm meant to be, Eli. With you. Here."

He kissed the top of her head. "And I'm meant to be here with you. This is our home, Mara. Our sanctuary. Not just for the animals, but for us too." He paused, his gaze distant for a moment, as if recalling a faint memory. "The Seattle offer... it seems so insignificant now, doesn't it? Like a ghost from a past life."

"A ghost that served its purpose," Mara agreed, her voice firm. "It was the catalyst, wasn't it? The final push that made me realize where my heart truly belonged." She took a sip of her wine, savoring the moment. The lingering scent of the storm had finally dissipated, replaced by the sweet, enduring fragrance of commitment, of a future built on shared values and unwavering love. This wasn't just about saving animals anymore; it was about saving herself, about finding her own safe harbor, and about building a life that was as sturdy and as warm as the rescue itself. The turning tide had brought them to this shore, a place of peace and purpose, where their love story, like the enduring spirit of Port Blossom, was just beginning to bloom. The challenges hadn't broken them; they had forged them into something stronger, something more beautiful, a testament to the enduring power of connection, resilience, and a love that had found its truest home.

CHAPTER SIX

Building on Solid Ground

The lingering warmth of the celebratory evening settled around Mara and Eli like a comforting blanket, but even as they savored the quiet afterglow, their minds were already turning to the future. The immediate crisis had passed, the frantic scramble for survival had subsided, replaced by a profound sense of accomplishment and a renewed belief in their shared purpose. Yet, they both understood that the true work, the work of building a lasting legacy, had only just begun. The community's outpouring of support had been a powerful testament to the rescue's value, a validation that resonated deeply within them. However, as Eli had wisely pointed out on countless occasions, a strong foundation wasn't built on sentiment alone; it required careful planning, diligent execution, and a forward-thinking approach that anticipated challenges and embraced opportunities.

"We did it, Mara," Eli said, his voice soft as he held her close that night, the soft moonlight filtering through their bedroom window. "We weathered the storm. And the community... they showed up in ways we could only have dreamed of."

Mara leaned into him, her heart swelling with gratitude. "They did. And it's incredible. But you're right. This can't just be about reacting to emergencies. We need to ensure this place, this haven, is here for the long haul. For every animal that needs us, for years and years to come."

Their shared vision for the animal rescue had always been a powerful anchor in their relationship, but the recent trials had forged it into something even more robust. The chaotic days of the crisis had inadvertently highlighted areas where their existing structures were strained, and now, with a clear mind and a united front, they were ready to address those vulnerabilities head-on. The first and most critical step, they agreed, was to solidify their financial footing. While the recent influx of donations had been a lifeline, relying solely on such unpredictable surges was no longer a viable long-term strategy. They needed a more structured, diversified approach to funding, one that could sustain their operations through leaner times and provide the capital for future expansion and improvements.

"We need to formalize our financial oversight," Mara stated, her brow furrowed in concentration as they sat at their usual breakfast table a few days later, a stack of financial reports spread between them. "The passion and goodwill are invaluable, but we need a committee, a dedicated group of individuals who can help us navigate the complexities of budgeting, fundraising, and grant management with a more strategic lens. People who understand finance, who are committed to our mission, and who can help us diversify our revenue streams."

Eli nodded, his pen hovering over a notepad. "I've been thinking about that too. We can't afford to be solely reliant on the next grant application or the next unexpected donation. We need to cultivate a broader base of support. Think about recurring donations, corporate sponsorships, perhaps even establishing a planned giving program for those who want to leave a lasting legacy. And we need to be more proactive in exploring opportunities for earned income, where appropriate. Maybe workshops, educational programs for the community, or even a small retail component selling branded merchandise."

The idea of a formal financial oversight committee was met with enthusiasm from several key members of the community who had witnessed their dedication firsthand. Mrs. Henderson, despite her busy schedule managing the local farm stand, readily agreed to lend her sharp business acumen, her pragmatic approach a perfect complement to Mara's compassionate vision. Mr. Abernathy, a retired accountant who had been instrumental in organizing the initial cleanup efforts and had a soft spot for animals, also stepped forward, offering his expertise in financial planning and auditing. Their involvement signaled a shift from ad-hoc problem-solving to systematic, sustainable growth. The committee's initial mandate was clear: to develop a comprehensive five-year financial plan, identifying key benchmarks for revenue generation, expenditure management, and capital investment.

"Beyond just grants, we need to cultivate deeper relationships with local businesses," Mara suggested during one of their early committee meetings. "Maya's bakery has been incredible, but imagine if we had a few more businesses like hers committed to regular contributions, or sponsoring specific programs. Perhaps we could offer them visibility at events, naming rights for kennels, or opportunities for their employees to volunteer as a team-building exercise. It's a win-win: they get positive PR and community engagement, and we get a more predictable stream of income."

Eli expanded on this, his mind already envisioning the practicalities. "We can create different sponsorship tiers. A 'Bronze Paw' for smaller businesses, a 'Silver Leash' for medium-sized enterprises, and a 'Golden Heart' for our larger corporate partners. Each tier would come with a bespoke package of benefits. It's about showing them the tangible impact their support has, not just on the animals, but on the entire Port Blossom community. We can highlight success stories, share the data on how many animals we've rehomed, the number of educational programs we've run, the economic benefit of our presence in town through employment and local spending. It's about building a compelling case for their investment."

The committee also began to explore diversification beyond traditional fundraising. The idea of a 'Friends of the Rescue' membership program, offering exclusive updates, early access to adoption events, and special discounts at partner businesses, was gaining traction. This would not only provide a steady stream of smaller, recurring donations but also foster a stronger sense of belonging and investment among a wider segment of the community. They discussed the possibility of hosting ticketed fundraising events – perhaps a summer gala under the stars, a cozy winter craft fair, or even a fun, family-friendly pet-adoption festival that would draw people from neighboring towns.

"We need to be creative," Eli emphasized, his eyes alight with enthusiasm. "The people of Port Blossom have shown us they care. Now we need to give them diverse and engaging ways to show that care, ways that fit their individual capacities and interests. Not everyone can write a large check, but many people can commit to a monthly donation, or volunteer their time, or participate in an event. It's about building a robust ecosystem of support, a network of individuals and organizations who are invested in our long-term success."

The financial aspect, however, was only one piece of the long-term puzzle. Equally crucial was the expansion and refinement of their volunteer program. The recent crisis had revealed a surge of interest in volunteering, a testament to the community's renewed connection with the rescue. Now, Mara and Eli were focused on transforming that initial enthusiasm into a sustainable, well-managed force that could amplify their impact. This meant moving beyond simply assigning tasks to creating a structured program that offered training, clear roles, and opportunities for growth and recognition.

"We need to formalize the volunteer onboarding process," Mara explained during a planning session with Eli and their core team of dedicated volunteers, including Liam, whose passion for animal behavior had blossomed into a leadership role. "It's not enough to just have people show up. We need to ensure they are properly trained, that they understand our protocols, and that they feel valued and supported. We want them to feel like an integral part of the rescue family, not just temporary helpers."

They began developing a tiered volunteer system. 'General Volunteers' would assist with daily tasks like cleaning, feeding, and walking animals, requiring a foundational training session. 'Specialty Volunteers' would focus on areas requiring specific skills or expertise, such as animal socialization, basic grooming, or assisting with adoption counseling. This would involve more in-depth training modules, perhaps even workshops led by Dr. Ramirez and her team for those interested in animal first aid or behavior modification.

"Think about a 'Junior Volunteer' program for supervised teenagers, like Liam," Eli suggested, watching the young man passionately describe a new enrichment activity he'd designed for the shelter cats. "It's a fantastic way to instill responsibility and compassion from a young age, and it provides us with much-needed help, especially during busy periods. We just need to ensure proper supervision and safety protocols are in place."

Mara was particularly excited about the prospect of developing 'Ambassador Volunteers' – individuals who would represent the rescue at community events, educate the public about responsible pet ownership, and help foster new relationships with potential adopters and donors. This role would require strong communication skills and a deep understanding of the rescue's mission and values.

To facilitate this expansion, they decided to invest in a dedicated volunteer coordinator position, a role that would be filled by a passionate and organized individual tasked with recruitment, training, scheduling, and ensuring the well-being of the volunteer team. This was a significant commitment, but one they deemed essential for the rescue's sustainable growth. They also began planning regular volunteer appreciation events, not just formal celebrations, but small gestures of gratitude – a coffee and donut morning, a casual barbecue, or simply a heartfelt thank you note – to ensure their invaluable contributions were consistently acknowledged.

"The goal is to create a feedback loop," Mara explained to the volunteer team. "We want to hear your ideas, your concerns, your experiences. Your insights are invaluable to us. You are on the front lines, you see what works and what doesn't, and your input will directly shape how we evolve. We want this to be a place where you feel empowered, where you can learn, grow, and make a real difference."

Beyond fundraising and volunteer management, their long-term planning also encompassed a renewed focus on community outreach and education. The crisis had demonstrated the power of community connection, and they were determined to build on that momentum. They envisioned a rescue that was not just a place for animals in need, but a hub for animal welfare education and advocacy within Port Blossom.

"We need to be more visible, more accessible," Eli stated, outlining his ideas for expanding their community engagement initiatives. "Think about partnerships with local schools. We can develop age-appropriate presentations on topics like animal care, empathy, and the importance of spaying and neutering. We can host open house days, adoption fairs at central locations, and participate in local festivals and farmers' markets to increase our visibility and engage with the public. It's about building a proactive, preventative approach to animal welfare, not just reactive rescue."

Mara was particularly enthusiastic about developing educational workshops for pet owners, covering topics such as basic obedience training, understanding animal behavior, and providing enrichment for pets at home. "So many of the issues we see stem from a lack of knowledge or understanding," she mused. "If we can empower people with the right information, we can prevent animals from ending up in shelters in the first place. We can foster a culture of responsible pet ownership throughout Port Blossom."

They also committed to strengthening their relationships with other local animal welfare organizations, creating a network of collaboration rather than competition. This included working closely with the veterinary clinic, Dr. Ramirez, and her team, to streamline referral processes and ensure seamless transitions for animals needing specialized medical care. They began exploring opportunities for joint fundraising efforts and sharing resources, recognizing that a united front would amplify their collective impact on animal welfare in the region.

"It's about building a comprehensive ecosystem of care," Mara articulated, her eyes shining with purpose. "From prevention and education to rescue, rehabilitation, and rehoming, we want to be a central part of that continuum. We want to be known not just for saving animals in distress, but for fostering a community that deeply values and respects them."

The strategic planning process, while demanding, had a profound effect on Mara and Eli's relationship. The shared responsibility, the open communication, and the collaborative problem-solving solidified their partnership in a way that even the crisis itself hadn't quite achieved. They were no longer just two individuals running a rescue; they were co-architects of its future, their individual strengths complementing each other seamlessly. Eli's pragmatic business sense and strategic foresight, combined with Mara's deep empathy and intuitive understanding of animal behavior and community needs, created a powerful synergy.

"You know, before all of this," Mara said one evening, as they sat on their porch swing, watching the fireflies begin their nightly dance, "I sometimes felt like I was doing this all on my own. Even with the volunteers, it felt like my responsibility, my burden."

Eli wrapped an arm around her, pulling her closer. "I know. But look at us now. We're a team, Mara. A true partnership. We're not just building this rescue together; we're building our lives together, brick by brick, with the same dedication and care."

He paused, his gaze sweeping over the quiet grounds of the rescue, now bathed in the soft glow of the outdoor lights they had recently installed, a testament to their forward-thinking investments. "We've moved from crisis management to strategic development. It's a different kind of challenge, isn't it? Less about putting out fires and more about building a sustainable, thriving future. And I wouldn't want to be building it with anyone else."

Mara leaned her head on his shoulder, a deep sense of contentment washing over her. The path ahead was still long, filled with its own unique set of challenges and opportunities. But they were no longer navigating it alone, or with a sense of frantic urgency. They were moving forward with intention, with a shared vision, and with the unwavering confidence that, together, they were building something truly solid, something that would endure and make a lasting difference in the lives of countless animals and the community they both loved. The rescue was no longer just a place of refuge; it was becoming a beacon of hope, a testament to resilience, and a living embodiment of their enduring commitment.

Mara's embrace of home in Port Blossom wasn't a sudden epiphany, but a slow, dawning realization, like the gentle unfurling of a fern frond in the morning light. The frantic energy that had once propelled her, the constant quest for independence and a place where she truly belonged, had gradually softened, replaced by a deep-seated contentment that settled into her bones. She had arrived in Port Blossom seeking refuge, a temporary haven from a life that had felt too transient, too uncertain. But with each passing season, with every shared sunrise over the shimmering expanse of the ocean, and every quiet evening spent under the starlit sky, the town had woven itself into the fabric of her being.

The rescue, of course, remained her heart's work, the vibrant nucleus of her days. Yet, her world had expanded beyond its comforting boundaries. She found herself drawn into the gentle ebb and flow of Port Blossom's daily life, participating in the town's rhythms with an enthusiasm that surprised even herself. The weekly farmers' market, once just a place to pick up supplies, had become a social hub. She'd learned the names of the vendors, their stories, the nuances of their wares. Mrs. Gable, whose stall overflowed with sun-ripened tomatoes and fragrant herbs, always had a warm smile and a story about her grandchildren for Mara. Young Finn, with his perpetually flour-dusted apron, would offer her a sliver of his freshly baked sourdough, his eyes bright with the pride of his craft. These were not just transactions; they were moments of genuine connection, threads weaving her more firmly into the tapestry of the community.

She'd discovered a surprising joy in the predictable warmth of the local bakery, the comforting aroma of coffee and pastries a familiar balm. Conversations flowed easily over the counter with Sarah, the owner, who knew everyone's order by heart and had a knack for dispensing gentle advice along with their morning indulgence. Mara found herself lingering, not out of necessity, but out of a desire to simply

be there, to soak in the easy camaraderie. It was a far cry from the guarded interactions and hurried exchanges she had once known. Here, smiles were genuine, conversations were unhurried, and the sense of shared community was palpable.

Beyond the market and the bakery, Mara had begun to seek out other opportunities to connect. When the annual Port Blossom Summer Festival was announced, she didn't hesitate to volunteer. Gone was the apprehension, the fear of being an outsider. Instead, she found herself happily directing festival-goers, helping set up stalls, and even lending a hand with the children's games, her laughter mingling with the excited squeals of the young ones. She discovered a camaraderie among the volunteers, a shared purpose that transcended their individual lives. They were all contributing to something bigger than themselves, a collective effort that brought the town together. She even found herself striking up conversations with people she'd only ever seen in passing – the quiet librarian, the energetic postman, the retired fisherman who always seemed to have a twinkle in his eye. Each interaction was a small brushstroke, adding depth and color to her growing sense of belonging.

The rescue's expansion and the establishment of the financial oversight committee had, of course, demanded a significant amount of her time and energy. But even in the midst of strategic planning and fundraising initiatives, the underlying current was one of shared purpose and collective investment. When Mrs. Henderson, with her sharp business acumen, would propose a new revenue stream, or when Mr. Abernathy, with his meticulous eye for detail, would refine a budget, Mara felt a deep sense of partnership. This wasn't just *her* vision anymore; it was *their* shared endeavor, a testament to the community's faith and their collective commitment to the animals. This shared responsibility, this reliance on the wisdom and dedication of others, had lifted a weight she hadn't realized she was carrying. The desire for complete self-sufficiency, the notion that she had to be the sole architect of her own destiny, had been replaced by the profound strength found in interdependence.

Eli, of course, remained her steadfast anchor. Their relationship, forged in the crucible of shared challenges, had deepened into a partnership of mutual respect and unwavering affection.

He understood her past, her need for independence, and he celebrated her present, her embrace of permanence. He never made her feel as though her past desires were a betrayal of her current reality, but rather a natural evolution. His quiet pride in her growing connection to the town, his gentle encouragement for her to explore new avenues of community involvement, spoke volumes of his love and understanding.

"You know," Eli had said one evening, as they sat on their porch, the scent of salt and pine mingling in the air, "I never thought I'd see you so... rooted. You used to be like a wild bird, always ready to take flight."

Mara had smiled, leaning her head on his shoulder. "Maybe I just found the right nest, Eli. And it's not a cage, it's a home. A place where I can spread my wings, but always know I have a safe place to return to."

He had kissed the top of her head. "And you built this home, Mara. With your own hands, your own heart. You brought so much of yourself to Port Blossom, and in return, it's given you so much back. It's a beautiful thing to witness."

She found herself no longer yearning for the anonymity of a larger city, for the endless possibilities of a life unburdened by routine. The predictable rhythm of Port Blossom had become a source of comfort, not a limitation. The gentle ebb and flow of the tides mirrored the steady beat of her own heart. She had come to understand that true freedom wasn't about constant movement, but about finding a place where one's spirit could flourish, where roots could grow deep.

Her days at the rescue had a new texture. The frantic urgency of the crisis had given way to a more deliberate, sustainable pace. The structured volunteer program meant that tasks were handled with efficiency and care, allowing Mara to focus on the bigger picture – program development, strategic partnerships, and the ongoing nurturing of the rescue's spirit. She found a deep satisfaction in seeing the animals thrive, in witnessing the quiet triumphs of rehabilitation and adoption, knowing that this stability was the direct result of the diligent planning and community support they had cultivated.

One crisp autumn afternoon, as she walked along the harbor, watching the fishing boats bob gently in the water, a profound sense of peace washed over her. She remembered the restless nights spent dreaming of a life she couldn't quite define, a place of belonging that remained perpetually out of reach. Now, that yearning had been replaced by a quiet gratitude. The salty air, the cry of the gulls, the distant laughter of children playing on the beach – it all felt like an intrinsic part of her. She was no longer an outsider looking in; she was woven into the very fabric of this coastal haven.

She saw Mrs. Gable walking towards her, her arms laden with a basket of late-season apples. "Mara, dear!" she called out, her voice warm and familiar. "Just the person I was hoping to see. My grandson, little Timmy, has been asking about visiting the rescue again. He's fascinated by the new puppies you've taken in. Do you think he could come by next Saturday? I'll bring some of my apple pie for the volunteers."

Mara's smile was genuine, unforced. "That would be wonderful, Mrs. Gable. Saturday morning would be perfect. And I'll make sure the puppies are ready for some cuddles."

As Mrs. Gable continued on her way, Mara watched her go, a sense of profound connection settling over her. This was her life now. Not a life of constant striving for something more, but a life rich with the abundance of shared moments, of deep relationships, of a home that felt truly and irrevocably hers. The journey from independence to permanence had been a winding one, filled with unexpected turns and moments of doubt. But standing there, with the sea breeze in her hair and the familiar sounds of Port Blossom around her, Mara knew she had arrived. She had found her place, not by escaping her past, but by embracing her present, by choosing to build something lasting, something beautiful, something that was, in its truest sense, home. The life she and Eli were building together wasn't just a sanctuary for animals; it was a sanctuary for her own soul, a testament to the quiet power of choosing to belong.

Eli's settled contentment was a quiet force, a steady hum beneath the surface of their shared life in Port Blossom. The restless energy that had once defined him, fueled by the pursuit of scientific discovery and exploration, had found a new, more profound outlet. The decision to weave his life permanently with Mara's in this coastal town wasn't a compromise, but a conscious expansion of his purpose. He had arrived in Port Blossom with a keen intellect and a deep well of knowledge, but it was here, in the embrace of community and the tangible needs of the rescue, that his expertise found its most meaningful application. His days, once dictated by the unpredictable currents of research and fieldwork, now flowed with a satisfying rhythm, anchored by a shared vision and a profound sense of belonging.

The initial stages of establishing the rescue had been a whirlwind, a testament to Mara's vision and sheer determination. But as the operation stabilized, as the community rallied and the financial footing grew more secure, it was the natural next step for Eli to step more fully into the operational planning. He found himself drawn to the intricate details of animal care, not just as Mara's partner, but as a scientist with a unique perspective. His background, which had once taken him to remote ecosystems to study the delicate balance of life, now found its focus on the nuanced needs of injured and orphaned wildlife within Port Blossom's reach. He possessed a keen analytical mind, accustomed to dissecting complex problems and devising innovative solutions, and he saw the rescue as a living, breathing laboratory of compassion and scientific application.

He began by meticulously reviewing the existing rehabilitation protocols. His scientific mind, trained to identify variables and measure outcomes, saw opportunities for enhancement. He wasn't just looking at immediate care; he was thinking about long-term recovery, about how to best equip these animals for a return to their natural habitats. He started by focusing on the smaller, more manageable rehabilitation projects, using his systematic approach to refine methodologies. For instance, the care of injured seabirds, a frequent occurrence along the Port Blossom coast, became an area of particular interest. He delved into the latest research on avian rehabilitation, cross-referencing scientific journals with the practical observations of the rescue's dedicated volunteers. He noticed that while the basic care was excellent, there was room for improvement in the specific diets and the environmental enrichment provided to aid in their recovery.

Eli proposed a new feeding regimen for the recovering gulls, one that was more closely aligned with their natural diet, incorporating specific supplements to aid bone and feather regrowth. He meticulously tracked the progress of birds on the new diet, comparing their recovery rates and overall health to those who had been on the previous plan. The results were encouraging, showing a marked improvement in healing times and a reduction in relapses. He then turned his attention to the enclosures. Observing that the birds seemed to exhibit signs of stress in overly sterile environments, he suggested introducing natural elements – sand baths, varied perching options, and even small pools for preening and bathing. He documented the changes in the birds' behavior, noting a decrease in repetitive movements and an increase in natural foraging instincts, even within the confines of their recovery spaces. This data, meticulously collected and analyzed, provided a strong case for the implementation of these more nuanced, scientifically informed practices.

His involvement wasn't just about protocols; it was also about building capacity. He recognized that the success of any rehabilitation program rested on the knowledge and dedication of the people involved. He began organizing workshops for the volunteers, transforming his scientific insights into practical, accessible training sessions. He explained the underlying physiology of common injuries, the rationale behind specific treatments, and the importance of patient observation. He taught them how to identify subtle signs of distress or improvement, empowering them to become more effective caregivers. These sessions were not lectures; they were interactive dialogues, where Eli patiently answered questions, shared anecdotes from his past research, and fostered a collaborative learning environment. He found a quiet satisfaction in seeing the volunteers' eyes light up with understanding, their confidence growing with each new piece of knowledge they acquired. They, in turn, offered him their invaluable ground-level experience, pointing out practical challenges and offering insights that enriched his scientific approach.

Beyond the immediate care of the animals, Eli's strategic mind began to explore broader avenues of conservation. Port Blossom's proximity to the marine ecosystem offered a unique opportunity for collaboration. He initiated contact with the local marine biology research institute, a well-respected organization known for its work on coastal preservation. He proposed a partnership, one that would allow the rescue to benefit from their advanced research capabilities and diagnostic equipment, while the institute could gain access to valuable field data and direct observation of wildlife impacted by local environmental factors.

His first meeting with Dr. Anya Sharma, the lead marine biologist at the institute, was a revelation for both of them. Eli, usually reserved, found himself articulating his vision with passion, detailing how the rescue could serve as a vital data-gathering hub. He spoke of tracking the health of local seal populations, of monitoring the impact of pollution on seabird colonies, and of using rehabilitated animals as indicators of the broader health of the marine environment. Dr. Sharma, initially cautious, was impressed by Eli's scientific rigor and his genuine commitment to conservation. She saw the potential for a symbiotic relationship, where the rescue's hands-on approach could complement the institute's research, providing real-world context and valuable case studies.

Their initial collaborative project focused on understanding the prevalence of microplastic ingestion in local seabirds. Eli worked with Dr. Sharma to design a sampling protocol that could be integrated into the rescue's intake procedures. When a bird was admitted with suspected digestive issues, a small, non-invasive sample could be collected and preserved for later analysis at the institute. Eli also helped develop standardized observational checklists for volunteers to document any unusual findings during necropsies of deceased animals. This collaboration was not without its challenges; coordinating schedules, sharing resources, and ensuring consistent data collection required careful planning and open communication. But Eli's methodical approach and unwavering dedication smoothed the path. He facilitated regular meetings, acted as a bridge between the two organizations, and ensured that the lines of communication remained clear and effective.

The success of this initial project opened doors to further collaborations. They began to explore the possibility of tagging and releasing rehabilitated marine mammals, allowing Dr. Sharma's team to track their movements and survival rates in the wild. Eli, with his understanding of animal behavior and his network of contacts in the scientific community, was instrumental in securing the necessary permits and ethical approvals for these initiatives. He also proposed the development of an early warning system for harmful algal blooms, leveraging the rescue's network of fishermen and coastal residents to report unusual observations of marine life.

Eli's steady presence and his scientific acumen had a transformative effect on the rescue's operational framework. He brought a level of organization and strategic foresight that had been previously constrained by the immediate demands of rescue work. His ability to translate complex scientific concepts into actionable plans inspired confidence not only in the volunteers but also in the broader community. When Eli presented his findings on the success of the new rehabilitation protocols at a town hall meeting, the audience was captivated. He spoke with clarity and conviction, illustrating his points with compelling data and heartfelt anecdotes about the animals' recovery. He demonstrated how scientific innovation, coupled with community effort, could achieve remarkable results.

The financial oversight committee, which Mara had established to ensure the rescue's long-term sustainability, found Eli's contributions particularly valuable. His meticulous approach to planning and his understanding of resource allocation helped them identify areas where investments in specialized equipment or training could yield significant long-term benefits. He proposed a detailed plan for expanding the rescue's capabilities in treating marine mammal injuries, outlining the necessary equipment, the specialized training required for staff, and the projected costs and potential funding sources. His proposals were always data-driven, demonstrating a clear return on investment, not just financially, but in terms of increased success rates and expanded reach.

This expansion of Eli's role wasn't just about professional advancement; it was deeply personal. He found a profound sense of fulfillment in contributing to something tangible and meaningful, something that directly benefited the natural world and the community he had chosen to call home. He had spent years chasing scientific understanding in theoretical landscapes, but here, in Port Blossom, he was actively participating in the preservation of life. The tangible results of his work – a successfully rehabilitated seal released back into the ocean, a colony of birds thriving under improved care, a new partnership forged for greater conservation impact – were immensely rewarding.

He often found himself working alongside Mara, their shared passion a silent, powerful bond. While Mara was the heart and soul of the rescue, with her intuitive understanding of the animals and her unwavering compassion, Eli provided the structural integrity, the scientific bedrock upon which their efforts were built. They complemented each other perfectly. Mara's empathy drew people in, her warmth fostering trust and encouraging community involvement. Eli's logical approach and his ability to articulate complex ideas made their initiatives credible and sustainable. They would often spend evenings poring over spreadsheets, discussing research papers, or sketching out new enclosure designs, their conversation flowing easily, a comfortable blend of scientific discourse and shared dreams.

"You know," Mara had said to him one evening, her hand resting on his as they reviewed a grant proposal, "I used to think I needed to do everything myself. I thought being independent meant being alone in my efforts. But being with you, seeing you pour your intellect and your passion into this place... it's shown me that true strength lies in collaboration. In building something together."

Eli had squeezed her hand, his gaze warm. "And you showed me that purpose can be found not just in discovery, but in dedication. In nurturing and protecting what we have. I wouldn't trade this for all the exotic expeditions in the world."

His dedication extended beyond the formal structures of the rescue. He began volunteering his time to local schools, sharing his love for science and conservation with the younger generation. He would bring in rescued animals (safely and with appropriate precautions, of course) for educational talks, sparking curiosity and a sense of environmental responsibility in the children. He believed that by fostering a love for nature early on, they were cultivating the next generation of protectors, the future stewards of Port Blossom's precious ecosystem. He found immense joy in seeing the children's wide-eyed wonder, their eager questions, and the genuine care they began to show for the animals he introduced them to.

One particularly memorable occasion involved a young, injured owl that had been successfully rehabilitated. Eli brought the owl to the elementary school, and, under strict supervision, allowed the children to observe it from a respectful distance. He explained the owl's role in the ecosystem, its adaptations for nocturnal hunting, and the importance of preserving its habitat. The children were captivated, their hushed awe a testament to the power of direct experience. The following week, a group of students from that class organized a small fundraiser for the rescue, drawing pictures of the owl and selling them to their families. Eli was deeply touched by their initiative, seeing it as a clear indication that his efforts were resonating.

The impact of Eli's expanded role rippled outwards, strengthening the rescue's reputation and its connection to the wider community. His scientific credibility lent an air of authority to their work, attracting more volunteers, more donors, and more collaborative opportunities. He was instrumental in securing a significant grant from a national wildlife foundation, a testament to his meticulous planning and compelling presentation of the rescue's mission and impact. This grant allowed for the construction of a new, state-of-the-art rehabilitation facility, designed with Eli's input to optimize animal care and research capabilities.

He also spearheaded the development of a citizen science program, encouraging local residents to report sightings of marine life and any unusual environmental observations. This initiative tapped into the collective knowledge of Port Blossom's inhabitants, transforming them from passive observers into active participants in conservation efforts. Eli designed the program's protocols, developed user-friendly reporting tools, and led training sessions for volunteers. The data collected through this program proved invaluable, providing early warnings of potential environmental threats and offering insights into the seasonal movements of marine species.

Eli's journey in Port Blossom was a testament to the idea that purpose can evolve, that expertise can find new and fulfilling applications. He had arrived with a scientist's mind, and he had become a guardian of the natural world, a pillar of the community, and a devoted partner. His contentment wasn't derived from personal achievement alone, but from the profound satisfaction of contributing to a legacy of care and conservation, a legacy he was building, day by day, alongside Mara, in the heart of their adopted home. He found a deep, abiding joy in this tangible work, in the steady progress of healing and the enduring strength of community. The scientific challenges still called to him, but now, they were intertwined with a deeper, more resonant purpose: the thriving of life itself, in the wild and in the hearts of the people who called Port Blossom home.

The lingering aftershocks of the near-crisis had, paradoxically, woven a stronger thread of connection between Mara, Eli, and the heart of Port Blossom. The vulnerability they had all experienced, the collective breath held and then released, had served as a potent reminder of their interdependence. It wasn't just the rescue that was a community resource; the town itself, with its interwoven lives and shared spaces, was a living organism that thrived on mutual support. Mara, ever attuned to the pulse of the town, felt this shift most acutely. She saw how the shared ordeal had softened edges, encouraged open dialogue, and fostered a renewed appreciation for the efforts of those who dedicated themselves to the well-being of others, be it human or animal. Eli, too, found himself more deeply rooted. The urgency of the situation had dissolved any lingering reservations he might have harbored about fully committing to Port Blossom. His scientific mind, while always seeking solutions, now recognized the immense value of collective action, of a community united in its purpose.

Their involvement began to extend beyond the immediate needs of the rescue. The town council, recognizing the valuable expertise and unwavering dedication Mara and Eli had demonstrated, began to seek their input on matters that touched upon Port Blossom's environmental future and its development. Mara, with her innate understanding of the local landscape and its delicate ecosystems, became a natural advocate for sustainable practices. She found herself attending town planning meetings, not as an outsider, but as a stakeholder deeply invested in the town's long-term health. Her contributions, often focusing on the impact of proposed developments on local wildlife habitats and water quality, were always grounded in practical knowledge and a genuine love for the natural beauty that defined Port Blossom. She spoke passionately about the need to preserve the coastal dunes, not just for their aesthetic appeal, but for the vital role they played in protecting the shoreline from erosion and providing sanctuary for a myriad of bird species. She also emphasized the importance of managing wastewater runoff, drawing parallels to the challenges they faced at the rescue with pollutants affecting marine life.

Eli, meanwhile, found a different, yet equally vital, avenue for his expertise. His scientific background, particularly his understanding of ecological principles and his methodical approach to problem-solving, made him an invaluable asset to the town's burgeoning environmental protection committee. He began by offering his analytical skills to assess the effectiveness of existing recycling programs, identifying bottlenecks and proposing data-driven improvements. He then moved on to more complex issues, such as the impact of increased boat traffic on the local seal population. He presented research papers, translated complex scientific data into easily digestible summaries for the committee, and helped them develop strategies for mitigating noise pollution and reducing the risk of boat strikes. His calm, rational approach often served as a grounding influence during heated discussions, allowing for more productive resolutions. He meticulously researched the migratory patterns of local fish species, providing crucial information that informed discussions about fishing regulations and the establishment of marine protected areas. His ability to foresee potential ecological consequences of proposed actions, backed by solid scientific evidence, earned him significant respect.

One particularly impactful initiative they spearheaded together was the expansion of educational outreach programs, starting right at the rescue itself. Mara and Eli recognized that fostering a sense of stewardship among the younger generation was paramount to ensuring Port Blossom's future environmental health. They transformed a quiet corner of the rescue into a vibrant educational hub, hosting regular workshops for local children. These sessions were far from passive lectures. Children, ranging from eager kindergarteners to inquisitive middle schoolers, were invited to actively participate. They learned about the anatomy of different seabirds, dissecting owl pellets (under Eli's careful supervision, of course) to identify the remnants of their prey, a tangible lesson in the food chain. They engaged in craft activities, creating bird feeders from recycled materials, understanding the importance of providing supplemental food sources during harsh weather.

Eli often led sessions focused on the scientific aspects of rehabilitation. He would explain, in age-appropriate terms, how broken bones healed, the principles of fluid balance in dehydrated animals, and the importance of a balanced diet for recovery. He used visual aids, often photographs and short videos from the rescue's operations, to illustrate his points, bringing the complex world of veterinary science to life. He would emphasize the importance of observation, teaching the children how to identify subtle signs of distress or improvement in animals, empowering them to become more observant and empathetic. The rescue's resident ambassador animals, those too injured to be released but perfectly healthy and content, became invaluable teaching tools. A calm, rehabilitated hawk perched on a gloved hand, its keen eyes observing the hushed, fascinated children, was a far more powerful lesson than any textbook could offer.

Mara, with her boundless warmth and natural rapport with children, guided them through the emotional aspects of animal welfare. She spoke about the importance of compassion, of understanding that every creature, no matter how small or seemingly insignificant, deserves kindness and respect. She would share heartwarming stories of animals that had overcome adversity, emphasizing the role of human intervention and care in their recovery. The children's faces would light up as they learned about the arduous journeys of injured seals or orphaned otters, their empathy deepening with each narrative. They were taught about responsible pet ownership, the impact of litter on wildlife, and the significance of respecting natural habitats.

These workshops weren't confined to the rescue's grounds. Mara and Eli actively sought opportunities to bring their educational mission into the broader community. They partnered with local schools, offering to visit classrooms and deliver engaging presentations. Eli brought his specialized knowledge to bear, preparing interactive lessons on marine biology, explaining concepts like photosynthesis in kelp forests and the intricate symbiotic relationships within tide pools. He'd often set up mini-aquariums, showcasing local marine invertebrates and explaining their ecological roles, much to the delight of the students. Mara would focus on the rescue's work, sharing success stories and explaining the vital role volunteers played. She'd often bring along materials for a hands-on activity, like creating miniature rescue kits for stuffed animals, a playful yet informative way to reinforce the lessons learned.

Their involvement in town meetings also grew organically from their deepening commitment. Initially, they attended out of necessity, to advocate for the rescue or for specific environmental concerns. But as they became more visible and their contributions more valued, they found themselves participating in broader community discussions. Eli, initially reticent in public forums, found his voice when discussing issues that required logical analysis and evidence-based reasoning. He learned to navigate the often-passionate discourse of town hall meetings, presenting his findings clearly and concisely, always with a focus on finding practical, community-benefiting solutions. He was instrumental in advocating for the implementation of a comprehensive waste management plan, presenting data that demonstrated the long-term economic and environmental benefits of reducing landfill waste and increasing recycling rates. His objective approach, combined with his genuine care for Port Blossom, made him a trusted voice.

Mara, on the other hand, was a natural at galvanizing support and fostering a sense of shared responsibility. She had a knack for articulating the emotional core of an issue, connecting with residents on a personal level. When discussions arose about the need for a new community center, or for improvements to local parks, Mara was often the one who could articulate the vision for how these spaces could enhance the quality of life for all residents, fostering social connection and providing opportunities for recreation and learning. She would speak about the importance of safe, accessible spaces for children to play, for seniors to gather, and for families to connect, reminding everyone that a strong community was built on shared experiences and mutual support. Her passionate pleas for preserving the town's green spaces, highlighting their benefits for both physical and mental well-being, resonated deeply with many residents.

Their home, once a quiet sanctuary, had become a hub of community engagement. Evenings were often filled with the gentle murmur of conversations as neighbors stopped by to discuss a local initiative, seek advice on an environmental issue, or simply share a cup of coffee and a friendly chat. Mara and Eli found immense satisfaction in this interconnectedness. They were no longer just residents of Port Blossom; they were an integral part of its fabric, their lives interwoven with the town's well-being and its future. The rescue, once the sole focus of their community efforts, had become a catalyst, a beacon that illuminated the path towards a more engaged, more compassionate, and more sustainable Port Blossom. They had arrived seeking refuge, and they had found something far more profound: a community that had embraced them, and in turn, had been enriched by their presence, their expertise, and their unwavering commitment to building a better tomorrow, together. The shared vulnerability had forged a bond, and their subsequent actions had cemented their place, not just as residents, but as true stakeholders in the heart and soul of Port Blossom. This deep integration meant that every decision, every proposed change, was now viewed through the lens of its impact on the entire community, a collective consciousness that Mara and Eli had helped to nurture and strengthen. They understood that building on solid ground wasn't just about financial stability or robust infrastructure; it was about the strength of human connection, the shared vision for a thriving future, and the unwavering commitment to protecting the precious ecosystem they all called home.

The soft glow of the lighthouse, a familiar sentinel against the encroaching twilight, cast long shadows across their living room floor. Outside, the rhythmic sigh of the ocean provided a comforting soundtrack to their quiet evening. Mara and Eli, nestled on the worn, comfortable sofa that had witnessed so many of their shared moments, found themselves in a space of profound contentment. The days, once filled with the frantic energy of crises and the quiet hum of rebuilding, now held a new cadence, one of thoughtful planning and blossoming hope. The near-disaster that had tested their resilience had, in a beautiful and unexpected way, clarified their purpose and deepened their commitment to each other and to Port Blossom.

"Remember when we first talked about what 'forever' might look like?" Mara mused, her fingers tracing the intricate patterns on a woven throw pillow. Her voice was a low murmur, imbued with a warmth that always settled Eli's soul. "It felt so... abstract then. Like sketching on fog."

Eli chuckled, his arm tightening around her. "And now it feels like we're laying the foundations. Solid concrete, not just sketches." He leaned his head against hers, inhaling the subtle scent of sea salt and lavender that always clung to her. "What's on your mind tonight, then? Beyond the fog?"

Mara turned in his embrace, her eyes, the color of a stormy sea, meeting his. "So much. And yet, it's all coming into focus. The rescue, for one. It's thriving, isn't it? We've built something truly remarkable, something that feels... permanent. But I've been thinking about growth. Not just in terms of the animals we care for, but in terms of space. We're bursting at the seams sometimes, aren't we?"

Eli nodded, his gaze distant for a moment as he pictured the bustling sanctuary. "You're right. The expanded rehabilitation areas have helped, but the educational wing... and the administrative offices... We're definitely at capacity. I've been looking at that undeveloped parcel of land adjacent to the main property. It's mostly marshland now, but with careful planning, and a significant investment in eco-friendly construction, we could potentially double our footprint. Imagine a dedicated research lab, a proper lecture hall for the outreach programs, maybe even a small, contained aviary for animals undergoing long-term recovery who benefit from naturalistic settings. It would solidify our role not just as a rescue, but as a center for marine conservation education and research for the entire region."

"A research lab!" Mara's eyes sparkled. "Eli, that's brilliant. You could finally have the space to pursue those deeper studies into migratory patterns and the long-term effects of microplastics.

And the lecture hall... think of the possibilities! We could host visiting scientists, offer specialized workshops for veterinary students, really elevate the profile of what we do here." She paused, a thoughtful frown creasing her brow. "It would be a huge undertaking, though. The fundraising alone..."

"I know," Eli said, squeezing her hand. "But we've built credibility. The success of the recent initiatives, the positive press, the growing support from local businesses and even some larger environmental foundations... I believe it's achievable. We could start with a phased approach. Focus on securing the land first, then perhaps a capital campaign specifically for the research facilities. It would require a significant leap of faith, but look at where we've come from. We've tackled seemingly insurmountable challenges before. This is just a different scale."

Mara leaned her head on his shoulder, a contented sigh escaping her lips. "It's a beautiful vision, Eli. A legacy. And it fits perfectly with what I've been dreaming about for our own little corner of Port Blossom." She hesitated, then her voice dropped to a softer, more intimate register. "Our home. I've been looking at old blueprints, you know, the ones from when the house was first built. It has such good bones. But imagine... if we were to expand. A small extension, just enough for a dedicated study for you, filled with your books and equipment, and perhaps a sunroom for me, overlooking the bay. A place where we could truly unwind, where our work doesn't constantly seep into our personal space."

Eli's smile was gentle. "A sunroom. I can see it. Sunlight streaming in, you with your sketchpad, and the sound of the waves. And my study... finally, a place where I don't have to clear off the dining table every time I want to spread out some data. We could even incorporate some sustainable design elements – rainwater harvesting for the garden, solar panels discreetly integrated into the roof. Make it a model of what we advocate for."

"Exactly!" Mara enthused. "A home that reflects our values, inside and out. And with that... with that comes a desire for something more, doesn't it?" Her gaze met his, a question in their depths that needed no words.

Eli's heart swelled. He knew where this conversation was leading, and it was a destination he had yearned for with every fiber of his being. He reached up, gently brushing a stray strand of hair from her cheek. "It does, doesn't it?" he said, his voice thick with emotion. "I've thought about it too, Mara. So much. With the rescue on solid ground, and our home becoming the sanctuary we envision... it feels like the right time. The absolute right time."

Mara's hand covered his on her cheek. "A family," she whispered, the word barely audible. "Our own little Port Blossom family. It feels both incredibly daunting and wonderfully inevitable."

"It is," Eli agreed, his thumb caressing her skin. "Daunting because it's a profound responsibility, and wonderful because... well, because it's with you. I can't imagine bringing a child into this world with anyone else. You have such an incredible capacity for love, for nurturing. You've already shown that with every creature we've nursed back to health. Imagine that love poured into a child."

"And you," Mara countered, her voice catching slightly. "Your patience, your intellect, your quiet strength. You'll be such a grounding presence. You'll teach them to observe, to question, to understand the world around them with curiosity and respect. You'll pass on your love for science, for understanding how things work, and I'll... I'll make sure they know how to find the magic in it all. How to appreciate the wild beauty of this place, how to be kind, how to stand up for what's right."

"We'll be a team," Eli stated, a certainty in his tone that banished any lingering doubt. "Just like we are with everything else. We'll navigate the sleepless nights and the endless questions together. We'll build them a childhood filled with the scent of the sea, the cry of the gulls, and the knowledge that they are loved, deeply and unconditionally."

He pulled her closer, their bodies fitting together as if they were made for each other, which, Mara thought, they undoubtedly were. "It's funny," she murmured, nuzzling into his chest. "A few years ago, I would have been terrified of this conversation. The idea of combining our lives, let alone starting a family, felt like a monumental risk. But with you... it feels like coming home. It feels like the most natural, most beautiful progression of everything we've built."

"That's because it's built on solid ground, Mara," Eli said, his voice resonating against her. "Not just the land beneath our feet, or the foundations of the rescue, but the foundation of trust, of shared values, of unwavering love that we've built between us. We've faced storms, and we've come through them stronger. This... this is about building a future, not just surviving the present. It's about creating something that will last, something beautiful, something that carries on the spirit of what we believe in."

They sat in comfortable silence for a long time, the weight of their shared dreams settling around them like a warm blanket. The lighthouse beam swept across their faces, illuminating the quiet joy and profound peace that had replaced the anxiety of their past. The uncertainty had dissipated, leaving behind a crystal-clear vision. It was a vision of continued dedication to the natural world they so dearly loved, of nurturing growth in both their professional and personal lives, and of raising a family rooted in the very heart of Port Blossom.

Mara envisioned their future home, a haven of tranquility, a place where the gentle rhythm of the tides would lull their children to sleep. She saw Eli, his face illuminated by the soft glow of a desk lamp, sharing his knowledge with them, his passion for discovery igniting their own. She saw herself, perhaps with a sketchpad in hand, teaching them the names of the seabirds, the language of the waves, the importance of compassion for all living things.

Eli, in turn, saw the expanded rescue, a beacon of hope and knowledge, its wings reaching further, its impact rippling outward. He saw their children, their bright young faces alight with wonder, exploring the new educational facilities, their curiosity sparked by the wonders of marine life. He saw their home, a testament to their shared values, a place of warmth and inspiration. He saw the profound happiness that would bloom from their shared commitment, a happiness that was not fleeting but enduring, deeply intertwined with the very fabric of Port Blossom.

The possibility of a family, once a whisper on the edge of their consciousness, was now a vibrant, tangible presence. It was a natural extension of their love, their shared purpose, and their deep roots in this coastal haven. They spoke of names, of nursery rhymes they'd learned, of the simple joys of watching a child take their first steps on sandy shores. These were not fanciful dreams; they were concrete aspirations, grounded in the deep well of love and respect they held for each other.

"We've come so far," Mara said softly, her voice filled with a quiet reverence. "From strangers, to colleagues, to partners, to... this." She looked up at him, her gaze unwavering. "I feel like we're standing at the edge of something truly extraordinary, Eli. Not just for us, but for Port Blossom. We're not just building a life; we're building a legacy. A legacy of care, of dedication, of a deep, abiding love for this place and for each other."

Eli's response was a tender kiss, a silent affirmation of her words, of their shared destiny. In that moment, bathed in the ethereal glow of the lighthouse, they were not just Mara and Eli, rescuers and environmental advocates. They were architects of their own profound future, their hearts aligned, their souls intertwined, ready to embrace every joy, every challenge, and every beautiful possibility that lay ahead, together, on the solid ground of Port Blossom. The map of their future was no longer a sketch in fog; it was a beautifully detailed, vibrant tapestry, woven with threads of purpose, love, and an unwavering commitment to a life lived fully, deeply, and together. Their shared vision was not a distant horizon, but a bright, warm sun rising on a new day, a day filled with promise and the enduring strength of their union.

CHAPTER SEVEN

Seeds of Commitment

The comfort of their shared silence was a language all its own, spoken in the gentle rhythm of their breathing and the soft murmur of the sea. Mara's head rested on Eli's chest, the steady beat of his heart a reassuring anchor. The conversation about their future, once a tentative exploration, had blossomed into a quiet certainty, a shared blueprint for a life they were both eager to build. Yet, as Eli held her close, a new thought began to take root in his mind, a burgeoning desire that went beyond the shared vision of a home and family. It was a yearning to solidify their connection in a way that spoke not just of partnership, but of an enduring, unwavering commitment.

He found himself replaying their journey, a mental film reel spooling through his mind. The chaotic beauty of their first meeting, amidst the frantic activity of a rescue mission, seemed a lifetime ago. He remembered Mara's fierce dedication, her eyes alight with compassion as she worked tirelessly to mend injured wings and soothe frightened creatures. He'd been drawn to her then, to her spirit, to her inherent goodness. And over the months and years that followed, that initial spark had ignited into a steady flame, fueled by shared challenges, mutual respect, and a love that had grown as deep and vast as the ocean itself. They had weathered storms, both literal and figurative, their bond forged in the fires of adversity and tempered by countless moments of quiet understanding and unwavering support.

The rescue, their shared passion, was more than just a sanctuary for animals; it was the crucible where their own love had been refined. Every success, every setback they had navigated together, had woven them closer, their lives becoming inextricably entwined. Now, as they stood on the precipice of even greater aspirations – expanding their reach, building a home that was a true reflection of their values, and perhaps, one day, welcoming children into their lives – Eli felt an overwhelming need to mark this profound stage of their relationship. He wanted to ask Mara to be his wife.

The idea, once it settled, felt both exhilarating and a little daunting. He wanted the proposal to be as unique and meaningful as their story. It couldn't be a fleeting gesture, a cliché borrowed from a movie. It had to be a reflection of *them*. He envisioned something that would encapsulate their shared history, their love for Port Blossom, and their dedication to the life they were building, brick by brick, wave by wave.

He started to sketch out possibilities in his mind, his thoughts a jumble of heartfelt intentions and logistical considerations. He considered the place where it all began, the heart of the rescue.

Perhaps amidst the gentle sounds of recovering seabirds, under the watchful gaze of the lighthouse that had become their silent confidante. He imagined a moment of quiet intimacy, perhaps after a particularly successful release, when the air was thick with accomplishment and the salty tang of the sea. He could speak of their journey, of how she had brought light and purpose into his life, and then ask her to embark on the ultimate adventure with him.

But then his mind would wander to their home, to the comfortable intimacy of their shared life. He pictured the cozy evenings on the sofa, the quiet mornings watching the sunrise paint the sky. Their home was their haven, a sanctuary built on their love and their shared dreams. A proposal there would feel deeply personal, a testament to the everyday magic of their relationship. He could create a space, perhaps by the fire on a cool evening, or in the garden as the scent of honeysuckle filled the air, and simply ask her to be his forever.

He even considered the natural beauty of Port Blossom itself. The rugged coastline, the hidden coves, the expansive, star-dusted skies. He thought of the quiet moments they had shared exploring these places, discovering them together. A proposal on a windswept cliff, with the vast ocean stretching out before them, could be incredibly romantic. He could speak of the boundless nature of his love, as vast as the horizon, as enduring as the tides.

Each idea held its own charm, its own resonance. But Eli knew that the most important element wasn't the location, but the sincerity. He wanted to articulate, in words and in action, the depth of his feelings, the profound gratitude he felt for having found Mara. He wanted to convey that his love wasn't just an emotion, but a commitment, a promise to stand by her, to support her, to grow with her, through all the seasons of their lives.

He began to jot down fragmented thoughts in a small, worn notebook he kept in his desk drawer – the one that was already filled with notes on marine biology, rescue protocols, and the occasional grocery list. Now, it was becoming a repository for his deepest hopes. Words like "legacy," "partners," "home," and "forever" began to fill the pages, interspersed with sketches of rings and diagrams of the rescue's expansion plans. He found himself writing down anecdotes, small moments that had cemented his love for her. The way she hummed off-key when she was concentrating, the fierce protectiveness she displayed towards even the smallest injured creature, the quiet strength that radiated from her in times of crisis.

He wanted the proposal to be a surprise, but not a shock. He wanted it to feel like a natural, beautiful culmination of everything they had built. He realized that the very act of planning it was a continuation of their shared endeavor. He was building something new, something precious, with the same care and intention that they poured into the rescue, into their home, into their relationship.

He considered the timing. He wanted to propose when they were both feeling settled, when the dust of recent challenges had fully settled, and the promise of their future felt clear and bright. The conversation they'd recently had about expanding the rescue and their vision for their home had felt like a significant turning point. It was a moment where their individual dreams had coalesced into a shared aspiration, a testament to their alignment. This felt like the right time to solidify their commitment to that shared future, not just in terms of their work, but in terms of their lives.

Eli knew that Mara wouldn't want anything ostentatious. Her heart lay in authenticity, in genuine connection. A public spectacle would likely make her uncomfortable. What she craved, he knew, was sincerity, a quiet declaration of love that resonated with the truth of their shared experience. He thought about the small, secluded beach they had discovered on the northern coast, a place of serene beauty where they had once spent an entire afternoon watching seals play in the surf. It was a place that held no grand significance in the history of the rescue, but it was a place that held immense significance for *them*. It was a place where they had simply been Mara and Eli, two souls finding solace and joy in each other's company, surrounded by the wild, untamed beauty of the coast.

He imagined them walking along the shoreline, the waves lapping gently at their feet. He could speak of the peace he found in her presence, the way she made even the most ordinary moments feel extraordinary. He could talk about how the vastness of the ocean mirrored the depth of his love for her, a love that was constantly shifting, always evolving, yet always profound. And then, as the sun dipped below the horizon, painting the sky in hues of orange and purple, he could ask her to be his wife. It felt... right. It felt like a proposal that would honor their journey, their love for nature, and the quiet strength of their bond.

He also thought about incorporating elements of the rescue itself. Perhaps a small, symbolic gesture, something that represented the healing and hope they brought to the world. He mused about the possibility of involving some of the more long-term residents of the sanctuary, animals that had become familiar faces, creatures that Mara had a particular soft spot for. He pictured a moment where a rehabilitated bird, strong and ready for release, took flight just as he asked the question. Or perhaps a gentle dolphin, a creature known for its intelligence and grace, could be part of the scene, a silent witness to their commitment. He knew that whatever he chose, it had to feel natural, not forced, and it had to be something that Mara would cherish.

He spent evenings poring over old photographs, not just of the rescue, but of their shared life – a candid shot of them laughing during a downpour, a quiet moment captured at a local festival, a selfie taken after a long day of work, their faces smudged with dirt but their eyes bright. He was looking for inspiration, for a reminder of the joy and love that had carried them through every stage of their relationship. He wanted to weave those memories into the fabric of his proposal, to show her that he remembered, and cherished, every step of their journey together.

He even considered a treasure hunt, a whimsical trail leading Mara through significant places in Port Blossom – the spot where they'd first rescued a stranded otter, the old lighthouse keeper's cottage that now housed their administrative offices, the quiet cove where they'd once watched a pod of whales breach. Each clue could be a reminder of a shared memory, a milestone in their relationship, leading her finally to him, ready to ask for her hand. It felt playful, adventurous, and deeply personal, a reflection of the vibrant energy that they brought to their lives together.

However, the idea of a treasure hunt also felt a little elaborate, perhaps too much for Mara's understated nature. He knew her best, her preference for quiet sincerity over grand gestures. He gravitated back to the more intimate settings, the moments of shared peace. He was looking for a way to speak directly to her heart, to articulate the profound impact she had on his life.

He began to draft the words he would say, scribbling them on scraps of paper, then transferring them to his notebook. He wanted to convey not just his love, but his deep respect for her, for her strength, her intelligence, her compassion. He wanted to acknowledge the incredible partnership they had built, the way they complemented each other, the way they made each other better. He wanted to express his desire to continue building that partnership, to make it official, to weave their lives together into a single, beautiful tapestry.

He thought about the proposal as a bridge, a structure that would connect the life they had built to the life they would continue to build. It was a commitment to the future, grounded in the strength of their past and the richness of their present. He knew that this was more than just a question; it was a declaration of a lifetime of love, of dedication, of shared dreams. And he wanted to get it absolutely right, to capture the essence of their unique story, the story of Mara and Eli, and the beautiful life they were creating in Port Blossom. The journey of planning this proposal was, in itself, a testament to the love and care he had for her, a love that was as deep and as vast as the ocean that cradled their beloved Port Blossom.

Mara found herself standing at the edge of the familiar, yet increasingly welcoming, expanse of permanence. The lingering tendrils of apprehension that had once coiled around her heart, whispering doubts about commitment and forever, were finally receding, replaced by a burgeoning sense of peace. It wasn't a sudden, dramatic shift, but rather a gentle unfolding, like the slow unfurling of a sail catching the breeze. Each day spent with Eli, each shared sunrise over the glittering waters of Port Blossom, each quiet evening spent poring over rescue plans or simply lost in each other's company, chipped away at the last remnants of her fear. Her trust in Eli, in their shared life, and in the future they were meticulously crafting, had deepened into something as solid and enduring as the ancient lighthouse that guarded their coastline.

She caught herself smiling more often, a genuine, unforced smile that reached her eyes, a stark contrast to the guarded expressions she'd worn for so long. The future, once a nebulous and somewhat terrifying concept, now shimmered with an inviting warmth. She found herself not just accepting the idea of a shared life with Eli, but actively anticipating it. It was a subtle yet profound transformation. The knot of anxiety that used to tighten in her stomach whenever they discussed long-term plans had loosened, replaced by a flutter of excitement. She was no longer just watching their lives intertwine; she was actively weaving herself into the tapestry, eager to see the full, intricate pattern emerge.

One evening, as they sat on their porch, the salty air carrying the distant cries of gulls, Mara found herself initiating a conversation that would have once sent her into a spiral of internal debate. "Eli," she began, her voice soft but steady, "I was thinking about the expansion plans for the rescue... and then, well, about *us*." She paused, searching his face for any sign of surprise or discomfort, but found only his usual steady gaze, filled with a familiar warmth. "Have you ever thought about... a family? Not just the rescue, I mean. Our own." The word 'family' hung in the air, no longer a loaded term, but a hopeful aspiration.

Eli turned to her, his expression shifting from contemplation to a profound tenderness. He reached out, his calloused fingers gently tracing the curve of her jaw. "Mara," he said, his voice a low rumble, "I've thought about it more times than I can count. Every time I look at you, I see it. I see the laughter of children echoing in our home, the way you'll teach them to be kind and strong." He paused, his thumb brushing a stray strand of hair from her cheek. "And I see you, always you, being the heart of it all."

A wave of emotion washed over Mara. It wasn't the overwhelming, paralyzing fear of being tied down, but a profound sense of belonging, of being seen and cherished for exactly who she was. She leaned into his touch, her eyes closing for a moment. "It used to scare me, you know," she admitted, her voice barely a whisper. "The idea of... forever. Of being this completely committed. I always felt like I was holding my breath, waiting for something to shatter."

Eli drew her closer, his arm wrapping securely around her shoulders. "And now?" he prompted gently.

Mara opened her eyes and met his gaze, a radiant smile blooming on her face. "Now," she said, the word filled with a newfound conviction, "now I feel like I can finally exhale. Like I'm exactly where I'm supposed to be, with exactly who I'm supposed to be with. It doesn't feel like a trap, Eli. It feels like... coming home."

The word 'home' resonated deeply within her. Port Blossom, once a place she'd found refuge, had become more than that. It was the backdrop to their shared life, the stage upon which their love story was unfolding. Their small cottage, with its creaking floorboards and the scent of salt and old books, was no longer just a shelter, but a sanctuary. It was filled with the echoes of their conversations, the warmth of their shared silences, the tangible presence of their growing love. And Eli, with his quiet strength and unwavering devotion, was the anchor that made it all feel so profoundly real, so undeniably hers.

She found herself openly discussing marriage with him, not with the hesitant, almost apologetic tone of someone testing the waters, but with the eager anticipation of someone planning a delightful future event. She'd point out quaint little chapels on their drives, or comment on the practicalities of choosing wedding bands, all with a lightness that surprised even herself. She remembered the first time the word "marriage" had been uttered in their presence. It had been during a casual conversation with old Mrs. Gable, the town's unofficial historian, who had a penchant for matchmaking and an even greater penchant for oversharing. Mara had felt a prickle of unease, a familiar urge to retreat, but Eli had simply squeezed her hand, his gaze reassuring. Now, the mere mention of it brought a soft glow to her cheeks and a flutter of excitement to her chest.

"Imagine," Mara had mused one afternoon, as they watched a pod of dolphins arc gracefully through the waves, "a small ceremony. Just us, maybe a few close friends from the rescue, and then... a picnic on the beach. Nothing elaborate, but... meaningful."

Eli had turned to her, his eyes sparkling. "Meaningful," he echoed, a slow smile spreading across his face. "I like the sound of that. And I like the idea of us, on the beach, with the ocean as our witness." He pulled her into a gentle hug, inhaling the scent of her hair. "Mara, there's not a single detail of our future that I wouldn't want to plan with you. Not one."

This willingness to share every aspect of their future, from the mundane to the momentous, was what truly solidified her growing trust. Eli didn't just accept her; he actively encouraged her to embrace the life they were building together. He listened to her ideas, no matter how small or seemingly insignificant, and treated them with the same respect he gave their most ambitious rescue plans. He valued her input, her perspective, her very presence in his life. It was a far cry from the guarded independence she had once clung to so fiercely.

Her journey of self-discovery had been a long and winding one, marked by moments of doubt and vulnerability, but it had led her here, to this place of profound security. She felt truly at home in her love for Eli, a love that was no longer a fragile seedling but a strong, deeply rooted tree, its branches reaching towards a boundless sky. She no longer felt the need to guard her heart, to build walls against potential hurt. Instead, she found herself opening it, letting the warmth of their shared life flood in, transforming every corner.

She remembered a conversation they'd had just a few months prior, about the possibility of starting a family. At the time, Mara had felt a familiar tremor of fear, a subtle withdrawal. She'd acknowledged the idea, but her response had been cautious, non-committal. Eli, with his usual understanding, hadn't pushed. He'd simply said, "Whenever you're ready, Mara. We'll take it one step at a time." And that, more than anything, had allowed her to slowly, surely, shed her fear. His patience, his unwavering support, had created a safe space for her to grow, to trust, to embrace the idea of a future that included children, a shared home filled with the sounds of family, and the enduring bond of marriage.

Now, when Eli spoke of their future, of a home filled with the laughter of children and the quiet comfort of shared years, Mara found herself not just listening, but contributing. She'd share her own nascent dreams, picturing bedtime stories read by the fireplace, the smell of baking bread wafting from their kitchen, the joy of watching a child take their first wobbly steps on the sand. These were no longer abstract notions; they were vivid, tangible possibilities, painted with the colors of their shared love and Eli's steadfast devotion.

She realized, with a quiet sense of awe, that she had stopped bracing for impact. The constant vigilance, the expectation of disaster, had faded. In its place was a profound and settled peace. She trusted Eli implicitly. She trusted their love. She trusted that they were building something strong, something that could withstand whatever life might throw at them. This wasn't just about romantic love; it was about a deep, abiding partnership, a shared commitment to weathering life's storms together, hand in hand.

One crisp autumn evening, as they walked along the deserted beach, the moonlight casting a silvery path across the water, Mara found herself stopping and turning to Eli. The air was cool and carried the briny scent of the sea. He looked at her, his expression open and questioning.

"Eli," she began, her voice hushed by the vastness of the ocean surrounding them, "I think... I think I'm ready."

His brow furrowed slightly, a question in his eyes. "Ready for what, Mara?"

She smiled, a soft, radiant smile that mirrored the moonlight. "Ready for all of it," she said, her gaze steady and unwavering. "For forever. For a family. For... for us. Whatever that looks like."

Eli's breath hitched. He reached out, his hands cupping her face, his touch gentle yet firm. "Mara," he whispered, his voice thick with emotion, "you have no idea how long I've waited to hear you say that." He pulled her into a tight embrace, his heart beating a steady rhythm against hers. In that moment, surrounded by the endless expanse of the sea and sky, Mara knew with absolute certainty that she had found her home, not just in Port Blossom, but in the arms of the man who had shown her the true meaning of love and commitment. The seeds of commitment, so carefully planted, had finally taken root, blossoming into a future she was no longer afraid to embrace, but eager to live.

The air in Port Blossom thrummed with a palpable energy, a vibrant hum that mirrored the tide as it retreated, revealing the bounty of the shore. The successful recovery of the stranded whales had been more than just a triumph of skill and dedication; it had ignited a spark, a collective surge of pride and a shared sense of accomplishment that permeated every corner of their coastal town. Mara and Eli, standing hand in hand on the docks, watching the last of the research vessels depart, felt the warmth of that shared spirit settle around them like a comforting embrace. It was in these moments, surrounded by the familiar scent of salt and brine, the cries of gulls overhead, that Mara felt the deepest connection to this place and to the man by her side.

"They're gone," Eli said, his voice a low murmur, a note of quiet satisfaction in his tone. "All accounted for. Back where they belong."

Mara squeezed his hand. "Thanks to all of us," she replied, her gaze sweeping across the harbor, where fishermen were already mending nets, their faces etched with the day's work but their eyes alight with a shared sense of purpose. "It felt like the whole town was out there with us, didn't it?"

Eli nodded, his thumb gently stroking her knuckles. "It did. And it's that spirit, that connection, that we need to keep alive, Mara.

The rescue is just one part of it. It's about more than just the animals. It's about Port Blossom itself. About its heart."

His words resonated with a truth that Mara had come to understand deeply. The rescue center, while her passion and a vital part of her life, was inextricably linked to the well-being of the town. Their shared success had woven a stronger thread between them all, a testament to what they could achieve when they came together. And as the adrenaline of the whale rescue began to ebb, a new idea began to take shape, not just in Mara's mind, but seemingly in the collective consciousness of Port Blossom.

"We should celebrate," Mara said, the words bubbling up, spontaneous and clear. "We should celebrate what we've done. And... and what we *are*."

Eli turned to her, his eyes questioning, but with a spark of understanding igniting within them. "Celebrate?"

"Yes," Mara affirmed, a smile spreading across her face, a smile that reached her eyes and crinkled their corners. "A big celebration. Something that brings everyone together. Something that shows off what Port Blossom is all about. The rescue, of course, but more than that. The artists, the musicians, the food... everything that makes this place special."

Eli's smile mirrored hers, growing wider and more confident with each passing second. He laced his fingers through hers, his gaze intent. "A festival?" he ventured, his voice filled with a dawning excitement. "A Seaside Sanctuary Festival?"

"Exactly!" Mara exclaimed, the name rolling off her tongue, feeling perfectly right. "A Seaside Sanctuary Festival. To celebrate the recovery, to thank everyone who helped, and to show the world, and ourselves, just how strong this community is. How resilient."

The idea, once spoken aloud, took on a life of its own. It was as if the very air of Port Blossom was waiting for such a proclamation, ready to embrace it. Over the next few days, as Mara and Eli discussed the nascent plans, the concept of the Seaside Sanctuary Festival began to blossom from a simple celebration into a grand vision, a vibrant tapestry woven with the threads of community spirit and shared purpose.

"It needs to be more than just a thank you," Mara mused one evening, as they sat at their kitchen table, a scattered array of notes and sketches spread between them. "It needs to be a showcase. A way to secure ongoing support for the rescue, and for all the good work happening here."

Eli nodded, his brow furrowed in concentration as he sketched a rough layout of the town square. "Absolutely. We can highlight the success of the whale rescue, of course. Have displays, information booths about marine conservation. But you're right, it needs to be broader. We need to involve everyone."

And involve everyone they did. The initial conversations, tentative and hopeful, soon turned into enthusiastic planning sessions. Mara and Eli found themselves at the center of a whirlwind of activity, their shared vision quickly becoming a collaborative project. They spoke with Martha from the Port Blossom bakery, whose blueberry scones were legendary, about a special festival edition. Old Man Hemlock, the weathered fisherman who had navigated the treacherous currents during the rescue, offered to organize a display of vintage fishing equipment, alongside stories of Port Blossom's maritime history.

The town square, usually a quiet hub of daily life, was envisioned as the heart of the festival. Mara imagined it transformed, draped in colorful bunting, with stalls showcasing the talents of local artisans. She saw Sarah, the potter whose delicate ceramic sea creatures had become treasured souvenirs, arranging her wares next to Thomas, the woodcarver whose driftwood sculptures captured the essence of the ocean's power. There would be local musicians, their melodies echoing through the salty air, their songs telling tales of the sea and the town.

"We can set up a dedicated 'Rescue Hub'," Eli suggested, his eyes gleaming with enthusiasm. "Not just information, but interactive exhibits. Maybe a 'Touch Tank' with some of the smaller, non-endangered sea life we've rehabilitated. Something for the kids to learn from and be excited about."

Mara pictured it vividly: children's faces alight with wonder, their small hands tentatively reaching out to touch a starfish or a tiny crab. It was precisely this kind of engagement, this fostering of a connection with the natural world, that the rescue center strived for.

The planning process itself became a joyous, unifying endeavor. Mara and Eli found themselves meeting with the town council, discussing permits and logistics with a shared sense of purpose. They consulted with the local school principal about organizing a children's art competition, with the theme "Our Ocean, Our Future." The response was overwhelmingly positive. Teachers were eager to incorporate lessons on marine life and conservation into their curriculum, and the children's anticipation was infectious.

"It's more than just a party, isn't it?" Mara said to Eli one evening, as they reviewed a list of potential volunteers. "It's a statement. A declaration of what Port Blossom stands for."

Eli wrapped an arm around her, pulling her close. "It is," he agreed, his voice warm and steady. "It's a symbol of our collective resilience. Of our commitment to this place, and to each other. And to the creatures we share this planet with."

He kissed her temple, his gaze filled with a profound tenderness. "And it's a testament to you, Mara. To your vision. You took that moment, that success, and you saw something more. Something bigger."

Mara leaned into his embrace, feeling the familiar comfort of his presence. "We saw it together, Eli," she corrected softly. "This is *our* festival. *Our* town. *Our* future."

The weeks leading up to the Seaside Sanctuary Festival were a blur of organized chaos. Volunteers from all walks of life pitched in. Surfers helped set up stages, retired teachers organized craft stalls, and even the notoriously taciturn lighthouse keeper, old Silas, offered to serve as a 'safety marshal,' ensuring everyone stayed within designated areas near the water.

Mara found herself delegating tasks, trusting the expertise and enthusiasm of those around her. She learned to let go, to empower others, a skill that had once been a struggle for her fiercely independent nature. Now, it felt natural, an extension of the deep trust she had in Eli and in the community they were a part of. She saw her own growth reflected in the way she approached this monumental undertaking, with a blend of strategic planning and open-hearted collaboration.

Eli, with his steady pragmatism and his knack for problem-solving, was instrumental in managing the more technical aspects – the power supply, waste management, and ensuring the safety of the beachfront areas. He worked tirelessly, often alongside Mara, their shared efforts a silent, powerful affirmation of their partnership. They would spend late nights poring over budgets, coordinating with suppliers, and then, exhausted but exhilarated, they would steal a quiet moment together, a shared glance that spoke volumes of their shared journey and the exciting future they were building.

One of Mara's favorite aspects of the planning was liaising with the local artisans. She had always admired their dedication to their craft, their ability to translate their passion into tangible works of art. She spent hours visiting their studios, hearing their stories, and seeing firsthand the unique contributions they would bring to the festival. There was Eleanor, whose intricate shell jewelry whispered tales of the ocean's depths, and David, the local chef, who was already planning a "Taste of Port Blossom" food stall, featuring sustainable seafood and locally sourced produce.

"This festival," Mara said to Eli, as they watched a group of children excitedly paint a mural on a large canvas designated for the event, "it's not just about raising money or awareness. It's about reaffirming our connection to this place. To the environment, and to each other."

Eli came up beside her, his arm brushing hers. "It's about laying down roots, Mara. Deeper roots. Showing that we're not just visitors or temporary residents. We're part of the fabric of Port Blossom."

The word 'roots' resonated deeply with Mara. It was a concept she had grappled with for so long, the fear of being tied down, of losing her freedom. But now, surrounded by the vibrant energy of her community, by the tangible evidence of shared effort and collective joy, she understood that true freedom wasn't in detachment, but in connection. In belonging.

The day of the Seaside Sanctuary Festival dawned with a sky of brilliant, cloudless blue, the kind of perfect weather that Port Blossom residents often attributed to good luck, or perhaps, a benevolent sea. As Mara and Eli stood on the edge of the bustling town square, the scene unfolded before them like a dream realized. Colorful tents dotted the landscape, their awnings fluttering in the gentle sea breeze. The air was alive with the murmur of excited voices, the tantalizing aromas of local cuisine, and the infectious rhythm of live music.

Children, their faces painted with whimsical sea creatures, darted through the crowds, their laughter echoing like a joyous symphony. Families strolled, browsing the stalls, their expressions a mixture of curiosity and delight. The 'Rescue Hub' was a hive of activity, with volunteers eagerly sharing information about the center's work and the importance of marine conservation. The interactive exhibits were a huge success, captivating both young and old with their engaging displays.

Mara watched as Eli, his usual calm demeanor now tinged with a proud excitement, addressed a crowd gathered near the main stage. He spoke with passion about the recent rescue, about the dedication of the volunteers, and about the ongoing need for community support. His words were met with enthusiastic applause, a resounding affirmation of their shared efforts.

Later, as Mara stood on a small, elevated platform, the spotlight illuminating her and Eli, she felt a surge of emotion that threatened to overwhelm her. She looked out at the sea of faces – familiar, friendly, and filled with a genuine warmth. There was Martha, beaming from behind her stall of freshly baked goods. There was old Man Hemlock, regaling a group with tales of legendary catches. There were the artists, their creations proudly displayed, and the musicians, their melodies weaving through the heart of the festival. And there, at the center of it all, was Eli, his hand finding hers, his steady gaze a constant reassurance.

"Welcome, everyone," Mara began, her voice clear and strong, carrying over the gentle hum of the festival. "Welcome to the first annual Seaside Sanctuary Festival! Today, we celebrate more than just a recent success; we celebrate the heart and soul of Port Blossom. We celebrate our connection to the sea, to its creatures, and most importantly, to each other."

She spoke of the rescue, of the teamwork and the unwavering dedication that had made it possible. But she also spoke of the broader vision – of a community that cared, that acted, that worked together for the greater good. She spoke of the artists who brought beauty, the chefs who brought flavor, the musicians who brought joy. She spoke of the shared commitment that bound them all together, a commitment to preserving the natural beauty of their home and to supporting the vital work of the rescue center.

"This festival," she continued, her voice filled with a heartfelt sincerity, "is a vibrant symbol of our collective resilience. It's a testament to what we can achieve when we stand united. And it's a promise – a promise to continue caring for our oceans, for our wildlife, and for this incredible community we are so fortunate to be a part of."

As she spoke, Mara felt a profound sense of belonging, a deep and settled peace that radiated through her. The fear, the apprehension that had once been her constant companions, had long since faded, replaced by a quiet confidence and an unshakeable sense of purpose. She looked at Eli, his eyes reflecting the same profound joy and pride she felt, and knew, with absolute certainty, that this was where she was meant to be.

The festival continued throughout the day, a kaleidoscope of activity and shared joy. Families picnicked on the beach, their laughter mingling with the sound of the waves. Children chased seagulls, their faces flushed with excitement. Artisans sold their creations, their hands calloused but their spirits bright. Musicians played, their melodies filling the air with a sense of celebration and community.

As the sun began its slow descent towards the horizon, casting a warm, golden glow over the scene, Mara and Eli found themselves walking hand in hand along the water's edge, the gentle waves lapping at their feet. The day had been a resounding success, exceeding even their wildest expectations.

But for Mara, the true success lay in the feeling of unity, the palpable sense of shared ownership and pride that permeated the festival grounds.

"We did it," Eli said, his voice soft, filled with a quiet satisfaction. He squeezed her hand. "We really did it."

Mara leaned her head on his shoulder, breathing in the salty air. "We did," she agreed, a contented sigh escaping her lips. "And it's just the beginning, isn't it?"

Eli turned to her, his gaze warm and full of love. "It is, Mara. This is just the beginning. A celebration, yes, but also a foundation. A promise of what's to come." He paused, his thumb gently stroking her cheek. "A promise of our future, together."

The Seaside Sanctuary Festival was more than just an event; it was a tangible manifestation of their shared commitment, a vibrant declaration of their love for each other and for the community they had chosen to build their lives in. It was a testament to the power of unity, the strength of resilience, and the enduring beauty of a shared dream, coming to life on the shores of Port Blossom. The seeds of commitment, so carefully nurtured, had blossomed into something truly extraordinary, a beacon of hope and a promise of a brighter future for all.

The salty tang of the ocean was an ever-present perfume in Port Blossom, a scent Mara had grown up with, a scent that clung to Eli like a second skin. But as he steered his small fishing boat south along the rugged coastline, the air seemed to carry a different weight, a more personal resonance. The rhythmic chug of the engine was a steady heartbeat against the vastness of the sea, a fitting soundtrack for the conversation he was about to have. He was heading to see Mara's father, a man he respected deeply, a man whose quiet strength and unwavering love for his daughter had shaped Mara into the woman Eli adored.

Old Man Hemlock, as he was affectionately known by the townsfolk, lived in a small, weathered cottage perched on a bluff overlooking a secluded cove. It was a place where time seemed to move at the pace of the tides, where the only rush was the ebb and flow of the water against the shore. Eli had visited before, always as Mara's companion, a welcome guest in their shared world. But today was different. Today, he was coming not as a guest, but as a supplicant, seeking a blessing that felt as vital and profound as the ocean itself.

As he neared the cove, he cut the engine, the sudden silence amplifying the gentle lapping of waves and the distant cries of gulls. The cottage, modest and unassuming, exuded a sense of peace. Smoke curled lazily from its chimney, a comforting sign of life within. Eli secured his boat to the small, sturdy dock, his movements deliberate and unhurried. He took a deep breath, the cool, crisp air filling his lungs, preparing himself for the sincerity that this moment demanded. He wasn't here to impress; he was here to connect, to be honest, and to ask for something deeply meaningful.

He walked up the worn path, his boots crunching on the gravel. The garden, though untamed, was full of life – hardy succulents clinging to rocks, vibrant wildflowers blooming in defiance of the salt spray. It was a reflection of Mara's own resilient spirit, her ability to thrive in any environment. He reached the porch and knocked, a firm, steady rap that echoed slightly in the quiet air.

The door opened, and there he was. Elias Hemlock, his face a roadmap of a life lived under the sun and sea, his eyes, a clear, piercing blue, held a warmth that immediately put Eli at ease. He stood a little straighter, a respectful smile gracing his lips.

"Eli," Mr. Hemlock said, his voice a low rumble, like distant thunder. "To what do we owe the pleasure?" There was no surprise in his tone, only a gentle inquiry, a quiet acceptance of whatever brought Eli to his doorstep.

"Mr. Hemlock," Eli began, his voice steady, though his heart gave a noticeable thump. "It's good to see you. I hope I'm not disturbing you."

"Never," the older man replied, stepping aside. "Come in, come in. The kettle's just gone on. And it's Elias, my boy. We've shared enough fish and weather to dispense with formalities." He gestured for Eli to enter the cozy cottage, its interior filled with the comforting scent of wood smoke and something faintly herbal.

Eli stepped inside, his gaze taking in the simple, functional space. Fishing nets hung from the walls, interspersed with framed photographs of Mara at various stages of her life – a gap-toothed child beaming from a sandy beach, a teenager with a determined glint in her eyes, a young woman standing beside a rescued seal. Each image was a testament to the love and pride Elias Hemlock held for his daughter.

They settled into worn, comfortable chairs by the hearth, the fire crackling merrily. Mr. Hemlock poured two mugs of steaming tea, handing one to Eli. The silence that followed was not awkward, but comfortable, a shared understanding that words would come when they were ready.

Finally, Eli cleared his throat. "Mr. Hemlock," he began, meeting the older man's gaze directly. "I've come today because... well, because Mara means the world to me. More than words can say." He paused, searching for the right way to articulate the depth of his feelings. "I've never met anyone like her. Her passion, her kindness, her... her light. She's the anchor of my life, and I can't imagine a single day without her."

Elias Hemlock listened intently, his gaze never wavering from Eli's face. He didn't interrupt, simply nodded as Eli spoke, his presence a solid, reassuring force.

"I love her, Mr. Hemlock. I love her deeply and truly," Eli continued, his voice gaining conviction. "And I want to spend the rest of my life with her. I want to build a future with her, here, in Port Blossom, where she's always felt most at home.

I want to support her dreams, her work at the rescue center, everything that makes her who she is."

He took a slow sip of his tea, the warmth spreading through him. "I know I'm not from here originally, not like Mara. But I've come to love this town, and I've come to love the people who make it special. And there's no one more special to me than your daughter." He looked around the room, his eyes settling on a framed photo of Mara with a playful otter. "I want to give her the kind of life she deserves, a life filled with love, security, and the freedom to continue doing the incredible work she does."

Eli set his mug down, his hands clasped together. He met Elias Hemlock's eyes again, his heart open and vulnerable. "I know how much she means to you. And I promise you, Mr. Hemlock, I will always cherish her, protect her, and love her with everything I have. I want to be more than just someone she loves; I want to be someone you can trust, someone who will always have her best interests at heart. I... I would be honored if you would give me your blessing to marry Mara."

The words hung in the air, heavy with sincerity and hope. Eli felt a tremor of anxiety, the vulnerability of the moment almost overwhelming. He had laid his heart bare, and now, he waited for the judgment of the man who had raised the woman who had captured his soul.

Elias Hemlock remained silent for a long moment, his blue eyes, which had seemed so sharp and observant, now softened with a profound understanding. He looked past Eli, his gaze drifting towards the window, towards the shimmering expanse of the ocean that had shaped his own life and the lives of his family.

Then, he turned back, a slow, genuine smile spreading across his weathered face. He extended a hand, not to shake Eli's, but to place it gently on his shoulder. The grip was firm, conveying a strength that belied his age.

"Eli," he said, his voice softer now, imbued with a warmth that Eli hadn't heard before. "I've seen the way you look at my Mara. I've seen the way she looks at you. And I've seen the way you both care for this town, for the creatures that need our help. You've brought a light into her life, a happiness that shines from her like the sun on the water."

He squeezed Eli's shoulder, his gaze filled with a quiet respect. "You speak of love and commitment, and I see that in you. You have a good heart, Eli, and you have a deep respect for what matters. My Mara... she's always been independent, strong-willed, but she needs someone to stand beside her, to share her burdens and celebrate her triumphs. And I believe, with all my heart, that you are that man."

He paused, his eyes twinkling. "She's a handful, you know," he added with a wry smile. "Don't let that calm exterior fool you. She's got a fire in her belly that could warm the whole coast. But that's why we love her, isn't it?"

Eli chuckled, a release of tension he hadn't realized he was holding. "That she is," he agreed, his own smile widening.

"So, yes, Eli," Elias Hemlock said, his voice firm and clear, the finality of his words bringing a wave of relief and joy to Eli. "You have my blessing. My heartfelt blessing. Take care of my Mara. Love her as you do, and I know she'll make you the happiest man on this earth. And if you ever need anything, a hand with the boat, or just a bit of advice on dealing with a stubborn woman, you know where to find me."

Tears pricked at the corners of Eli's eyes, a testament to the emotional weight of the moment. He clasped Elias Hemlock's hand, the handshake firm and reciprocal this time, a bond forged not just between two men, but between two families, united by their love for one remarkable woman.

"Thank you, Mr. Hemlock. Elias," Eli said, his voice thick with emotion. "Thank you. I won't let you down. I promise."

"I know you won't," Elias said, his smile reaching his eyes. He released Eli's hand, then clapped him on the back. "Now, let's finish this tea. And then, you can tell me all about how you plan to keep that firecracker of a daughter of mine happy."

As they sat there, sipping their tea, the conversation flowed easily. Eli shared more about his hopes and dreams for his future with Mara, and Elias, in turn, shared stories of Mara's childhood, anecdotes that revealed the depth of her character and the unwavering love that had always surrounded her. It was a conversation that felt like a new beginning, a cementing of their connection, not just as father-in-law and future son-in-law, but as men who both deeply loved the same extraordinary woman. The journey back to Port Blossom felt lighter, the engine's hum now a joyous anthem, carrying him towards the woman who was now, officially, his future.

The sun, a molten orb, began its slow descent towards the horizon, painting the sky in hues of apricot, rose, and amethyst. The salt-laced breeze, which had carried the scent of brine and possibility all day, now softened, whispering secrets to the gentle waves lapping at the shore below. Mara and Eli found themselves on the familiar porch swing, its rhythmic creak a soothing counterpoint to the symphony of the ocean. It was a rare stillness, a pocket of peace carved out of their bustling lives, and it felt like a gift.

Mara leaned her head against Eli's shoulder, the solid warmth of him a comforting anchor. Her fingers traced the worn wood grain of the swing's armrest, a silent acknowledgment of the countless hours they had spent here, often lost in conversation, but sometimes, like tonight, simply existing together. The immensity of the sea stretching before them mirrored the immensity of the feelings that had bloomed between them, a landscape as vast and as breathtaking as the view.

"Remember when we first met?" Mara's voice was soft, a murmur against the gentle roar of the waves. "It feels like a lifetime ago, and yet, just yesterday. So much has happened, hasn't it?" She squeezed his hand, her thumb stroking the back of his. "I'm... I'm so grateful, Eli. For everything. For you. For us."

Eli turned his head, his gaze meeting hers. His eyes, usually alight with a playful spark, held a profound tenderness now, a depth that spoke volumes without a single word. He brought her hand to his lips, pressing a gentle kiss to her knuckles, his touch sending a shiver of warmth through her.

"Grateful?" he echoed, his voice a low, resonant rumble that vibrated through her. "Mara, I'm the one who should be grateful. You came into my life like a beacon, showing me a path I didn't even know I was looking for. You brought color to my world, a sense of purpose I'd been missing." He paused, his thumb stroking her skin. "Every day with you feels like... like finding a treasure I never expected. You are, without a doubt, the best thing that has ever happened to me."

Mara smiled, a genuine, heartfelt smile that reached her eyes. She loved the way he spoke, the sincerity that laced every word. It wasn't about grand declarations or poetic flourishes; it was about the quiet, unwavering truth of his feelings. "We've certainly navigated some choppy waters, haven't we?" she mused, a hint of a playful challenge in her tone. "From almost sinking your boat to dealing with my stubborn streak..."

Eli chuckled, a deep, rich sound. "And I wouldn't trade a single one of those moments," he said, his arm tightening around her. "They've made us stronger, haven't they? Made us appreciate what we have even more. I've never been more certain about anything in my life, Mara. Not about the tides, not about the catch, not about anything. I'm certain about us. About my love for you. About wanting to spend every sunrise and every sunset with you."

He turned her slightly, so she was facing him fully on the swing. The fading light cast a soft glow on her features, highlighting the curve of her cheekbones, the gentle slope of her nose, the sparkle in her eyes that always captivated him. He saw not just the woman he loved, but the vibrant spirit that had drawn him in from the very beginning – her fierce compassion, her unyielding determination, her infectious laughter. He saw the Mara who nurtured injured seabirds back to health, the Mara who stood up for what she believed in, the Mara who, with a single glance, could make his world feel right again.

"I've thought a lot about our future," he continued, his voice dropping to a near whisper. "About what comes next. And the answer is always the same. It's you, Mara. It's building a life with you, right here, in this town that means so much to us both. It's waking up next to you every morning, and falling asleep in your arms every night. It's sharing in your joys and being there for you through any challenges. It's... it's everything."

Mara's breath hitched. She knew what he was saying, the unspoken question that hung in the air between them, heavy with anticipation and yet so light with the certainty of his love. She met his gaze, her heart swelling with a mixture of joy and a quiet, profound understanding. The journey they had taken, both individually and together, had led them to this very moment, this nexus of shared dreams and unwavering commitment.

"I feel it too, Eli," she confessed, her voice barely audible above the ocean's murmur. "This... this deep knowing. That you are where I'm meant to be. That we are meant to be." She reached up, her fingers gently caressing his cheek, tracing the line of his jaw. "You've given me so much. You've made me feel seen, truly seen, in a way I never have before. You believe in me, even when I doubt myself. And that... that's a gift beyond measure."

The silence that settled between them was not an emptiness, but a fullness, a rich tapestry woven from shared experiences, unspoken affections, and the promise of a future yet to unfold. It was a silence that spoke of trust, of comfort, of a love that had weathered storms and emerged stronger, brighter, more resilient. The gentle sway of the porch swing, the rhythmic crashing of the waves, the distant cry of a lone seagull – all of it coalesced into a harmonious backdrop for their shared intimacy.

Eli leaned closer, his forehead touching hers. He could feel the gentle rise and fall of her chest, the steady beat of her heart a mirror to his own. He inhaled her scent, a subtle blend of sea salt and her own unique fragrance, and felt a profound sense of peace wash over him. This was it. This was the quiet culmination of all their hopes, all their dreams.

"I want to ask you something, Mara," he murmured, his voice laced with emotion. "Something I've wanted to ask you for a long time. But I wanted to wait for the right moment, for a moment like this, when we're just us, with nothing else around to distract us." He pulled back just enough to look into her eyes, his own filled with an earnest intensity. "Mara, will you marry me?"

The question, though anticipated, still sent a thrill through Mara, a cascade of emotions that left her breathless. She saw the sincerity in his eyes, the vulnerability, the unwavering hope. This wasn't a question born of obligation or fleeting passion; it was a question born from the deepest recesses of his soul, a testament to a love that had grown and deepened with every shared smile, every comforting touch, every whispered secret.

She didn't hesitate. The answer was as clear and as unwavering as the tides. A broad smile bloomed across her face, her eyes shining with unshed tears of pure joy. She reached for his hands, intertwining her fingers with his, their connection a silent, powerful affirmation.

"Yes, Eli," she whispered, her voice thick with emotion. "Yes. A thousand times, yes."

Eli's face lit up, his relief and happiness radiating from him. He pulled her into a tight embrace, holding her as if he would never let go. Mara melted into him, feeling the solid strength of his arms, the steady beat of his heart against hers. The world outside their embrace faded away, leaving only the two of them, bathed in the fading light, their future stretching out before them, as vast and as beautiful as the ocean at dusk.

As they held each other, the comfortable silence returned, but now it was imbued with a new layer of meaning. It was a silence of shared promises, of a future secured, of a love that had found its true north. The gentle creak of the swing, the rhythmic pulse of the waves, the soft whisper of the wind – they were no longer just sounds of the evening; they were the soundtrack to their newfound commitment, a prelude to the beautiful chapter they were about to begin together. The seeds of commitment, nurtured through shared experiences and a love that had blossomed in the heart of Port Blossom, had finally taken root, promising a future as rich and enduring as the ocean itself. Eli's careful planning, the unspoken anticipation that had buzzed beneath the surface of their days, had now found its joyous resolution. They were embarking on a new adventure, one that would be built on the foundation of their deep and abiding love, a love that was as constant and as powerful as the tides themselves. The evening, once a quiet moment of reflection, had transformed into a profound affirmation of their shared destiny, a testament to a love that was as deep as the ocean and as bright as the stars that would soon begin to pepper the darkening sky.

CHAPTER EIGHT

The Festival and the Question

The air in Port Blossom had taken on a new energy, a vibrant hum that vibrated through the very cobblestones of the streets and the weathered planks of the boardwalk. It was the palpable buzz of anticipation, the collective breath held just before a grand performance. The Seaside Sanctuary Festival, a beacon of hope and a testament to the town's enduring spirit, was fast approaching, and the preparations were in full, glorious swing.

Mara, her usual organizational prowess amplified by a joy that seemed to radiate from her very being, moved through the grounds of the rescue center with a practiced, energetic stride. She was a whirlwind of color and purpose, her laughter ringing out as she directed volunteers, her eyes sparkling with an infectious enthusiasm. The rescue grounds, normally a place of quiet healing and focused care, were transforming. Bunting, in shades of ocean blue and sandy beige, fluttered from lampposts and the sturdy oak trees that dotted the perimeter. Hand-painted signs, each bearing the charmingly imperfect calligraphy of local schoolchildren, announced the various attractions: "Bake Sale Bonanza," "Craft Corner Creations," and the ever-popular "Seafood Shanty."

Eli was her steadfast anchor, his presence a comforting constant amidst the delightful chaos. He moved with a quiet efficiency, his strong hands adept at setting up the main stage, a robust structure that would soon host local musicians and storytellers. He was coordinating the placement of the food stalls, ensuring a smooth flow for the anticipated crowds, and overseeing the delivery of much-needed supplies. While Mara was the effervescent conductor of the festival orchestra, Eli was the skilled stage manager, ensuring every prop was in place, every cue was hit, and the entire production ran without a hitch. Their communication was a language honed by shared experience, a series of nods, gestures, and murmured words that conveyed volumes. A glance from Mara, a slight tilt of her head, and Eli understood precisely where the artisanal soap vendor needed to be positioned. A subtle adjustment of his hand, a knowing smile, and Mara knew the sound system for the main stage was being meticulously checked.

"The tide charts are all accounted for, Mara," Eli called out, his voice carrying easily over the din of hammers and happy chatter. He was leaning against a stack of hay bales destined for seating around the storytelling circle. "The fishermen have promised the freshest catch for the grill, and Old Man Hemlock is personally overseeing the oyster shucking. He said he'd only allow it if he could personally ensure 'peak brininess.' You know how he is."

Mara grinned, tying off a bright blue ribbon on a trestle table laden with handmade knitted goods. "Peak brininess," she repeated, her eyes crinkling. "That's high praise indeed coming from Hemlock. Tell him the seagulls will be performing a review and he must meet their exacting standards." She paused, looking around at the bustling scene. "It's incredible, isn't it? Look at everyone. Every single person here has a story, a connection to the Sanctuary, or just a pure love for this town. It feels... bigger than just a fundraiser."

And it was. The Seaside Sanctuary Festival was more than just a means to secure vital funding for the wildlife rescue center. It was a tangible manifestation of Port Blossom's collective heart. The generosity poured in from every corner of the community. Local businesses, from the bustling bakery that had donated a mountain of pastries to the quiet bookstore that had curated a special selection of nautical tales for the silent auction, had opened their coffers and their hearts. Even the usually reclusive artist, Silas Blackwood, known for his moody seascapes, had contributed a stunning watercolor of the lighthouse, his signature grumbling softening to a gruff approval of the festival's purpose.

"It is," Eli agreed, walking over to join her. He gently brushed a stray strand of hair from her forehead, his touch sending a familiar warmth through her. "It's a celebration of what we've built, of what we've overcome. Remember when this place was just a dream, Mara? And now... look." He gestured with a sweeping arc of his arm, encompassing the vibrant activity. "This is Port Blossom, at its finest. Together. United."

The sentiment resonated deeply with Mara. She remembered the early days, the endless meetings, the quiet doubts that had sometimes shadowed even her most optimistic moments. She remembered the initial hesitation from some of the older residents, the ingrained skepticism that whispered of fleeting fads and dashed hopes. But Eli, with his steady belief and unwavering support, had been her rock. And the town, slowly but surely, had come to embrace the vision, to see the vital importance of the Sanctuary, and to feel the pride of contributing to something truly meaningful.

The rescue grounds themselves were a testament to this growing pride. Children, their faces smeared with the remnants of paint from an earlier decorating session, helped arrange chairs for the storytelling tent, their small hands eager to contribute. Teenagers, their usual boisterous energy channeled into productive tasks, meticulously set up the games area, their friendly competition evident even in the way they stacked beanbag toss targets. Even the older generation, the keepers of Port Blossom's history and traditions, were actively involved. Mrs. Gable, her silver hair neatly pinned, was overseeing the sorting of donated books, her keen eye ensuring only the best found their way to the auction tables. Mr. Henderson, the retired fisherman with hands like gnarled oak, was painstakingly mending fishing nets that would be repurposed into decorative bunting.

"Sarah's team is almost done with the 'Adopt-a-Seabird' stall," Mara reported, checking her clipboard. "They've got all the bios ready, and they're setting up the little donation envelopes. I think the idea of sponsoring a named bird is really going to resonate with people."

"It will," Eli said, his gaze softening as he watched a young girl carefully place a fluffy toy penguin on a shelf. "It's about making that connection, isn't it? Taking something abstract, like fundraising, and making it personal. These birds, they're not just statistics. They're individuals with personalities, with stories of survival and recovery. Just like us."

He met Mara's eyes then, and in that shared glance, the unspoken understanding passed between them. The festival wasn't just about the physical sanctuary they were building for injured wildlife; it was about the emotional sanctuary they had found in each other, and the community's sanctuary from the storms, both literal and figurative, they had weathered.

The logistical details, while extensive, were being managed with remarkable efficiency, a testament to the dedication of the core organizing committee. Lena, the ever-organized owner of the local bakery, had taken charge of the food and beverage logistics. Her team was a well-oiled machine, coordinating with local farmers for fresh produce, negotiating with suppliers for biodegradable plates and cutlery, and ensuring a diverse range of delicious options would be available, from hearty chowders to delicate pastries. Mark, the owner of the town's hardware store, had taken on the Herculean task of ensuring all the physical infrastructure was sound and safe. He'd personally inspected every tent pole, reinforced every temporary structure, and even organized a team of volunteers to manage waste disposal and recycling, a crucial element in their commitment to sustainability.

Even the entertainment schedule, a complex puzzle of local talent and community participation, was falling into place. The town's beloved folk band, "The Salty Dogs," had agreed to headline the main stage, their lively jigs and sea shanties guaranteed to get toes tapping. Young aspiring musicians from the local school were also scheduled to perform, a chance for them to share their budding talents with their community. The storytelling tent, a cozy haven under a canopy of canvas, would feature readings of local maritime legends and heartwarming tales of rescue and resilience, read by some of Port Blossom's most cherished residents.

Mara moved towards the main stage where Eli was supervising the placement of sound equipment. "Have we heard back from the lighthouse keepers about the evening illumination?" she asked, her voice carrying a note of hopeful inquiry. "I was thinking, as a special touch, they could project a soft beam out over the water just as the stars come out. A little nod to the Sanctuary's guiding light."

Eli straightened up, wiping a bead of sweat from his brow. "I spoke with Captain Davies this morning. He's all for it. He said they'll synchronize it with the lighting of the bonfire down on the beach. A beautiful visual, he called it. And he even offered to have one of the younger keepers come down and talk about the history of the lighthouse to the kids at the storytelling tent."

"Oh, that's wonderful!" Mara's face lit up. "That's exactly the kind of personal touch that makes this festival so special. It's not just about the money; it's about sharing the stories, the history, the very soul of Port Blossom."

She looked around again, a sense of profound gratitude washing over her. This wasn't just her project, or Eli's; it was a shared endeavor, a collective outpouring of love and support. She saw the genuine smiles on the faces of the volunteers, the easy camaraderie between people who might not otherwise interact, the shared purpose that had woven them all together. It was a beautiful tapestry, each thread contributing to the vibrant, resilient pattern of their community.

The scent of popcorn and freshly baked bread began to mingle with the ever-present aroma of the sea, a tantalizing prelude to the culinary delights that awaited. Children darted between stalls, their excitement a tangible force, while adults chatted, their conversations punctuated by laughter and the occasional shared memory. The festival grounds, a hive of activity just days before, were now a vibrant tableau of community spirit, alive with the promise of a day filled with joy, connection, and the enduring strength of Port Blossom. Mara and Eli, standing amidst the joyful bustle, shared a look, a silent acknowledgment of their shared accomplishment, and the deep, abiding love that had fueled their journey to this vibrant moment. The festival was more than just an event; it was a living, breathing testament to everything they held dear.

The air, already thick with the promise of sea salt and summer festivities, seemed to hold its breath as a car, unfamiliar yet possessing a certain understated elegance, navigated the winding lane leading to the rescue center. It wasn't a vehicle typically seen in Port Blossom, its polished chrome and sleek lines a stark contrast to the sturdy, well-loved pickups and sedans that usually traversed these roads. Eli, who had been meticulously checking the tension on a guy rope for the main stage, straightened up, a flicker of curiosity in his eyes. He recognized the make, a detail that pricked at a memory he'd long tried to keep tucked away.

Mara, her hands dusted with flour from a brief foray into the bake sale tent, followed his gaze. "Is that someone lost?" she mused, a friendly concern coloring her tone. "We're not officially open for another hour, but I suppose we can point them towards the parking area."

Eli didn't respond immediately. He watched as the car pulled to a smooth stop near the entrance to the festival grounds, not haphazardly, but with an almost practiced precision. The driver's door opened, and a figure emerged, tall and broad-shouldered, with a familiar set to his jaw and a shock of dark hair that, even from this distance, looked uncannily like Eli's own, albeit styled with a deliberate, almost corporate neatness. A wave of something akin to unease, a cold, unwelcome guest, washed over Eli. He knew that gait, the way the man held himself, an air of contained energy that could either be confidence or a carefully constructed defense.

"Eli?" the man called out, his voice carrying on the gentle breeze, a voice that Eli hadn't heard in person for... how long had it been? Five years? Six? Time had a way of blurring the edges of painful memories, but the sound of that voice, so unequivocally his brother's, was sharp and clear, cutting through the festive atmosphere like a shard of ice.

David. His older brother, David.

Eli's hands clenched into fists by his sides. He hadn't expected this. Not here. Not now. Not ever, if he were being completely honest. David was a phantom from a life Eli had carefully disentangled himself from, a life of expectations, of unspoken resentments, of a deep, aching chasm that had opened between them years ago and never seemed to close.

Mara, sensing the sudden shift in Eli's demeanor, turned to look at him, her brow furrowed with concern. "Eli? Do you know them?"

He managed a tight nod, his gaze still fixed on the approaching figure. "Yeah," he said, his voice rougher than he intended. "Yeah, I know him. That's... that's my brother."

David navigated the uneven ground with an ease that suggested he wasn't entirely unfamiliar with less-than-manicured landscapes, though Eli suspected the effort was more about projecting an image than actual comfort. He wore a crisp, pale blue shirt, its sleeves rolled to the elbows, revealing tanned forearms. His jeans were dark and immaculately pressed, a stark contrast to the comfortable, lived-in attire of the festival volunteers. He looked... successful. Polished. The kind of man who commanded boardrooms, not community festivals.

As David drew closer, the subtle tension in Eli's shoulders became more pronounced. He could feel Mara's gaze, questioning but not intrusive. He offered her a weak smile, a silent plea for understanding, before turning to face his unexpected visitor. The years had etched subtle lines around David's eyes, but the arrogant tilt of his chin remained, as did the faint smirk that always seemed to hover at the corners of his lips, a smirk that Eli had learned to interpret as a prelude to judgment.

"Well, well," David said, stopping a few feet away, his eyes sweeping over the bustling scene with a detached amusement. "Eli. Still playing in the dirt, I see." His gaze flickered to Mara, a quick, appraising glance that held no warmth. "And you've found yourself a... partner in crime?"

The familiar condescension stung, a subtle jab that Eli had endured for years. He resisted the urge to retort, to let the years of pent-up frustration spill out. This wasn't the place. This wasn't the time. The festival, Mara, the Sanctuary – they deserved better than to be caught in the crossfire of his and David's fractured history.

"David," Eli said, keeping his voice level, a practiced neutrality that masked the turmoil beneath. "What are you doing here?"

David's smirk widened. "Can't a brother come to support his... dedicated sibling?" He gestured vaguely around them. "Heard there was some sort of shindig going on. Figured I'd drop by, see what all the fuss was about." He paused, his eyes finally settling on Eli, a subtle challenge in their depths. "Been a while, hasn't it, Eli? Thought I'd see how the prodigal son was faring."

The air crackled with unspoken history. Eli remembered the arguments, the raised voices, the accusations hurled across the vast expanse of their differing visions for their lives. David, the golden child, the one who had followed the predetermined path of corporate success, of financial security, of a life meticulously curated to impress their parents. And Eli, the dreamer, the one who had always felt like a disappointment, who had dared to forge his own way, a way that David clearly still saw as a childish indulgence, a waste of potential.

Mara, bless her observant heart, stepped forward, a small, placid smile gracing her lips. "Welcome to the Seaside Sanctuary Festival," she said, her voice warm and inviting, a stark contrast to the icy undertones of the brothers' exchange. "I'm Mara, Eli's partner. We're so glad you could make it. We're just getting ready to open, but there are plenty of activities for everyone."

David turned his attention to Mara, and for the first time, Eli saw a flicker of something other than amusement in his brother's eyes – a hint of surprise, perhaps, or even grudging respect for her unwavering composure. "David Thorne," he introduced himself, extending a hand, his grip firm and confident. "Eli's... older brother. Apparently."

Mara shook his hand, her smile never faltering. "It's lovely to meet you, David. Eli's told me so much about you."

Eli winced internally. He doubted he'd told David anything remotely positive in years, and he certainly hadn't spoken of him to Mara in a way that would warrant such a diplomatic platitude. He wondered what fabrication Mara's words might be.

David's gaze, however, seemed to hold a question, a silent probing that Eli couldn't quite decipher. Was he genuinely curious about Mara? Or was he simply looking for another angle, another weakness to exploit?

"Has he now?" David's voice was smooth, almost silken, but Eli detected the subtle shift, the undercurrent of something sharper. "I find that hard to believe. Eli wasn't always one for sharing the details of his... unconventional life choices."

"Well," Mara replied, her tone light, "he's a man of many surprises." She shot Eli a playful wink, a gesture that sent a wave of warmth through him, a silent acknowledgment of their shared understanding, their shared world. It was a world David had no part in, a world he had actively chosen to exclude himself from.

Eli cleared his throat, stepping slightly in front of Mara, a subtle but clear territorial marker. "David, the festival officially opens in an hour. There's a designated parking area over by the north gate. We can show you where it is." He deliberately omitted any mention of David being a guest, framing his arrival as a logistical necessity.

David chuckled, a low, rumbling sound that held no genuine mirth. "No need to fuss, Eli. I'll find my way. I'm not entirely incapable of navigating a small-town fair." He paused, his eyes again locking with Eli's. "Though I must admit, I'm impressed. Didn't think you had it in you to pull something like this off. Looks like a lot of people turned out."

His words, meant to be a backhanded compliment, landed like a poorly aimed dart. Eli felt a surge of defiance. "It's not just 'something like this,' David. It's for the Seaside Sanctuary. We rescue and rehabilitate injured marine wildlife." He allowed a touch of pride to color his voice. "It's important work."

David raised an eyebrow, a gesture that conveyed polite skepticism. "Important, you say? And all these people... they're genuinely interested in saving seals and seagulls?" He let out a soft, disbelieving laugh. "Or are they just here for the free food and the opportunity to ogle the local talent?"

The dismissiveness was palpable. It was the same old David, the one who saw the world in black and white, in terms of profit margins and tangible achievements, incapable of understanding the value of altruism, of community spirit, of a passion project that didn't offer immediate financial returns.

Eli took a deep breath, trying to quell the rising tide of anger. "They're here because they care, David. Because they believe in what we're doing. Port Blossom is a community that looks out for its own. And that extends to its wildlife, too."

David merely shrugged, his gaze drifting towards a group of children enthusiastically helping to arrange colorful cushions for the storytelling tent. "Remarkable," he murmured, though his tone suggested the opposite. "Still, it's a... quaint little endeavor. I imagine the overheads must be astronomical. How are you funding all this, Eli? Another one of your 'generous benefactors'?" The emphasis on "generous benefactors" dripped with sarcasm.

The implication was clear: Eli was a charity case, a perpetual recipient of handouts, unable to stand on his own two feet. It was a narrative David had long cultivated, a narrative that conveniently overlooked Eli's own hard work and dedication.

"We're funded by donations, grants, and events like this," Eli stated firmly, meeting his brother's gaze. "And yes, we have people who believe in our mission and contribute financially. It's called community support, David. Something you might not be familiar with, given your... secluded existence."

The barb landed, and David's smirk faltered for a fraction of a second. He recovered quickly, however, his jaw tightening almost imperceptibly. "Secluded? I'm merely... pragmatic, Eli. I invest in things that have a tangible return. Things that build a future, not drain resources on... sentimentality."

"Sentimentality is what drives people to help," Mara interjected smoothly, stepping between them again, her presence a calming force. "It's what makes them want to contribute to something bigger than themselves. And you know, David, there's a certain return in that, too. A sense of fulfillment. A connection to something meaningful."

David looked at Mara, a complex mixture of curiosity and suspicion in his eyes. He seemed to be assessing her, trying to understand her role in Eli's life, and perhaps, to gauge the depth of her commitment. "Fulfillment," he echoed, the word sounding foreign on his tongue. "An interesting concept. I prefer a more... concrete ROI."

Eli felt a familiar weariness settle over him. Arguing with David was like trying to steer a ship against a hurricane; futile and exhausting. He knew his brother's mindset, etched in stone by years of a privileged, sheltered life. David saw the world as a series of transactions, of power plays and financial gains. He couldn't fathom a life driven by passion, by compassion, by the simple desire to make a difference.

"We're opening soon," Eli said, his voice firm and final. "We'll be setting up a donation booth inside. Perhaps you'd like to contribute to our cause, David? A little seed money to get the seals thinking about their future returns." He deliberately used David's own language, a subtle dig at his perceived shallowness.

David's eyes narrowed, a flicker of genuine irritation finally breaking through his carefully constructed facade. "Don't patronize me, Eli," he said, his voice dropping to a low, dangerous tone. "I came here to... observe. Not to be lectured by my younger brother on the finer points of charity." He glanced at his watch, a gesture that screamed impatience. "I'll be around. Don't expect me to be queuing up for a soggy hotdog, though. I have certain standards, you see."

With that, David turned on his heel, his movements precise and deliberate, and walked away, leaving behind a ripple of awkward silence. He didn't look back. He didn't offer any further explanation for his presence. He was simply there, an uninvited guest, a stark reminder of a past Eli had tried to leave behind.

Mara watched him go, her expression thoughtful. When she turned back to Eli, her eyes were filled with a mixture of concern and a quiet resolve. "He's... a lot," she said softly, her voice barely above a whisper.

Eli let out a long, shaky breath, the tension in his shoulders finally easing slightly. He ran a hand through his hair, the gesture one of pure exhaustion. "Yeah," he admitted. "He's... always been a lot."

"Are you alright?" Mara's hand gently touched his arm, her touch a soothing balm.

He met her gaze, finding solace in the warmth and sincerity he saw there. "Yeah," he said, a little more firmly this time. "I'm alright. Just... unexpected. He hasn't been around for years. And for him to just show up here, now..." He trailed off, the implications swirling in his mind. David's motives were always complex, always layered with unspoken agendas. What was he really after? Was this a genuine, albeit bizarre, attempt at reconciliation? Or was he here to scrutinize, to judge, to find fault in the life Eli had built for himself?

"Whatever his reasons," Mara said, her voice steady, "he's here now. And we'll deal with it. Together." She squeezed his arm. "You've built something incredible here, Eli. Something he can't take away from you, no matter how much he might want to."

Her unwavering belief in him, in their shared vision, was a powerful anchor in the swirling uncertainty David's presence had introduced. He knew she was right. He wouldn't let his brother's unwelcome arrival derail the joy and purpose of the festival. He wouldn't let David's cynicism dim the light they had worked so hard to create.

"You're right," Eli said, a renewed sense of determination settling over him. He met Mara's gaze, a silent promise passing between them. "We'll deal with it. He's just another... unexpected visitor. And we'll make sure he sees what we're all about." He even managed a small, genuine smile. "Maybe he'll even be impressed. Or at least, he'll have to admit that our 'quaint little endeavor' is a lot more successful than he anticipated."

Mara returned his smile, her eyes twinkling. "That's the spirit. Now, come on. We've got a festival to open. And who knows? Maybe David will surprise us all."

Eli doubted it, but he appreciated Mara's optimism. He knew, with a certainty that chilled him to the bone, that David Thorne's visit was not going to be a simple, fleeting stop. The past, it seemed, had a way of catching up, even in the most unexpected of places, and he had a feeling that this particular reunion was far from over. But for now, he would focus on the present, on the vibrant energy of the festival, and on the woman beside him, who was, as always, his unwavering strength. He took her hand, their fingers intertwining, and together, they turned back to the growing throng of eager attendees, ready to welcome them to a day of celebration, purpose, and undeniable community spirit. David Thorne's arrival had cast a shadow, but it was a shadow that wouldn't be allowed to extinguish the sunlight.

Mara's Intuition

The cacophony of the festival was a living, breathing entity, a joyous symphony composed of laughter, music, and the happy chatter of a community coming together. Stalls brimmed with handcrafted treasures and the tantalizing aroma of local delicacies, each vendor a testament to the vibrant spirit of Port Blossom. Children, their faces painted with whimsical designs, darted between the legs of adults, their excitement a palpable force. Mara, as she had done countless times before, found herself swept up in the exhilarating energy, her attention split between ensuring the smooth flow of the event and soaking in the infectious good cheer.

Yet, amidst the delightful chaos, a subtle thread of disquiet began to weave its way through Mara's awareness. It wasn't a tangible disturbance, no misplaced item or minor squabble. It was a feeling, a quiet hum beneath the surface of Eli's usual calm, a tension that seemed to emanate from him in almost imperceptible waves. She'd seen him on countless event days, witnessed his quiet competence, his steady hand guiding everything from setup to breakdown. But today, there was a subtle difference, a flicker in his eyes that was more than just the usual pre-event jitters.

From her vantage point near the information booth, where she was helping a young volunteer organize the festival map, Mara found her gaze drifting towards Eli. He was engaged in conversation with Mrs. Gable, discussing the placement of the antique quilt display, his smile polite and engaging. But then, his eyes, as if drawn by an invisible current, flickered in her direction. For a fleeting moment, their eyes met, and Mara saw it – a peculiar mix of excitement and a gnawing anxiety, a vulnerability that belied his outwardly composed demeanor. It was a look that tugged at her heart, a silent question she couldn't quite decipher.

He looked away quickly, a faint blush tinging his cheeks, and turned his attention back to Mrs. Gable, his voice a little too even. Mara's brow furrowed. It wasn't just the usual stress of a large gathering. This felt... different. More personal. She'd noticed him stealing glances at her throughout the morning, brief, almost furtive looks that held a depth of emotion he wasn't articulating. It reminded her of the way he used to look at her when he was about to broach a difficult topic, or when he was wrestling with a decision he knew would impact them both.

Could it be David's arrival? It was certainly a seismic event, a ghost from Eli's past materializing at their doorstep on one of their most important days. The tension of that encounter had been thick enough to cut with a knife, and Mara had felt the ripple effect of it in Eli. He'd been visibly shaken, and though he'd put on a brave face, she knew his brother's presence was a significant disruption. David Thorne was a force, a stark embodiment of a world so different from the one Eli had so painstakingly built here in Port Blossom.

But as she continued to observe Eli, even from a distance, Mara sensed that David was only part of the equation. There was something else, something simmering beneath the surface, an internal narrative playing out within him. He seemed to be constantly assessing the crowd, not just for logistical purposes, but as if searching for something, or perhaps, trying to prove something. He'd spoken to her before David's arrival about his desire for the festival to be a resounding success, a testament to the Sanctuary's vital work and the community's unwavering support. And now, with David watching, the stakes felt exponentially higher for Eli.

Mara excused herself from Mrs. Gable, her mind already formulating a plan. She needed to check on the volunteers at the craft tent and ensure the face-painting station was adequately stocked. But her path naturally led her towards the main stage area, where Eli was now overseeing the final checks on the sound system. As she approached, she saw him pause, his hand hovering over a cable, his gaze once again drifting towards her. This time, the look was more prolonged, a silent confession of unspoken thoughts.

"Everything alright over here, Eli?" she asked, her voice deliberately light, a gentle probe.

He started slightly, as if pulled from a deep reverie. "Yeah, Mara. Perfect. Just making sure everything's humming along." He gestured towards the stage, a broad, confident sweep of his hand that didn't quite reach his eyes. "The band's ready, the sound's good. We're all set."

She stepped closer, her eyes scanning his face. The lines around his eyes seemed a little deeper today, and there was a faint tremor in his jaw that he was trying to mask. "You seem a little... on edge," she observed softly, her gaze unwavering. "More than usual for festival day."

Eli offered a small, self-deprecating laugh, but it sounded hollow. "Just the usual butterflies, you know. Big turnout today. Want to make sure it's all perfect for everyone." He avoided her gaze, busying himself with straightening a microphone stand. "Especially with... with David here."

The mention of his brother hung in the air, a tangible weight. "He's making you nervous," Mara stated, not as a question, but as a gentle acknowledgement.

Eli sighed, finally meeting her eyes. The anxiety was still there, but now, mixed with a flicker of something else – a raw honesty. "He's always... critical. He sees everything I do through a lens of judgment. And today, with him watching, it feels like... I don't know. Like I have to prove something. Not just to him, but to myself, I guess." He rubbed the back of his neck, a familiar gesture of his unease. "He thinks this is all some kind of fanciful hobby. He doesn't understand the passion, the dedication it takes. He doesn't understand *us*."

Mara's heart ached for him. She knew how much this festival, and the Sanctuary, meant to Eli. It was his life's work, his passion, his sanctuary. And for his brother, the one person from his past who represented everything he had rejected, to be here, witnessing it all with what Eli perceived as disdain, was undoubtedly a heavy burden.

"He can't understand," Mara said, her voice firm and reassuring. "Because he's not looking with the right eyes. He's looking for profit margins and tangible returns, like he told me. He doesn't see the value of what we're doing here. He doesn't see the community, the hope, the lives we're saving." She reached out, her hand finding his, her touch grounding him. "And you don't have to prove anything to him, Eli. You've already proven it to me. You've proven it to everyone here who believes in this place."

Eli's fingers tightened around hers. The touch seemed to anchor him, to pull him back from the brink of his anxiety. He looked at her, his eyes filled with a deep gratitude that spoke volumes. "I know," he murmured. "But it's hard not to let it get under my skin. Especially when he's standing right there, questioning everything."

"Let him question," Mara said, her gaze steady. "We'll answer him with our actions. With the success of this festival. With the gratitude of every creature we help. That's our answer, Eli. And it's a damn good one." She squeezed his hand, a silent promise of unwavering support. "Besides," she added with a playful wink, "maybe he'll surprise us. Maybe he'll see the magic, too."

Eli managed a genuine smile this time, the tension in his shoulders visibly easing. "I doubt it," he said, but his voice lacked the edge of his earlier apprehension. "But I appreciate you saying it. And I appreciate you." He paused, his gaze lingering on her, a warmth spreading through him that had nothing to do with the summer sun. "You're the reason I can even do this, you know. You're my anchor."

Mara's heart swelled at his words. It was moments like these, these quiet acknowledgments of their shared journey, that solidified their bond. "We're each other's anchors, Eli," she replied softly. "And we're doing this together." She released his hand, a sense of purpose settling over her. "Now, come on. We have a festival to run. And I think the kettle corn stand is about to run out of its first batch."

As they walked away, Mara kept a subtle eye on Eli. He was still glancing towards David's general direction every so often, but the anxiety had subsided, replaced by a quiet determination. The nervousness hadn't entirely vanished, she suspected, but it was no longer the dominant emotion. Her intuition told her that Eli's internal struggle was far from over, that David's presence would continue to cast a long shadow. But it also told her that Eli was stronger than he gave himself credit for, and that together, they could weather any storm, even one brewed by the complicated dynamics of his past. She couldn't shake the feeling that this festival, this seemingly joyous occasion, was also a subtle turning point, a test of Eli's resolve, and she was ready to stand by him, every step of the way. The festival was in full swing, and while David Thorne was a knot in the tapestry of the day, Mara knew that Eli's strength, and their shared commitment, would ultimately prevail.

The afternoon sun, once a vibrant blaze, had softened into a warm, honeyed glow, casting long shadows across the festival grounds. The initial rush of attendees had ebbed, leaving a gentler hum of activity. Families strolled, children chased stray balloons, and the aroma of kettle corn and grilled onions hung pleasantly in the air. It was a moment of comfortable reprieve, a breath between the morning's energetic opening and the evening's anticipated music performance. Eli, having just finished a quick debrief with the volunteers at the petting zoo, found himself lingering near the edge of the bustling marketplace, observing the contented flow of the crowd. He was taking a moment to appreciate the tangible success of the day, the palpable joy that permeated the air – a testament, he felt, to the hard work of everyone involved.

It was then that he noticed David. Not the boisterous, dismissive David he'd braced himself to face, but a David who stood slightly apart from the throng, his gaze fixed not on the stalls or the games, but on the makeshift enclosure where the rescued puppies tumbled and played. There was a stillness about him, an uncharacteristic pensiveness that Eli found disarming. He hadn't sought out Eli since their tense arrival earlier that morning, and Eli, caught between apprehension and a grudging curiosity, hadn't approached him either.

As if sensing Eli's gaze, David turned. His expression wasn't the usual smug confidence or veiled disdain. Instead, Eli saw a flicker of something akin to... regret? He hesitated, then began to walk towards him, his movements deliberate, not hurried.

The festival's soundtrack, a cheerful medley of folk music and distant laughter, seemed to recede, leaving a pocket of quiet anticipation between them.

"Eli," David said, his voice softer than Eli remembered, devoid of its usual sharp edge. He stopped a few feet away, his hands clasped loosely in front of him.

Eli braced himself, a familiar knot of defensiveness tightening in his stomach. "David. Enjoying the... spectacle?" He couldn't keep the sarcasm entirely out of his tone.

David's gaze drifted back to the puppies, a faint smile touching his lips. "They're remarkable," he said, his voice laced with a genuine warmth that surprised Eli. "The way they're being cared for, the sheer amount of work... it's impressive. More than I expected."

This was a new tack. Eli remained guarded. "It's what we do here."

David finally met Eli's eyes, and the sincerity there was unmistakable. "Eli, I... I owe you an apology."

The words hung in the air, heavy with years of unspoken grievances. Eli blinked, taken aback. An apology? From David? It felt as foreign as a blizzard in July. "An apology for what, exactly?" Eli asked, his voice carefully neutral, though his mind raced through a litany of past offenses.

"For... everything," David said, his shoulders slumping slightly. "For the way I've dismissed your choices. For the way I've belittled what you've built here. For not understanding, not even trying to understand." He took a deep breath. "I came here with a preconceived notion of who you were, what you were doing. I saw your life in Port Blossom as a retreat, a failure to launch, compared to my own path." He looked directly at Eli, his eyes clear and steady. "I was wrong. Terribly wrong."

Eli felt a strange unclenching within him. The years of feeling inadequate, of feeling judged by his successful, driven brother, had taken their toll. Hearing David admit fault, seeing him vulnerable, was disarming. "You always thought this was a waste of time," Eli said, the old hurt surfacing, but with less bite.

"I did," David admitted without hesitation. "And that was my blindness. I was so caught up in my own world, my own definition of success, that I couldn't see the value in yours. Not just the rescue, Eli, though that's a monumental achievement in itself. But the community you've fostered. The genuine happiness I see on people's faces. The purpose that shines through everything you do." He gestured vaguely at the vibrant scene around them. "This isn't a retreat, Eli. This is a foundation. A damn strong one."

Eli listened, a profound sense of disbelief warring with a burgeoning sense of relief. He searched David's face for any hint of insincerity, any glint of his old condescension, but found none. There was only a quiet earnestness, a raw honesty that resonated deep within him.

"I've been doing a lot of thinking, lately," David continued, his gaze sweeping across the festival. "More than I probably ever have in my life. My own path... it's been successful, by all outward measures. But it's also been... hollow. Lacking something. And watching you, seeing the passion and the dedication you pour into this, seeing the tangible good you're doing... it's made me re-evaluate a lot of things." He met Eli's gaze again. "I don't expect you to forget the past, Eli. I know I've hurt you. But I want to try. I want to understand. And I want to be a brother to you, not just a judgmental shadow."

The air between them, once charged with unspoken animosity, now felt lighter, filled with the potential for something new. Eli found himself taking a step closer, the defensiveness he'd carried for so long beginning to crumble. "I... I don't know what to say, David. I wasn't expecting this."

"I know," David said, a small, almost sheepish smile playing on his lips. "And I'm not asking for instant forgiveness. Just... an opening. A chance." He looked at the rescued animals again. "This place, the Sanctuary, it's a testament to your character, Eli. To your resilience. And I'm... I'm proud of you. Genuinely proud."

The word 'proud' landed with an unexpected weight. Eli had craved that acknowledgement from his brother for years, and to hear it now, in this setting, amidst the vibrant chaos of the festival, felt surreal. It was a balm to a wound he hadn't realized was still so raw.

"Thank you, David," Eli said, his voice thick with emotion. He felt a lump form in his throat, and he swallowed hard. "That... that means a lot."

David nodded, his expression softening further. "I've been observing, too. Watching how you interact with people, how you handle the challenges. You've got a strength that I always underestimated. And Mara... she's a remarkable woman. You two... you're a team. A good one."

The mention of Mara brought a warmth to Eli's chest. He glanced towards the main stage, where Mara was now coordinating with the band's lead singer, her usual grace and efficiency on full display. To hear David acknowledge their partnership, and to do so with apparent respect, was another significant hurdle cleared.

"She is," Eli agreed, a genuine smile finally breaking through. "She's everything."

"I can see that," David replied. He paused, then extended his hand. "So, is this the beginning of... not being estranged brothers?"

Eli looked at David's outstretched hand, a symbol of reconciliation offered amidst the joyous celebration of life and second chances. He hesitated for only a moment before reaching out and clasping it firmly. The handshake was solid, the connection immediate and surprisingly comforting.

"I hope so, David," Eli said, meeting his brother's gaze. "I really hope so."

As they stood there, hands clasped, the sounds of the festival swelling around them – the laughter of children, the strumming of a guitar, the happy barks of a newly adopted terrier being carried away by its beaming new owners – something shifted. The years of bitterness, the resentment, the distance, began to dissipate, replaced by a fragile sense of hope. David's apology, so sincere and unexpected, had not only begun to mend old wounds but had also eased the burden Eli had been carrying, the pressure to prove himself to his brother. It was a moment of profound connection, forged in the heart of the very community Eli had dedicated himself to building, a testament to the power of second chances and the enduring strength of family, even when it had been broken. The festival, it seemed, was not just about celebrating the rescued animals; it was also about the unexpected healing that could bloom in the most unlikely of circumstances.

The sky was a canvas of deepening hues, the fiery oranges and soft purples of sunset bleeding into one another, painting a breathtaking panorama over the ocean. The festival, once a vibrant, buzzing hive of activity, was now settling into a contented twilight. The air, still carrying the sweet scent of kettle corn and the distant echo of music, was infused with a sense of peaceful closure. Families, their faces flushed with the day's enjoyment, began to drift towards the exits, their laughter softening into fond farewells. Children, their energy finally waning, were being cradled in tired arms, their eyes heavy with the day's adventures.

Eli stood on a gentle rise overlooking the expanse of the festival grounds, Mara's hand warm and secure in his. The press of the crowd had receded, leaving them in a pocket of quiet intimacy. He felt it then, a profound sense of rightness settling deep within him, a quiet joy that resonated with the very soul of the day. It wasn't just the palpable success of the festival, the record number of adoptions, the overwhelming generosity of the community, or the unexpected, heartfelt reconciliation with his brother, David. It was Mara, standing beside him, her presence a constant, steady warmth. He looked at her, really looked at her, and saw not just the woman he loved, but the embodiment of everything good that had come into his life. Her smile, still present from a shared joke with a departing volunteer, was radiant, her eyes reflecting the fading light of the sun and the promise of the stars.

He felt a familiar flutter in his chest, a nervous excitement that had been building all day, a quiet anticipation that had been simmering beneath the surface of every interaction, every successful moment. It was more than just a good day; it was a turning point. The Sanctuary was thriving, his family ties were strengthening, and Mara... Mara was his anchor, his confidante, his everything. This felt like the culmination of everything he had worked for, everything he had hoped for, and it was all happening in this perfect moment.

He squeezed her hand, a silent question in his touch. Mara turned to him, her brow furrowing slightly in a question of her own. "Everything okay?" she asked, her voice soft, a gentle melody against the murmur of the receding crowd.

Eli's smile widened, a genuine, unrestrained beam that reached his eyes. "More than okay, Mara," he said, his voice a little rough with emotion. He started to lead her away from the main thoroughfare, away from the lingering pockets of festival-goers, towards a more secluded spot on the edge of the grounds. They walked in comfortable silence, the crunch of gravel beneath their feet the only sound accompanying the gentle sigh of the ocean in the distance.

They found their way to a small, grassy knoll that offered a spectacular, unobstructed view of the sea. The last rays of the sun kissed the waves, turning them into shimmering paths of liquid gold. The air here was cooler, carrying the crisp, salty tang of the ocean, a refreshing contrast to the mingled scents of food and excitement that still clung to the air closer to the festival. He could hear the rhythmic lullaby of the waves, a soothing balm to his racing heart. It was a place of quiet solitude, a world away from the joyful chaos of the festival, yet intrinsically connected to its spirit of renewal and hope.

Eli turned to face Mara fully, releasing her hand only to gently cup her face. Her skin was warm beneath his touch, her eyes wide and questioning, yet filled with an unspoken trust. He saw a flicker of surprise, then a dawning realization, in her gaze. He had planned this, had anticipated this moment for weeks, but now, standing here, with her looking at him, he felt a surge of overwhelming emotion that threatened to steal his breath.

"Mara," he began, his voice hushed, as if he were afraid of breaking the spell of the evening. "This day... it's been... everything I hoped it would be. The festival, the Sanctuary... it's all going so well. And then there's you." He paused, searching her eyes, wanting to convey the depth of his feelings without faltering. "You've been... you are... the most incredible part of it all. You make everything brighter, stronger. You make me... better."

He took a deep breath, the salty air filling his lungs, steadying him. He could feel her heart beating beneath her thin sweater, a frantic echo of his own. He saw a hint of tears welling in her eyes, and it spurred him on. "I can't imagine my life without you, Mara. You've brought so much joy, so much purpose, so much love into my world. And today, seeing everything come together, seeing David... seeing him

see what we've built... it's made me realize something very clearly."

He lowered his hands from her face, stepping back slightly, his gaze never leaving hers. The anticipation in the air was palpable, a tangible force that seemed to hum between them. He reached into his back pocket, his fingers fumbling slightly with the worn velvet of a small box. As he pulled it out, the subtle glint of metal caught the last vestiges of sunlight.

Mara's breath hitched, her hands flying to her mouth. Her eyes widened, filling with unshed tears that now shimmered like fallen stars. The world around them seemed to fade into a soft blur. The sounds of the festival, the distant laughter, the gentle roar of the waves, all receded, leaving only the thunder of his own heartbeat and the soft, hopeful sound of Mara's ragged breath.

"Mara," Eli said again, his voice barely above a whisper, his own emotions threatening to overwhelm him. He knelt down before her, the damp grass cool beneath his knees. He opened the box, revealing a delicate, antique-inspired ring, its simple diamond catching the light and throwing tiny rainbows against the darkening sky. "Will you... will you marry me?"

He held his breath, his gaze fixed on her face, every atom of his being focused on this single, monumental question. The silence stretched, filled only by the symphony of the sea and the frantic beating of his own heart. He watched as a single tear escaped Mara's eye, then another, tracing glistening paths down her cheeks. A slow, radiant smile spread across her face, a smile that encompassed all the joy, all the love, all the hope that had bloomed between them.

She didn't speak for a long moment, and in that sliver of time, Eli's heart performed a series of frantic acrobatics, a whirlwind of hope and fear. But then, she nodded, her entire body trembling with emotion. And then, finally, her voice, thick with tears and unshed joy, broke the silence.

"Yes," she whispered, her voice choked with feeling. "Oh, Eli, yes!"

Her "yes" was a cascade of pure emotion, a sound that resonated through him, washing away years of doubt, years of striving, years of quiet longing. He stood, pulling her into his arms, holding her tightly as if he would never let go. Her tears dampened his shirt, but he didn't care. They were tears of happiness, of profound love, of a future unfolding before them.

He felt her arms tighten around him, her face buried against his chest. Her muffled sobs were sounds of pure relief and overwhelming joy. He held her, rocking her gently, murmuring reassurances, his own voice thick with emotion. The setting sun cast a warm, golden glow over them, a celestial spotlight on their shared moment of profound happiness. The festival, a testament to second chances and enduring love for animals, had become the backdrop for their own beautiful, blossoming future. The quiet knoll overlooking the sea, bathed in the soft twilight, was now etched in his memory as the place where his greatest dream had come true. He knew, with an absolute certainty that settled deep in his soul, that this was not just the perfect moment; it was the beginning of their forever. The journey they had taken to get here had been filled with challenges, with moments of doubt and uncertainty, but looking at Mara, feeling her in his arms, he knew that every step had been worth it. He had found his home, not in a place, but in her. And as the first stars began to prick the darkening sky, he felt a profound sense of peace, a deep contentment that promised a lifetime of shared sunsets, quiet mornings, and unwavering love. This was more than a proposal; it was a promise, a declaration, a testament to the enduring power of love to heal, to build, and to create something truly extraordinary. He kissed the top of her head, breathing in the scent of her hair, a scent that was now inextricably linked with the intoxicating aroma of the sea and the sweet promise of their shared future. The festival was winding down, but their own celebration was just beginning.

CHAPTER NINE
A Promise by the Sea

The gentle caress of the sea breeze whispered secrets through Mara's hair as she clung to Eli, her heart still doing a joyous, frantic dance against his. The echo of her "yes" seemed to hang in the twilight air, a sweet melody that intertwined with the rhythmic lullaby of the waves. Eli's arms were a sanctuary, a comforting embrace that spoke of security and a love so profound it felt like coming home. He held her as if he'd never let go, and in that moment, she knew he wouldn't. The soft glow of the lanterns from the receding festival grounds cast a warm, golden hue, painting them as the sole focus in a world that had suddenly narrowed to just the two of them. It was a moment suspended in time, a perfect, breathtaking culmination of everything they had ever hoped for.

Eli finally pulled back, his hands still cradling her face, his thumb gently tracing the path of a tear that had escaped her eye. His own eyes, pools of deep affection, were fixed on hers, reflecting the nascent stars that were beginning to pepper the darkening sky. "Mara," he began, his voice a low rumble, laced with an emotion that resonated deep within her soul. "Look at us. Right here. Right now."

He drew a deep, steadying breath, the salty air filling his lungs and anchoring him to the present. "I've replayed this moment a thousand times in my head," he confessed, a shy smile playing on his lips. "Planned it, dreamed it, worried myself sick over it. But you... you always manage to make even my most elaborate fantasies pale in comparison to the reality of being with you."

He guided her hand, his own palm warm and solid against hers, and led her a few steps away from the grassy knoll, towards the edge of the bluff where the ocean stretched out before them, a vast, inky expanse meeting the horizon. The sound of the waves crashing against the rocks below was a powerful, constant presence, a reminder of the enduring, untamed beauty of nature, a beauty that mirrored the wild, exhilarating love that had bloomed between them.

"Remember our first meeting?" Eli's voice was soft, nostalgic, as if he were conjuring the memory for both of them to share. "At the old animal shelter, before the Sanctuary was even a whisper of a dream. You were wrestling with that enormous, slobbery Newfoundland, trying to get him into his kennel, and he was having none of it. Covered in drool, looking completely exasperated, but your eyes... they were so full of kindness, even when you were practically being flattened by his enthusiasm."

Mara laughed, a soft, delighted sound. "He was a gentle giant, just misunderstood. And you, you walked in, all quiet confidence and ready to help, and I thought you were the most handsome man I'd ever seen, even with your jeans splattered with God knows what."

"And you," Eli countered, his gaze unwavering, "were a force of nature. A whirlwind of compassion and determination. I knew then, even before I knew, that you were something extraordinary. That you were someone I wanted to keep close."

He squeezed her hand, pulling her gently closer. "And then there were the late nights, weren't there? The ones spent poring over blueprints, debating paint colors for the veterinary clinic, dreaming up fundraising events. The exhaustion, the setbacks, the moments when it felt like we were drowning in paperwork and unanswered emails. But through it all, you were there. Your unwavering belief, your steady calm, your ability to find the humor in even the most stressful situations."

He paused, his gaze sweeping across the darkening seascape. "I remember one particular night, after a disastrous grant application that had been rejected. We were sitting here, on this very bluff, feeling utterly defeated. The wind was howling, and the rain was coming down in sheets. I thought we were going to have to give up. But you... you just looked out at the ocean, and you said, 'The tide always turns, Eli. We just have to wait for it to turn in our favor.' And you were right, weren't you?"

Mara leaned her head on his shoulder, a contented sigh escaping her lips. "We always found a way. Together."

"Together," Eli echoed, the word a sweet affirmation. He tilted her chin up, his eyes searching hers with an intensity that made her breath catch. "And it wasn't just about the Sanctuary, was it? It was about us. About building something that was ours. Remember the day we rescued that litter of abandoned kittens from the old abandoned barn? So tiny, so vulnerable. We stayed up all night, feeding them with droppers, keeping them warm. You held one, no bigger than my hand, against your chest, and you whispered to it, 'You're safe now, little one. You're loved.' That was it, Mara. That was the moment I knew for certain that my place was by your side, protecting you, loving you, building a future with you."

He stepped back, his hand moving slowly to his back pocket. The worn velvet of a small box, familiar and yet thrillingly new, emerged. The soft twilight caught the subtle glint of metal as he pulled it free.

Mara's heart leaped into her throat. She knew. She *felt* it, a seismic shift in the atmosphere, a prelude to a moment she had dreamed of, a moment she had dared to hope for. The world around them seemed to hold its breath, the sea's roar softening to a hushed murmur, the wind its gentle sigh.

Eli's hand trembled as he opened the box. Inside, nestled against dark velvet, lay a ring. It was exquisite, a delicate band of rose gold, its intricate filigree work reminiscent of the sea's delicate patterns. At its center, a small, pear-shaped diamond, cut to capture and refract light, sparkled with a soft, ethereal glow, like a captured moonbeam. It was perfectly Mara, understated yet captivating, a reflection of her own quiet strength and inner radiance.

"Mara Ellison," Eli began, his voice thick with unshed emotion, cracking just slightly. He knelt before her, the damp grass cool beneath his knees, his gaze never leaving her face, his eyes shining with a love so pure it brought tears to her own. "You are the kindest, the most compassionate, the most determined woman I have ever known. You've filled my life with laughter, with purpose, with a love I never thought I deserved. You are my anchor, my confidante, my best friend. You make every single day brighter, and every challenge easier to face. You are, quite simply, my everything."

He held the ring out, the delicate diamond catching the last sliver of the setting sun. "I can't imagine a single day without you by my side. I want to wake up next to you every morning, to share every sunrise and every sunset with you. I want to build a lifetime of memories with you, of rescue missions and quiet evenings, of adventures and of simply being together. You've already given me so much, more than I could ever ask for. But there's one more thing I need from you. One thing that will make my life complete."

He met her tear-filled gaze, his own eyes glistening. "Mara, will you marry me?"

The question hung in the air, suspended between the sky and the sea, between the past and their shared future. Mara felt a wave of overwhelming emotion wash over her, so potent it threatened to sweep her off her feet. She saw not just Eli, the man she loved with every fiber of her being, but the culmination of all their shared dreams, the promise of a future built on a foundation of unwavering love and mutual respect. She saw their life together, a tapestry woven with threads of compassion, resilience, and an abiding joy.

A sob, born of pure, unadulterated happiness, escaped her lips. She nodded, unable to speak, her throat tight with emotion. Eli's breath hitched, his gaze fixed on her, his hope palpable. Then, with a watery smile, Mara found her voice, her whisper carrying on the ocean breeze.

"Yes," she breathed, the word a soft exhalation of pure, unadulterated joy. "Oh, Eli, yes! A thousand times, yes!"

The world exploded into color and sound for Mara. Eli surged to his feet, pulling her into a fierce embrace. She melted into him, her arms wrapping around his neck, her face buried in his shoulder, the scent of him, of salt and of the sea, and of pure, unadulterated love, filling her senses. Her tears, no longer tears of trepidation but of overwhelming happiness, soaked his shirt, and he held her just as tightly, murmuring reassurances, his own voice thick with emotion. The ring, a tangible symbol of their commitment, was still clutched in Eli's hand, waiting for its rightful place on her finger. The golden light of the setting sun bathed them in its warm embrace, a celestial benediction on their profound moment of connection.

The festival's happy conclusion had ushered in the beginning of their own extraordinary story, a story etched in the sand, whispered by the waves, and sealed with a promise by the sea.

The words tumbled out of Eli, each syllable a carefully chosen testament to their shared journey, and Mara felt a cascade of emotions wash over her. Her vision blurred, not from sadness, but from a happiness so profound it felt like a physical force, pushing against the very edges of her being. She saw it all in those fleeting moments: the hesitant first glances, the awkward conversations, the shared dreams that had slowly, steadily, woven themselves into the fabric of their lives. She saw the late nights fueled by coffee and unwavering optimism, the moments of doubt that had flickered but never truly ignited into despair, because Eli had always been there, a steady beacon. Her own journey, from the quiet skepticism that had once clouded her heart to this absolute, undeniable certainty, felt like a miracle. She had entered Port Blossom with a fragile hope, a need to prove herself, and she was leaving, or rather, embarking on a new chapter, with a love that was as vast and encompassing as the ocean stretching before them.

The memory of her initial reservations, the quiet anxieties that had whispered doubts in the dark, now seemed like distant echoes from another lifetime. She had worried about her place, about whether she truly belonged, about the possibility of being swept away by a love that felt too big, too brilliant. But Eli, with his quiet strength and his boundless compassion, had not only met her fears but had gently, irrevocably, dismantled them. He had seen her, truly seen her, past the defenses she had unknowingly erected, and had loved her for the person she was, not for the person she thought she should be. His gaze, right now, was a mirror reflecting back to her a self she had only dared to dream of: loved, cherished, and utterly, blissfully accepted.

And then, the question. "Mara, will you marry me?" It wasn't just a question; it was an anchor, a promise, a declaration of a future built together. The simplicity of his words belied the immense weight of their meaning. The world seemed to tilt on its axis, and in that glorious, breathtaking moment, there was no past, no future, only the exhilarating, vibrant present. The air crackled with unspoken emotions, a symphony of their intertwined destinies. Her heart, which had been performing a frantic drum solo against her ribs, now settled into a rhythm of pure, unadulterated joy. She could feel the tremor in his hand as he held the ring box, a testament to his own vulnerability and the depth of his feelings. It was a silent plea, a desperate hope, and she wanted nothing more than to grant him that joy.

"Yes," she whispered, the word barely a breath, yet it carried the weight of every joy, every shared laughter, every tender touch, every quiet moment of understanding that had led them to this precipice. It was a sound born from the deepest wellspring of her soul, a sound that resonated with the truth of her heart. But a whisper felt too small, too fragile for the magnitude of what she was feeling. She needed him to hear it, to feel it, to know the absolute certainty that had settled within her. Her throat tightened, not with fear, but with an overwhelming sense of gratitude and love. She found her voice again, stronger this time, imbued with a conviction that echoed across the twilight sea.

"Oh, Eli," she breathed, the endearment a soft caress. "Yes! A thousand times, yes!" The words burst from her, a joyous release, a tidal wave of affirmation that swept away any lingering vestiges of doubt. She saw his breath hitch, his eyes widen, and a slow, radiant smile spread across his face, a smile that mirrored the dawning of a new day. It was a smile that held the promise of all the tomorrows they would share, a smile that spoke of a love that had found its home. She didn't wait for him to move; she surged forward, her own feet carrying her into his arms, into the sanctuary of his embrace.

Her arms wrapped around his neck, pulling him close, her body molding against his as if they were two pieces finally reunited. She buried her face in his shoulder, inhaling his scent – the clean, invigorating aroma of the sea, the subtle warmth of his skin, and something else, something uniquely Eli, a scent that was as comforting as a familiar lullaby and as exhilarating as a first kiss. Tears, unchecked and unrestrained, streamed down her face, dampening his shirt, but they were tears of pure, unadulterated happiness. Each one was a tiny pearl of joy, a testament to the love that had blossomed between them. He held her just as tightly, his arms a strong, protective circle around her, murmuring soft, reassuring words against her hair. His voice, usually so steady, was thick with emotion, a mirror of her own overwhelming feelings.

"You're crying," he murmured, his voice rough with a tenderness that made her heart ache in the best possible way.

She pulled back just enough to look at him, her eyes shining with unshed tears. "Of course, I am," she managed, her voice still a little shaky. "This is... this is everything, Eli. Everything I've ever wanted." She reached up, her fingers tracing the curve of his jaw, feeling the slight stubble, the warmth of his skin. "I love you so much," she whispered, the words inadequate, yet spoken with every fiber of her being.

His hand came up to cup her cheek, his thumb gently brushing away a stray tear. His gaze was unwavering, filled with a love so deep, so pure, it stole her breath. "And I love you, Mara. More than words can say. More than I ever thought possible." He shifted slightly, his hand moving to his back pocket. The small velvet box, the vessel of their future, was still clutched in his other hand. He opened it again, the delicate rose gold ring catching the last vestiges of the twilight.

With a gentle movement, he guided her left hand, his own hand trembling slightly as he slid the ring onto her finger. It was a perfect fit, a seamless union of metal and skin, of promise and commitment. The small, pear-shaped diamond seemed to capture the dying light, casting a soft, ethereal glow that illuminated her hand, her face, their shared moment. It was more than just a piece of jewelry; it was a tangible symbol of their bond, a whispered promise of forever. She turned her hand over, admiring the way the light danced within the facets of the stone, a tiny beacon of their love.

"It's beautiful, Eli," she whispered, her voice choked with emotion. "It's perfect."

"You are perfect, Mara," he said, his voice a low, resonant rumble that vibrated through her. He pulled her back into his embrace, holding her close, their bodies fitting together as if they had been made for each other. The rhythmic sound of the waves crashing against the shore below seemed to underscore the profound peace that had settled within her. The festival's joyous conclusion had been a beautiful prelude, but this, this quiet moment by the sea, sealed with a promise and a ring, was the true beginning.

They stood there for a long time, simply holding each other, the silence between them filled with the unspoken language of love. The salty air caressed their faces, and the distant calls of seabirds seemed to echo the melody of their hearts. Mara felt a profound sense of contentment, a feeling of finally being home, of belonging. She thought of all the possibilities that lay before them, the adventures they would embark on, the challenges they would face, the quiet evenings spent simply being together. She pictured their life in Port Blossom, a life woven with the threads of their shared passions, a life dedicated to compassion, resilience, and an unwavering love.

Eli finally stirred, his lips brushing against her temple. "We should probably head back," he murmured, his voice laced with a reluctance to break the spell. "Your family will be wondering where we've disappeared to."

Mara nodded, a small smile playing on her lips. "Yes," she agreed, her voice soft but firm. "But first." She pulled back again, her eyes locking with his. She cupped his face in her hands, her gaze filled with an emotion so potent it made his breath catch. "Thank you, Eli. For seeing me. For loving me. For making me believe in forever."

He leaned into her touch, his eyes closing for a brief moment. "Thank you, Mara. For being you. For giving me a future I never dared to dream of." He opened his eyes, and the intensity of his gaze made her heart flutter. "I can't wait to start our life together, Mrs. Ellison."

The playful moniker sent a thrill through her. "And I can't wait either, Mr. Hayes," she replied, her voice laced with amusement and affection. She leaned in and kissed him, a soft, tender kiss that spoke of deep affection and the promise of more to come. It was a kiss that sealed their commitment, a kiss that tasted of the sea and of forever.

As they turned to walk back towards the gentle glow of the festival grounds, Mara's hand found Eli's, her fingers interlacing with his. The weight of the ring on her finger was a comforting presence, a constant reminder of the promise they had made. The path ahead was unknown, full of the uncertainties of life, but with Eli by her side, she felt ready for anything. The joy that had blossomed in her heart was a vibrant, unyielding force, a testament to the enduring power of love, a love that had found its true home by the sea, under the watchful gaze of the stars. Port Blossom, once a town of tentative beginnings, now felt like the beginning of everything. The sea breeze, which had once whispered secrets of doubt, now carried on its currents the sweet, joyous melody of their shared future.

The lingering magic of the proposal still hummed beneath Mara's skin as she turned, hand clasped securely in Eli's, back towards the twinkling lights of the Port Blossom festival. The salty air, once a whisper of uncertainty, now felt like a celebration carried on the breeze, a joyful current guiding them back to their waiting loved ones. Each step was lighter, infused with a giddy joy that threatened to bubble over into spontaneous laughter. The ring on her finger, a cool, beautiful weight, was a constant, thrilling reminder of the words spoken, the promise made, the future stretching out before them, vast and luminous as the sea itself. Eli's thumb brushed against her knuckles as they walked, a silent reassurance, a testament to the solid, unwavering ground they now shared.

As they neared the heart of the festival, the cheerful din of music and conversation grew louder, a symphony of Port Blossom's vibrant spirit. Faces turned towards them, illuminated by the warm glow of lanterns and the camaraderie of a community celebrating. A collective murmur rippled through the crowd, growing into a wave of recognition as they saw the radiant smiles on Mara and Eli's faces, the unmistakable glow of newfound happiness. Then, it erupted. A spontaneous eruption of cheers, applause, and delighted exclamations. It wasn't a planned announcement, but the sheer, palpable joy radiating from the couple was infectious, a beacon that drew everyone in.

Mara's heart swelled, a little overwhelmed by the outpouring of affection. She saw familiar faces – Mrs. Gable, her eyes crinkled in a delighted smile, waving enthusiastically; the fishermen from the docks, their rough hands clapping together with gusto; the younger families, their children squealing with excitement. It felt like the entire town had been holding its breath, waiting for this moment, and now, it was finally here, a shared exhale of pure delight. Eli squeezed her hand, his own gaze sweeping over the jubilant faces, a warmth spreading through him that had nothing to do with the mild evening air. He met Mara's eyes, and in that shared glance, they understood that this joy wasn't just theirs; it belonged to Port Blossom too, a testament to the resilience and hope that had woven them all together.

And then, Mara saw him. Standing a little apart from the main throng, his hands tucked into his pockets, was David. For a moment, a flicker of apprehension tightened in her chest, a residual echo of the past. But as David's gaze met hers, it wasn't judgment or bitterness she saw. It was something far more profound, far more unexpected. A genuine smile, slow and sure, spread across his face. It was a smile of acceptance, of peace, and as he stepped forward, his hand reaching out to clap Eli firmly on the shoulder, Mara felt a significant weight lift from her own shoulders. It was more than just a friendly gesture; it was an olive branch extended, a silent acknowledgment of a shared journey, and a true reconciliation. Eli turned, his smile widening as he clasped David's hand, the handshake firm and full of unspoken understanding. In that moment, the lingering shadows of past conflict dissolved, replaced by the bright, promising light of a united future.

The rest of the evening became a blur of shared happiness. Friends, old and new, flocked to them, offering heartfelt congratulations, tight hugs, and teasing whispers about wedding plans. Mara found herself recounting the proposal, her voice still tinged with disbelief and wonder, while Eli, ever the steady anchor, fielded questions with his characteristic warmth and humor. They were showered with well wishes, their engagement quickly becoming the talk of the festival, a joyous ripple spreading through the already celebratory atmosphere. It felt as though every single person in Port Blossom had played a part in their journey, from the initial uncertainty to this moment of pure bliss, and their collective joy amplified their own.

Old Man Hemlock, who had initially been so wary of Mara's arrival, hobbled over, his weathered face alight with a rare, toothy grin. "Well now, young lady," he rasped, his voice surprisingly strong, "looks like you've finally managed to reel in the best catch Port Blossom has to offer. Glad to see it. Truly glad." He patted Eli's arm, his touch surprisingly gentle. "You two," he declared to no one in particular, but to everyone nonetheless, "you're a good pair. A very good pair indeed."

Even the usually reserved Captain Thorne, the harbormaster, approached, his stern demeanor softening into a genuine smile. He offered Eli a firm handshake, his eyes twinkling. "Hayes, I always knew you had a good head on your shoulders, but this... this is exceptional. Congratulations to you both. May your voyages together be long and prosperous." His words, so carefully chosen and earnest, held a deeper meaning, a recognition of the profound commitment they were embarking upon.

The air thrummed with a collective sense of accomplishment and shared joy. The successful rescue mission, the rebuilding efforts, the quiet strength that had emerged from adversity – all of it seemed to culminate in this beautiful, spontaneous celebration of love and commitment. The festival, which had already been a vibrant testament to Port Blossom's spirit, took on a new dimension. It transformed from a celebration of resilience into a celebration of hope, of new beginnings, and of the enduring power of human connection. The music seemed to play a little louder, the laughter a little brighter, the stars above shining a little more brilliantly.

Someone – Mara couldn't quite recall who – started singing an old folk song about love and home, and soon, others joined in, their voices rising in a harmonious chorus that echoed across the bay. Lights from the fishing boats bobbing gently in the harbor winked like scattered diamonds, mirroring the constellation of emotions swirling within Mara. She looked at Eli, his face bathed in the warm glow of the lanterns, his eyes reflecting the same profound happiness that she felt. He leaned down and whispered something in her ear, a private jest about how they'd have to start planning a wedding, and she laughed, a clear, bell-like sound that seemed to weave itself into the tapestry of the night.

As the evening wore on, the spontaneous celebration began to wind down, not with a sudden stop, but with a gradual ebb, like the tide receding after a joyful high. People began to drift away, their faces still alight with the shared warmth, their goodbyes carrying promises of future visits and continued celebrations. Mara and Eli found themselves lingering near the water's edge, the gentle lapping of waves a soothing counterpoint to the day's emotional crescendo. They held each other close, the silence between them comfortable, filled with the unspoken language of their souls.

"I can't believe this is real," Mara murmured, resting her head against Eli's chest, listening to the steady beat of his heart. "It feels like a dream."

Eli's arm tightened around her. "It's real, Mara," he said, his voice a low, comforting rumble. "It's as real as the sand beneath our feet, as real as the salt in the air, as real as the love I have for you." He tilted her chin up, his gaze tender. "And it's just the beginning."

He spoke of their future, of building a life in Port Blossom, of the small cottage they'd talked about, of the possibility of a family, of the quiet mornings and the adventurous afternoons they would share. His words weren't grand pronouncements, but quiet promises, woven with the fabric of everyday life, yet they held the weight of forever. Mara listened, her heart overflowing, absorbing every word, every sentiment. She saw it all unfold in her mind's eye – the warmth of their shared hearth, the laughter echoing through their home, the quiet companionship of years lived side-by-side.

The earlier apprehension she'd felt about her place in Port Blossom had completely vanished, replaced by an unshakeable sense of belonging. This town, once a place of tentative beginnings, now felt like home, a place where her heart had found its anchor, its true north. The sea breeze, which had once whispered secrets of doubt and uncertainty, now carried on its currents the sweet, joyous melody of their shared future, a future sealed by a promise made by the sea, under the watchful gaze of the stars, and celebrated with the heart and soul of a town that had become their own.

"We should head back soon," Eli said, his voice laced with a gentle reluctance to break the spell. "Your family will be wondering."

Mara nodded, a small smile playing on her lips. "Yes," she agreed, her voice soft but firm. "But first." She pulled back slightly, her eyes locking with his. She cupped his face in her hands, her gaze filled with an emotion so potent it made his breath catch. "Thank you, Eli. For seeing me. For loving me. For making me believe in forever."

He leaned into her touch, his eyes closing for a brief moment. "Thank you, Mara. For being you. For giving me a future I never dared to dream of." He opened his eyes, and the intensity of his gaze made her heart flutter. "I can't wait to start our life together, Mrs. Ellison."

The playful moniker sent a thrill through her. "And I can't wait either, Mr. Hayes," she replied, her voice laced with amusement and affection. She leaned in and kissed him, a soft, tender kiss that spoke of deep affection and the promise of more to come. It was a kiss that sealed their commitment, a kiss that tasted of the sea and of forever. As they turned to walk back towards the gentle glow of the festival grounds, Mara's hand found Eli's, her fingers interlacing with his. The weight of the ring on her finger was a comforting presence, a constant reminder of the promise they had made. The path ahead was unknown, full of the uncertainties of life, but with Eli by her side, she felt ready for anything. The joy that had blossomed in her heart was a vibrant, unyielding force, a testament to the enduring power of love, a love that had found its true home by the sea, under the watchful gaze of the stars. Port Blossom, once a town of tentative beginnings, now felt like the beginning of everything.

The hum of the festival still resonated in the air, a cheerful echo of the momentous events of the evening, but as Mara and Eli walked hand-in-hand away from the main throng, a different kind of resonance settled between them. It was a quieter symphony, one played out in the subtle shifts of their posture, the gentle pressure of their clasped hands, the shared breaths that seemed to sync with the rhythm of the waves still a gentle murmur against the shore. The proposal, more than just a question and an answer, had been a pivot point, a definitive turn towards a future they had only dared to whisper about until now. The weight of the ring on Mara's finger was a tangible anchor, grounding her in a reality that felt both breathtakingly new and profoundly familiar. It was the weight of permanence, of a commitment that felt as deep and enduring as the ocean stretching out before them, a silent testament to the promise they had made not just to each other, but to the life they were now actively choosing to build.

Mara's gaze drifted from the twinkling lights of Port Blossom, her heart swelling with a feeling that transcended simple happiness. It was a profound sense of security, a deep, settling peace that had been elusive for so long. The years of uncertainty, of feeling adrift, of questioning her place in the world, seemed to recede with each receding wave. Here, with Eli, the uncertainty had dissolved, replaced by a quiet, unwavering conviction. This was home. This was where she belonged. The image of their future, once a hazy, aspirational vision, now coalesced into sharp, vivid detail. She saw the small cottage they'd discussed, the one with the sea-facing porch, bathed in the soft glow of morning light. She saw laughter filling its rooms, the comforting rhythm of everyday life, the quiet understanding that would pass between them without a single word. It wasn't a dream anymore; it was a meticulously crafted blueprint, laid out with love and intention, and she felt an overwhelming sense of fulfillment in having finally stepped onto the path that would lead them there. Eli's thumb traced a slow, reassuring circle on the back of her hand, and she felt a surge of gratitude for his steady presence, his unwavering belief in them. He had seen her, truly seen her, past the defenses she had built and the doubts she had harbored, and he had loved her anyway. More than that, he had chosen her, actively and with all his heart, and in that choice, she found a completeness she had never imagined possible.

Eli, too, felt a profound satisfaction bloom within him, a deep contentment that settled into the very marrow of his bones. It wasn't the thrill of a victory, or the relief of a burden lifted, but the quiet, powerful joy of having intentionally built something meaningful. His life, once a series of solitary endeavors, now had a center, a focal point around which everything else revolved. Mara was that center, the radiant sun around which his world now turned. He had always been a man who valued purpose, who sought to contribute, to build, to leave a positive mark. But now, his purpose was inextricably linked with Mara, with their shared future, with the creation of a life that was not just successful in the eyes of the world, but rich in love, in connection, in shared meaning. He thought of the challenges they had already navigated, the moments of doubt and fear, the quiet resilience they had shown individually and together. Each hurdle overcome had only served to strengthen their bond, to deepen their understanding of each other's strengths and vulnerabilities. It was a partnership forged in shared experience, tested by adversity, and now, solidified by an unshakeable love.

He felt a quiet pride in the life they were building, a life that was a testament to their commitment to each other, to their shared values, and to the enduring power of human connection. He had always believed in the importance of community, of finding a place to belong, and with Mara by his side, he knew they had found it in Port Blossom, in this vibrant, resilient town that had embraced them both.

Their understanding of each other had evolved into something far more profound than they could have ever anticipated. It was a language spoken not just in words, but in shared glances, in the comfortable silences, in the intuitive way they anticipated each other's needs. The honesty that had been the bedrock of their initial connection had deepened, allowing them to bare their souls to each other without fear of judgment. Mara knew Eli's quiet strength, the unwavering moral compass that guided him, and the gentle empathy that lay beneath his often-reserved exterior. She saw the passion that ignited him when he spoke of his work, of the sea, of their shared future, and it filled her with a quiet admiration. Eli, in turn, understood Mara's innate kindness, her fierce loyalty, and the creative spirit that had always burned brightly within her, even when circumstances had tried to dim its flame. He saw the depth of her emotions, the way she felt things with a rare intensity, and he cherished that about her, that vibrant aliveness that drew him in and held him captive. Their shared challenges had acted as a crucible, refining their connection, burning away any superficiality and leaving behind a core of unshakeable trust. He knew she would be his rock, his confidante, his greatest supporter, and she knew he would be hers.

He squeezed her hand, a gesture that sent a warm tremor through her. "You know," he said, his voice a low rumble that seemed to vibrate with contentment, "I used to think I had my life all figured out. That I had a clear path laid out before me." He chuckled softly, a sound of genuine amusement. "But it was all just... pieces. Scattered. It took you, Mara, to bring all those pieces together, to give them context, to make them make sense. You're the heart of it all." His words, so simple and direct, resonated deeply within her. She understood exactly what he meant. Her own life had felt like a collection of disparate experiences, a series of moments that didn't quite connect to form a cohesive whole. It was only through their relationship, through their shared dreams and their commitment to building a life together, that those fragments had coalesced into something solid, something meaningful, something that felt like her own.

"And you," Mara replied, her voice soft with emotion, her gaze locked on his, "you've given me a home. Not just a place, but a feeling. A sense of belonging that I've longed for my entire life. Before you, I was always looking for my anchor, for that one place where I could finally exhale and just... be. And I found it with you. In you." The sea breeze, carrying the scent of salt and possibility, seemed to wrap around them, a silent witness to their shared vows. They weren't just making promises to each other;

they were promising to be the home for each other, the anchor that would steady them through life's inevitable storms.

The conversation flowed easily, the silences between their words as comfortable as their spoken sentiments. They spoke of the practicalities, of course – the cottage, the renovations, the possibility of starting a small business together, a shared dream that Mara had long harbored and Eli had enthusiastically embraced. But more than the logistics, they spoke of the intangible, of the everyday moments that would weave the fabric of their life together. The quiet mornings with coffee on the porch, watching the sunrise paint the sky. The shared meals, the comfortable companionship of evenings spent reading by the fire. The laughter that would fill their home, born from shared jokes and inside stories that would accumulate over the years. They spoke of raising a family, of the children who might one day fill their lives with a different kind of joy, a joy that would be a testament to the love that had brought them together.

"I want our home to be a place of warmth and laughter," Mara said, her eyes shining with a vision she could now clearly see. "A place where everyone feels welcome, where conversations flow easily, and where there's always an extra plate at the table."

Eli's smile was warm and genuine. "That's exactly the kind of home I've always envisioned, too," he replied. "A place that reflects who we are, individually and together. A place that's filled with love and life." He paused, his gaze thoughtful. "And it will be. Because you'll be there. You make everything brighter, Mara."

His words were a balm to her soul, soothing the last vestiges of self-doubt. She knew, with an absolute certainty, that she was enough. That she was worthy of this love, this commitment, this beautiful, unfolding future. The external validation, the cheers of the festival, the congratulatory nods from the townsfolk – they were all wonderful, but the true validation came from within, from the deep, unwavering certainty of Eli's love and her own capacity to love him in return. Their bond was no longer a fragile sprout, vulnerable to the slightest gust of wind. It was a deeply rooted tree, its branches reaching towards the sky, its foundation solid and unshakeable.

As they continued their walk along the deserted stretch of beach, the moon casting a silvery path across the water, Mara felt a profound sense of gratitude wash over her. Gratitude for the journey that had led her here, for the unexpected turns and the difficult lessons, for the moments of doubt that had ultimately led her to this place of unwavering faith. Gratitude for Eli, for his unwavering love, his steadfast support, his ability to see the best in her, even when she struggled to see it herself. He had not just proposed marriage; he had offered her a partnership, a shared adventure, a life built on the solid ground of mutual respect, unwavering honesty, and a love that felt as vast and as deep as the ocean that surrounded them.

"I promise you, Eli," Mara said, her voice firm and clear, echoing the sentiment of their earlier exchange, "that I will always strive to be the partner you deserve. I'll be your confidante, your biggest supporter, and your truest friend. I promise to cherish this life we're building, to nurture our love, and to always find my way back to you, no matter what storms may come."

Eli stopped, turning to face her fully. He reached out, gently cupping her face in his hands, his touch warm and grounding. His eyes, reflecting the moonlight, held a depth of emotion that stole her breath. "And I promise you, Mara," he said, his voice thick with feeling, "that I will love you fiercely and faithfully. I will protect your heart, cherish your dreams, and stand by your side through every season of our lives. You are my home, my heart, my forever. I promise to never take a single moment with you for granted."

Their lips met then, a kiss that was both a reaffirmation of their vows and a silent testament to the profound understanding that now existed between them. It was a kiss filled with the promise of shared tomorrows, of a love that would continue to deepen and grow with each passing day. It was a kiss that spoke of a shared vision, a unified purpose, and a love that had found its truest expression by the sea, under the watchful gaze of the stars, and in the quiet, unwavering certainty of their hearts. The future, once a nebulous concept, now shimmered before them, a landscape of shared dreams waiting to be explored, a testament to the fact that they had not just fallen in love, but had chosen to build a life, together, on the most solid foundation of all:

unwavering love and commitment. The proposal was not an end, but a beautiful, luminous beginning.

The lingering echoes of the festival began to fade, the vibrant energy of the day softening into the hushed reverence of twilight. Above them, the sky transformed into a vast, inky canvas, pricked with the first hesitant gleams of stars. Mara and Eli found themselves drawn away from the last vestiges of celebration, their steps carrying them along the deserted stretch of beach where the gentle rhythm of the waves provided a soothing soundtrack. The air, now cool and carrying the clean scent of salt, seemed to hold a promise of its own, a quiet prelude to the future they had so joyfully embraced. Their clasped hands, a familiar comfort, tightened almost imperceptibly as they navigated the soft sand, a silent acknowledgment of the profound shift that had occurred between them. The engagement, so joyous and definitive, had set their hearts alight, and now, with the quietude of the night embracing them, their thoughts naturally drifted towards the next beautiful step: their wedding.

"Can you believe it?" Mara's voice was a soft murmur, barely disturbing the peaceful hush. She squeezed Eli's hand, her gaze lifted to the burgeoning constellations. "It feels like just yesterday we were... well, just us. And now..." She trailed off, the unspoken words – *and now we're getting married* – hanging sweetly in the air between them. The sheer wonder of it all, the speed with which their lives had intertwined and blossomed, still held a certain delightful disbelief.

Eli's thumb brushed gently against the back of her hand, a gesture of quiet reassurance and shared marvel. "I know," he replied, his voice a low, resonant hum that seemed to vibrate with the same contentment that filled her. "It feels like a dream, doesn't it? But a good dream. The best kind." He tilted his head, his gaze meeting hers, his eyes reflecting the nascent starlight. "And it's a dream we're building together."

Their conversation, previously centered on the immediate joy of their engagement, now began to weave the delicate threads of their upcoming wedding. It was a topic that had been hinted at, speculated about in hushed tones by well-meaning friends and family, but now, it was theirs to explore, to shape, to imbue with their own unique essence. They spoke not of grand, impersonal spectacles, but of a celebration that would be as authentic and heartfelt as their love for each other, and as deeply rooted in the very fabric of Port Blossom as they themselves were becoming.

"I've been thinking," Mara began, her voice growing more confident, a spark of excitement igniting within her. "About the wedding. I don't want anything... ostentatious. It needs to feel like *us*."

Eli nodded, his expression mirroring her sentiment. "Absolutely. No towering ice sculptures or thirty-tier cakes. We're not those people, are we?" He chuckled, a warm, genuine sound. "I've always imagined something that honors this place, this community that's welcomed us so warmly. Somewhere with the sea as our backdrop, the sound of the waves a constant reminder of... well, of this." He gestured vaguely towards the expanse of water stretching out before them, the moonlight painting a shimmering path across its surface.

Mara's eyes lit up. "The rescue grounds!" she exclaimed, a vivid image forming in her mind. "Imagine it, Eli. The old boathouse, decorated with wildflowers and soft lights. And the ceremony, right there on the bluff overlooking the water. We could have it at sunset, when the sky is all shades of orange and pink." She could picture it so clearly: the salty breeze catching the veil, the laughter of their loved ones mingling with the cry of the gulls, the vast, endless ocean bearing witness to their vows. It felt perfectly, unequivocally *them*.

Eli considered it, his brow furrowed in thought for a moment, then a broad smile spread across his face. "That's perfect, Mara. Absolutely perfect. I can already see it. Your father walking you down that little path, everyone looking out at the sea. It would be so... real. So meaningful." He squeezed her hand again. "And the rescue grounds... it's a place that means so much to this town. It feels right to be married there, doesn't it? To start our married life with a connection to something so vital and enduring."

"Yes," Mara agreed wholeheartedly. "And after the ceremony, we could have a reception. Not a stuffy ballroom, but something more... relaxed. Maybe down at the old fish market? We could have string lights strung across the space, and long tables filled with incredible local seafood. Everyone mingling, laughing, dancing under the stars." She imagined the scent of brine and cooking fish, the lively chatter of friends and family, the joyful chaos of a celebration that felt more like a grand family reunion than a formal event.

"I love that idea," Eli said, his voice filled with genuine enthusiasm. "A true Port Blossom celebration. Local food, local music, and all our favourite people. It wouldn't just be about us exchanging vows; it would be about us sharing our joy with the community that's become our home." He paused, his gaze thoughtful. "We could ask the fishermen to bring in their best catch of the day. And the bakers... Mrs. Gable's pies would have to be there, of course."

Mara laughed, picturing the formidable Mrs. Gable, her stern exterior hiding a heart of gold, beaming with pride as her famed blueberry pie graced their wedding tables. "Definitely Mrs. Gable's pies," she agreed. "And maybe some of the local artists could display their work? It would be like a mini-festival, a celebration of everything we love about this place." The vision was becoming more vivid, more tangible with each shared word. It was a wedding infused with the spirit of Port Blossom, a testament to the life they had chosen and the community that had embraced them.

They continued to walk, the conversation flowing seamlessly, their imaginations painting a shared canvas of their future. They spoke of the ceremony itself, of the vows they would exchange. Mara envisioned simple, heartfelt promises, spoken with sincerity and love. Eli agreed. He wanted their vows to be a reflection of their deep commitment, their understanding of each other, and their shared hopes for the life they would build.

"I want our vows to be honest," Eli said, his voice serious. "To speak of our partnership, our respect for each other, and our unwavering belief in what we have."

"And to be filled with love, of course," Mara added, her hand finding his again. "Love, and a little bit of humor. We need that, don't we?"

"Always," Eli confirmed with a smile. "Humor will be essential for navigating life's inevitable... surprises."

They pictured a small, intimate gathering, a circle of their dearest friends and family, those who had supported them, cheered them on, and perhaps even played a role in bringing them together. They didn't envision hundreds of distant acquaintances; their focus was on the people who truly knew and loved them, the ones who would celebrate their union with genuine joy.

"It's about the people who have witnessed our journey," Mara mused. "The ones who have seen us through the ups and downs. They deserve to be there, to share in our happiness."

"Exactly," Eli agreed. "Our chosen family. Everyone who has made us feel so welcome here. It's a celebration of our love, yes, but also a celebration of the connections we've forged, both individually and as a couple."

The idea of a wedding that was both deeply personal and intrinsically linked to their community resonated with both of them. It was a reflection of the life they were building – one that was grounded, authentic, and rich with shared experiences. The thought of their wedding being a beautiful tapestry woven with threads of their personal story and the vibrant spirit of Port Blossom filled them with an immense sense of anticipation.

"And the music," Mara continued, a new idea sparking. "I was thinking, instead of a typical wedding band, we could have some of the local musicians play. Maybe that folk band from the tavern, the one that plays such lively jigs. Or even just a few acoustic sets throughout the evening. It would add such a special touch."

Eli's eyes gleamed with appreciation. "Mara, you're on fire tonight. That's a brilliant idea. It keeps with the theme, doesn't it? Celebrating Port Blossom through and through. I can already hear the music, feel the energy." He pulled her gently closer, their bodies aligning in a comfortable embrace. "It's going to be the most wonderful celebration. I can feel it."

The prospect of their wedding, once a distant and somewhat abstract idea, was now taking shape, becoming a vibrant, tangible reality. The details, once fuzzy around the edges, were sharpening into focus, each element carefully chosen to reflect their shared values and their deep affection for each other and for the community they now called home. It wasn't just about a ceremony; it was about the beginning of a new chapter, a declaration of their commitment to a life lived fully, deeply, and together.

"I can't wait," Mara whispered, leaning her head against Eli's chest, the steady beat of his heart a reassuring rhythm against her ear. The stars above seemed to twinkle a little brighter, as if in silent affirmation of the beautiful future they were so enthusiastically planning. The wedding, a symbol of their enduring love and their shared dreams, was no longer a distant aspiration, but a joyous anticipation, a promise whispered to the sea and to each other, a celebration waiting to unfold.

CHAPTER TEN

Wedding Bells in Port Blossom

The starlit walk along the shore had ignited a fire of shared dreams, and as dawn painted the sky in soft hues of rose and gold, Mara and Eli's conversation continued indoors, fueled by strong coffee and an even stronger sense of purpose. The abstract beauty of their beachside discussion now needed to be grounded in tangible plans. The romantic whispers of their ideal wedding were ready to transform into concrete decisions, each one a deliberate stroke in the masterpiece of their future.

"So, the rescue grounds," Mara began, her eyes sparkling with a blend of excitement and practicality. "It's perfect in my mind, and I know it's where you've always envisioned it too. But we need to think about the logistics." She pulled out a notebook and a pen, a familiar professional instinct kicking in, though the subject matter was infinitely more personal than any project she'd tackled before. "The bluff is beautiful for the ceremony, but what about... everything else? Seating, an arch, sound system for vows? And the reception at the fish market.

It's charming, but it's a working space. We'd need to consider decorations, catering setup, flow for guests..."

Eli leaned over the table, his arm brushing hers, a silent anchor in the whirlwind of planning. "I agree. The vision is clear, but we need to make it happen. And who better to help us bring this vision to life than our Port Blossom neighbours?" He smiled, a genuine, reassuring smile that always settled her nerves. "The beauty of this place is its people. We're not going to outsource everything to strangers miles away. We're going to lean into the community that's already embraced us."

Mara's pen hovered over the page. "You're right. It should feel like Port Blossom, from start to finish." She paused, a new thought blossoming. "The rescue... it's so central to us. It's where we met, where so much of our story has unfolded. What if the ceremony wasn't *just* on the bluff overlooking the water, but actually *in* the grounds? Imagine the garden area, the one bordering the sea path. It's already so beautiful, with those old stone walls and the climbing roses. We could have the ceremony there, surrounded by the animals."

Eli's eyes widened, a slow grin spreading across his face. "The rescue garden. Mara, that's brilliant! It's even more personal. We could have the dogs there, maybe some of the more relaxed cats. Not in the middle of it all, of course, but part of the atmosphere. It would be such a unique touch, and it would genuinely represent us. Plus, it's a beautiful, natural setting that won't need much embellishment." He tapped his chin thoughtfully.

"We could set up benches, with a clear aisle leading to a simple archway decorated with local wildflowers and perhaps some soft fabric. We'd need to coordinate with Sarah, of course, but I'm sure she'd be thrilled."

"Exactly!" Mara felt a surge of exhilaration. "Sarah would absolutely love it. She's been so supportive of us, and she knows how much the rescue means to me. We could even have a little donation box for the rescue at the entrance, as a subtle nod to our passion. And think about the photos! The animals, the gardens, the sea in the background… it would be magical." She scribbled down 'Rescue Garden Ceremony' and added a little heart next to it. "And for the reception… the fish market is still a great idea for the atmosphere, but maybe we could have the catering and the main gathering space slightly more… established? What about the old boathouse, after all? It's connected to the rescue grounds, it has that rustic charm, and it offers more protection from the elements than an open-air market space. We could still have seafood stalls and food trucks from local vendors set up just outside, so we get that vibrant market feel, but the boathouse can be our main dining and dancing area."

Eli nodded, picturing it. "The boathouse. Yes, that's a fantastic compromise. It's got history, it's got character, and it's conveniently located. We could string fairy lights through the beams, use long wooden tables, and have a dance floor in the centre. It feels… right. It's functional and romantic. And it keeps everything relatively contained, making logistics easier for everyone." He paused, his gaze distant for a moment. "For vendors... we absolutely need to go local. For catering, I'm thinking of the small, family-run seafood restaurant down by the harbour. They do the most incredible grilled fish, and I know they cater small events. They'd be thrilled to be part of it."

"Oh, 'The Salty Siren'!" Mara exclaimed. "Their chowder is legendary! Yes, they would be perfect. And for the cake... we *have* to have Mrs. Gable. There's no question. Her apple pie is a Port Blossom institution, but her cakes are equally divine. Imagine her lemon drizzle cake with elderflower frosting. It would be heavenly." She added 'Catering: The Salty Siren' and 'Cake: Mrs. Gable' to her notes. "And flowers? We need someone who understands the local flora. Maybe that little florist shop on Main Street? The one with the wild, unstructured arrangements."

"'Blooms & Buds'," Eli supplied. "Agnes there has an incredible eye for natural beauty. She could create something that feels organic and wild, perfectly suiting the rescue garden setting and the boathouse vibe. We wouldn't want anything too stiff or formal. Think driftwood accents, sea glass, and lots of greenery interspersed with local blooms." He reached for her hand, his thumb stroking her knuckles. "And for music, what did we discuss? Local musicians, right?"

"Absolutely," Mara confirmed, her heart swelling with the shared vision. "The folk band from 'The Tipsy Mermaid' tavern. They're lively and fun, and they know all the old sea shanties and jigs. We could have them play during the reception, and perhaps have a quieter acoustic set during the ceremony or cocktail hour. Someone like Liam, the young guitarist who busks down by the pier. His music is so soulful." She wrote down 'Music: The Tipsy Mermaid Band + Liam'. "This is all coming together so beautifully, Eli. It feels so intrinsically *us*."

"It does," he agreed, his voice warm. "And it's not just about us. It's about celebrating Port Blossom too. Every vendor we choose, every detail we select, is a way of honouring this place and the people who have made it our home. It's a celebration of our love, yes, but it's also a celebration of our integration into this wonderful community." He squeezed her hand. "We're not just getting married; we're solidifying our place here."

Mara leaned her head against his shoulder, a contented sigh escaping her lips. "It feels right. Every step of it. I've always dreamed of a wedding that felt personal and meaningful, not just a grand production. And this... this is beyond my wildest dreams." She thought about the little touches that would make it unique. "What about favours? Something small, a token of our appreciation. Maybe little jars of local honey from the apiary just outside of town, or handmade soaps from that artisan soap maker on the coast road?"

"Both excellent ideas," Eli said, his mind already whirring with possibilities. "The honey would be lovely, especially with the bee motifs we could incorporate into the décor. Or the soaps... we could have them custom-scented with coastal herbs. We should definitely look into both. It's these little details that make a wedding memorable, isn't it? The things that tell a story."

"And the invitations," Mara mused, flipping to a new page in her notebook. "We need someone to design them. Something that reflects the feel of the rescue garden and the boathouse. Elegant, but not stuffy. Natural, but refined."

"There's a graphic designer who works out of the old lighthouse building," Eli recalled. "He does a lot of branding for local businesses, and his style is very clean and artistic. I think he'd be perfect. He'd be able to capture that coastal charm we're going for." He traced the outline of her hand. "We'll need to set a date, of course. Have you thought about that?"

Mara's brow furrowed slightly. "That's the big one, isn't it? I was thinking... not too soon, but not too far away either. I want to savour the engagement, but I also don't want to wait so long that the momentum fades. Perhaps late spring? When everything is in full bloom at the rescue, and the weather is usually beautiful. Early May, perhaps? It feels like a time of renewal, a perfect metaphor for a new beginning."

Eli considered it. "Late spring sounds lovely. It gives us enough time to plan properly without feeling rushed, and it aligns with the natural beauty we want to showcase. May... yes, I like the sound of that. May 18th, perhaps? It's a Saturday, and it falls just after my birthday, making it a celebratory month all around."

"May 18th it is," Mara declared, writing it down with a flourish. "Now, the guest list. This is where it gets tricky. We want it to be intimate, but who do we leave out?"

"Our closest friends and family," Eli stated firmly. "The people who have been instrumental in our lives, who have supported our journey here. Our parents, of course. Your sister and her family. My brother. A few of our oldest friends from university who have always been there for us. And of course, the Port Blossom crew – Sarah, Captain Ben, the Gables, the owners of 'The Salty Siren' and 'The Tipsy Mermaid'. They've become our family here."

Mara smiled at the inclusion of their Port Blossom friends. "Yes, absolutely. It needs to feel like a celebration of our love, but also a celebration of the community that has embraced us. It's about sharing our joy with the people who have witnessed our journey, both individually and as a couple." She looked at her list, the names starting to take shape. "We'll need to be disciplined, though. No inviting distant cousins twice removed."

"Agreed," Eli chuckled. "Discipline will be key. But it will be worth it to have a truly intimate and meaningful gathering." He brought her hand to his lips, kissing her knuckles. "This is all coming together so beautifully, Mara. You have such a clear vision, and I love how you're weaving our love story with the essence of Port Blossom."

"And you, my love," Mara replied, her voice soft with affection. "You're the anchor. You keep me grounded when my imagination starts to run wild, and you elevate every idea with your own wonderful perspective. It's our shared vision, isn't it? A perfect Port Blossom wedding."

The afternoon unfolded with a quiet intensity, their shared excitement a palpable energy in the room. They discussed the ceremony itself, the readings they might include, the music that would accompany their entrance and exit. Mara envisioned a reading of a poem that spoke of finding home in unexpected places, while Eli considered a passage from a favourite book that celebrated enduring love and partnership. They agreed on simple, heartfelt vows, promises spoken not just to each other, but to the life they were building together in Port Blossom.

"I want our vows to reflect our growth," Eli said, his gaze earnest. "To acknowledge where we've come from, and to pledge our commitment to where we're going. To promise not just love, but also friendship, support, and an unwavering belief in each other."

"And laughter," Mara added, a playful glint in her eye. "We need to promise to always find the humour in things, even when life throws us curveballs. Because knowing us, there will be curveballs."

Eli laughed, a deep, resonant sound. "Oh, there will be curveballs. But we'll face them together. And we'll laugh. Always."

As the sun began its descent, casting long shadows across the room, Mara and Eli looked at their notes, a tangible representation of their dreams. The rescue garden ceremony, the boathouse reception, the local vendors, the intimate guest list – it all felt so perfectly aligned with who they were, and who they were becoming. It was more than just a wedding plan; it was a blueprint for a life deeply rooted in love, community, and the breathtaking beauty of Port Blossom. The perfect day was no longer a distant fantasy, but a clearly charted course, and they couldn't wait to set sail.

The air in Port Blossom, usually infused with the briny scent of the sea and the gentle hum of everyday life, now thrummed with an anticipatory energy. It was a Friday afternoon, and the quiet coastal town was slowly but surely transforming into a hub of joyous reunions and excited chatter. Cars bearing out-of-state license plates began to dot the picturesque streets, their occupants eager to witness the culmination of Mara and Eli's love story. The invitations, designed with the delicate touch of the lighthouse graphic designer and reflecting the rustic charm of the boathouse and the wild beauty of the rescue garden, had done their job – drawing a beloved constellation of faces to their doorstep.

Mara stood at the window of their cozy cottage, watching a familiar, sturdy sedan pull up to the curb. A broad, beaming smile spread across her face as her father, Arthur, emerged, his gait a little less steady than it used to be, but his eyes radiating an unmistakable pride and delight. He carried a small, wrapped gift, and his shoulders seemed to shed a lifetime of unspoken worries as he strode towards her. Their reunion was a soft, tender moment, filled with the quiet understanding that comes from years of shared history and a daughter's blossoming happiness. Arthur's voice, usually gruff with the weight of responsibility, was thick with emotion as he hugged her. "My Mara," he murmured, his voice cracking. "You look... you look like you've found your harbour."

"I have, Dad," she replied, squeezing him tight. "And you're a big part of why." She led him inside, where Eli was waiting with a warm embrace and a genuine handshake that spoke volumes about their burgeoning father-son bond. Eli's brother, David, arrived shortly after, his presence a quiet reassurance. The initial awkwardness that had once shadowed their interactions had long since faded, replaced by a newfound respect and affection. David, ever the steady support, had taken it upon himself to help with some of the more logistical aspects of the wedding, his keen organizational skills a welcome asset. He and Eli shared a camaraderie that Mara found deeply comforting, a testament to their shared journey and the healing power of time and forgiveness. David's easygoing nature and his genuine happiness for Mara and Eli were a balm, solidifying the sense of family that was growing around them.

As the afternoon deepened, a steady stream of familiar faces began to arrive. Mara's closest friends from her life before Port Blossom, women who had navigated the choppy waters of early adulthood alongside her, started to pull into town. There was

Chloe, with her infectious laughter and an uncanny ability to make anyone feel like the most important person in the room; Sarah, the pragmatic artist whose sharp wit was matched only by her fiercely loyal heart; and Jessica, the quiet observer whose thoughtful insights often cut through the noise. Seeing them, Mara felt a rush of mingled emotions – nostalgia for shared memories, gratitude for their unwavering support, and a deep sense of satisfaction that they were here to witness this new chapter of her life.

Chloe was the first to burst through the cottage door, her arms already outstretched. "Mara! Oh, my gosh, you look absolutely radiant!" she exclaimed, her eyes sparkling as she took in Mara's flushed cheeks and the undeniable glow of happiness that seemed to emanate from her. Their embrace was a tangle of laughter and happy sighs. "I can't believe it! You're actually getting married! And here! In this... this picturesque little paradise!" Chloe's gaze swept around the cottage, taking in the nautical touches and the vase of wildflowers on the table. "It's perfect. It's so *you*, Mara."

Sarah arrived next, a sketchbook tucked under her arm. She offered a more reserved, but no less heartfelt, hug. "Hey, you," she said, her voice warm. "Looks like you've finally found your happy place. And I'm not just talking about Eli," she added with a wry smile, nudging Mara playfully. "Though he is a pretty fantastic addition to the scenery." Sarah's critical artist's eye quickly took in the surroundings. "This town... it's got character. And you've certainly embraced it. I love what you've done with the place." She gestured towards the small garden visible through the window. "That little patch of green looks so vibrant."

Jessica arrived last, carrying a beautifully wrapped box. Her greeting was a quiet, sincere hug. "Mara. It's so good to see you so happy," she said softly. "Really, truly happy." She handed Mara the gift. "Just a little something. A reminder of our adventures, and a wish for many more, with Eli by your side."

As Mara opened the gift, a delicate silver locket etched with a compass rose, her eyes welled up. It was the perfect symbol of their shared past and the new directions their lives were taking. "Oh, Jessica, it's beautiful," she whispered, fastening it around her neck. "Thank you."

The arrival of these cherished friends marked a significant shift. It was one thing for Mara and Eli to share their dreams and plans with each other, and another entirely to have the people who had shaped their individual journeys bear witness to their shared future. These women, who knew Mara's past so intimately, could now see the profound peace and joy that Port Blossom and Eli had brought into her life. They saw not just a woman in love, but a woman who had found a deep sense of belonging, a place where her passions could flourish and her heart could find its truest home.

Eli, observing these reunions with a quiet satisfaction, felt a profound sense of gratitude. He saw the genuine warmth in his future father-in-law's eyes, the easy camaraderie between him and David, and the unquestioning love his closest friends offered Mara. It was a tapestry of connection, woven with threads of shared history, present joy, and hopeful anticipation. The influx of loved ones was more than just a social gathering; it was a testament to the strong bonds they had forged, both individually and as a couple. Each arrival, each shared laugh, each embrace, was another brick laid in the foundation of their shared life, reinforcing the sense of community that had already become so dear to them.

The town itself seemed to embrace the growing throng of guests. The 'Tipsy Mermaid' pub was busier than usual, its usual clientele now mingling with unfamiliar faces, all sharing in the collective excitement. The aroma of freshly baked goods wafted from 'Gable's Bakery', hinting at the sweet delights that awaited. Even 'The Salty Siren', known for its no-nonsense efficiency, had a cheerful buzz about it as locals and visitors alike discussed the upcoming nuptials. Captain Ben, his weathered face crinkling into a perpetual smile, was seen offering impromptu tours of his boat, the 'Sea Serpent,' to anyone who expressed an interest, his voice booming with tales of the sea and, more recently, of the remarkable couple getting married.

Mara's father, Arthur, found himself drawn into conversations with Eli's brother, David. They spoke of their children, of the journeys that had led them to this point, and of the immense joy they felt at seeing Mara and Eli so happy. Arthur confided in David about his initial apprehension when Mara had first spoken of moving to Port Blossom, a small coastal town he knew little about. "I worried, you know," Arthur admitted, his gaze drifting towards Mara, who was laughing with her friends. "Worried she was chasing a dream that was too... remote. But seeing her now, seeing the light in her eyes, and the strength she's found here... and Eli, what a fine young man he is. He's good for her. He's her anchor."

David nodded, a gentle smile playing on his lips. "Eli's found his anchor in Mara, too. They're good for each other. It's rare, isn't it? To see two people fit together so perfectly. It makes you believe in that kind of enduring love." He clapped Arthur on the shoulder. "You've raised a remarkable daughter, Mr. Davies. Truly remarkable."

Meanwhile, Mara's friends were getting a crash course in the unique charm of Port Blossom, guided by Mara herself. They marvelled at the rescue grounds, the sea cliffs, and the quaint shops along the harbour. They listened, captivated, as Mara recounted tales of the animals she'd nursed back to health, the storm that had brought her and Eli together, and the quiet beauty of their daily lives.

"So, the ceremony is actually going to be *here*?" Chloe asked, eyes wide as she surveyed the rescue gardens. "Surrounded by... animals?"

"Well, not exactly *in* the enclosures," Mara clarified, laughing. "But the grounds, yes. It's where we first really connected, Eli and I. It's so important to me. And it's beautiful, isn't it? Those old stone walls and the roses... Agnes from 'Blooms & Buds' is going to decorate with local wildflowers and driftwood. It'll be magical."

Sarah, ever the observer, took it all in with a keen eye. "I can see it," she mused, already picturing the scene. "The natural light, the textures... it's going to be incredibly photogenic. And the reception at the boathouse? That's brilliant. So much character." She looked at Mara, her expression soft. "You've really built something special here, Mara. Something real."

Jessica, with her quiet grace, surveyed the bustling activity around the rescue. "It's more than just a place, though, isn't it?" she observed. "It's a community. You've all welcomed each other. It feels... genuine."

As the sun began to dip towards the horizon, painting the sky in hues of orange and purple, a sense of quiet contentment settled over Mara and Eli. The cottage was filled with the comforting presence of loved ones, the air alive with shared laughter and the murmur of happy conversations. They had planned a wedding, yes, but in the process, they had also gathered their worlds, bridging the old and the new, the familiar and the emerging. The arrival of family and friends was the final, perfect flourish, a vibrant affirmation of the love they shared and the rich, fulfilling life they were building together in the heart of Port Blossom. The town, once just a picturesque backdrop for their romance, had become a living, breathing celebration, its embrace extending to everyone who had come to share in their joy. The anticipation for the wedding day itself was palpable, a sweet melody building to a crescendo, promising a celebration as unique and as beautiful as the love it honoured.

The air in the Port Blossom rescue grounds the following morning buzzed with an energy distinctly different from the usual quiet dedication of animal care. Today, a festive undercurrent flowed through the familiar routines. Mara, her heart brimming with a joy that felt as expansive as the ocean vista, surveyed the scene with a smile that could melt glaciers. It was the morning of her wedding to Eli, and true to their shared ethos, the beloved animal rescue was not just a backdrop, but an integral, breathing part of their celebration.

A gentle nudge against her hand drew her attention. Bartholomew, a venerable old retriever whose gentle eyes had seen countless seasons at the rescue, sat patiently at her feet, a satin ribbon tied loosely around his neck. Beside him, looking a little bewildered but impeccably groomed, was a sleek black cat named Luna, whose usual aloofness had been replaced by a surprising eagerness. These two, along with a surprisingly well-behaved terrier mix named Pippin, who had a penchant for chasing squirrels with more enthusiasm than skill, were to be their special attendants. Bartholomew, with his dignified bearing, would proudly carry the ring pillow, a small, hand-stitched creation adorned with tiny paw prints. Luna, perched in a specially designed, plush basket that Eli's brother David had ingeniously fashioned, would be carried down the aisle by a discreet volunteer, a regal procession of feline grace.

Pippin, meanwhile, was slated for a more whimsical role, trailing behind the flower girls, a mischievous but endearing addition to the bridal party.

Mara knelt, stroking Bartholomew's soft fur. "You've got a very important job today, old boy," she murmured, her voice thick with emotion. "You're carrying the symbol of our promise." Bartholomew responded with a contented sigh and a gentle lick to her hand, his wagging tail a silent affirmation. The idea of involving the animals had been one of the first discussions Mara and Eli had had about their wedding. For Mara, the rescue wasn't just a place of work; it was the crucible where her passions had solidified, where her resilience had been tested and proven, and most significantly, where her path had irrevocably intersected with Eli's. He had, after all, first seen her in her element, her dedication to a struggling fawn capturing his immediate attention and admiration. To have them play a part, however small, felt like a profound acknowledgment of their shared journey.

Eli, with his usual calm competence, was overseeing the final arrangements for the animals. He'd worked with a local trainer, a kind woman named Clara who was a regular volunteer, to ensure the animals involved were comfortable and understood their roles. "Bartholomew's already had his pre-wedding pamper session," Eli reported, a fond smile playing on his lips as he joined Mara. "Clara says he's a natural. And Luna... well, Luna is tolerating the basket with regal disdain, which I'm taking as a win." He chuckled, wrapping an arm around Mara's waist. "Who knew our wedding would involve more animal wrangling than actual planning?"

"It wouldn't be *our* wedding if it didn't," Mara replied, leaning into him. "Think of it as a dress rehearsal for life with two humans and a small zoo."

David, ever the pragmatist, had ensured the logistics were seamless. Specially designated, quiet areas were set up near the ceremony site, complete with water bowls, comfortable bedding, and discreet barriers, ensuring that any of the rescue animals who weren't directly involved in the ceremony could still feel present and a part of the joyous occasion without being overwhelmed. These areas were adorned with tasteful floral arrangements, mirroring those used in the main ceremony, creating a sense of unity. A few of the older, calmer residents of the rescue, like a wise old owl named Archimedes who resided in a spacious aviary that overlooked the ceremony site, or a pair of affectionate alpacas named Willow and Finn who lived in a paddock bordering the gardens, were given prime viewing spots. They couldn't participate directly, of course, but their presence served as a gentle, constant reminder of the life and purpose that Mara poured her heart into.

As guests began to arrive, their initial surprise and delight at seeing the animal attendants quickly turned into a collective warmth. Laughter rippled through the air as Pippin, in a moment of pure terrier exuberance, attempted to chase a stray butterfly, only to be gently redirected by a volunteer. Children squealed with delight at the sight of Bartholomew, his earnest demeanor melting their hearts. The inclusion of the animals wasn't a mere gimmick; it was a heartfelt expression of the couple's identity, a testament to the love and dedication that defined them.

Arthur, Mara's father, watched the proceedings with a proud smile. He'd been initially perplexed by the idea of dogs and cats as wedding participants, but seeing Bartholomew's serene composure and the sheer joy it brought Mara, he'd come to understand. "She's always had a way with them," he'd remarked to David earlier, gesturing towards a particularly shy fox kit that was being coaxed into its enclosure by Mara. "A gentle touch, a patient heart. It's a gift." He admired the way Mara's friends, Chloe, Sarah, and Jessica, were interacting with the animals, their initial hesitation replaced by genuine affection. Chloe was cooing over a litter of kittens, Sarah was sketching Bartholomew with rapid, expert strokes, and Jessica was quietly stroking the nose of a rescued pony. It was a scene of unadulterated happiness, a testament to the life Mara had cultivated.

The ceremony itself unfolded against the breathtaking backdrop of the sea, the gentle murmur of the waves a natural soundtrack to their vows. When Bartholomew, with a practiced paw, nudged the ring pillow towards Eli, a collective sigh of adoration swept through the assembled guests. Luna, in her basket, let out a soft trill that seemed to punctuate the solemnity of the moment. It was a scene that was both deeply personal and universally touching. Eli's eyes, when he looked at Mara, held a depth of emotion that transcended words. He saw not just the woman he loved, but the fierce advocate, the compassionate caregiver, the woman whose spirit was as untamed and beautiful as the wild coast they called home.

Mara, in turn, saw in Eli a steadfastness that mirrored the ancient cliffs, a kindness that was as profound as the ocean's depths, and a love that was as unwavering as the lighthouse's beam. Their vows, exchanged under the vast expanse of the sky, were imbued with the spirit of the rescue – a promise of protection, of unwavering support, and of a love that would always seek to heal and to nurture.

The reception, held at the rustic boathouse, continued the theme of heartfelt inclusion. While the primary focus was on celebrating with their human loved ones, small touches ensured the animal element remained present. Guests were treated to a "Paws for a Cause" station, where they could learn about the rescue's ongoing needs and make donations if they wished. A beautifully crafted photo booth featured props like dog ears, cat whiskers, and miniature watering cans, encouraging playful interactions. And, in a particularly touching gesture, Mara and Eli had arranged for a professional photographer to capture candid moments of the animals interacting with guests throughout the day. These images, later compiled into a special album, would serve as a lasting reminder of how deeply intertwined their lives and passions were.

During the toasts, Eli's best man, his brother David, spoke with genuine warmth. "I've always known Eli to be a man of integrity and deep loyalty," David began, raising his glass. "But seeing him with Mara... it's like watching two halves of a whole find each other. Mara, you've brought a light into his life that's truly remarkable. And you've done it while building something incredible here at the rescue. You've saved countless lives, and you've saved each other, in a way. To Mara and Eli – may your love be as strong as the tides, as deep as the ocean, and as endlessly giving as your hearts."

Mara's maid of honor, Chloe, followed, her voice bright and full of emotion. "When Mara first told me about Port Blossom, about the rescue, I admit, I pictured her surrounded by quietude and... well, maybe a few very well-behaved sheep. But what she's created here is a vibrant, beating heart. It's a testament to her spirit. And Eli, you are clearly her perfect counterpart, her calm in the storm, her anchor. Seeing you two together is like watching a perfectly executed rescue – all grace, strength, and a whole lot of love."

Later in the evening, as the band played a lively tune, Mara noticed Arthur standing by the edge of the boathouse, watching a group of younger guests interacting with a shy, one-eyed rabbit named Patches, who had been brought out under strict supervision. Arthur's face, usually etched with a certain gravity, was relaxed, a soft smile playing on his lips. He caught Mara's eye and gave her a nod, a silent acknowledgment of her happiness and the unique world she had built.

Eli, pulling Mara onto the dance floor, whispered, "You know, I think Bartholomew might be enjoying the music more than anyone." He indicated the old retriever, who was lying contentedly near the edge of the dance floor, his tail thumping a gentle rhythm against the wooden planks.

Mara laughed, her head resting on his shoulder. "He's got good taste. Just like his humans." As they swayed together, surrounded by the warmth of their loved ones and the quiet presence of their animal family, Mara felt a profound sense of peace. This was more than just a wedding; it was a declaration of their life together, a beautiful fusion of their individual passions and their shared future. The rescue, the animals, the sea – they were all woven into the fabric of their love story, making their celebration not just memorable, but truly, deeply their own. The gentle lapping of the waves against the boathouse pilings seemed to whisper a benediction, a promise of many more joyous days to come, filled with love, laughter, and the unwavering spirit of rescue.

Mara's Vows

The salt-laced breeze, a familiar caress against her skin, seemed to carry the weight of generations of Port Blossom whispers, a chorus of encouragement for the momentous step she was about to take. Standing beside Eli, his hand warm and steady in hers, Mara felt a profound sense of rightness, a quiet joy that settled deep within her bones. The gentle murmur of the ocean, the rustling leaves of the ancient oak that served as their natural canopy, and the adoring faces of their friends and family created a tapestry of love and support, a sacred space for the words that had been brewing in her heart for months. She met Eli's gaze, and in his eyes, she saw not just the man she loved, but the reflection of a journey that had brought them both to this beautiful precipice. The vows she had penned were not just promises to him, but declarations of a self she had fought to discover, a self he had helped her to truly see.

She began, her voice clear and steady, resonating with a newfound strength. "Eli," she started, the name a warm ember on her tongue. "When I first came to Port Blossom, I was a creature of the wild, much like the animals I sought to protect. I built walls, not of stone, but of self-reliance, of a fierce independence that I mistook for strength. My heart was a sanctuary, yes, but one I kept guarded, fearing that vulnerability would be a weakness I couldn't afford. I believed that true strength lay in standing alone, in weathering every storm with only my own resilience as my shield." She paused, a soft smile touching her lips as she looked at him. "And then you arrived, like a steady beacon in my often-turbulent sea. You didn't try to breach my walls, Eli. Instead, you patiently sat by them, offering a consistent warmth, a quiet understanding that slowly, so slowly, began to melt the ice. You saw the fear beneath the fierce, the longing beneath the independence, and you loved me not in spite of it, but because of it. You showed me that vulnerability isn't a weakness, but the very foundation of true connection. You taught me that true strength isn't in enduring alone, but in the courage to lean on another, to share the burdens and the joys, and to build something beautiful together."

Her fingers tightened slightly around his. "You have a remarkable way of seeing the best in everyone, even when they can't see it in themselves. You saw the potential in this broken-down rescue, and you saw the potential in me. You didn't ask me to change, but your presence inspired me to evolve. You championed my dreams, celebrated my successes, and held me through my deepest doubts. You became my confidant, my partner, my greatest supporter, and the gentle hand that guided me towards a love I never truly believed I deserved. Your unwavering faith in me has been the cornerstone of my own self-belief. You are my calm in the storm, my anchor in the wild currents of life, and the most beautiful constant I have ever known."

Mara's gaze swept over the familiar faces surrounding them – her father, his eyes glistening with pride; Chloe, her maid of honor, offering a teary smile; and Eli's family, their warmth radiating towards her. She felt a surge of gratitude for them, for their acceptance, and for the community they had all built together. "Today, standing here," she continued, her voice growing more resonant, "I choose you, Eli. I choose this life we are building, brick by brick, in this wild, beautiful place we call home. I vow to honor the courage you've helped me find, to nurture the trust you've so freely given me, and to love you with an honesty that mirrors the clarity of the ocean on a perfect summer's day. I promise to be your steadfast companion, your confidante, and your greatest admirer. I promise to face every challenge with you, to celebrate every triumph with you, and to build a future filled with laughter, adventure, and a love as deep and enduring as the tides that shape our shores."

She looked back at Eli, her heart overflowing. "I vow to cherish our shared purpose, to continue to advocate for those who cannot speak for themselves, and to make our home a haven of compassion and kindness, just as you have made my heart a haven for you. I promise to always listen, to always support, and to always love you, not just for who you are today, but for the ever-evolving, wonderful person you will become. You are my greatest rescue, Eli, the one I will dedicate my life to cherishing and protecting. My heart is yours, completely and without reservation, for all of our days." The final words hung in the air, a whispered promise carried on the wind, sealing her commitment not just to Eli, but to the life they had chosen together, a life rooted in love, purpose, and the unwavering spirit of Port Blossom. She felt a profound sense of release, of peace, as if a heavy burden had been lifted, replaced by an exhilarating lightness. Her journey had led her here, to this moment, to this man, and to the undeniable truth of her own capacity for love and commitment.

Eli's Promises

Eli's smile was a sunbeam, warm and genuine, reflecting the pure joy that radiated from his soul. He squeezed Mara's hand, his thumb tracing a gentle path across her knuckles, a silent communication of the deep emotion swelling within him. The gentle applause from their assembled loved ones, a soft ripple of appreciation for Mara's heartfelt words, faded into a backdrop as he turned his full attention to her, his gaze holding hers with an intensity that spoke volumes. The world around them seemed to soften, the vibrant hues of the coastline and the azure sky deepening as if in reverence to the moment. He cleared his throat, the sound a low rumble that drew Mara's complete focus, a prelude to the promises he was about to make.

"Mara," he began, his voice a rich baritone, imbued with a tenderness that made her heart flutter. "Looking at you today, standing here, radiating that incredible light you've always possessed, it's... it's everything I ever dreamed of, and so much more." He paused, a soft chuckle escaping him, a sound that was pure Eli. "You spoke of walls, and of a wildness you carried. And I saw it, I truly did. But what you might not have realized, my love, is that I wasn't looking at walls. I was looking at a magnificent, untamed spirit, a fierce protector with a heart as vast and deep as the ocean itself. And I was utterly captivated."

His eyes crinkled at the corners as he remembered. "I remember the first time I saw you truly let your guard down. It was during that terrible storm, the one that threatened to wash away half the docks. You were out there, long after everyone else had retreated, with a little injured gull in your hands, your face streaked with rain and salt, but your eyes – they were alight with a fierce determination to save it. In that moment, I didn't see someone struggling. I saw the embodiment of everything I admired: courage, compassion, and an unwavering commitment to life. That's when I knew. That's when I knew with absolute certainty that you were the one. The one I wanted to share every sunrise and every storm with."

He continued, his voice growing more passionate. "You see the best in others, Mara, but you have a remarkable blindness to the incredible best in yourself. You inspire me, not just to be a better man, but to be a better version of the man I already was. You challenged me, in the most beautiful ways, to step outside my comfort zone, to be more open, more vulnerable, and more appreciative of the simple, profound beauty of life. You taught me that true strength isn't about always being the protector, but about the courage to also be protected, to allow oneself to be loved and cherished. You've shown me that partnership isn't about two halves making a whole, but about two complete souls choosing to intertwine, to share their strengths and to lift each other up when they falter."

Eli's gaze softened, a profound love shining in his eyes. "When you spoke of your journey to Port Blossom, of finding your way, I felt like I was embarking on a parallel journey. Meeting you wasn't an accident, Mara. It was fate nudging me in the right direction, leading me to the woman who would become my greatest adventure, my truest home. You are the missing piece I never knew I was searching for, the anchor that grounds me, and the wind that fills my sails. You have a way of making the ordinary extraordinary, of finding magic in the mundane, and of filling our lives with a love that feels both wild and wonderfully familiar."

He lifted their joined hands, bringing hers closer to his lips and pressing a soft kiss to her knuckles. "Today, I vow to you, Mara, that I will be your steadfast partner. I promise to cherish your wild spirit, to encourage your every dream, no matter how big or small, and to be the unwavering support you have so readily offered me. I promise to listen, to understand, and to always choose you, even when the path ahead is uncertain. I promise to build this life with you, here in Port Blossom, with the same dedication and love that you pour into every creature you rescue and every person you touch. Our home will be a sanctuary of shared laughter, of quiet comfort, and of a love that grows deeper and richer with each passing season."

Eli's expression was one of unwavering devotion. "I vow to never take your love for granted, to continuously work to earn your trust and your heart, every single day. I promise to be the calm in your storm, the steady hand in your moments of doubt, and the loudest cheer at your triumphs. I promise to learn from you, to grow with you, and to love you with an intensity that mirrors the vastness of the sky above us and the depth of the sea beside us. You are not just my wife, Mara; you are my confidante, my best friend, and the keeper of my heart. You are my Port Blossom, my forever home, and I can't imagine a single day without you by my side. I love you, Mara, more than words can ever say, and I commit my life, my heart, and my soul to you, now and always."

The sincerity in his voice, the raw emotion that painted his features, left Mara breathless. His promises weren't just words; they were a tangible extension of the man she knew and adored, a testament to the profound bond they shared. As his final words echoed in the gentle breeze, a profound sense of peace washed over her. His vows, like hers, were not just about the present, but about a future they would actively create, a testament to their shared journey and their unwavering commitment to each other. The world around them seemed to shimmer with a newfound brilliance, the vows they had exchanged weaving an invisible, unbreakable thread between their souls, anchoring them in the enduring love that had blossomed in Port Blossom.

CHAPTER ELEVEN

Forever Starts Now

The air thrummed with a joyous energy, a palpable extension of the love that had just been sealed. The garden, bathed in the soft, golden light of the setting sun, transformed into a kaleidoscope of laughter, music, and contented chatter. Fairy lights, strung between ancient oak trees, began to twinkle, mirroring the constellations that were slowly emerging in the darkening sky. It was a scene of pure, unadulterated celebration, a testament to the deep affection that Mara and Eli had cultivated, not just for each other, but for the vibrant community of Port Blossom that had gathered to witness and honor their union.

The gentle murmur of conversations, punctuated by bursts of hearty laughter, created a symphony of happiness. Guests mingled, their faces alight with shared joy. Old friends reminisced, new acquaintances were forged, and everyone present felt an undeniable sense of belonging, a collective warmth that emanated from the central figures of the day. Mara, her heart still buoyant from Eli's deeply touching vows, felt an overwhelming sense of gratitude wash over her. She squeezed Eli's hand, her fingers lacing with his, a silent reaffirmation of the promises they had just exchanged. He returned the squeeze, his thumb stroking her palm, his gaze unwavering, a constant reminder of the profound connection that now bound them.

The clinking of glasses signaled the start of the toasts, each one a heartfelt offering to the newlyweds. Eli's father, a man of quiet dignity and immense pride, was the first to speak. His voice, though a little raspy with emotion, carried across the gathering. "To Mara and Eli," he began, raising his glass. "To a love that has bloomed as beautifully as this garden, and as strong as the tides that grace our shores. Mara, you have brought such a radiant light into our son's life, and by extension, into our family. Eli, you have always shown a remarkable capacity for love, but with Mara, you have found your true north, your anchor. May your journey together be filled with endless adventures, unwavering support, and a love that deepens with every passing year. To Mara and Eli!" A chorus of "To Mara and Eli!" echoed, followed by the satisfying sound of glasses meeting.

Next was Sarah, Mara's oldest friend, her eyes sparkling with unshed tears. "To Mara," she said, her voice clear and strong. "My dearest Mara. I've known you since we were little girls, building sandcastles that the ocean always claimed. But you, my friend, you were always building something more. You built resilience, you built kindness, you built a heart that could hold the entire world. And then you met Eli. And in his eyes, I saw something new – a reflection of the love you so freely give, finally being returned in full measure. Eli, you have a rare gift for seeing the true essence of people, and in Mara, you found a treasure beyond compare. Thank you for loving her, for seeing her, for cherishing her. May your love be a beacon, guiding you through all of life's seasons. To Mara and Eli!"

The toasts continued, each speaker weaving a narrative of Mara and Eli's journey, their shared dedication to the animal rescue, and the undeniable strength of their bond. There were anecdotes that brought tears to the eyes and stories that elicited roars of laughter. The mayor, a jovial man with a booming voice, spoke of their contributions to Port Blossom, of how their work, both together and individually, had enriched the town. He recounted the time Mara, with Eli's help, had single-handedly rescued a stranded dolphin during a particularly fierce storm, a testament to her unwavering compassion. He also spoke of Eli's quiet leadership, his ability to inspire those around him, and how he had found his perfect partner in Mara.

As the evening deepened, the music swelled, and the dance floor, a clearing under the canopy of stars, beckoned. Eli turned to Mara, his eyes alight with an invitation. He took her hand, his touch sending a familiar thrill through her. "May I have this dance, my wife?" he murmured, his voice a low, intimate rumble. Mara's heart soared. "I'd be honored, my husband," she replied, her voice soft. They moved onto the dance floor, and as Eli pulled her close, Mara rested her head against his chest, the steady rhythm of his heartbeat a comforting counterpoint to the lively music. They swayed, lost in their own world, the gentle murmur of the crowd fading into a distant hum.

The next dance was a lively folk tune, and Mara found herself laughing as Eli twirled her around, his steps surprisingly agile. Around them, friends and family joined in, forming a joyous circle. The children, their faces flushed with excitement, chased each other between the legs of the dancers, their giggles weaving into the fabric of the celebration. Mara watched them, a smile playing on her lips. This was their community, their chosen family, all gathered here to celebrate the beginning of their forever.

Later, as they sat at a small table, the remnants of their wedding cake before them, Eli reached for Mara's hand. "Are you happy?" he asked, his gaze searching hers. Mara's smile was radiant. "More than words can say," she whispered. "This is... perfect, Eli. Everything I could have ever dreamed of."

"And it's only the beginning," Eli said, his voice filled with a quiet certainty. "We have so many more sunsets to watch, so many more adventures to embark on. And I can't imagine a single one without you by my side." He leaned in, his lips brushing against hers in a tender kiss. "You are my Port Blossom, Mara. My home. My forever."

The celebration continued late into the night, a tapestry woven with threads of joy, love, and community. As the last of the guests departed, leaving behind a garden dotted with discarded confetti and the lingering scent of flowers, Mara and Eli stood hand in hand, the soft glow of the fairy lights illuminating their faces. The quiet hum of the night was a gentle lullaby, a prelude to the lifelong symphony of love they were about to compose, together, in their beloved Port Blossom. The stars above seemed to wink in approval, bearing witness to a love story that had found its perfect beginning, under the watchful gaze of the ocean and the embrace of a town that had become their home. The lingering warmth of the celebration settled around them, a cozy blanket woven from shared laughter and heartfelt wishes, promising a future as bright and enduring as the love that had brought them to this beautiful moment.

The symphony of toasts, each a carefully crafted melody of sentiment, continued to weave its spell around the garden. Eli's father had set a tone of heartfelt sincerity, and Sarah had followed with a testament to enduring friendship. Now, it was Mara's father's turn. He rose from his seat, a man whose quiet strength had always been a bedrock for Mara, and a gentle smile played on his lips as he surveyed the gathered guests, his eyes eventually finding Mara and then Eli. The twinkle in his gaze, a familiar one, spoke of a father's deep love and quiet contentment.

"To Mara and Eli," he began, his voice a low baritone that carried a warmth as comforting as a hearth fire. He paused, his gaze sweeping over his daughter. "Mara, my dearest girl. Watching you grow up has been the greatest adventure of my life. I've seen you navigate life's storms with a courage that has always amazed me, and I've seen you find joy in the simplest of things, a trait I've always admired. You've always had a spirit that yearned to make a difference, a heart that bled for those less fortunate, whether they walked on two legs or four." He chuckled softly, a sound that drew affectionate smiles from around the tables. "And you've always done it with a grace and determination that made me incredibly proud. I remember when you were no older than ten, and you decided our backyard needed a 'rescue center' for every stray cat and bird that dared to wander in. Eli, you were always at the ready, your pockets full of the treats you'd 'borrowed' from your mother's pantry, helping Mara wrangle our reluctant patients."

He turned his attention to Eli, his expression one of profound approval. "And then, Eli came along. From the moment Mara brought you home, I knew there was something special about you. It wasn't just the way you looked at her, though that was enough to warm any father's heart. It was the way you understood her, the way you met her passion with your own steady strength, the way you saw the world through her compassionate eyes. You share a vision, a purpose, a love for this community and for the creatures that inhabit it. You are not just a partner to Mara; you are her confidant, her rock, her greatest supporter. And for that, Eli, I am eternally grateful." He raised his glass higher, his voice resonating with emotion. "It takes a special kind of person to truly see my Mara, to cherish her quirks, to celebrate her triumphs, and to be her steady hand during difficult times. You, Eli, are that special person. May your life together be as rich and as full of love as the life you've already built for yourselves here in Port Blossom. To Mara and Eli! To a future as bright as the stars above us tonight!"

A resounding chorus of "To Mara and Eli!" filled the air, followed by the clinking of glasses. Mara's eyes welled up, and she squeezed Eli's hand, her heart overflowing with the love and pride radiating from her father. Eli's answering squeeze was firm and reassuring, his gaze a silent promise that he would always be worthy of that trust.

The next toast was met with a wave of anticipation. Eli's best man, his brother David, was known for his wit and his unwavering loyalty. He stood, a tall, charismatic figure with a mischievous glint in his eyes that always managed to find its mark. He held his glass, waiting for the gentle murmurs to subside, his smile broad and genuine.

"Alright, everyone," David began, his voice carrying a warm, boisterous energy. "For those of you who don't know me, I'm David, Eli's older (and, dare I say, wiser) brother. And let me tell you, watching Eli, my sometimes-stubborn, always-determined, incredibly kind brother, fall in love with Mara has been... well, it's been something else. Honestly, I'm still trying to figure out how she managed to rope him in so completely." He winked at Mara, who playfully rolled her eyes. "No, in all seriousness," he continued, his tone softening, "Eli and Mara are the perfect storm. And I mean that in the best possible way. Eli, you've always been the planner, the one with the five-year forecast. Mara, you're the spontaneous adventurer, the one who'd chase a wild idea across town just to see if it was worth catching. And somehow, it just... works.”

He turned to Eli, his expression turning more serious, though the warmth never left his eyes. “Eli, you’ve always had a good heart, but Mara... Mara amplified it. She showed you that the grand plans, the meticulous schedules, were all the more beautiful when punctuated by moments of pure, unadulterated joy. She taught you to embrace the unexpected, to find magic in the everyday, and to never, ever underestimate the power of a good belly laugh. And Mara,” he shifted his gaze back to his sister-in-law, his voice filled with affection, “you found in Eli a man who not only respects your wild spirit but cherishes it. You found a home in his steadiness, a safe harbor for your adventurous soul. He’s the anchor that keeps you grounded when you’re ready to set sail for the moon, and you’re the wind in his sails, pushing him to explore horizons he never knew existed.”

David raised his glass. “They say opposites attract, but I think Eli and Mara are more like two perfectly complementary pieces of a puzzle. They fit together so seamlessly, enhancing each other’s strengths, softening each other’s edges. They’ve built a life together founded on respect, on shared dreams, and on a love so deep it’s woven into the very fabric of their being. They are a testament to what happens when two souls align, when two hearts beat as one. So, here’s to the happy couple! May your adventures be grand, your laughter be loud, and your love grow deeper with every passing year. To Eli and Mara!”

The cheers that followed were enthusiastic, a true reflection of the affection everyone present held for the newlyweds. The air was thick with shared happiness, a palpable sense of community celebrating the union of two souls who were clearly meant to be. Each toast, from the loving words of Mara's father to the witty affection of David, had added another layer to the beautiful tapestry of their wedding day. They spoke not just of the couple, but of the strong bonds that held Port Blossom together, a town that embraced and celebrated love in all its forms. These were not just words; they were blessings, woven into the fabric of a future that was just beginning to unfold, a future that promised to be as bright and as full of promise as the twinkling lights now illuminating the garden, mirroring the stars above. The collective sentiment was clear: this was more than just a wedding; it was the radiant dawn of a shared forever, witnessed and supported by everyone they held dear.

The last of the heartfelt toasts had faded, leaving behind a resonant warmth that settled over the garden like a soft blanket. The celebratory hum of conversation resumed, interspersed with laughter and the clinking of glasses, but for Mara and Eli, a new melody was about to begin. The gentle swell of the ocean, a constant, soothing presence in Port Blossom, seemed to grow more pronounced, a natural soundtrack to the unfolding magic of their evening. As the last rays of the sun dipped below the horizon, painting the sky in hues of lavender and rose, the fairy lights strung through the trees began to twinkle, mirroring the emerging stars.

Eli turned to Mara, his eyes, a warm hazel that always seemed to hold a universe of affection for her, sparkling with a gentle intensity. He offered her his hand, a silent invitation. "Ready?" he murmured, his voice a low rumble that vibrated through her.

Mara's heart fluttered, a familiar sensation that had been a constant companion since she'd first realized the depth of her feelings for Eli. She slipped her hand into his, her fingers finding their perfect fit. "More than ready," she whispered back, her gaze meeting his. The air between them crackled with an unspoken promise, a culmination of shared dreams and a lifetime of whispered hopes.

As they walked towards the center of the cleared garden, where a small, starlit dance floor had been set up, a hush fell over the guests. A musician, positioned discreetly beneath the boughs of an ancient oak, began to play. The melody was a slow, achingly beautiful waltz, a song that seemed to have been plucked from the very heart of their shared memories. It was a tune they had danced to on countless nights, under skies both clear and clouded, a testament to the quiet, enduring rhythm of their love.

Eli gently took Mara's waist, drawing her close. She rested her head on his shoulder, the familiar scent of him – a blend of sea salt, his favorite worn leather, and something uniquely Eli – enveloping her. His arms tightened around her, a gesture of possessiveness and profound tenderness that made her feel both utterly cherished and completely safe. They began to sway, their movements fluid and natural, as if they had been practicing this dance their entire lives.

The world narrowed to this single, perfect moment. The murmurs of the guests faded into a distant hum, the fairy lights became a shimmering halo around them, and the vast expanse of the starry sky above felt like a private, celestial canopy. They were no longer just Mara and Eli, the bride and groom, surrounded by friends and family. In this dance, they were simply two souls, finally and irrevocably intertwined, moving to the silent cadence of their own hearts.

This dance was more than just a tradition; it was a physical manifestation of their journey. It was a testament to the winding path they had navigated, a path that had begun with tentative steps, navigated through moments of doubt and fear, and had ultimately led them here, to this unwavering certainty, this profound and all-encompassing love. Each step they took was a reflection of the challenges they had overcome, the compromises they had made, and the unwavering support they had always offered each other.

Mara closed her eyes for a moment, breathing in the cool night air, the scent of jasmine from the garden, and the undeniable presence of Eli. She remembered the early days, the hesitant conversations, the unspoken attraction that had simmered beneath the surface. She remembered the fear that had threatened to pull them apart, the anxieties that had whispered doubts in the quiet hours of the night. But Eli had always been there, a steady, unwavering force, his belief in them a constant anchor. He had seen past her insecurities, her sometimes-brash exterior, to the vulnerable heart beneath. He had loved her not in spite of her flaws, but because of them, understanding that they were as much a part of her as her strengths.

Eli, too, was lost in the swirling emotions of the moment. He felt the steady beat of Mara's heart against his chest, a rhythm that had become the most comforting sound in his world. He remembered the first time he had truly *seen* her, not just as the vibrant, passionate woman he had always admired, but as the woman he couldn't imagine a future without. It had been a moment of quiet revelation, a dawning realization that his own dreams were inextricably linked to hers. He had been drawn to her fierce independence, her unwavering commitment to her causes, her infectious laughter that could light up even the darkest room. But it was her kindness, her deep well of empathy, that had truly captured his heart. She saw the world with a clarity and compassion that inspired him daily.

He held her a little tighter, his thumb tracing a gentle circle on her back. "You're beautiful," he whispered, the words a simple truth that felt inadequate to capture the depth of his feelings.

Mara lifted her head, a soft smile gracing her lips. "So are you," she replied, her voice thick with emotion. "Thank you, Eli. For everything."

He leaned down and kissed her forehead, a gesture of pure, unadulterated adoration. "There's nothing to thank me for," he murmured against her skin. "This is just the beginning."

The music continued, a gentle ebb and flow that mirrored the gentle rhythm of their breathing. They turned slowly, their movements effortless, a dance of two souls finally in perfect harmony. The other guests had formed a respectful circle around them, their faces alight with joy, their presence a silent testament to the love that surrounded this couple. Children, momentarily forgetting their exuberance, watched with wide, fascinated eyes, perhaps catching a glimpse of a love story unfolding before them.

As they danced, Mara felt a profound sense of peace settle over her. The anxieties that had once plagued her seemed to melt away, replaced by an unshakeable conviction. This was right. This was real. Eli was her home, her safe harbor, her forever. She had found her equilibrium in his presence, and he, in turn, had found a wild, beautiful spark in hers. They were the perfect balance, two halves of a whole, destined to navigate the complexities of life together.

Eli felt it too, a profound sense of rightness. All the planning, all the effort, all the hopes and dreams had converged on this single, luminous moment. He looked at Mara, her eyes reflecting the starlight, her smile radiating a happiness that mirrored his own. He saw the future stretching out before them, a vast landscape of shared adventures, quiet mornings, and the enduring comfort of knowing they would face it all together. The gentle lapping of the waves against the shore seemed to whisper a lullaby, a promise of continuity and peace.

The song began to draw to a close, the final notes lingering in the air like a whispered promise. As the music softened, Eli brought Mara to a gentle stop, their foreheads touching. They remained in each other's embrace, the world outside their bubble of shared intimacy momentarily suspended. The fairy lights twinkled, the stars bore witness, and the ocean sang its eternal song.

"I love you, Mara," Eli said, his voice raw with emotion.

"And I love you, Eli," she replied, her voice equally filled with the weight of that sacred declaration.

The kiss that followed was not a passionate, fiery embrace, but something far more profound. It was a kiss of profound understanding, of unwavering commitment, of two souls acknowledging the sacred bond that had been forged between them. It was a kiss that sealed not just their vows, but their shared future, a promise whispered on the ocean breeze, under the vast, star-dusted canvas of their forever.

As the last notes of the waltz faded completely, a ripple of applause spread through the guests, a wave of genuine warmth and heartfelt congratulations. Eli and Mara pulled apart, still holding hands, their eyes locked, a silent acknowledgment passing between them. They had shared their first dance as a married couple, and in that dance, they had reaffirmed the deepest truths of their love. The journey had been long, winding, and at times, uncertain, but here, under the watchful eyes of the stars and the gentle caress of the ocean breeze, they knew, with an unshakeable certainty, that their forever had truly begun. The night was young, and their life together, a grand adventure waiting to unfold, had just taken its first, perfect step.

The final notes of their first dance as husband and wife had melted into the gentle murmur of the celebrating crowd, but for Mara and Eli, the resonance of that shared rhythm lingered, a silent echo of the vows they had just exchanged. The fairy lights strung through the ancient oaks overhead cast a warm, inviting glow, illuminating the faces of their loved ones, each one a testament to the journey that had brought them to this moment. The air, still carrying the scent of jasmine and the salty tang of the sea, felt alive with a palpable sense of joy and a quiet, profound contentment.

Mara leaned her head back against Eli's shoulder, a sigh of pure happiness escaping her lips. The world had tilted on its axis, not in a dizzying spin, but in a gentle, perfect realignment. The anxieties that had once felt like heavy weights had evaporated, replaced by a lightness of being she hadn't realized was possible. She felt seen, understood, and loved in a way that went deeper than words, a truth mirrored in the steady beat of Eli's heart against hers. This wasn't just the culmination of a wedding day; it was the inauguration of a new chapter, one written in shared dreams and an unwavering commitment to a life built on purpose and compassion.

Eli's arms tightened around her, a silent affirmation of the sentiment. He knew, with a certainty that settled deep into his bones, that this was more than a union of two people; it was the formal intertwining of two lives, two souls, and two deeply held passions. The rescue, a beacon of hope for so many animals in need, was not merely an entity they supported; it was an intrinsic part of their shared identity, a living, breathing testament to the values they held dear. Today, as they had pledged their love to each other, they had also reaffirmed their dedication to its future, their vows extending beyond their personal commitment to encompass the well-being of the sanctuary and the community it served.

As they slowly detached from their embrace, the warm applause of their guests washed over them, a wave of genuine affection that warmed them from the inside out. Mara caught sight of her parents, their eyes shining with pride and a quiet understanding, and her heart swelled. Her mother squeezed her father's arm, a small, knowing smile playing on her lips, a silent acknowledgment of the journey Mara had undertaken, the growth she had experienced, and the profound happiness she had found. Across the garden, the rescue volunteers, their faces etched with a familiar blend of dedication and joy, beamed at them, a silent reassurance of their continued partnership.

Eli met the gaze of his own parents, his father giving him a firm, approving nod, his mother's eyes glistening with unshed tears of happiness. They had always understood his deep connection to the animal kingdom, his innate desire to protect and nurture. Seeing him now, with Mara by his side, their shared vision for the rescue solidified by their marital bond, was a moment of profound fulfillment for them.

The success of the festival, which had seamlessly woven itself into the fabric of their wedding day, had been more than just a financial boon for the sanctuary; it had been a resounding testament to the community's unwavering support. The joyous atmosphere, the shared laughter, the children's delighted squeals as they interacted with the adoptable animals – it had all painted a vivid picture of a Port Blossom that understood the importance of compassion and collective care. Mara remembered the initial anxieties, the delicate balance of blending such a significant personal event with the vital work of the rescue. But with each passing hour, it had become clear that the two were not mutually exclusive, but rather, beautifully synergistic. The wedding had become an extension of the sanctuary's mission, a public declaration of its enduring value.

The integration of the rescue into their wedding had been a thoughtful, deliberate choice, a way of honoring the place it held in their hearts. From the carefully chosen floral arrangements featuring wildflowers that mimicked the sanctuary's meadows, to the adoption station set up discreetly near the reception area, every detail had spoken of their commitment. Even the wedding favors, small, handcrafted birdhouses, were a tangible reminder of their shared passion for wildlife. The children, particularly, had been enthralled. A group of them had gathered around a specially designated "Meet and Greet" area, their faces alight with wonder as they gently petted a calm, older dog named Gus, a long-term resident of the sanctuary who had, for the day, become an ambassador of sorts. Gus, with his soulful eyes and gentle demeanor, had captivated them, his presence a living embodiment of the second chances the rescue provided.

Mara watched as a young girl, no older than seven, with pigtails and a bright pink dress, whispered something into Gus's ear, her small hand stroking his soft fur. The sheer innocence and burgeoning empathy in that gesture brought a fresh wave of emotion to Mara's chest. This was why they did what they did. This was the future they were nurturing, not just for the animals, but for the children of Port Blossom, who were learning invaluable lessons in kindness and responsibility.

Eli's hand found hers, his thumb brushing over her knuckles in a comforting gesture. "They're amazing, aren't they?" he murmured, his gaze following hers to the scene with Gus. "The way they connect. It's... everything."

Mara squeezed his hand. "It is," she agreed, her voice a little thick. "Seeing all this, all these people coming together, it just... it reinforces why we fight so hard for them."

The festival had indeed been a resounding success. The adoption event, held earlier in the afternoon, had resulted in four successful placements – a timid tabby cat named Luna, a boisterous terrier mix named Buster, a pair of bonded rabbits, and a quiet, elderly Labrador named Daisy, who had found her forever home with a kind, retired couple who promised her endless belly rubs and soft blankets. Each successful adoption was a victory, a testament to the tireless efforts of the sanctuary staff and volunteers. And now, with the wedding reception in full swing, the energy remained high, a celebratory hum that amplified the joy of those reunions.

The financial contributions from the festival and the generous donations made throughout the day were substantial, ensuring that the sanctuary's vital work could continue uninterrupted. There were plans for expansion, for new enclosures, for more specialized veterinary care – dreams that had, until now, felt perpetually just out of reach. But today, surrounded by this outpouring of love and support, those dreams felt tangible, achievable. The wedding had served as a powerful catalyst, drawing attention to the rescue's needs and galvanizing the community in a way that even the most well-intentioned fundraising event couldn't fully replicate.

Eli leaned in, his lips brushing against Mara's ear. "Tonight," he whispered, his voice a low, intimate rumble, "we celebrate this beautiful beginning. And tomorrow, we get back to work, with a renewed sense of purpose. This life we're building, Mara, it's going to be extraordinary."

Mara turned to face him fully, her eyes shining. "It already is, Eli," she said, her voice filled with conviction. "It already is." The life they were building was not just about grand gestures or public events; it was in the quiet mornings they would share, the late nights spent tending to a sick animal, the shared exhaustion and the shared triumphs. It was in the understanding that passed between them without a word, the unspoken acknowledgment of their shared responsibility and their shared love.

The presence of the rescue animals at the wedding hadn't been a disruption; it had been a celebration of life itself. A few well-behaved, leashed dogs, accompanied by their dedicated handlers, had mingled with guests, their wagging tails and happy panting adding to the festive atmosphere. They weren't just pets; they were living examples of the sanctuary's impact, their presence a constant, joyful reminder of the mission that bound Mara and Eli together. A particularly charming golden retriever, known for his boundless enthusiasm and tendency to "hug" people, had managed to charm almost every guest, his affectionate nudges and happy barks eliciting laughter and smiles. He was a testament to the transformative power of love and care.

Mara thought about the sheer amount of planning that had gone into making this day a reality, the intricate dance of coordinating a wedding with the operational needs of a busy animal sanctuary. There had been moments of doubt, of overwhelming logistics, but Eli's steady presence, his unwavering belief in their ability to make it work, had always been her anchor. He possessed a remarkable ability to see the big picture while meticulously managing the details, a skill that had proven invaluable. He had a knack for finding solutions, for anticipating potential problems, and for rallying the troops with an infectious optimism.

She recalled a particular instance during the setup, when a crucial delivery of hay for the sanctuary's horses had been delayed, threatening to disrupt the feeding schedule. Eli, without a hint of panic, had personally driven to a neighboring farm, negotiating a temporary loan of several bales, ensuring the animals were cared for without missing a beat. It was this kind of unwavering dedication, this proactive problem-solving, that Mara admired so deeply. He didn't just talk about his passion; he lived it, breathed it, and made it happen.

And Mara, in her own way, complemented his strengths. Where Eli was the calm, strategic leader, Mara was the passionate advocate, the one who could connect with the animals on an almost intuitive level, who saw their individual stories and advocated for their unique needs with fierce determination. She had a way of making people understand the depth of the animals' suffering and the profound joy of their recovery, her words imbued with a raw honesty that resonated deeply. Their partnership, in both their personal lives and their shared work, was a testament to the power of complementary strengths, a beautiful symphony of dedication and compassion.

As the evening progressed, the dance floor filled with guests, a vibrant tapestry of swirling colors and joyous movement. Mara and Eli, now fully immersed in the celebratory spirit, found themselves drawn into the revelry, their hands held tightly, their smiles radiating a shared happiness. They danced with friends, with family, their laughter intermingling with the music, each interaction a reinforcement of the community that supported their endeavors. They were not just marrying each other; they were embracing a shared life, a shared purpose, and a shared future, with the Port Blossom Animal Rescue at its very heart.

The rescue, in many ways, had been the architect of their relationship. It was where they had first met, a shared space of dedication and purpose. It was where their bond had solidified, through late-night shifts, shared moments of despair and elation, and the quiet understanding that comes from facing challenges together. The animals, in their silent, unconditional way, had brought them together, and it was only fitting that their union would be a celebration of that shared foundation.

Mara looked around at the faces illuminated by the fairy lights – the volunteers who had worked tirelessly, the donors who had opened their hearts, the friends and family who had offered unwavering encouragement. She saw not just a wedding party, but an extended family, a network of support that would continue to nurture the sanctuary long after the last of the champagne had been savored. This day was a testament to what could be achieved when a community rallied around a shared cause, when individual passions converged into a collective force for good.

Eli, sensing her thoughtful gaze, leaned in. "Thinking about everything?" he asked softly.

Mara nodded, a contented sigh escaping her. "Just... grateful. Grateful for this moment, for all of them, for us. For the rescue." She paused, her gaze sweeping over the lively scene. "It's more than just a place, isn't it? It's a promise. A promise to them," she gestured towards the few well-behaved canine guests, "and to each other."

Eli's eyes met hers, a depth of emotion swirling within them. "It's our forever, Mara," he said, his voice laced with a profound sincerity. "Our shared forever, built on love, and hope, and the unwavering belief that every life deserves a chance." He raised his glass, catching the light. "To our forever."

Mara raised her glass, her heart soaring. "To our forever," she echoed, her voice strong and clear. The clinking of their glasses was a small sound in the grand scheme of the night, but to them, it was a resonant declaration, a silent promise whispered on the ocean breeze, a commitment etched into the very fabric of their souls. The rescue, now more than ever, was inextricably woven into the tapestry of their marital bond, making their life together not just a journey of love, but a testament to a shared purpose, a purpose that promised to enrich their lives, and the lives of countless creatures, for all the years to come. The enduring heart of the rescue beat in time with their own, a rhythm of hope, resilience, and a love that had found its truest, most meaningful expression.

The salt-laced air of Port Blossom had a different kind of sweetness now, a comfort that seeped into Mara's bones. Months had woven themselves into a comfortable tapestry of married life, each thread a shared moment, a quiet understanding, a deepening love. The frantic energy of their wedding day had settled into a serene rhythm, a life built not just on grand pronouncements but on the gentle, consistent hum of shared existence. Mornings began with the ritual of coffee, brewed strong and dark, savored on their small porch overlooking the shimmering expanse of the ocean. Eli would often sit beside her, his arm a familiar weight around her shoulders, his gaze lost in the distant horizon, a quiet contentment settling over him. These were the moments Mara had always craved, the tranquil pauses in a life that had, until Eli, felt like a constant scramble. Now, there was a sense of arrival, a feeling of belonging that resonated deeper than any professional accomplishment.

Their days were intrinsically linked to the Port Blossom Animal Rescue, the beating heart of their shared life. The wedding had been a magnificent launch, a powerful infusion of resources and community spirit, but the real work, the day-to-day dedication, was an ongoing testament to their commitment. Mara found herself instinctively anticipating Eli's needs at the sanctuary, her movements in sync with his, a silent dance of efficiency and shared purpose. She would be checking on the newly arrived litter of kittens, their tiny cries a symphony of vulnerability, while Eli was overseeing the construction of a new, larger enclosure for the rescued farm animals. The scent of hay, disinfectant, and the undeniable, earthy aroma of animals was no longer just the smell of work; it was the fragrance of their life together.

One sun-drenched afternoon, Mara found herself assisting with a particularly challenging intake – a nervous, once-stray dog named Shadow, whose eyes held a perpetual flicker of fear. Eli had brought him in, his voice calm and reassuring as he explained the dog's history of neglect. Mara, with her innate gentleness and profound understanding of animal behavior, sat patiently outside Shadow's kennel, speaking in soft, low tones, her movements slow and deliberate. She offered no immediate touch, no forceful encouragement, simply her quiet presence, a silent promise of safety. Eli watched from a distance, a soft smile playing on his lips, a familiar swell of pride in his chest. He knew that Mara's connection with these animals was a gift, a rare ability to bridge the chasm between fear and trust, a skill that made their shared mission not just effective, but profoundly humane.

Later, as the last rays of the sun painted the sky in hues of orange and purple, they found themselves cleaning out stalls together, their movements synchronized, their conversation a comfortable blend of rescue updates and mundane observations. "Did you see Mrs. Henderson's face when she met Buster again?" Mara asked, a grin lighting up her face as she shoveled straw. "She practically glowed. He's so good with her grandson." Buster, the boisterous terrier mix adopted during the wedding festival, had found a perfect match with a family whose youngest member had been struggling with anxiety. The rescue wasn't just about saving animals; it was about weaving them into the fabric of the community, creating connections that healed and enriched lives.

Eli chuckled, his strong hands working efficiently. "He's got that effect on people. Remember how scared he was when he first came to us? Bouncing off the walls, a ball of pure, unadulterated chaos." He paused, leaning against the wooden fence. "It's moments like that, Mara, seeing them find their people, seeing them thrive... that's what makes it all worthwhile. That's our happily ever after, isn't it? Not just for us, but for them."

Mara's heart swelled at his words. He understood. He understood the deep, soul-satisfying reward that came from their shared work, the quiet triumphs that were more precious than any personal accolades. Their life together was a testament to that understanding, a continuous unfolding of shared purpose. Evenings were often spent curled up on the sofa, the gentle glow of a reading lamp casting shadows on their faces, a book shared between them, or simply the comfortable silence of two souls at peace. Sometimes, they would listen to the distant cries of the resident owls at the sanctuary, a reminder of the lives they were protecting, a soft lullaby to their shared existence.

The integration of their personal lives with the rescue had been seamless, not forced or contrived, but a natural evolution. Mara had discovered a knack for organizing community outreach events, transforming what could have been mundane fundraisers into engaging, educational experiences. She'd orchestrated a "Paws and Pages" day at the local library, where children could read to the adoptable dogs, a program that had not only boosted adoptions but fostered a love of reading and compassion in the younger generation. Eli, ever the pragmatist, had developed more efficient systems for animal care and veterinary partnerships, ensuring the rescue's long-term sustainability. They were a well-oiled machine, a partnership built on mutual respect and a shared vision.

One blustery autumn evening, as the wind howled outside their cottage, they sat by the fireplace, mugs of steaming tea warming their hands. The crackling fire cast a warm, flickering light on their faces. "I was thinking about that day," Mara said softly, her gaze fixed on the dancing flames. "The wedding. It feels like a lifetime ago, and yet, just yesterday. It was so much more than just a wedding, wasn't it?"

Eli reached for her hand, his thumb tracing the familiar lines of her palm. "It was the beginning of everything," he agreed, his voice a low rumble. "The official start of our forever. And it wasn't just about us, was it? It was about what we could build, together, for this place, for these animals, for this community." He squeezed her hand. "Every day, I wake up and I realize how lucky I am. To have you, to have this life. It's everything I ever dreamed of, and more."

Mara leaned her head against his shoulder, a wave of pure contentment washing over her. The anxieties that had once plagued her seemed like distant echoes, shadows of a past life. Here, in the warmth of their home, with Eli by her side, she felt a profound sense of peace, a deep-seated joy that radiated from within. Port Blossom had become more than just a town; it was their anchor, their sanctuary, the place where their love had blossomed and where their shared purpose found its truest expression.

The Port Blossom Animal Rescue continued to flourish. The successful wedding and festival had brought a wave of new volunteers and a significant influx of donations, allowing them to expand their facilities and offer more specialized rehabilitation programs. They had welcomed a rescued eagle with a damaged wing, a family of orphaned deer, and even a grumpy old tortoise named Sheldon who, despite his initial reluctance to socialize, had eventually become a beloved, albeit slow-moving, fixture. Each new arrival was met with the same dedication, the same unwavering commitment to providing a safe haven and a second chance.

Mara often found herself reflecting on how far they had come, from the initial anxieties of blending their wedding with the rescue's operational needs to the comfortable synergy they now shared. It hadn't always been easy, but their love, their shared passion, and their unwavering belief in their mission had seen them through every challenge. They had learned to communicate not just with words, but with glances, with shared smiles, with the quiet understanding that comes from building a life together, brick by brick, paw print by paw print.

As the seasons turned, their life together in Port Blossom continued to be a beautiful testament to the power of love, dedication, and a shared dream. The sea breeze whispered through the ancient oaks, the laughter of children echoed from the rescue's play areas, and the quiet contented purrs of adopted cats filled their home. It was a happily ever after not of grand pronouncements or fairy-tale endings, but of the enduring, everyday magic of a life lived with purpose, with passion, and with an abundance of love. Their days were filled with the quiet joy of knowing they were making a difference, of building a future not just for themselves, but for all the creatures who had found a home, and a family, in the heart of Port Blossom.

Glossary

Back Matter

Port Blossom: A charming, coastal town known for its tight-knit community and the thriving Port Blossom Animal Rescue.

Paws and Pages: A community outreach program designed to encourage reading and compassion in children by having them read to adoptable animals.

Shadow: A nervous, once-stray dog rescued by Eli and nursed back to trust by Mara.

Buster: A boisterous terrier mix adopted during the wedding festival, known for his positive impact on his new family.

Sheldon: A grumpy, elderly tortoise who eventually becomes a beloved fixture at the rescue.

Humane Society of the United States: www.humanesociety.org

ASPCA (American Society for the Prevention of Cruelty to Animals): www.aspca.org

Local Animal Shelter Directories (searchable online by region)

Books and research on animal behavior and rehabilitation (specific titles available upon request from the author).